Helen Newman Wood

Silver Spurs and a Twelve Pound Heart

The Book Guild Ltd

First published in Great Britain in 2023 by
The Book Guild Ltd
Unit E2 Airfield Business Park,
Harrison Road, Market Harborough,
Leicestershire. LE16 7UL
Tel: 0116 2792299
www.bookguild.co.uk
Email: info@bookguild.co.uk
Twitter: @bookguild

Copyright © 2023 Helen Newman Wood

The right of Helen Newman Wood to be identified as the author of this
work has been asserted by them in accordance with the
Copyright, Design and Patents Act 1988.

All rights reserved. No part of this publication may be
reproduced, transmitted, or stored in a retrieval system, in any form or by any means,
without permission in writing from the publisher, nor be otherwise circulated in
any form of binding or cover other than that in which it is published and without
a similar condition being imposed on the subsequent purchaser.

This work is entirely fictitious and bears no resemblance to any persons living or dead.

Typeset in 11pt Minion Pro

Printed and bound by CPI Group (UK) Ltd, Croydon, CR0 4YY

ISBN 978 1915352 873

British Library Cataloguing in Publication Data.
A catalogue record for this book is available from the British Library.

For Mum, Dad, Marcus and Tabitha.

One

Twenty-four-year-old Katie Holland stirred her vegetable soup with a rather bent spoon that had been stolen from the café down the road.

'Homemade soup again, Katie? You are eating healthily. Did we overindulge during the festive period?' Mrs Hicken gave a tinkly laugh as she arranged the blue pashmina over her shoulders and then wafted out of the office on a cloud of Chanel.

Smiling sweetly until her boss turned away, Katie then narrowed her brown eyes and stuck two fingers up at the Versace that was stretched to its limit over Mrs Hicken's enormous backside.

From the desk opposite came a splutter of stifled laughter. 'I know who's been overindulging over the festive period, and it's not Skinny Minnie over there.' Trish nodded at Katie and the rest of the office murmured in agreement.

Katie knew that Mrs Hicken wouldn't be having vegetable soup for lunch, and if she did, she would probably report that the Asian-inspired aromatic vegetable broth, with coconut milk, pak choi and shiitake mushrooms, was *celestial*. Last week, she had floated back into the office raving about the baked celeriac, smoked trout and caper salsa at the new pop-up bistro in Kensington. The week before, it was how *divine* the beef carpaccio with Gorgonzola Piccante and Tardivo di Treviso had tasted in the posh restaurant in Mayfair.

Mrs Hicken always lunched out with her clients and returned to the office with her podgy cheeks flushed with lunchtime Chardonnay. Friday lunches were always an extended affair and, knowing that they would not see their boss until after three o'clock, Trish threw her empty yoghurt pot in the bin and took a bottle of red nail polish from her handbag.

'Coming, Katie?' Lauren was pulling on her coat. 'We're going to McConnell's. According to Old Hicken, the pan-fried salmon and watercress sauce is supposed to be *heavenly.*'

'No thanks.' Katie shook her head with a rueful smile, her long, brown hair sweeping around her shoulders. 'I've got my soup today, thanks. Maybe another day?'

'Definitely,' Lauren squeezed Katie's arm and joined Becky making for the door.

Katie looked down again at her cooling bowl. Having had no breakfast, she was absolutely starving, but vegetable soup was the last thing she felt like eating. Taking a spoonful, she watched Trish painting the nails on her left hand with caring precision.

Her co-workers all assumed she was eating this wonderous, fat-busting soup for the benefit of her health, and she had done nothing to suggest otherwise. There was something embarrassing about being so short of money, and for the first time in her life, Katie was discovering that looking well-heeled on a non-existent budget was an artform.

She made excuses when her colleagues were going for a drink after work, saying she was meeting friends elsewhere in London. And despite the monotony of the soup diet, it was something of a blessing as it gave her a ready-made excuse if she was invited out for lunch. She dreaded the day one of her fellow employees discovered that the soup regimen was not a choice and that all she could afford to buy in the grocery department was a bag of vegetables and a loaf of bread.

The first time she had braved the Saturday market, the nice man who ran the vegetable stall had given her a wink and the bag of stewing vegetables at a discounted price as she was thirty pence short.

'Best come here after four, princess. I'll keep a bag for you, if you want one every week?'

When she nodded, he muttered that Gloria with the artisan bread, five stands further down the row, was selling off her London Bloomer Bread "Meryl Streep" and added two Granny Smiths and a pomegranate to Katie's bag.

The potatoes, carrots, cabbage, onions and turnip made a pan of soup on a Sunday afternoon which lasted until the following Saturday, as long as Katie limited herself to only a small portion at lunchtimes. By Thursday evening, when the bloomer was a bit too stale to swallow in public, she scraped off the mouldy blue spots, cut what was left of the loaf into chunks and grilled them until they turned golden-brown.

Wincing as the spoon scratched the bottom of the bowl, Katie recalled the moment yesterday when her bank card had been declined in the discount shop. She had only wanted to buy toothpaste and shampoo, but as her emergency credit card was hidden between the pages of a paperback in her room, she had been forced to leave the shop as quickly as she could while the lady behind the till gave her a pitying look. After going back to her digs and realising that it was two weeks until payday, she had upturned her car in total desperation and unearthed two pounds and seventeen pence in sticky, discoloured coins.

Feeling as though she had won the lottery, Katie was planning to stop at the discount shop again this evening and had decided that if she used the bar of soap in the communal bathroom to wash her hair, she could splurge on some conditioner as well as toothpaste.

The credit card hidden in-between the pages of Jilly Cooper's *Riders* had been taken out strictly for emergencies. The emergencies so far had consisted of a packet of cheap and not very sharp razors which left her legs covered in shaving burn, a tub of horribly greasy moisturiser to try and combat the razor burn, seven cocktails after work on the last Friday before Christmas and a new suit from the charity shop.

The new suit was unquestionably classed as an emergency purchase because staggering to the bus stop after the seven cocktails, she had tripped and landed face down in someone's regurgitated Tikka Masala and Pea Pilau. Despite scrubbing the jacket and skirt with her flatmate's shower gel in a fairly drunken state that evening, the stain had refused to budge, and she had been forced to plunder fifteen whole pounds on someone's shiny-elbowed cast off.

Having finished painting her toenails, Trish took a small mirror and a pair of tweezers from her top drawer and began to pluck her eyebrows. Trish was also a junior in the company, and Katie assumed by the packed lunches and DIY beauty treatments at her desk on a Friday, she also didn't have much spare money. Eating their pre-made lunches together at their desks was a stark contrast to Lauren and Becky, who lunched out every day and got their nails and waxing done by the illegal workers at Ellie's further down the Caledonian Road.

'What have you got to do this afternoon?' Trish was leaning over the little mirror on her desk pulling her right eyebrow taught.

'Reference checks, on the couple moving into that place on Derby Road.'

Trish looked across in amazement. 'I can't believe you found someone to rent that – it's tiny.'

'I know,' Katie furrowed her brow. 'But it was the only property we had in their price range.'

'I don't know how anyone can afford to rent in London, that's why I still live at home.' Trish was pulling at her left brow and plucking wildly.

'Tell me about it. I pay a fortune, and it's not exactly the Ritz.'

'Why don't you look for somewhere else? There's always rooms to rent on the Cally Road, and it would save your tube fare if you could walk to work.'

'But the rent would be twice as much as I'm paying now.' Katie was about to add that as she had no money on her Oyster card, she had been walking the three miles to work for the past two weeks anyway but stopped herself. She knew from past experience that if she admitted to strolling around North London alone in the dark, Trish would regale her with a tale about someone she had once known being raped and murdered as they made their way home from work one evening. And the daily commute was terrifying enough without hearing Trish's dramatic anecdotes. Katie always walked purposely, with her headphones in her ears but with no music playing so she could listen to what was happening behind her. If someone fell into step in her wake, she would start speaking very loudly on her mobile phone and stop walking, hoping they would pass by and let her continue on her journey. There had been one frightening experience when a drunk had grabbed her shoulder and she had thumped him with her handbag, only to hear him apologising in a slurred Northern accent and asking where the nearest tube station was. Despite hating where she lived, there was always a huge sense of relief when the house came into view, and Katie had to force herself not to run the last fifty metres past the ladies of the night who waited for punters at the bus stop across the road.

The tall, brown house in Stamford Hill where Katie rented a room was freezing cold, but as the offices of Hicken Lettings were tropically warm, she was always at her desk at eight and didn't leave until after six, making Mrs Hicken think she had the most marvellous work ethic. Keeping warm in this way also meant Katie could avoid having to talk to her housemates, who were seriously strange.

There was Sam, who worked in a pizza restaurant and ate microwaved margherita for every meal; Matt, the builder who left cement dust in huge, hand-shaped marks all over the kitchen and skid marks down the back of the toilet. Orchid was an exotic dancer who dripped bright pink hair dye all over the bathroom, and sixty-seven-year-old Olive washed her knickers in the kitchen sink in-between stints at the nearby library.

The house was filthy as none of them ever cleaned up. Orchid slept all day, worked all night and made her presence felt by the smell of cannabis wafting from her room, her crotchless knickers left drying on the towel rail in the bathroom and several tubes of lubricant in the fridge that no one else would admit to owning. Matt ate fish and chips out of their paper in the lounge every night; Olive hung out her weary, grey underwear on a makeshift line across the hall; and there was always pubic hair in the shower.

Last week when Katie had complained she was cold, Matt had sniggered that she was welcome to warm up in his bed, as he wouldn't kick her out for farting. Sam had then suggested that they could toss a coin to see who got first dibs, which made Katie feel slightly sick and remain in her bedroom every evening since.

'Are you coming for a drink after work tonight?' Trish was holding the mirror above her upturned face so she could examine her finished brows.

'I can't,' Katie lied. 'I'm meeting up with some friends.'

Moving from Dorset at the beginning of November, Katie had initially tried hard to adapt to London life but, used to the slower pace of the countryside, she hated the crowds, the noise and the faceless bustle of London. Having no money and no friends to do the things her parents had told her she was missing out on in Dorset, Katie resented her father daily for setting her up in this crap and boring job.

Edward Holland ran a land agency in Dorset and wanted Katie to start at the bottom and work her way up. After all, he had said, just look at him – he had started as the tea boy and now had his own company with five offices in Dorset and Hampshire.

When her dad had proudly told her that he had got her a job in London, Katie had gone ballistic.

'You have to control everything, don't you? You couldn't have let me find a job on my own!'

'You can't go swanning off to New Zealand to play polo every bloody winter!' Eddie bawled back. 'You've got to get a proper job and join the real world; after a year in London, you can come and work for me.'

'I don't want to work for you,' replied Katie fiercely. 'I'd rather spend the rest of my life stuck in a lift with a naked Piers Morgan.'

Being five foot six, slim and pretty with her high cheekbones and slanted brown eyes, Katie had never been short of work. Unfortunately, the kind of work Katie wanted to do, her father saw as a complete and utter waste of time and far removed from what he considered to be a career. Six years ago, after finishing her A levels, Eddie had begrudgingly paid for her to attend the Royal Agricultural College, where Katie had sailed through a degree course in International Equine Studies and Land Management. Eddie's hopes that she would then find a "real job" were thoroughly thwarted when Katie promptly signed up for a twelve-week course at the Southern Riding Centre in Gloucestershire, to gain her coaching qualifications so she could teach people to ride. The winter after passing her teaching exams, she had groomed for a polo team under the New Zealand sun and, after picking up further connections in the southern hemisphere, had flown out the following winter to work in an event yard. Both jobs had provided free air fares, board and lodgings, meaning Katie not only got to play polo and event but was also able to put money aside to compete her own horse from her Dorset base during the English summer. She was already planning her next jaunt back to the eventing yard in New Zealand, leaving England as usual in the autumn when her father found out and subsequently hit the roof.

Katie was an intelligent girl. She knew that if she went back to New Zealand, her dad would rant on and on to her mother about the wasted university fees, so she had found a room to rent and moved to North London to start the job that he had created for her. The overwhelming homesickness during those early days in the capital had made her remain in the city every weekend. She knew that going back to Dorset's high hedgerows and thatched cottages would make coming back to London even harder. Filling her Instagram feed with images of the famous London sights for her friends in New Zealand, she added art galleries and museums for the benefit of her mum, who assumed her reluctance to leave London was because she was having a fabulous time. Katie was aware that anyone who knew London well would have rumbled her straight away, because every attraction on her Insta feed was free to visit.

'Trish, Katie!' She jumped as Rob roared into the office in his usual whirlwind fashion, bringing a blast of cold January air with him. 'My son's playing in a sponsored football match this weekend, raising money for the school. I don't suppose I could press you to sponsor him, could I?' He rattled a metal biscuit tin that was half full of notes and coins.

Trish was plugging her hair straighteners into the extension lead under her desk and said in a muffled voice that she had left her purse at home.

'Oh, Rob,' Katie put down her crooked spoon on a piece of scrap paper. 'I don't think I have any cash on me either.' She searched in her handbag for her purse with a slightly sinking heart. 'I've only got two pounds and some shrapnel.' She dropped the two tacky pound coins into his box and gave him her best attempt at a smile.

'That's really kind,' he said warmly. 'Every little helps, thanks.'

Fuck, thought Katie.

True to form, a grinning and shiny-eyed Mrs Hicken swept back into the office at twenty-past three, bursting with lamb flatbread, pickled cucumber, elderflower yoghurt and lemon posset. Disappearing into her office for what she thought was a tiny secret snooze, she accidentally slammed the door so hard that Lauren's framed Letting Agent Certificate fell off the wall.

At quarter to five, having slept off the three large glasses of wine on her squashy leather sofa, Mrs Hicken was putting on her coat when Katie knocked on her door. Two minutes later, she was frantically fanning herself with a copy of *House Letting Monthly*.

'*Leave?* But you have only been here for five minutes, and Eddie was adamant I was to train you up properly. That's why he offered so much for... oh, forget it.' She dropped the magazine on top of a brochure for a block of new apartments in the East End. 'Leave?' she repeated in amazement.

Katie looked down at her neatly typed resignation on the desk. 'I've got some holiday to use, so would it be okay to finish now?'

Mrs Hicken sighed heavily. 'No, it would not. Take your holiday and come and see me when you get back; we can talk then. January is such a gloomy month; you're just suffering from post-Christmas blues.' Mrs Hicken was back to waving her hands around like an air traffic controller. 'Go abroad; get some sun for a few days. Come and see me next Friday.'

Thinking of the seventeen pence in her purse and the credit card bill she couldn't afford to pay, Katie decided that some sun was definitely off the cards.

Two

Three hundred miles north of London, Shelley McNeil was glaring in disbelief at a twenty-year-old Irishman who was obviously about to become her ex-colleague.

'You can't just *leave!*' she shrieked, seeing the bin bags full of belongings rammed into the back seat of Seamus's very battered Ford Focus. 'You need to tell Roger that you're going, give him a chance to get someone else.'

'Shelley, me darlin' I'm absolutely done with working for a clapped-out has-been who keeps all the best horses for himself and leaves me with all the shit,' he lit a cigarette and exhaled, 'making me look like I cannot ride in a taxi with the focking door shut.'

'Seamus please, can't we just talk about this?' Shelley's Glaswegian accent was becoming more pronounced, and her green eyes were open very wide, as she was forced to walk more quickly alongside the moving car. 'It's getting dark.'

'Luckily, me car has these wonderful tings called "lights".' Seamus smiled as he changed gear and Shelley had to run to keep up. 'I'm off home to God's own country. Good luck to y' and tanks for everythin', and to tell y' the God's honest truth, Shelley, I've never been all that keen on focking Scotland.'

'It's *Northumberland*, Seamus; we're thirty miles south of the border.'

Seamus moved his cigarette to the other side of his mouth. 'Still too close for me, me darlin'. Farewell, and I'm sure we'll meet again.'

'Seamus, please, just stop for a minute and we can talk about this.'

'Me darlin', there's nothing to talk about, and I'm simply goin' home.'

Shelley slammed her hand on the windscreen. 'Stop, for the love of God, just stop!'

'Don't you worry about me, me darlin'. I'll be catchin' the first sailing back to the motherland in the mornin'.'

'I'm not bloody concerned about you making the ferry home; I'm more concerned that you're leaving me and Roger with no bloody work rider!' Shelley was almost sprinting as Seamus accelerated.

'I'm sure, another pretty little ting will be along to take my place in the blink of an eye. Now, if you don't mind…' he took his cigarette out of his mouth and pretended to aim its glowing tip at Shelley's hand on the open window.

Giving a yell, she jumped back and could hear the sound of his laughter as he drove away. As she watched the dark-green car disappear up the long drive into the gloom, his skinny white arm waved a final adieu out the window.

Catching her breath, she pulled out her phone from the back pocket of her jeans. 'Roger? Seamus has just done a bunk. Okay, okay, keep your pants on, I'm on my way.'

∼

Shelley used the small step at the back door to Athward Hall to lever off her muddy wellies and pushed open the huge door with her shoulder. Patting Otter, the black Labrador, and accepting his slobbery gift of one of Roger's shoes, she made her way to the warmth of the kitchen.

Roger Fleming Bowen, wearing his usual uniform of jeans and a torn rugby shirt, was standing by the large, scrubbed table; his pale-blue eyes were flashing; and his strong, square jaw was clenched in temper.

'He just fucking drove off?' he asked incredulously.

Calmly handing him his shoe, she nodded and lifted the kettle off the simmering plate of the Aga to see if there was enough water for a coffee. 'Said he was sick of you having all the best horses and leaving him with the rubbish.'

'And you never noticed that he'd packed up all of his possessions in the flat?' Roger threw the shoe back to Otter who picked it up and wandered off to his basket.

Shelley stopped spooning sugar into a mug and glared at him. 'Is it my fault now?'

Roger's rigid six-foot frame stooped slightly, and he ran a hand through his blond hair. 'Of course not,' he handed her his mug and watched her add a large spoonful of coffee granules.

'What will you do? Advertise?'

Roger swallowed a mouthful of coffee then shook his head. 'It was horrendous the last time I advertised for staff. All of them were useless. Straight from a six-week course of lessons at the local riding school, thinking they could ride fit event horses—'

'Apart from me,' put in Shelley tartly.

'Well, you'd had a seven-week course at the local riding school, so you were head and shoulders above the other muppets.' His mouth quivered into a smile, and Shelley saw his jawline was softening.

'Sometimes, I seriously wonder why I put up with you and your fantastic sense of humour.'

'Do you know of anyone looking for a job?' He sat down at the table and flicked through *Horse & Hound* to the situations vacant at the back of the magazine.

Shelley thought for a moment. 'The only person I would love to have on the team was packed off in the autumn by Daddy-Dear to sit behind a desk at some property company in London. She was on my coaching course at the Southern Riding Centre; I ended up going to New Zealand with her for six months afterwards. Really good rider, used to event her own horse every summer on the southern circuit.'

Roger's white-haired housekeeper shuffled into the kitchen, carrying a load of washing in a grey plastic basket. There was a silence as she lowered the wooden pulley and began carefully laying items of clothing across the rails.

'Are you talking about the lassie from the chalk cliffs?' Mrs Royal shook a pair of paisley-patterned boxer shorts vigorously.

'Ring her.' Roger suddenly realised Otter was destroying his shoe and jumped up to retrieve it.

'I will. Later.'

'Now,' he replied slowly.

After Shelley had left, Roger sat in silence, occasionally drumming his fingers on the table. Shelley was a good head girl. Brought up in Glasgow and leaving school at the earliest opportunity, she had brought a wealth of knowledge to his yard. She was tough and looked after the horses and other members of staff firmly but fairly. When she had applied to join his team last year, he had been surprised that she wanted to move on from the prolific show jumping yard of Danny Jenks' and her beloved Scotland, but after having her in situ for a few weeks, he had seen that what Danny had lost, he had gained. The other benefit to Shelley was that she didn't fancy him and, in her straight-to-the-point attitude, had made this clear to him in her interview. She had a sharp tongue, and if something wasn't quite right, she was the first person to point it out; she was also very quick-witted and the queen of wisecracks. Now twenty-seven, and despite being ten years his junior, Shelley was able to offer advice to him in a way that no one else really could, not even his paternal grandmother who lived in the West Lodge half a mile away from the Hall. Roger thought ruefully that Shelley was probably the first female and purely plutonic friend he had ever had.

~

Shelley checked her watch as she left the Hall and pulled her woolly hat over her tight blonde curls to make the short walk to the stables. It was four-thirty; bloody Seamus couldn't even wait until the end of the day to go. She would miss his Irish sense of humour and his ability to ride even the trickiest of horses. Brightening somewhat, she realised she wouldn't miss him stuffing his sweaty socks down the side of the sofa or the towering dirty crockery collection in his bedroom.

It was dark now, but the sky was clear, and the air was bitterly cold, indicating there was going to be a hard frost that night. As she walked through the navy-blue gates onto the cobbles, Jules and Caitlyn were sweeping the stable yard.

'Okay, you obviously both heard him. Seamus has gone back to Ireland, so until the boss finds another work rider, you're both stuck with just me.'

Jules, in her red, fitted jacket, straightened blonde hair looking almost white in the stable lights, was the first to stop sweeping. 'I'm glad he's gone; I didn't like him.'

'I didn't mind him.' Caitlyn kept sweeping in a workmanlike fashion. Her wellingtons were strained around her chunky calves, and half of her curly red hair had fallen out of its ponytail. 'He was fooking lazy though.'

~

With the horses settled for the night, it was a little after five o'clock when Shelley opened the door to her flat above the stables. Settling on the sagging sofa with a cup of tea, she sent a voice note to Katie asking how her flashy London job was going.

After a bath, a Cup a Soup and four pieces of toast, she listened to Katie's reply.

'London is bloody awful,' Katie's voice was quiet. 'I handed in my notice this afternoon. Dad's going to have a fit, but I don't care; I can't do another day in the office watching the clock. Mrs Hicken has told me to take a week off and speak to her next Friday, but I'm not bloody going back.'

Shelley tapped the microphone button on her phone. 'Come and stay with me for a few days, if you want?'

'Do you really mean that? Because I would love it, anything to avoid going home and to get away from here. Will you send me the postcode?'

'I'll WhatsApp it to you. Come any time you like, but it's not a good forecast for this weekend.'

'Are you sure that's okay? I don't want to be in the way if you've got to work.'

Shelley laughed. 'You won't be in the way, but you'll end up riding, meaning you won't be able to cross your legs by the second day as you haven't sat on a horse since October.' After a pause, Shelley tapped her phone again. 'Not that crossing your legs has ever been your strong point anyway.'

'You're such a cow sometimes, and *you* can talk,' came Katie's reply.

~

Roger ate his way through the pork casserole that Mrs Royal had left for him without tasting it. He was thinking about Shelley, wondering if she had contacted her friend yet. He was tempted to message her to remind her, but in fairness, Shelley never forgot to do anything that she said she would.

It was after nine, but he still had emails to answer and an owner to ring. Charles Dee had bought the difficult liver chestnut horse called The Mechanic rather cheaply, as no one else seemed to be able to get a tune out of him. Not only was Roger enjoying schooling the horse, but Shelley was also enjoying hacking him out. They had only had the horse in the yard for two weeks, but Charles wanted a progress report. Picturing Charles with his thinning red hair and his suit jacket straining across his beer belly, Roger picked up his phone. Managing to keep the call to under ten minutes, which was something of a triumph, he whistled for Otter, put on his coat and went outside.

Roger had inherited Athward Hall when he was twenty-five after both his parents had been killed in a car crash. His father, having fallen asleep at the wheel, had died instantly, but his mother had clung to life for two days with Roger at her bedside, until she succumbed to her massive head injury. His grief at losing them both so suddenly had played a huge hand in his hasty marriage a year later. He had been infatuated with the elegant brunette Elizabeth De'Alba, and they had married at her family estate in Leicestershire six months after their first date. During their short courtship, they were the golden couple who people turned up at parties and balls just to see. Both were six feet tall with athletic frames and he as fair as she was dark; they exuded glamour and money, and Roger, with his hair cut short which emphasised his chiselled good looks, was the pin-up of horsey teenage girls across the country.

Elizabeth hunted three times a week and was renowned for being a brave, practically suicidal rider. She would jump the biggest part of a hedge if it was the shortest route, and despite what she told *Horse & Hound* about her horses being loved and part of the family, if one went lame, it was sold off cheaply so it could be quickly replaced.

Returning home to Athward after their honeymoon in the Caribbean, Roger realised that he had nothing in common with her except the hunting field. In turn, Elizabeth discovered that the hunting in Northumberland was not as glamorous as in the home counties. Used to being regularly photographed for *Horse*

& Hound in her beautiful navy hunting coat, she felt she had lost her identity now she was merely known as Roger's wife. As the marriage limped on, Roger found that Elizabeth neither knew nor cared about the methods of schooling a top-level event horse. At the time, he was short-listed for the British team, and the final nail in the coffin came when she took his prospective Olympic horse hunting and it broke its leg.

Despite being the third generation of Fleming Bowens to live at Athward Hall, Roger's only close family was his grandmother, who kept watch over the comings and goings with her binoculars at the west entrance of the drive to the Hall.

Hearing Otter pushing his way through the frosty undergrowth at the side of the drive, Roger took his phone out of his coat pocket. 'Still up, Granny? Yes, a swift nightcap would be perfect.' He called to Otter and strode confidently on through the darkness.

Wigeon, Victoria Fleming Bowen's black Labrador, flumped her tail on the floor as Roger opened the front door to West Lodge. Victoria was wearing her nightgown and had put on a red velvet smoking jacket and pale-pink cashmere bed socks to keep out the cold until bedtime. Once she had been a tall woman, but now in her mid-eighties, her frame had buckled, and she walked in a stilted fashion owing to the arthritis in her hips. Despite the hour, Victoria's thinning brown hair was swept neatly off her face, and as removing her make-up was her final task of the day, she still had a thin black line painted across her upper waterline, enhancing her clear blue eyes. She patted Otter in welcome but did not acknowledge her grandson until she had poured them both a whisky from the decanter on the sideboard.

'Trouble?' she asked as they clinked crystal.

'Seamus decided at four o'clock that he would much prefer to be back home in Ireland.'

The small lounge with its crackling woodburning stove was warm after the icy air outside, and Roger could feel his cold cheeks reddening.

Victoria watched the muted television for a moment; they were advertising exercise bicycles on QVC. 'Good rider,' she said eventually. 'But a bit of a scallywag when it came to stable management.'

'Really?' Roger looked up in astonishment. 'How do you know?'

'Well firstly, whichever horse he was riding always had wood shavings in its tail, and secondly, Caitlyn told me that she always had to clean his boots before a competition.'

Roger placed the back of his hand against his flushed cheek.

'I wouldn't dream of telling you your job, Roger, but sometimes I think you need to teach a little less and be on your own yard more.'

'Teaching brings in the money.' Roger swirled his whisky around the glass.

'I understand that,' replied Victoria gravely. 'But you must miss absolutely nothing regarding your own horses. You can't leave it all to Shelley.' She took a mouthful of Glenfiddich.

Roger's phone vibrated in his pocket. He hadn't finished reading Shelley's message when his grandmother asked when the new girl was starting.

Three

Katie had been awake most of the night, drifting in and out of the most horrible dreams.

At five-thirty, after waking from a dream which involved Rob from Accounts, a stolen metal biscuit tin containing a hundred quid and Matt the builder in just his boxers, she had given in and got up. She had been intending to leave London after eleven o'clock, by which time all the shoppers would be safely ensconced in whatever shop was promoting slashed prices as part of their January sale. But as she was up and awake, she decided to shower, pack and go. Knowing she was about to escape, leaving London could not come quickly enough.

Retching, she used a handful of toilet paper to scrape the short, pink, curly hair from the floor of the shower and cleaned her teeth as she waited for the water to get hot. As she washed her hair with the slightly grimy bar of soap from the sink, through the steam she took in Matt's razor lying on the bench next to a shrinking blob of shaving foam, Orchid's tiny red and black bra on the top of the heated towel rail and Olive's enormous grey knickers on the bar underneath. There were two filthy mugs growing mould on the cabinet in the corner, a half-drunk glass of something with a slice of lemon in it, a pizza box at a jaunty angle in the cement-encrusted bucket they used as a bathroom bin and several pieces of dental floss lying on the floor beside it. A half-smoked spliff was balanced on the windowsill, and as the Fray Bentos pie tin that was used as an ashtray was overflowing, someone had taken to putting their fags out in the parched soil of the yellowing spider plant.

Being a Saturday, none of her housemates were awake when she left at quarter-past six. Writing "away for a week" on the back of an empty envelope she found Olive was using as a bookmark in her *Cooking in a Bedsitter* recipe book, she stuck it to her bedroom door and wondered if Olive had tried the Shrimp Wiggle or the Lamb Tomato Quickie.

As she tiptoed down the hallway carrying her bags to the front door, Olive's door swung open. Standing in her colossal billowing nightie, her grey hair, usually pinned up on top of her head, was hanging long past her shoulders. Saying she had heard someone moving about, Katie replied that she was going to Northumberland for a week to stay with a friend.

'I hope you've packed a Kuala Lumpur.' Olive wiped the dust off the brass number on her door with the long sleeve of her nightshirt. 'It's bladdy cold up North.'

'I've locked my room.'

Olive nodded. 'That's good, darlin', I'll keep an eye on it 'til you're back. Enjoy yourself, love, and will I save that bowl of vegetable soup in the fridge goin' to waste and 'ave it for my lunch today?'

Katie replied with a grin that she was most welcome to it.

∼

Leaving London and Capital Radio behind, she made it all the way to Weatherby before she had to stop for petrol. After filling the tank and paying for the fuel with her illicit credit card, she pulled into the car park. Feeling sleepy, she climbed onto the back seat of her car and, looking at the pocket on the back of the passenger seat where she had found Rob's son's sponsorship money two days previously, she fell asleep.

Waking just before eleven, freezing cold but rejuvenated after half an hour's sleep, she shivered fiercely as she ate the packet of Monster Munch that the credit card had paid for earlier and prepared to set off for the last leg of the journey. Christ it was cold; she turned the heater up. Putting Athward Hall's postcode into her phone, she saw that the blue dot of her destination was in the middle of nowhere. As she rejoined the motorway traffic, she listened to the local radio weather report before her thoughts turned to Shelley.

If you'd rung Shelley at three in the morning and told her you were in France with three horses, only one shoe, an annoying tramp hanging around and a tax return you couldn't complete, Shelley would have found a way of sorting everything out.

They had hit it off instantly at the Southern Riding Centre. Katie with her long, brown hair and Shelley with her blonde ringlets were easily the most popular girls in the halls of residence and were the heart of any practical jokes and tricks. As alcohol was banned from any part of the complex, they began brewing their own incredibly potent banana wine in the attic, the wine being gradually decanted through a long tube fed through a trapdoor and into Shelley's room. Unaware that the longer the wine brewed, the stronger it became – and after one poor seventeen-year-old trainee was hospitalised with alcohol poisoning after drinking a pint of it – Shelley and Katie had come clean. On the verge of being sent home, it was only their course manager, who pleaded that the centre needed their high pass rates to lure future students to the course, who had saved them both.

After finishing the course, Katie was already lined up to go to New Zealand for six months to groom in a polo yard. Knowing that Shelley was going to have to look for a job back home in Scotland or return to her parents' home on a council estate in

Glasgow, Katie had made a phone call, organised the visa and had taken Shelley with her.

It was almost one o'clock when the A1 narrowed to single carriageway and, looking down to the right, Katie saw the dense bank of threatening clouds hanging over the grey North Sea. Despite the watery sun behind her, the landscape was bleak, the barren black hedges creating boundaries between the orangey-brown fields of clay and the green turf dotted with sheep. Finding it hard to comprehend that she was driving the main route from London to Edinburgh, Katie found the road was continuing between walls of rock which had obviously been blasted away to allow the new, straighter sections of the highway to resume its route to Scotland. Colossal snowflakes were beginning to drift down to the ground as she turned off the trunk road, and she found she could no longer see the sea through the storm. She watched the white flakes in hypnotic fashion as they drifted down to the windscreen, melting as they met the warm glass, and followed the slippery, twisting road carefully as it dropped down towards the coast. The travel news broke through her music, warning that there were long tailbacks at the Angel of the North, heavy snow showers would continue across the region throughout the afternoon and temperatures tonight would dip to minus five in rural areas. A yellow gritting lorry travelling quickly through the blizzard back up to the A1, its orange lights flashing, made her start as it splattered her car with grit. Snow in Dorset didn't last long, and the snowflakes were never as big as these; it was as if a crazed pillow fight had unexpectedly become violent, and goose feathers were floating down from the strange yellowy-grey sky.

The road wound from left to right, and after five miles, there was a wobbly looking signpost where Katie could just make out the words "Athward 3 miles" in worn black writing. The narrower road took her straight through the middle of the charming village of Athward. The houses were mostly built of shadowy Whinstone, but Katie noticed an estate of light-coloured new builds to the left as she went past the "please drive slowly through our village" sign. The snow was still falling heavily, laying white pages across the slate rooftops and smothering the road ahead of her. The red-haired vicar closing the metal gate to the churchyard, her dog collar visible above her half-fastened coat, gave a cheery wave through the silent-falling flakes. Katie continued past the little white hotel and saw that there was a small shop with bags of logs outside gathering snow, next to the triangular-shaped village green. Further on, there was a pub, and through the window, Katie could see people standing around the bar beneath the swinging sign proclaiming it was the "Cup and Kettle".

Leaving the village behind, the road suddenly swung to the right before straightening out. The snow was blowing in thicker blasts from the sea, and Katie slowed down as she found all she could see was the hedge on the left of the road. Shelley had warned her that there was no sign to Athward Hall, and as the huge pillars appeared through the blizzard, she braked hard, and the car briefly slid on the coating of snow on the road. Turning between the pillars, she glanced at the small lodge with its navy door on her right and then at the single track of the drive which stretched out in front of her. After half a mile, the towering stark trees and low-growing evergreens thinned out, and the Hall, in its golden sandstone, reared up in front of her. Following Shelley's instructions, she followed the driveway to the left towards the stable yard.

Parking beside the tall stable buildings next to the yard gates, Katie got out of the car and stood in the falling snow, listening to the strange silence it was creating. She inhaled the wonderful aroma of horses and sweet-smelling haylage and raised her eyes towards the sky, blinking as the snowflakes landed on her face. Pulling on her coat, she walked through the open gates and found herself in the most beautiful square, cobbled stable yard.

From where she stood in the middle of the yard, no stables were visible through the high windows, and she found the boxes were accessed by wide doorways on two sides. On her right there was a huge arch in the building, and standing under it out of the snow, Katie found there were three stables off to her left and right. The navy glossed door in front of her was slightly ajar, and after tentatively pushing it open, she found herself in a vast tack room. Logs crackled merrily in the old cast-iron grate in the far corner, and Katie walked over to it, past the bridles hanging on the left of the room. Warming her hands in the heat, she turned to look at the racks of saddles which almost reached the high ceiling. There was a tall, barred window with the shutters pulled back above a Belfast sink, in which navy bandages were soaking in soapy water, and on the table in the middle of the room, there stood a heap of old *Horse & Hound* and *Stable Tattle* magazines, along with several empty crisp packets, a woolly hat and a half-eaten Pot Noodle with a fork still stuck in it. Katie thought the tack room was an awful lot warmer and cleaner than the bathroom in Stamford Hill.

Hearing someone approaching, she hurriedly made her way to the doorway and collided heavily with a very tall man. Gasping as her face smacked against his chest, she was overwhelmed by the smell of Hugo Boss and felt his hands gripping her arms firmly to keep her upright.

'Sorry.' She felt dizzy from the force of the impact.

Roger slowly let go of her and looked down with an expression of amusement twinkling in his blue eyes. 'Are you alright? You almost knocked me over.'

'Possible grade-three concussion, but I'm sure I'll recover.' She touched her nose gingerly.

'You must be Katie?' He spoke in a deep, clipped voice, slightly posh and as though his brain was already moving on to the next task.

'Yes.' She placed her index fingers into the corners of her eyes to remove the tears.

'Roger,' he smiled at her, 'and now that I've just nearly broken your nose, let me help you with your bags to the flat.'

24

'It's okay.' Katie found she was unable to take her watering eyes off him; he was even more handsome than she had thought possible.

'It's the very least I can do; the girls are riding out at the moment, but given the weather, I don't think they'll be too long.'

Carrying the two bags from her car back into the yard, he led her to a small blue door with a tiny glass window, on the opposite side of the yard to the tack room. Turning the round metal handle smoothed by the hands of many grooms before, he pushed open the scratching door, flicked the light switch and a single bulb lit up a set of curved and worn stone stairs. He gave her a smile as he handed her the bags and turned back to the yard. Closing the door, Katie peeped through the dirty window and watched him answer his phone as he walked back to the tack room in the snow. Taking a deep breath and touching her bruised nose again, she began to climb the stairs. There were several split logs on every stone step, and at the top, the steps curved to the right where there was another door. Opening it, she had to step up into the flat and found she was standing in a small space with a long, very narrow pale-blue galley kitchen in front of her, with a hot water tank at the far end half hidden by an orange curtain. The low window on the left looked onto the drive as it swept around the outside of the stable yard, and behind the door to her right was a small bathroom. The door in front of her opened into a lounge where Katie felt heat like the office of Hicken Lettings. There was a table and two chairs underneath the window on the right that overlooked the yard and two exceedingly small, very worn sofas on either side of a little black log burner which was burning gleefully, creating friendly orange flames. The two doors that were either side of the log burner both had Yale locks fitted and, not wanting to pry, she sat on the sofa nearest to the stove and contemplated messaging her mum.

A week, she thought. Almost a whole week to not have to endure Matt's bloody fish and chips and the smell of Sam's microwaved pizza. Thinking of the seventeen pence to her name and an ever-increasing credit card account, that she knew she could only pay the minimum payment on, she started to panic. Knowing she had to do something to take her mind off her increasing debts, she found a pair of Shelley's boots by the door and a very torn coat and went down to the stables. After tidying six boxes, she heard the muffled sound of horseshoes approaching through the snow.

Looking over the grooming kit and propped up dressage whips on the windowsill, she saw Shelley leading a liver chestnut across the yard. There was a very thin girl with a fully made-up face and almost white-blonde hair getting off a dark-coloured horse and a not-very-slim red-haired girl still in the saddle, feet out of the stirrups, chatting madly to no one in particular.

'For God's sake stop bloody talking, Caitlyn!' Shelley yelled. 'Get him inside out of the cold!'

Giving a grin, Katie put down her wheelbarrow and ran out onto the snow-covered cobbles to give Shelley a hug.

'Why didn't you message me when you got here?' Shelley wailed. 'We've been for miles because I thought you must have been held up.'

Katie replied that she could have robbed the entire tack room and stolen all the horses, but Roger had found her and had shown her the flat.

'You mean the *Dorchester*,' Shelley put in.

'Why the *Dorchester*?' asked Katie, imitating Shelley's dramatic tone.

'Because it's so rough,' Shelley laughed. 'Come on, let's get out of this damn white stuff.'

Following her into a stable at the top of the yard, Katie watched as Shelley took off the horse's tack and, leaving the exercise sheet over his quarters, vigorously towel dried his head and neck.

'It should be gone by tomorrow afternoon,' said Shelley, alluding to the snow. 'Bloody nightmare.'

'I love it,' enthused Katie. 'How often does it snow here?'

'Often, but as we're so near the sea, it has to be seriously cold before it lies for long.'

'It feels like Christmas.'

'Only without the day off, the presents, crackers and sledging.'

At six o'clock, Shelley poured two large vodka and tonics and put a shepherd's pie in the oven, saying she hoped Katie was hungry. After the vegetable soup diet, the shepherd's pie was the best thing Katie had ever tasted.

'I didn't know you could cook like that.' Katie was using a piece of bread to wipe her plate clean; after having only a packet of Monster Munch all day, she was absolutely starving.

'I can't.' Shelley put her plate on the lounge floor. 'But Roger's housekeeper, Mrs Royal, can.'

'Oh my God, he's to die for, isn't he?' Katie reached for another slice of bread. 'I never thought he was as good looking as that. Although he did nearly knock me out when I crashed into him.'

Shelley lay back on her sofa and unfastened the button on her jeans. 'So, he measures up to the photos of him that you used to have on your bedroom wall?'

Katie laughed. 'Up until now, I thought those photographs were cleverly taken, but he really is that gorgeous from every angle.'

'You're not allowed to shag him.' Shelley was smiling as she shook her head. 'If you do, I can't have you back to stay. He's got a foul temper as it is, I would hate to see him sexually frustrated at the same time.'

'Really?'

'What? About not shagging him or his foul temper?'

'He comes across as being so nice, I can't believe he ever loses his temper.'

'Oh, believe me, it's fucking ferocious; he's had Caitlyn in tears a few times when he's lost his rag. Thankfully, it doesn't happen that often.' Shelley watched as Katie finally put her knife and fork together. 'Anyway, tell me about that hot bloke you were seeing last summer. What happened to him?'

'I wasn't as keen on him as he was on me. I tried loads of times to dump him, but he just didn't get it. That was the only good thing about moving to London, being able to finally get rid of him, and even then, he said he would come to London every weekend. Dad was mad as Jamie's dad is on the local show committee and he wanted to be invited to join.'

'And Daddy-Dear packed you off to London to stop you "horsing around" as he calls it?'

Katie nodded. 'I hate it, Shell – I've got no money – I've lived on vegetable soup for weeks, and I'm sick of using shit toothpaste and washing-up liquid instead of shampoo because it's all I can afford. I've got a credit card and seventeen pence to my name.'

Shelley laughed and Katie had to smile; it sounded ludicrous.

'You must be earning plenty,' Shelley took a slug of vodka and tonic, 'how come you're skint? Are you spending it all on foundation and fashion magazines?'

'Minimum wage, and the room rent is extortionate. That's why yesterday I told Old Hicken to shove her job.'

'What's Daddy-Dear said about that?' Shelley's blonde eyebrows were raised.

Katie wrinkled her nose. 'I *might* not have told him yet. Because Hicken's told me to take a week's holiday to think about it, I've got time to think of something.'

'For the love of God, you're going to give Eddie a heart attack.' Shelley shook her head. 'Why don't you speak to your mum? She couldn't stand being in London either.'

'She told me she loved it,' said Katie in disbelief.

'She hated it! When I stayed with you after we came back from New Zealand, she told me she couldn't wait to get back to the country.'

'I'll ring her tomorrow.'

Shelley knew that she wouldn't. Katie had always been the one with the money, the supportive mother driving the lorry all over the country so her daughter could compete, the one with the connections in Australia and New Zealand, even being able to hook Shelley up with a job in an event yard over there at a week's notice. Now, although Katie was unaware of it, Shelley was holding all the cards.

'Look, you must be knackered. You were up at stupid o'clock this morning and have driven halfway up the country. Go to bed, and I'll even let you have a lie-in tomorrow and won't drag you out of bed to muck out. I'll be in for coffee about nine; make sure the kettle's on.'

After Katie had gone to bed, Shelley drained the last of her vodka. Picking up her phone, she messaged Roger, asking him who he wanted Katie to ride tomorrow. Surprised that he answered immediately, Roger replied he wanted her to hack out Paperchase with her, Jules and Caitlyn and then jump him in the school. Raising her eyebrows, she replied with a "K", which she knew would wind him up as he never used text speak in his messages. Yawning, she carried the plates into the kitchen, stoked the burner with three more logs in the hope it would last until morning, cleaned her teeth and fell into bed.

∼

Woken by the sound of chatter and Radio 1 floating up from the stable yard the next morning, Katie took a sip from the glass by her surprisingly comfortable bed and winced as the icy water hit her teeth. Dressing quickly and rushing to the heat of the log burner, she pushed back the orange velvet curtains in the lounge. The yard beneath the Dorchester was still white, but the snow on the roof opposite was beginning to melt and drip into the gutter. Looking at her watch, she quickly went into the cold kitchen and filled the kettle.

With her riding hat and boots being safely encompassed at her home in Dorset and not wanting to alert her parents to the fact that she was having a cheeky week away in Northumberland, Katie found herself wearing Shelley's second-favourite boots, jacket and a hat unearthed from the enormous tack room.

Shelley, riding The Mechanic who was the horse Katie had watched her untacking the day before, shouted that they would take the top route as it was definitely gritted.

'What do you mean "definitely gritted"?' queried Katie as she led Paperchase towards the mounting block in the yard.

Shelley turned The Mechanic carefully on the liberally salted cobbles. 'If Caitlyn's Uncle Tommy has been on the gritter, he always grits the top road to the village.'

'And if Uncle Tommy hasn't been on the gritter?' Katie swung herself into Paperchase's saddle and rode up to Shelley.

'Then we take the track through the woods or use the school,' replied Caitlyn cheerfully.

As they trotted around the gritted roads, Katie watched Shelley ignoring The Mechanic as he shied at a female cyclist clad in yellow Lycra and then turned her attention to her companions.

Jules, her make-up perfect under her velvet hat in her beautifully fitted riding jacket, was riding the little brown horse called Brogue, and Caitlyn, in her yellow, oversized high-visibility coat and her non-stop chatter, was allowing Lightoller to slop along in a world of his own.

Caitlyn's stirrup clinked against Katie's as they trotted up a hill on the way home. 'What do you think of him?' she dropped her eyes, gesturing to Paperchase.

'He's very nice,' Katie patted the beautiful dark neck. 'But he's much better at turning left than right. Do you ride him much?'

Caitlyn's pale-blue eyes widened. 'Not very often, just for hacking. I don't know anything about schooling.'

'Schooling is easy, all you've got to do is walk, trot and canter, on both reins in the correct outline.' Katie smiled.

'Perhaps you'd like to school Paperchase when we get back,' said Jules acidly, who had been schooling him herself for the past two weeks.

'Where do you live?' Caitlyn's freckled cheeks were turning pink.

'London now, Dorset originally.'

'I've always wanted to live in London, just for all that partying.' Caitlyn pulled Lightoller back to a walk as she saw Shelley was slowing The Mechanic.

'You need a very flash job to be able to afford the partying,' Katie confessed.

'Do you not have a flash job?' asked Jules.

'Not at all,' replied Katie flatly. 'I have a horrible job that my dad found for me to stop me working with horses.'

'Some dull admin post,' said Jules in a bored voice.

'Actually, I work for a letting agency.'

'Like I said, an admin post.'

Katie looked at her in annoyance before her eyes travelled downwards and she coolly told Jules her girth was loose.

'I love working with ponies,' Caitlyn was trying to tie her hair back, 'but me and Jules aren't full-time here, and last year, after I was eighteen, I got a job at the Cup and Kettle behind the bar, so I do that as well.'

'Do you have another job?' Katie directed the question at Jules, who was lowering her leg after tightening her girth.

The blonde woman stared at her. 'I go to the gym and do yoga four times a week, I haven't time for another job.'

Katie ignored the edge to her voice. 'And you both live in the village?'

'Yes,' Caitlyn was searching her pockets for a hanky, 'I live with my parents in Cheviot View, and Jules lives in the estate by the church.'

'Is that the new build I saw when I drove through yesterday?'

'Yes,' said Jules slickly, 'I'm not a *real* local, like Caitlyn.'

Caitlyn blew her nose noisily. 'I keep telling you, Jules, you moved here over ten years ago, that makes you a local.'

Jules made a snorting sound as she eased Brogue into a jog to catch up with Shelley, leaving Katie and Caitlyn to catch eyes for a second.

'You're not really a local unless—'

'Your great-grandfather was born here,' finished Katie. 'And even then, you'd still be called the "new people".'

Caitlyn giggled. 'How do you know?'

'Small villages in Dorset are just the same. Were you and Jules at school together?'

'Fook no, she's twenty-six.'

Katie looked ahead to Jules's rigid back riding in front of her. Jules was either as hostile as this with everyone she met or had taken a dislike to her. Maybe she shouldn't have said anything about Paperchase as Jules had obviously taken the comment personally.

'She's like that with everyone,' said Caitlyn, as if she knew what Katie was thinking. 'It's really weird because her mum and dad are really nice. That was her mum who passed us on her bike a few minutes ago.'

Looking at the snow-covered hedges and the white fields at the side of the road, Katie realised that she didn't care what Jules thought of her, she was away from London and sitting on a horse again. Her stomach dropped slightly when she thought of her dad, who was currently under the impression that she was happily working in the office job that he had generated for her. She still had a few days to think of something, and her rent at Stamford Hill was paid to the end of the month. It was the wrong time of year to be going back to New Zealand, but she could ring Brett and ask if he would have her back. Smiling to herself, she knew Brett would take her back tomorrow if he could.

'Are you looking forward to going back to London?'

'No.' Katie leant forward and stroked Paperchase's neck.

'Why?' Caitlyn had her eyes wide open again.

'I hate it. If you want, I'll take you back with me on Friday and you can see how awful it is.'

'I've never been to London. The idea of living there is nice, but I don't think I could leave here.'

'Believe me, here is much nicer,' said Katie grimly.

Roger had slipped back unnoticed to the yard and, standing in the shadows of the arched walkway that led from the stable yard to the outdoor school, he watched Katie jumping Paperchase over the coloured show jumps. He admired the light style of riding and the enthusiasm and encouragement that was flowing from her into the horse. Paperchase was a nervy character and Roger was kicking himself for letting Jules ride him so much, especially when he heard Katie shout to Shelley that the horse was as stiff as a board on his right rein.

He had looked up Katie's competition record on the British Eventing website; he had rung the Southern Riding Centre; he had even tracked down the polo yard and the eventing yard on the other side of the world to gain an unofficial curriculum vitae. Catching Shelley's questioning eyes from the edge of the school, he smiled back at her and nodded.

～

At ten o'clock on Monday morning, Roger picked up his phone with a sigh and rang his head girl. 'I think I am going to have to deal with a situation,' he began.

'What do mean *a situation*? Can't you just say *shout at someone* instead?' Shelley yawned and sat up in her bed. 'And why are you ringing me on my day off?'

'Jules has just asked me if she could apply for the position of work rider.'

Shelley blew out a lungful of air loudly. 'Well, I suppose you have to admire the ambition and confidence in her own ability.'

'She's going to be pissed off, and you know she will take the most enormous huff.'

'An award-winning huff, but she's only here because she wants to get into your pants. Why do you think she straightens her hair and wears her best breeches every day?'

'I thought her hair was just naturally very straight,' said Roger smoothly.

~

On Thursday afternoon, Shelley and Katie were coming down the Dorchester's stone stairs when Shelley realised her phone was ringing on the lounge table.

'Wait for me in the tack room, unless you can find Jules or Caitlyn, they'll show you the tack for Bean.' She turned and ran back up the steps to the flat.

'Forget that,' she said five minutes later as Katie was looking in confusion at Bean's bridle. 'Go and see Roger; just open the back door and shout. I'll school her.' She ushered Katie out of the stable with a grin. 'Just try not to shag him.'

As Katie left for the Hall, Shelley shouted for Jules.

'Did you give Katie the tack for this horse?' she asked furiously.

Refusing to meet her eyes, Jules agreed that she had.

'So, you'll know that this is Lightoller's.' She threw the bridle at her. 'I won't have you trying to mess things up on my yard, so don't even try it.'

'Keep your knickers on,' Jules picked the bridle up from the floor. 'I just made a mistake, and I'm sure *Zara Phillips* would have realised the bridle was too big when she went to put it on.'

'Tindall,' said Shelley shortly.

'What?'

'She's been Zara Tindall since she got married about ten years ago.'

Jules rolled her eyes.

'And I'm still waiting for the right bridle,' snapped Shelley.

Before Katie's hand had made contact with the handle, the back door to Athward Hall flew open. Mrs Royal was drying her hands on a tea towel, and she quickly shepherded Katie inside.

'Well, you must be Katie,' she spoke with a slow but strong

Northumbrian accent. 'I'm Mrs Royal, Roger's housekeeper. Now come in, lass, and let's have a nice cup of tea – bring your boots in and put them in here.' She gestured to a small room on the left with a line of coats hanging above a row of boots.

For a single bloke, thought Katie, Roger seemed to have an awful lot of coats and boots.

Mrs Royal, in her blue tabard, led Katie through a kitchen with a washing machine and tumble drier and little else, into another kitchen with a pale-blue Aga and a scrubbed wooden table. Roger was sitting in the only armchair in the room, stockinged feet resting on the table and his phone clamped between his ear and shoulder as he flicked through a heap of paperwork. He smiled at Katie in greeting, and she was mortified to feel a weakening in her knees.

'Now, I've made a fruitcake and it's lovely.' Mrs Royal poured her a cup of tea from the blue and white teapot. 'Would you like a piece?'

'No thank you, Mrs Royal, I've just had lunch.'

Katie pulled a face as she sipped the well-stewed tea and looked around at the photographs on the walls. They were all of Roger, jumping enormous fences or looking incredibly handsome in his top hat and tails, trotting among the flowers of a dressage arena.

Mrs Royal reappeared with a slab of fruitcake the size of a paperback book and a slice of Wensleydale on a tea plate. 'I brought you a piece anyway, in case you fancy a nibble later,' she whispered as Roger supressed a smile.

'You really shouldn't do that,' said Katie as Roger finally put down his phone and rolled his neck to relieve the tension.

'What?'

'Hold your phone between your ear and shoulder; it's really bad for affecting your alignment.' She mimicked how he had been holding the phone.

'I'd never thought about it.' He sounded surprised.

Shit, she thought, *I shouldn't have said that.* 'It's like a teenage girl who tips sideways in the saddle, usually because they play a lot of hockey.' She stopped abruptly as she saw Roger had his head on the side, smiling at her.

'Have you enjoyed being here this week?'

'I really have, except my seat bones are on fire and I can't cross my legs because my thighs are so sore.'

'Too long out of the saddle.' He picked up the fruitcake. 'Were you going to eat this?'

She shook her head.

'Katie, I would like to offer you a job.' He stopped, seeing her shocked expression. 'You don't have to accept it.'

'What kind of job?'

Roger got up, lifted one of the Aga hotplate covers and put the kettle on. 'Well, judging by this fruitcake, I seem to have a rather good housekeeper, but if you were interested in riding some of the novices for me this season?' He was standing close to her, and she saw how very tall he was.

Katie opened her mouth, but no sound came out.

'Brett Taylor was very complimentary about you; he even asked if you were thinking of going back to New Zealand.'

'You rang Brett?' she asked in amazement.

'Of course. I trust Shelley implicitly, but I'm certainly not going to invite someone to join my team without doing my homework.'

'Did you ring anyone else?'

'The Southern Riding Centre, Mark Ruepert. Do you want me to go on?'

'Have you ever thought about joining MI5? Because they could probably really use someone like you.'

'Think about it.' He finished the fruitcake. 'When do you have to be back in London?'

'Officially, tomorrow afternoon to see my boss, but I'm not going.' She snapped the piece of cheese in half. 'I'll just go to Stamford Hill and empty my room.'

'Are you sure?' Roger was looking at her intently. 'It's a big decision to move this far.'

'I've worked in New Zealand; Northumberland isn't as far from Dorset as that is.'

'You don't have to decide now; you can take some time.'

'I don't need to.' She looked at the boiling kettle. 'Do you want me to make the coffees?'

Four

It was a cold but bright morning in Dorset. Glittering patches of frost were lying in the shadows where the sun had not yet reached, and Joanna Holland's thoroughbred's breath was forming huge, slow moving clouds in front of them as she rode him home to Mairhead House.

She hadn't heard from Katie since Tuesday night, and as they usually spoke at least twice a week, Joanna wondered idly if her daughter had found a new boyfriend. She had sounded distracted during their last call, and Joanna had been given the feeling that she wasn't alone. She hoped Katie hadn't begun a relationship with the huge-handed builder or the flaky-looking boy who worked in the pizza restaurant; Eddie would have a seizure.

Joanna worried about her daughter living in London, knowing that she would be far happier in the country, working outside and not stuck in a static job behind a desk. She sighed as she smoothed a strand of Nightshade's mane onto the correct side; she should have been firmer with Eddie when he had suggested that Katie needed to get a proper job, but her husband couldn't comprehend a world outside his own.

Now fifty years of age, Joanna still rode every day and

competed during the summer months. Nightshade was an ex-racehorse, and after owning him for eighteen months, retraining him and introducing him to the world of eventing, she had plans to sell him in the spring and look for something else to bring on and sell. She had heard from the Hansford family only yesterday, the people who had bought Katie's event horse, Grenadier. They were thrilled with him, and having had the horse since the end of November and doing some winter dressage and show jumping with him, Annabel was looking forward to competing him when the eventing season began in March.

Seeing a tractor approaching carrying a ragged round bale of hay in front of it on its forks, Joanna placed a calming hand on Nightshade's neck and gave Jamie the driver a wave as he passed. Poor Jamie, every time Joanna went into the village shop, Jamie's mother Rhoda insisted on telling her that heartbroken Jamie still hadn't got over Katie moving to London. Unlike Rhoda, Joanna appreciated that the only benefit in Katie moving to the capital was that she had stopped stringing Jamie along, and he was saving a lot of money, as his riding lessons had been costing him a fortune.

As the cobb and thatch of Mairhead House nestling at the bottom of the hill came into sight through the leafless oak trees, Joanna recalled how delighted Eddie had been last summer when he discovered his daughter was finally dating a farmer's son and not, as he put it, "some long-haired surfer who can't afford socks or someone who stinks of horse piss". The problem, Joanna surmised, was that Jamie had desperately tried to learn everything there was to know about horses, mistakenly thinking that he and Katie could have something in common to talk about at length. He had bought books on three-day eventing and dressage and had even taken riding lessons in secret, so he could surprise Katie with a romantic ride through the bluebell-blanketed woods. Joanna had gently tried to discourage him from his equestrian endeavours, especially after one disastrous day at Mellington horse trials when he had told Katie that if she'd been using a pelham and running martingale, Grenadier wouldn't have refused fence seven on the cross country.

Whereas Joanna tried to quietly dissuade Jamie from becoming involved in the horsey world, Eddie positively encouraged it, telling Jamie it was the way to Katie's heart. Joanna felt that Eddie had a truly short memory, because thirty-one years ago, Eddie had also disastrously tried to take up riding in an aim to impress her nineteen-year-old self.

As Eddie had often seen Joanna riding through the narrow lanes around Mairhead House, he assumed that riding a horse was like driving a car and didn't have any riding lessons before hiring a horse to ride at the Dorset Hunt's opening meet.

After three large glasses of whisky, he thought he looked very dashing in his new riding kit and had been photographed several times for the local paper. Unfortunately, as the field set off, Eddie found he was advancing towards an enormous hedge at a tremendous pace and found that this crazed creature he was astride didn't stop when you shouted "whoa". He managed to cling on as they raced past the other riders, too scared to even feel like an utter buffoon, but when the wise old hireling decided that jumping the huge hedge into the next field was completely out of the question, he shuddered to a jolting halt, throwing his inexperienced rider over his head. Eddie not only broke a shoulder, a collarbone and several ribs, but he also punctured a lung, and to add insult to quite serious injury, Joanna was completely unaware of the carnage behind her and, after soaring over the hedge, had enjoyed a thoroughly wonderful day.

Although the dashing Eddie, with his dark hair and second-hand Porsche, did eventually manage to woo the beautiful Joanna, that was the very last time he had anything to do with a horse. It was therefore Joanna who had carted Katie and an assortment of ponies around Pony Club and then, as she got older, dressage lessons, show jumping training and British Eventing. Eddie did turn up on the odd occasion but, despite other fathers telling him his daughter was talented, he refused to see anything to do with horses as sport.

As a teenager, Katie had made her pocket money from the string of tricky children's ponies that arrived for two weeks' bed and breakfast at Mairhead House. Her methods were simple and worked with most bored and overweight ponies. She simply exercised them vigorously and then encouraged the small jockeys and parents to come and ride in front of her, so she could assess the problems which were persistently man-made. Being young, even the non-horsey parents were not intimidated by her and were able to ask questions about ponies and horse care that they would not have dared put to the tweed-wearing shooting stick brigade at Pony Club.

As Joanna walked to the back door of the house, hens clucking after her demanding kitchen scraps, Eddie rang her from the golf course.

'Your bloody daughter handed in her notice yesterday,' he roared.

'Always *my* bloody daughter when she's done something you don't like.' Joanna removed her boots with the metal bootjack.

'You can talk to her,' he barked and hung up without saying goodbye.

~

Joanna watched Katie's car pull up in the parking spot next to hers and switched on the kettle.

'You can't just walk out of a job, no matter how much you hate it,' said Joanna half an hour later.

'I didn't walk out,' objected Katie, 'I tried to hand in my notice last week, and the old bag told me to go away and get some sun.' She laughed without humour. 'Get some sun with seventeen pence to my name. Stupid cow.'

'Your dad got that job for you, and he's desperate to see you in a full-time job.' Joanna was nursing her coffee with both hands. 'Why didn't you tell me you were so short of money? I would have transferred some to you.'

'Because Dad was adamant that I had to do it by myself. Anyway, I've now got a full-time job,' Katie was flicking through *Horse & Hound*, 'with an immediate start, which is why I'm here to get my things.'

She turned the page to see a smiling Roger in his navy-blue jacket holding the reins of Paperchase, Brogue and Vision in front of his open tack room door, under the title "Behind the Scenes". She breathed in. From Monday, she would be working for him, riding those very horses that were gracing a two-page spread in the most famous equine magazine in the country.

'I hardly think your dad is going to be jumping through hoops when you tell him it's a full-time job with horses. Though,' Joanna paused, looking over Katie's shoulder, 'he is so incredibly good looking.'

'I presume you mean Dad and not Roger,' snapped Katie.

Joanna recovered herself. 'Well, both. Obviously. And I do recall you had posters of Roger Fleming Bowen on your bedroom wall during your Pony Club years.' She began loading their cups into the dishwasher. 'What is he like? Is he nice?'

'Very, or I wouldn't be going to work for him.' She flapped the magazine shut. 'I'll just get my car loaded and go.'

'You can't just turn around and go straight back. For goodness' sake, Katie, at least get a good night's sleep and travel up tomorrow.'

'To be honest, I can't face seeing Dad. He's just going to rant about how I'm throwing my life away, blah, blah, blah and I'm more than a bit worried that I'm just going to tell him to fuck off.' She pulled her hair into a ponytail.

'Why don't we go out for supper tonight? Just the two of us.'

'I'd really like that.'

'And you're sure? About moving to Northumberland?'

'Mum, there are literally thousands of people who would kill for this opportunity – he's one of the best trainers in the country.'

'I know.' Joanna ruffled her daughter's ponytail. 'Just, unfortunately, your father doesn't understand horses the way we do.'

Five

'We'll have to limit the vodka to weekends only,' Shelley panted as she hauled more of Katie's belongings up the stone stairs.

'And there's karaoke every Saturday in the Cup and Kettle – you'll have to come.' Caitlyn's face had gone crimson with the exertion of carrying a bag full of books on one arm and a body protector on the other. 'Lovely boots,' she nodded at Katie's black leather riding boots that were lying on top of the mountain of her possessions. 'And at least Mrs Royal's left you a beef casserole, so you don't have to cook tonight.' She looked longingly at the enormous dish covered in tinfoil.

'Caitlyn, would you like to stay for dinner in return for your help, and we can give you a lift home afterwards?' asked Shelley wearily.

'Oooh yes please! Thanks very much.' Caitlyn laid the body protector next to the boots on the top of the heap. 'Dad'll probably come and get me if I ask him.'

'For the love of God, did you have to bring so much stuff?' Shelley stared at the mound of what seemed to be all Katie's worldly goods. 'And are all your clothes *pink*?'

'It's my favourite colour,' Katie protested. 'And as I suspect my dad is going to change the locks now I'm gone, I wasn't leaving anything to chance.'

'What a lovely jacket!' Caitlyn was pulling clothes out of an Ikea bag. 'Could I borrow it some time?'

'Only if you cut off an arm,' said Shelley.

Jules had shown a cool attitude of displeasure when she heard that Katie was to be the new work rider. Worried by Shelley's straight-talking and direct approach, Roger had even broken the news to her himself.

'Am I not good enough?' Jules had whispered, her blue eyes brimming with tears, chin down so she was looking up at him through her dyed lashes, jumper so tight there was an offering of the treat that lay underneath.

Startled by such an obvious attempt at seduction, he had replied very firmly that she needed more mileage.

'Then she put her hand on my leg,' Roger shuddered at the memory, 'and said she would love to gain more mileage under me.'

Shelley had roared with laughter and, after wiping her eyes, had suggested that he should always be chaperoned in future. 'Must be over a year since you've had a groom throw themselves at you; you must be out of practice at brushing them off.'

Shelley hadn't mentioned Jules's icy lack of enthusiasm to Katie, but she made a mental note to put out feelers to see if any of the local yards had any grooming vacancies. Jules was a moody cow who pulled the whole yard down, and Shelley would have dearly liked to see her moving on. Horribly aware that Jules had a thumping crush on Roger, Shelley was also conscious that although Jules was good with the horses on the ground, she was a panicky rider and was incredibly huffy.

Caitlyn talked incessantly and often forgot things as she was so busy chatting, but she was a sweet person and not afraid of physical work. While Seamus had been at Athward Hall, the girls' weaknesses and lack of riding ability hadn't really shown; he was a fearless rider and had been like wallpaper paste sticking paper to the wall and binding the team together. In the days Shelley had been without him, she was made terribly aware that Caitlyn couldn't canter a circle on any horse in the yard and Jules turned green if she was asked to jump anything higher than sixty centimetres. Jules and Caitlyn's shortcomings were now being magnified by the arrival of Katie, who didn't think twice about suggesting they jump the fence instead of opening the gate. Jules was giving Shelley a constant headache; the green-eyed monster was making life as difficult as possible for Katie and never missed an opportunity to make a snide remark under her breath.

In the middle of February, when Katie had been at Athward for two weeks, it had all come to the point of explosion when the four of them were hacking out together and came across a fallen branch on a woodland track. After quickly checking the take-off and landing, Katie announced it was safe and should she go first with Tiger?

Shelley, looking at the white faces of Jules and Caitlyn, suggested they find a way around it.

'For God's sake, it's only a foot high.' Katie swung around, popped Tiger Lily over it and turned to wait for them.

Caitlyn, anxious to get the jump over with, hands sweating and knees shaking, trotted Brogue towards the branch. Brogue, feeling the obstacle was way too small in comparison to what he usually jumped, was suspicious and leapt a metre high over the branch, launching Caitlyn out of the saddle and onto the muddy ground.

Katie and Shelley, almost hysterical with laughter, told her that was called being "jumped off", and as Caitlyn got to her feet, Katie trotted off to retrieve Brogue. Not wanting to wait for Jules to faff about, Shelley aimed Lightoller at the branch as Katie returned Brogue to Caitlyn.

'Are you alright?' Shelley was trying not to laugh at Caitlyn who was absolutely covered in mud.

'Yes thanks.' Caitlyn sorted through her pockets, looking for a tissue to stem the flow of blood from her nose.

'Come on, Jules,' called Katie, 'keep your leg on and come in trot.'

Jules trotted Paperchase toward the branch, and he ground to a halt.

'You can't let him do that,' Katie warned. 'Turn him round and give him his head, he could step over that.'

Jules trotted him towards it for a second time and again he came to a standstill.

'For fucksake Jules!' yelled Katie crossly. 'You *can't* let him get away with that; he's nervous enough about something new. Come again and smack him with your whip down his shoulder, or do you want me to ride him over it?'

Livid with herself and hating Katie more than ever, Jules turned away and then trotted towards it for a third time. Half-heartedly flapping her whip down Paperchase's shoulder, the horse stopped in front of the branch before stepping over it with exaggerated care, one leg at a time.

Shelley and Caitlyn were howling with laughter, but Katie immediately slipped out of Tiger's saddle and handed her reins to Shelley. Taking Paperchase's reins, she told Jules to get off and ordered her to give her a leg-up.

Scarlet in the face, Jules refused.

'Get off him.' Katie pulled her foot from the stirrup.

'Let her get on him.' Shelley's tone was dangerous.

Hauling herself into the saddle and finding Jules's stirrups were too long for her, Katie rode Paperchase at the log. Jumping it without issue, she then turned him around and leapt over it half a dozen times more.

'Do you want to ride him home? Or do you want to ride Tiger?' she asked as she halted next to a furious Jules.

'Do you get a buzz out of making me look stupid?'

Katie looked at her quizzically. 'It's not all about you, Jules. Paperchase needs to know that he has to jump anything he's asked to, without questioning it,' she dismounted, 'even if it is only thirty fucking centimetres high.'

'You bloody love it, don't you?' Jules snatched Paperchase's reins. 'Roger thinks you're the next bloody Zara Phillips and all you can do is make other people look stupid, so you feel better about yourself.'

'Tindall,' muttered Shelley.

'I don't need to feel better about myself,' Katie replied coldly.

'You could have fooled me. You're obviously so much better than all of us; I'm not sure why you even bother to work here.' She led Paperchase over to the branch so she could stand on it to remount. 'Couldn't Mummy just have bought you some horses and then you could have stayed in Dorset.'

'Jules, that'll do,' said Shelley sharply. 'You wouldn't have spoken to Seamus like that so just pack it in.'

'Fuck off, Shelley.' Jules rode past her and began to ride away up the track.

'And don't fucking speak to me like that either,' Shelley yelled after her.

Katie said nothing as she climbed back onto Tiger. She hadn't wanted to make an enemy out of Jules, but it was clear that there was nothing she could do to placate her, and the mummy comment had really stung.

'You alright?' Shelley turned Lightoller in the direction of home.

'I wasn't trying to show off; the horse had to jump it.'

'I know.'

'She's going to be in a monumental huff now,' said Caitlyn woefully.

'She'll just have to get over it. How the hell did she think she could be a work rider if she's scared of jumping something as small as that?' Katie asked in amazement.

'I think she thought it was another route to Roger's bed,' Caitlyn sighed.

Athward Hall was preparing for the start of the eventing season in the middle of March, and there was a constant stream of horses coming in and out of the yard. Some came for a few weeks for schooling; others came for longer so Roger could compete them, and there were the faithful ones, who returned year after year.

Miss Mac was one of Roger's long-standing owners. Now in her mid-seventies, she enjoyed the craic at competitions and often came to see her horse Brogue at Athward Hall. Roger loathed owners who just dropped in, as they always seemed to turn up in the middle of a crisis, but Miss Mac was different; she didn't expect the yard to always be immaculate and understood that no one had time to chat. She was happy sitting in her very battered Subaru, with a flask of tea, Classic FM and her old Border Terrier for company while she watched them riding in the school.

This day however, she parked the Subaru in the middle of the stable yard and, helped by her stick – pure white hair standing up in shocks around her head – limped across the cobbles in her blue Crimplene trousers and bobbly green sweatshirt.

'Caitlyn! Could you bear to make me one of your marvellous tack room coffees?' She sat down heavily on the mounting block, tugging the collar of her shirt away from her neck, finding it was almost strangling her as she had sat down on the untucked tail.

Roger slid to the ground from The Mechanic's saddle. 'How are you today, Miss Mac?'

'What a nice-looking horse,' she answered, running a professional eye over The Mechanic. 'How is he bred?'

'Royal Beech.' Roger handed his reins to Jules and gave the horse a pat.

'Strong stamp of a horse.' She took her coffee from Caitlyn. 'Who owns him?' She was screwing up her eyes to watch The Mechanic being led away to his stable.

'Charles Dee, the garage owner.' Roger sat down next to her

on the mounting block and took off his hat. 'He got a good deal on him, but then no one has been able to stay on the horse long enough to find out if he's any good or not.'

'Weasel of a man.' Miss Mac took a mouthful of coffee. 'I've bought another horse,' she said in a conversational tone. 'Will you have room for him?'

'I'm sure we can find room for him – where and what has he come from?'

'He's that big grey horse that Petra Williams was riding last year,' Miss Mac took another gulp of her coffee, 'the one that kept carting her all over the place, do you remember, Roger?'

'I do.'

'He's well bred, by Knightsville, out of a Red Stamp mare. Of course, all Knightsville stock are renowned for being difficult, but I doubt you'll find him trying.'

They watched Katie leading Tiger out of her stable.

'What made you decide to buy another horse?'

'I always liked the look of the horse, and I heard through the grapevine that the owner could no longer afford Petra's fees to send him eventing again.'

'Has he been at Petra's all winter?'

Miss Mac nodded.

'She must have made a fortune charging the owner for the horse just standing in the field. You know that Petra won't be amused if he comes here?'

'I don't really care what Petra thinks,' said Miss Mac in a stern voice. 'Although yes, I appreciate that she doesn't like it when her horses go to the opposition.'

'It will be interesting to see what he's like; I hope you didn't pay too much for him.' Roger got up and walked across the yard to give Katie a leg-up.

'I made a sensible offer.' Miss Mac was feeling in her pocket for her cigars even though smoking was explicitly forbidden on the yard.

A lorry was pulling up at the yard gates and Roger recognised the cream and blue livery of the local horse transporters; he looked questioningly at Miss Mac.

'This is him being delivered,' she said calmly as she drained the last of her coffee and lit a cigar.

Katie was standing with her left leg raised, awaiting Roger's leg-up, and he hoisted her so hard that she almost went straight over Tiger's saddle and down the other side.

'Sorry, Katie.' He turned back to Miss Mac and pointed at the lorry reversing into the yard. 'This is him being delivered, now?' he asked in disbelief.

Miss Mac, for possibly the first time in her life, looked sheepish. 'Well, the owner had received another offer for the horse, so I thought it best to get him here before he changed his mind.'

Roger shouted for Shelley to get the isolation box ready and went to meet the driver.

Billy climbed out of the driving seat and greeted Roger warmly; he had delivered and collected a great many horses to and from Athward Hall over the years.

'Have you got a muzzle, Roger?' he asked as he let down the hydraulic ramp. 'The bastard had a chunk out of me arm when I was loading him.'

'Don't worry; we'll manage without.'

'In that case you can bring him out.' Billy was opening the partition to reveal a huge white horse, plastered with mud and wearing a very torn rug. 'I value me arms.'

As Roger went to untie him, Bluebell Folly flattened his ears against his head and lunged at him with incredibly big yellow teeth. Swearing and shouting for Shelley to bring a muzzle, Roger avoided the snapping teeth and tied the horse up again.

'What do you want first? His stable made up or the muzzle?' enquired Shelley in an exasperated voice.

Billy shook his head, 'I don't know what she does with them, Roger; every horse I pick up from Petra's is like this.'

'No bloody discipline and keeping them stabled for twenty-three hours a day sends them mad.' Roger held out his hand for the muzzle.

~

'So I said, "Steve, that's just not gentlemanly at all," and he looked at me as if I was dead rude or something.'

'What happened then?' asked Shelley in a bored voice, only asking the question because she knew it was expected.

'He took his hand off my boob and drove me home,' finished Caitlyn.

Katie tried not to laugh.

'I think I might have blown it.' Caitlyn had taken her feet out of Brogue's stirrups and was looking decidedly dejected.

'I think,' Shelley turned in her saddle to look at her, 'you definitely haven't blown it.'

Caitlyn's round face lit up. 'Do you think so? I really fancy him.'

Shelley had turned to face the right way again. 'If you'd *blown it,* he certainly wouldn't have taken you straight home.' She set off trotting up the hill.

Caitlyn trotted up beside Katie. 'Did she mean—'

'That's exactly what she meant,' replied Katie kindly.

At the top of the hill, they turned off the road and took the winding track that led down through the woods back to Athward Hall. The heavy rain the previous day had left puddles dotted along the track, and as Katie watched Caitlyn steering Vision around them, the Hall was suddenly visible through the empty trees.

'Tomorrow,' Shelley took off her hat and smoothed back her hair, 'we're taking Tiger, Brogue and Paperchase to Allerton. Roger is going to walk the cross country course this afternoon, so we don't need to leave until just before six.' She replaced her hat and fastened the chinstrap. 'That will get us there before seven, giving us an hour before Roger's first dressage test on Paperchase at eight, but as Brogue's cross country is last at twelve-thirty, we're in for a pretty frantic morning.'

'Why are we all going when he's only taking three horses?' Caitlyn ducked to avoid the low branch overhanging the track.

'Because Roger wants me,' Shelley clasped her hand to her chest theatrically, 'to pass on my incredible expertise to Katie and give you and Jules a refresher course in the joys of standing beside the lorry all day, waiting for Roger to hand you a sweating horse to wash off.'

As Katie was putting Paperchase's saddle on the wooden rack in the tack room, she noticed a parcel with her name on propped up against the wall next to the sink. Opening it, she found a jacket in Roger's navy-blue cross country colours with a note from him welcoming her to the team. She inhaled its scent of newness for a moment before unfolding it. On the back it had "Roger Fleming Bowen Eventing" in big gold lettering and her name embroidered on the front above the phone pocket.

'Yeah,' Jules came clattering in carrying Shelley's tack, 'don't get too excited; a jacket doesn't make you more popular.' She slammed the saddle on the rack with a crash, dropped the bridle on the floor and flounced out.

Katie watched her disappearing out of the door and once again thought what an absolute bitch she was. Having worked with the men on the polo yard in New Zealand, she was quite good at allowing the catty comments to wash over her, but it was tiring being guarded and defensive all the time. Katie much preferred the days at Athward Hall when Jules wasn't at work.

Jules aside, since moving into the Dorchester at the end of January, Katie had been very happy with life, and Shelley was easy to live with. Even if she did think it was normal to go into Katie's bedroom and borrow her clothes without asking first.

'I've got a hoodie exactly the same as that,' Katie said as they fought over the toaster one morning.

'No, you haven't,' Shelley smirked back.

Despite complaining that pink was not her colour, Shelley was often rummaging through Katie's wardrobe for something to wear.

'How can you be so organised at work and yet not be able to turn on a washing machine?' asked Katie crossly.

'I know how to turn it on.' Shelley examined a pale-pink rugby shirt before pulling it over her head. 'I turn it on and then forget to hang the bloody washing out when it's finished.'

Roger had also noticed a steady trickle of pink items inching their way into his yard and this had been the reason for Katie's first-hand encounter with the infamous Fleming Bowen temper.

Nervously sitting astride Paperchase at the equestrian centre, waiting to start her dressage test, Roger's roar of rage had nearly sent her into orbit.

'No bloody way!' he yelled, pointing at the horse's pink Swarovski-crystal-encrusted browband. 'Take it off, are you trying to give him a fucking complex?'

'He likes it,' Katie replied innocently.

'Let's get this straight right now, my horses do not wear pink. Not. Fucking. Ever.'

'It's only a bloody browband,' she muttered as she slid out of the saddle to change it.

'What's next?' he retorted. 'Diamond-coated plaiting bands and fucking glittery hoof oil?'

'Oooh, they sound lovely!' exclaimed Caitlyn, who then went red as he glared at her.

'Nothing pink or glittery, not ever,' Roger uttered through gritted teeth.

To his horror, Katie had then given him a nonchalant look and lifted her jacket to show him the sparkling diamante belt on her breeches, making Caitlyn almost fall over laughing.

It was strange, Katie thought, working for the man who she had been obsessed with while she was growing up and discovering that he was just a normal person. A very good-looking but normal person. But it had been obvious from her first day at work that all Roger was interested in was getting the best out of his horses and making her a better rider. That was the frustrating thing, Roger rode beautifully and even had the knack of riding smaller horses without dwarfing them with his height. She could watch him ride for hours; he made it look so easy, and even when a horse was being as obstinate as it could possibly be, he still sat peacefully in the saddle and, gradually, the horse would start to co-operate. It was infuriating sometimes, when she was fighting and working as hard as she could in the saddle and Roger would quietly ask if he could have a sit on the horse. Within minutes, the horse would be going beautifully, and Katie would be left feeling inadequate, asking in frustration what she was doing wrong. There was always a little smile before he answered her, and he would tell her she was trying too hard.

She picked up her new jacket again and grinned when she realised her name was embroidered in pink thread.

∽

Roger's navy-blue lorry with its blacked-out windows could carry six horses, and despite being only half-loaded for the first competition of the season, as there was little time between each horse's different phases, the Fleming Bowen team had a busy morning.

Jules had written the horse's times in the order they were to run on a piece of paper that was now pinned on the noticeboard in the lorry above the sofa. Shelley, knowing the times off by heart, told Katie, Jules, and Caitlyn to study it.

'There's eleven minutes between Paperchase's cross country and Brogue's show jumping, but at least as Roger will have to change his gear, he'll have to come back here to change horses.' Shelley glanced at the times. 'I wish you'd bloody print the start times,' she moaned. 'How on earth do I know who is dressaging, show jumping and cross countrying and at what time if I can't read your writing?' She stomped out to tack up Paperchase for his dressage.

With Roger mounted on Paperchase and Jules buffing his already immaculate boots with a duster, Shelley was already bringing Tiger off the lorry to start getting her ready for her dressage test. Caitlyn would accompany Roger and Paperchase to video the test on Roger's phone, and Jules was to take Tiger across to where the white boards of the dressage arenas lay, ready for Roger to get on her as soon as Paperchase's test was over.

Watching Roger's tall back and Paperchase's glossy black tail disappear through the horses and bodies in the lorry park, Katie realised that all eyes were on him. Many people called out a greeting, but some just nudged each other and gazed at him, hoping not to be caught looking.

'They really do think he's a god, don't they?'

'Who?' Shelley was removing the thick, protective travelling boots from Tiger's dainty grey legs.

'Roger.'

'They all think the sun shines out of his arse.' Shelley picked up Tiger's hind foot and began screwing a metal stud into the shoe. 'He could tell them all that their horses would show jump better without a girth to hold the saddle on and they'd believe him.'

Caitlyn skipped down the steps from the lorry's living area; despite the coldness of the early morning air, she had swapped her jeans for an exceedingly small pair of shorts which were rapidly disappearing up the crack of her ample backside. Feeling flush with life, she almost got as far as asking if a horse really would go better without a girth, before Shelley roared at her to catch up with Roger, stop treating the day as a fashion parade and pay bloody attention.

The morning passed in a blur of changing saddles, opening bottles of water for Roger, making coffee for the owners and hangers-on and loading items back into the huge lockers on the outside of the lorry. As soon as Tiger had come galloping over the cross country finishing line, Jules was waiting with Brogue so Roger could swap horses and go out on his third and final cross country of the day. Shelley poured out a bucket of water for Jules and Caitlyn to wash off the little grey mare and took Katie to the edge of the lorry park where they could catch a glimpse of the course.

They watched Roger and Brogue sail through the water complex down by the river, and while they waited for them to reappear at the bottom of the hill, the fence judge in front of them blew his whistle, and they saw a rider in bright orange colours riding a small black horse galloping up the hill towards them. The little black horse hesitated as he approached the first of the three fences, and with a slap of the whip and a shout of encouragement, he jumped the first, somehow clambered stickily over the second and third and was then galloping back down the hill to the sound of the rider's obvious delight.

'Takes all sorts,' muttered Shelley, offering her can of Coke to Katie. 'Has he said when he's going to put an entry in for you?'

Katie shook her head. 'He's not even said who I'd be riding.'

There was another blast on the whistle, and they both turned to look at the next competitor. The rider, with a face as red as a cherry, looked to be in his sixties, and as his enormous black and white horse saw the first fence, he baulked and slithered into the obstacle for a refusal.

'Number two-six-two, a first refusal at fence fourteen,' said the fence judge into his radio, as the OAP circled in a ragged trot and pointed his horse at the fence again.

The horse this time made an enormous effort to jump the fence, which put them too close to the second element and again he refused.

'A second refusal at fence fourteen for number two-six-two.'

The radio stuttered back to him, 'That's their fourth accumulated refusal; that's elimination.'

'I'm sorry, number two-six-two,' called the fence judge, 'but I'm afraid you're eliminated; could you leave the course at a walk, please?' The fence judge glanced down the hill. 'And I would make it quick because this one's coming with a rattle.' He gave a sharp blast on his whistle as Roger in his navy colours and Brogue's lovely brown face came thundering up the hill.

As Roger lined the horse up to the fence, he sat down in the saddle to slow the gait and shorten Brogue's stride. They met the fence perfectly, and Brogue landed neatly, took two strides, jumped the second element, took another stride, jumped cleanly over the third part and was galloping away from them towards the finish.

There was the sound of scattered applause from the small crowd that had gathered on the ropes, and a lady with two terriers told everyone that Roger was awfully good.

Shelley grinned at Katie as they turned to leave the group of spectators, and the terrier lady saw the name on the back of Shelley's jacket and blushed.

∼

Mrs Royal was there to greet them as the lorry rumbled slowly into the yard.

'Is everyone home safe?' Her white hair was flattened on one side of her head from her afternoon nap, and there was flour on the front of her floral-patterned tabard.

In reply to the chorus of yes, all horses and Roger were sound, she said there was a fish pie for Roger to put in the oven to warm through, and there was a lasagne that would feed four if they needed it in the Dorchester. She sat on the mounting block to watch the horses being unloaded, and as the task of emptying all the kit out of the lorry began, she eased herself upright and said that she had better be off.

'I've had a little tidy-up in the flat.' She patted Shelley's shoulder kindly as Shelley looked at her in horror.

'Please, no,' whimpered Shelley, 'not after the last time.'

Mrs Royal inclined her head. 'I haven't painted a *thing*, pet; I've just cleaned up a bit and put a load of washing in for you both.' She winked at Katie, advised her to mind her foot and announced she was off home.

'Dear God, no!' cried Shelley as she began hauling saddles out of the lorry's outside locker. 'For the love of God, Roger, why can't you keep your bloody housekeeper under control? The last time she *cleaned up a bit*, it was horrendous. She'd tidied my bloody knicker drawer and used the leftover paint from the show jumps to do the skirting boards and doors.'

'What was so bad about that?' Katie was carrying half-eaten haynets down the ramp. 'Did she find something battery-powered in your knicker drawer?'

'Thankfully no, but she'd ironed all my bloody thongs and the leftover paint was orange, pink and green.' Shelley winced at the thought. 'Seamus nearly had a coronary when he saw he had a pink bedroom door.' She put on a convincing Irish accent: 'To be sure, at least she's painted the focking skirting boards orange and green, I almost feel as though I'm back home in the Emerald Isle.'

'If she's only put some washing in the machine, I think you're both quite safe.' Roger was pulling his bag from the living area of the lorry and looking at his watch. 'It's ten-past three – turn out the three we've had away today, get the tack put away and Jules and Caitlyn can call it a day. I'll come down at half-past four to help you two do them up for the night.'

'I'll stay and help,' put in Caitlyn eagerly, thinking of Mrs Royal's lasagne sitting in the Dorchester.

'Who's off tomorrow?' Roger threw his bag onto his shoulder.

'Jules.' Shelley was walking past him with a heap of bridles.

Roger nodded. 'I'll school Bluebell and The Mechanic tomorrow morning; Shelley, Vision and Bean could do with a canter if they're going to Elleworth next weekend. And Jules? I'll give you a lift home now if you like?'

Jules felt her stomach flutter at the thought of being close and alone with Roger for the five-minute drive to her parents' house in Athward. Hastily, she ran into the tack room to grab her bag and stood behind the door to brush her hair.

Shelley watched them walk out of the yard together before asking Caitlyn, in her very best pained voice, if she would like to stay for dinner tonight.

'Oooh yes please,' she replied excitedly, 'I love Mrs Royal's lasagne.' She turned away from Paperchase to grin broadly at Shelley.

Paperchase, bored with waiting to be turned out in the field, promptly snapped his teeth at Tiger, who jumped back in alarm and trod on Katie's foot. Wincing in pain and telling Shelley that her comment about not wearing trainers on the yard wasn't helpful, she hobbled off to put the kettle on.

Mrs Royal's gorgeous lasagne did not redeem her from the "bit of washing" that she had done, because every item of clothing from both bedroom floors had been picked up and washed on the hottest wash the Dorchester's machine was capable of.

There was a heap of neatly ironed bed linen on the table in the lounge, but as Katie examined a bright pink bra that had once been white and a giggling Caitlyn was stretching what should have been a size twelve jumper over the small pedal bin in the kitchen, Shelley lost her temper and rang Roger to demand that he find keys for the unused Yale locks on both bedroom doors immediately.

'Why didn't you tell me that you couldn't lock the bedroom doors?' he asked in exasperation.

Shelley admitted that it had come in useful when Seamus had lived with her, as he had some nice T-shirts that she could unofficially borrow when she had run out of clean ones.

Six

'Please tell me you didn't buy that?' Shelley was gazing in dismay at the small lurid-green car that Caitlyn was emerging from.

'Dad won it in a card game.' She slammed the door shut, and Katie tried to ignore the piece of rust that had fallen onto the cobbles. 'Isn't it fab? Now Jules and I won't need lifts to work.'

'Do you have insurance?' Roger was dubiously running his eyes over the ancient bubble-shaped Nissan Micra, taking in the brown patches of corrosion and the almost-bald front tyres.

Shelley gave a honk of laughter. 'For the love of God, Roger, Barry won it in a game of cards; it probably hasn't got an MOT.'

'It's got a CD player,' said Caitlyn helpfully.

'Please be careful.' Roger shook his head.

'You should get one of those strips across the windscreen with "Cait and Joo" written on it.' Shelley was laughing.

Katie caught Jules's expression of revulsion and realised she would rather walk the two miles to work than be seen dead in the lime-green Micra. 'Caitlyn can give you a lift home tonight, Jules,' she told her sweetly.

Katie was fastening The Mechanic's noseband when Roger came into the stable.

'Don't wind her up,' he said quietly.

She looked at him sharply. 'I didn't!'

Roger raised his eyebrows sarcastically as he put on his hat.

'She's called me worse than shit, why shouldn't I wind her up?' she replied crossly.

'Be the grown-up.'

'Have you told her off as well? For being such a bitch?'

'You know, you really are very pretty when you're angry.'

She stared at him.

'Don't panic; it was just an observation.' He grinned at her as he led The Mechanic out of the stable.

It was hard enough to ignore the butterflies in her stomach whenever he was near her or the feeling of electrical energy that shot through her whenever he gave her a leg-up. Now, as Katie watched him walk the horse down the corridor to the yard, she told herself sternly that he was just being a man. *Don't even think about it*, she told herself, *he's the bloody boss and you don't need that kind of complication.*

Jules, walking into the stables, caught the fading expression on Katie's face and scowled. 'Sorry, did I just interrupt something?'

'Don't be stupid,' snapped Katie.

As Roger left all yard politics to Shelley, he was completely unaware how toxic the relationship was between Katie and Jules and how icy the atmosphere was when Jules was having one of her huffy days. These "mute days", as Shelley called them, had become much more frequent since Katie moved to Athward Hall, and since the incident at the fallen tree, Katie wasn't even trying to get along with Jules.

'Please try and get on with her,' begged Shelley as she and Katie rode together one morning. 'She's a pain in the arse when she goes into bloody silent mode.'

'Why should I bother?' Katie replied shortly. 'She goes out of her way to make everything difficult; I prefer it when she doesn't talk.'

'But me and Caitlyn don't,' argued Shelley. 'I know it's not your fault; I know she's a bitch, but please try?'

'Why doesn't he just get rid of her?'

'Because she lives five minutes away and is good with the horses.'

'And she's ready to hop into bed with him if he fancies it?'

Shelley laughed at her furious face. 'Definitely not. He much prefers brunettes.'

'If that was a dig, I'm not bloody rising to it.'

On one of the mute days, Shelley had taken Jules off into the Dorchester for a coffee and explained how her lack of communication was affecting the whole yard, horses included. Jules had drunk her coffee in silence and then, seeing a framed photograph on the wall of Katie and Grenadier jumping an enormous cross country jump, she'd suggested that the "horse must be really something because the rider is shit", at which point all professionalism in Shelley vanished like a puff of smoke.

'She's a brilliant rider, you spoilt little cow!' she yelled. 'And you might hate her because she pointed out that Paperchase works better on the left rein which you took as a bloody personal insult, but she's right – Paperchase is better on the left rein, and she picked up on it after sitting on the horse for five minutes!'

And Jules had stomped off down the stone stairs and slammed the outside door like a teenager.

'It was quite a feat to get it to slam,' Shelley confessed to Roger later. 'The bloody thing usually catches on the floor when you're trying to shut it.'

Jules, an only child born to middle-class parents, had been impossibly spoilt throughout her childhood. Moving from the outskirts of Newcastle to Athward had not suited her; Jules liked the city and hated the sleepy hamlet of Athward with its solitary pub and farming community.

After leaving school, she had half-heartedly started a beauty therapy course which had lasted two months and then a photography course which lasted a week. Other part-time jobs had followed – a trainee florist, a few shifts at the shop in Athward, even a six-month placement with a PR company in Newcastle – but in truth, Jules did not want to work. She wanted a rich man to sweep her off her feet so she could go to the gym, watch nail art tutorials on YouTube and be given unlimited funds for the salon and her wardrobe.

She had thought her chance had come when Roger had advertised for staff. Having ridden throughout her youth, Jules thought she was a good rider but had never ridden high-quality, fit and strong competition horses. Nevertheless, the chance to get to know Roger, and make him fall in love with her, was too strong a pull to ignore, and although she didn't want to work twenty hours a week, she had applied and got the job.

Like Katie, Jules had hero-worshipped Roger during her teenage years, and from the first time she saw Athward Hall and his beautiful, immaculate stables, she assumed it was champagne at eleven o'clock every morning and lobster for supper every night. Even if she had been close enough to Roger to see that it was usually coffee for breakfast and a hastily eaten beef stew on his knees in front of the television, she wouldn't have believed it. Jules held Athward Hall as a fantasy land in her head and waited for the day that Roger would ask her out on a date, expecting things to lead on from there. But so far, in the year she had worked for him, things hadn't quite gone to plan for Jules, and she suddenly found herself in unfamiliar territory when he had made no attempt to be anything other than her employer.

After a few weeks in his employment, she had even managed to blag a ticket to the local hunt ball and grabbed him for a kiss at the end of the night. Hoping that her mouth planted on his would lead to something more, she was left bitterly disappointed when he had laughed it off and then, to her annoyance, never mentioned it again. It was grating hugely on her that Roger was spending so much time with Katie. They spent hours in the school together while Shelley, Jules and Caitlyn took horses to them and led away the ones that had been worked. Conveniently forgetting that Roger had spent the same amount of time with Seamus when he first started work at Athward Hall, Jules got it into her head that Roger had a thing for Katie, which bolstered her jealously to gigantic proportions.

She bitched endlessly to Caitlyn, who refused to be drawn into a Katie-targeted bitchfest, arguing that Katie was nice and had even lent her a jacket for her date with Steve. Caitlyn didn't add that she couldn't fasten the jacket or that she had used a baby wipe to try and remove the pasta sauce that she had spilt down one of the lapels but had gone on to advise Jules in a motherly voice to give Katie a chance.

Jules had glowered at her and snarled that Roger had obviously only employed fucking Zara Phillips because he wanted to sleep with her.

'I didn't know he employed Zara Phillips,' replied Caitlyn excitedly.

With her very curvy figure and slightly frizzy red hair, Caitlyn was well liked, and the local boys were always buying her drinks at the Cup and Kettle. Jules, with her slender frame and beautiful, slim face was infuriated that they didn't do the same for her. She assumed it was because Caitlyn was a proper local, having been born in the village, whereas Jules's family had moved into the huge, modern house called Sweet Meadows when she was sixteen. The real reason, however, was that Jules was beautiful and a little bit posh, which, when combined with the occasional bitchy comment, made her look as though she thought she was a class above everyone else in the village. Caitlyn, on the other hand, was sweet, kind and, although not the brightest girl in school, always had a smile for everyone.

Caitlyn was also getting tired of Jules's black hatred of Katie, and several times she had swapped the wrong bridle, which Jules had left out for Katie, with the correct one.

In the middle of April, the famously naughty Mechanic was to have his first outing as part of the navy Fleming Bowen team. The horse had been working well at home, and Roger was looking forward to bringing him out in public, hoping to achieve something that previous riders had not. Looking up the horse's record on the British Eventing website, Roger had found that he had never had a fault in the cross country phase but had regularly knocked up (or rather down) a cricket score in the show jumping. His dressage marks were hardly inspiring either, and Roger was genuinely puzzled. The Mechanic had hardly knocked down a show jump at home and was schooling nicely.

Katie was also having her first outing as part of the team as Roger had entered Brogue for her to ride. In complete contrast to Roger's excitement about The Mechanic, Katie had been feeling sick with nerves for the last four days. She was relieved she was riding for Miss Mac, who she knew would be supportive whatever the result, but discovered that competing someone else's horse was decidedly more nerve-wracking than riding your own.

On Friday afternoon, Roger rang Katie from the Hall and told her to come up in an hour and they would drive over to Tillbridge and walk the course together.

As it was such a mild day, Caitlyn had tied The Mechanic up outside to wash his tail; Jules was sullenly cleaning tack and making sure Roger's bridles looked more polished than Katie's. Shelley was riding Tiger in the outdoor school, and she brought the grey horse into a halt as Katie called across from the gate. Telling her she was going to walk the course with Roger, Shelley stood up in her stirrups and began searching her jeans pockets, urging Katie to wait as she had something for her. 'Wait, wait, it's here somewhere.' Shelley was emptying sweet wrappers and tissues from the pockets of her jeans. 'There.' She handed something small to Katie.

It was a condom.

'Just in case you can't control yourself on the drive.' She rode away laughing.

Katie looked angrily at her departing back.

The course was bigger than Katie had anticipated, and the colour in her face depleted the further she and Roger walked.

'This is going to cause problems tomorrow.' Roger slapped the fallen tree trunk in front of them.

The tree trunk was at the top of a slope, so the horses would be landing on an incline before taking two strides and jumping down a small bank, then another three strides to jump up another narrow bank.

'We're four fences from home, so if I was riding Brogue tomorrow,' Roger smiled at her, 'I would bring him to the very right of the fence as he can be inclined to drift to the left.'

Katie nodded.

There were a lot of people walking the courses, and everyone stopped to speak to Roger, to ask him when he was next teaching at the local equestrian centre, how many horses he was bringing to the competition tomorrow and how they could ride the combination of fences that made up number eight A, B and C. He introduced Katie to everyone they met and, having been on the competition circuit for a month, there were faces Katie was starting to recognise.

'Roger, darling!' A tall, dark lady wearing an expensive puffa waistcoat kissed Roger on both cheeks. 'You must come for kitchen supper; I haven't seen you properly to talk to for weeks.'

'Petra,' Roger turned to Katie, 'have you met Katie, my work rider?'

Petra Williams looked down her slightly long nose at Katie from her superior height. 'From afar,' she said coolly. 'How are you getting on at Athward? I hope he's not working you too hard.' She gave a tinkly laugh which reminded Katie of Mrs Hicken. 'You must let me know when you have time to help with a new horse I've got.' Petra was staring deep into Roger's eyes. 'He's a wonderful horse but is incredibly headstrong, and I really could do with your expertise on the ground.' She placed a hand on his arm.

'Of course, any time. Do you want to bring him over next week?'

'I think it might be better for you to come and see him in my indoor school, Roger.' Her face had taken on a patronising expression. 'He's very naughty.'

'Ring me and we'll sort a time to suit.' Saying they must get on, he manoeuvred Katie onwards.

'Charming lady.' Katie felt like giving him the durex that was in her back pocket.

Roger wiped Petra's lipstick off his cheeks with the back of his hand. 'She's alright, but I wouldn't trust her.'

~

'Wouldn't trust her?' repeated Shelley as she watched Katie polishing her competition boots on the hearth of the Dorchester's log burner. 'Did he come up the Clyde in a tin bath? That's like saying Jack the Ripper was a little bit dodgy.'

Petra Williams had moved from Gloucestershire to Northumberland four years earlier after her husband had died from a long illness. As a fifty-year-old widow, no one could understand why she had moved so far north; after all, in Northumberland there were fewer eventing competitions, and you had to travel further to get to them. But the land prices were considerably less than the south, and Petra had bought Low Athward Farm at a quarter of what it would have cost had it been standing in Gloucestershire.

She had converted the farm buildings into stables, slapped in a horse walker, an indoor school and installed her string of talented but wasted event horses. She was nicknamed "Golden Knickers" on the circuit as her cross country colours were a rich dark yellow, which she referred to as "old gold", and all her horses' rugs, boots, brushes and buckets were the same colour. Being incredibly wealthy, she could afford to buy the best and most expensive horses and pay for lessons from the top instructors but, regrettably, none of this made her ride any better than mediocre. She could also afford to employ lots of staff, which meant most of them worked short hours, but most didn't stay long when they realised that if anything was less than what Petra considered perfect, the horse, or usually someone else, got the blame. It was never, ever Petra's fault.

'More than one person has suggested she moved up here for another reason.' Shelley watched as Katie buffed the polish off her right boot.

'What's that?'

'That Petra saw a single Roger as the perfect second husband.'

The next day, Brogue produced a good, solid dressage test and was very unlucky to have two show jumps down, putting him and Katie well down the order.

'Unlucky!' Miss Mac boomed as she limped up to the lorry. 'He dropped a toe on them! Thought they were going to stay up!'

'Unlucky,' agreed Roger, who was adjusting his stirrups on Lightoller.

Miss Mac leant heavily on her stick and patted Brogue's sleek neck. 'Now, are you ready for the fun part?'

Katie gave a weak smile in answer as she fastened her pink air jacket over the top of her navy team sweatshirt. In a nod to Roger, she hadn't put on her usual hat cover and was still wearing her black one after Brogue's show jumping.

'Do you usually cross country with a black hat cover?' Roger was waiting to ride to the start with her.

'No, but I thought you'd prefer black.'

'Don't tell me, your usual one is pink?'

'No!' shouted Shelley from inside the lorry. 'It's pink with silver stars and a silver pom-pom.' She threw it to Katie, who looked at Roger enquiringly.

He sighed. 'Change it if that's what you usually wear. But when everyone starts calling you "Pink Knickers" you'll be sorry, so don't say I didn't warn you.'

'Spoken by mister "Boring Boxers",' she replied as she looked him up and down in his navy colours.

Usually, as soon as she was in the saddle, the nerves disappeared. But today, the shaking hands and dry mouth got worse and as she rode Brogue between the white rails of the start box for her cross country; she thought she was going to be sick.

'Bit green about the gills,' Miss Mac muttered to Roger, who had eight more horses to start before him.

'She's finding riding for an owner quite a different experience to riding her own horse.' Roger was squinting as Katie and Brogue galloped towards the first fence.

They were over safely, and in silence, they watched the pair jump the next three fences before they disappeared out of sight.

'Nice rider.' Miss Mac had dropped her binoculars and was unscrewing the top off her hipflask. 'She's a lovely girl, Roger. It can't be much fun rattling around the Hall all on your own.'

Roger rode away to continue warming up Lightoller, thinking of the many times he had vowed to never get involved with his staff again.

In his younger days, he had slept with several of his grooms, and it had never ended well. Roger had initially thought working his way around the yard was an excellent way of getting over his short marriage, but what he saw as a quick shag or a casual arrangement had the girls ready to redecorate his house and move in.

He winced as he recalled the fiasco with the little blonde Jessica. He had been sleeping with her off and on for months and, returning home from a competition in the early hours of the morning after a thumping long drive, had found not only her ready and waiting in his bed, but also all the furniture and paintings in his house rearranged and his post opened. Then there had been the overdramatic Abi who, after turning up at the Hall one evening while Roger was having a dinner party, had begged and sobbed to be taken back and slid down the dining room window, like something from a Scream film, as his guests looked on in amusement.

Oh God, and then there had been Melissa, who had turned up uninvited to the hunt ball he was attending and had proceeded to throw every glass she could find at him after he'd danced with the complete stranger who had sat next to him at dinner.

He felt physically sick when he thought about the raven-haired Louise, her face twisted in hate as she screamed at him. It had taken a number of attempts to end it with her and she had rammed a kitchen knife into one of his car tyres on the day she finally left.

Jules made eyes at him persistently, and after the last time he had given her a lift home, he had made a pledge to never do it again. She hadn't entirely thrown herself at him but had sat as close to him as she could, never taking her eyes off him as he drove, constantly flicking her hair from her face. When he had pulled up outside her cream-coloured house and she had invited him in for a drink, as her parents were away overnight, he had told her as kindly as he could that she was very pretty but young and much too good to be with someone old like him.

Unfortunately, Roger telling her that she was pretty had only made Jules even more conceited and she now turned up to work wearing tops that left barely anything to the imagination. Much to Katie's delight, the early spring sun was ensuring that the strappy little tops left Jules with the most hideous tan lines; Shelley just thought that, judging by the erect nipples, Jules was freezing.

Shelley thought he was oblivious of Jules's intentions, but Roger was fully aware that if he clicked his fingers, Jules would have slid out of her clothes quicker than a rat running up a drainpipe. She was such a pretty girl but had a nasty streak to her, but Katie, well, Katie was different. She was incredibly attractive, with her beautiful, slanted brown eyes, her gorgeous figure and witty outbursts, but was strictly off-limits. She had a wisdom way beyond her years, probably because she had spent so much time working abroad, and Roger had lost count of the times that he had woken after dreaming about her and thought about messaging her.

Don't even think it, he told himself. *Getting involved with them screws up the whole yard – don't even consider it.*

Brogue galloped through the finish, and the commentator announced that Katie Holland was home but had twenty penalties to add after a refusal at fence eight.

Katie's face was shimmering with sweat and delight. 'What a horse, he was amazing.' She slackened her girth and jumped to the ground.

'What happened at number eight?' Roger leant across to pat Brogue's neck.

'My martingale snapped, and he was a bit distracted by it flapping around. I managed to get hold of it before I asked him to jump it again.'

'It snapped?' Roger hated tack breakages; it looked shoddy.

She held up the band that should have been attached to the girth between Brogue's front legs. 'Snapped,' she confirmed.

'That's annoying,' he frowned. 'But no harm done.'

'I'll take him back to the lorry. Good luck.' She grinned.

Roger watched her go and realised it was the first time he had seen her look genuinely happy.

The Mechanic was very highly strung during his dressage and produced a very tense test. He managed to control himself until the final trot down the centre line towards the judge, when he suddenly stood on his hindlegs and waved his front feet at them.

His show jumping was terrifying to watch as he rattled every fence, but the gods were obviously on Roger's side as, despite breaking a plastic pole and several containers of flowers, they only knocked down three fences. As Roger expected, he went clear over the bold cross country fences and gave him the most easy and enjoyable ride of the day.

It had been a good day, Miss Mac told Victoria Fleming

Bowen on the telephone that evening. Brogue had been incredibly good and, despite Katie's frustration regarding their refusal cross country, Miss Mac was pleased with the way the horse had gone. The girl could certainly ride, and Miss Mac thought it would be interesting to see what else Roger gave her to ride as the season progressed.

Seven

While Jules maintained her ice queen demeanour, Caitlyn was lavishing attention on her new car.

"The Bogiemobile", as Shelley called it, was held together with filler and the thick silver tape that was normally used to repair horse rugs and hold poultices onto horses' feet.

There had been one incident when the handbrake cable snapped and the Bogiemobile had slowly rolled into the wall at the side of the yard. Undeterred, Caitlyn had at first used T-Cut to try and hide the damage but eventually had to admit defeat and had stuck "slow down for horses", "my other car's a Porsche" and "honk if you had it last night" stickers over the worst of the dents.

Jules's parents were obviously just as horrified as she was by the uninsured and untaxed Bogiemobile, and Jules suddenly started arriving at work in a very smart, black Ford Fiesta.

Unlike Caitlyn's car, which was hoovered and cleaned every week, the Fiesta was an absolute tip inside, and after getting a lift up the drive to catch Vision and Bean from the field by Mrs Fleming Bowen's Lodge, Shelley was livid to find a piece of chewing gum stuck to the arse of her jeans.

They were still on the yard at seven o'clock, having taken a lorry load of horses for a late afternoon canter on the beach, when Roger appeared wearing a tuxedo and carrying a bottle of wine.

Katie wolf-whistled through her teeth as she took in his freshly washed hair and the broad shoulders under the beautifully tailored dinner jacket. Roger however, looked to be in a furious temper as he strode across the yard to Shelley.

'Caitlyn!' Shelley shouted a minute later. 'Roger's Discovery won't start – can you give him a lift across to the Major's on your way home? He's meant to be there for dinner in half an hour!'

'I'll finish what you're doing.' Katie took Caitlyn's broom. 'Go on.'

Two minutes later, there was the sound of an engine being reluctantly coaxed into life, and a plume of diesel fumes floated across the yard. Caitlyn drove into the yard, and after carefully turning the car around, Shelley opened the door with a flourish and gestured for Roger to get inside. Roger's eyes met Katie's for a second, and he saw she was trying hard not to laugh.

'I think it needs new spark plugs, Shelley.' Caitlyn had her foot firmly on the brake to make up for the lack of handbrake.

'It's a diesel, you muppet, it doesn't have spark plugs.'

Still Roger hovered.

'Maybe Jules should give him a lift.' Katie was leaning on her broom and was taken aback when Roger shot her a black look.

'For God's sake, Katie, Jules's car is like a skip. You're going to be late.' Shelley waved her arms at Roger. 'Just get in.'

Muttering something they couldn't hear, he gracefully folded his long legs into the footwell, and Shelley slammed the door shut which acted like a starting pistol. After a brief wheelspin, Caitlyn then accidentally selected fourth gear instead of second, so the Bogiemobile disappeared around the corner of the drive with its diesel engine growling unhappily.

Shelley and Katie were bent double with laughter.

'I haven't laughed so hard in ages.' Katie wiped her eyes. 'I'd better ring him and offer to pick him up; there's no way we should have subjected him to that.'

∼

A little after half-past ten, Katie was sitting in her car in the dark, outside Major Dawson's beautiful sandstone home waiting to drive Roger home.

'Thank you so much for not subjecting me to another terrifying ride in the Bogiemobile.' Roger fastened his seat belt. 'Dear God, what a nightmare driver, I have honestly never been so frightened in my life. I would rather ride Brogue around Badminton than get in a car with Caitlyn ever again.'

Immediately after Caitlyn had pulled out onto the main road at East Lodge, she had almost collided with a cyclist but had simply given the ashen-looking man a cheery wave and swerved around him and his bike lying in the road. Asking if she was going to stop to check that he was alright, Caitlyn had dismissed Roger with a flap of her hand, adding that he was always falling off his bike, and laughed that she might buy him stabilisers for Christmas.

Unwilling to disturb her concentration and her constant stream of chatter, Roger had shut his eyes when she had overtaken a tractor on a blind bend, and as the barriers had begun to descend at the railway crossing, Caitlyn had dropped a gear and hurtled between the flashing red lights yelling "weeeeeeee!".

Roger's face was so white when she had dropped him off, the Major had poured him a brandy assuming he had been in an accident with his car and hence, why he was being ferried around by his youngest girl groom, who had pulled up with a vain attempt at a handbrake turn, scattering his beautifully raked gravel all over his lawn.

'And now I know why we are using so much bloody silver tape!' he finished.

Katie laughed and then suddenly hit the brake as she saw the faint red taillight of the cyclist in front of her.

'Why on earth is she out so late?' Roger watched as Katie overtook the bike.

'Who?'

'Pippa, Jules's mum.'

'How do you know it's her?'

He chuckled. 'No one else would wear yellow Lycra, although I suppose it's marginally better than pink.'

Roger hesitated as he was about to close the car door outside Athward Hall. It was a still night with no wind, but after the warmth of the spring day, the air was cool. He shivered slightly as he adjusted to the cold after the warmth of the car.

He bent down to look at her. 'Would you like a drink?' he asked casually. 'As way of a thank-you for not running the gauntlet at the railway line.'

Feeling a jolt in her stomach as she looked into his clear blue eyes, Katie turned off the engine.

Never having been further than the two kitchens, she followed him through the door to the rest of the house and gave a little gasp when she saw the Baby Grand Steinway in the parquet-floored hall.

'Do you play?' She was touching the top of the piano.

'No.'

'Can I?'

'I don't know, can you?'

'A little.' She smiled at him as she pulled out the stool and sat down. Playing a chord, she pulled a face. 'When was it last tuned?'

'A long time ago. My mother played.'

'Sorry.' She was starting to close the lid.

'Don't be. Play something.'

'I haven't played for ages.'

'Play anything – it would be nice to hear it.'

'Like what? Pachelbel's Canon—'

'Christ no. That was played as my wife walked down the aisle towards me, and it still makes me feel nauseous.'

She played another chord, and he could see she was thinking. Suddenly playing a set of dramatic harmonies, she smiled at him before she launched into "The Ballad of Barry and Freda", making Roger laugh.

'You are too young to know this song.'

'Learnt it for an end-of-term party.'

He laughed and watched her as she played, her fingers easily finding the keys, her eyes bright with enthusiasm and the humour carrying in her voice. She looked so at home and confident, exactly how she looked when she was in the saddle.

She stopped abruptly and looked at him. 'I can't remember the next line,' she said impatiently.

Roger briefly creased his brow. 'Something about being jolly, I think?'

'How do you know?'

'My mother always wanted to play it; apparently it's very difficult.'

'It is.' She closed the lid carefully and stood up.

'Play the rest of it.'

'I can't, not while you're watching me.' She was blushing, thinking there was no way she could sing the line about being bent over backwards on a hostess trolley.

'Alright. In that case play it while I'm pouring the drinks.' He turned and went into the drawing room.

Roger listened as he poured her a vodka and tonic, shaking his head and laughing, he took a mouthful of his whisky and waited while she finished the song. She hesitated every now and again to recall the words, and after she finished, there was a moment of silence before she played a snatch of "A Thousand Miles" and "Don't Look Back in Anger" before she appeared at the door. He handed her the tumbler, and she began to examine the beautiful paintings on his drawing room walls.

'You play and you sing like that, but I have never heard you doing karaoke in the Kettle?'

'It's painful, listening to most of them makes my ears bleed.' She took a sip of her drink and studied the two paintings of Roger and his British team horse, Lyrical Prospects. One was them jumping the Vicarage Vee at Badminton and another was them soaring over the Cottesmore Leap at Burghley. 'He broke a leg, didn't he?'

'My then wife decided to take him hunting,' he said bitterly. 'He fractured a front leg, and she didn't even have the decency to stay with him until they shot him.' He took a gulp of whisky. 'We were short-listed for the Olympic team at the time, having being part of the team for the Europeans. I have never found another horse like him and, unfortunately, no one has come forward with one as good as him for me to ride.'

'They're lovely paintings, and he was a very handsome horse.'

Roger opened the doors to the terrace to let Otter out. 'The irony is, my wife had these two paintings commissioned for me as a wedding present.' He took off his jacket and threw it on the back of the sofa before he sat down.

There was a silence.

Katie had never heard him speak with such emotion before, realising that she knew nothing about his personal life apart from what she had read in the snipey Smith's Gossip Corner in *Stable Tattle* magazine. She took a sip of vodka, thinking of all the times she had turned to Smith's column before reading anything else in *Stable Tattle*, desperate to read who had behaved the most badly that week in the horse world. The column still ran in the weekly publication but was a much tamer affair these days after a successful jump jockey had taken the magazine to court for insinuating that he had a drug problem. In typical Smith's fashion, the magazine had denied it, arguing that they had written that the jockey in question enjoyed a coke after a win and they had meant the drink. Sadly, as the jockey had been banned from riding for cocaine use in the past, a huge and high-profile court case had ensued, and it had not ended well for either party.

Nine years ago, the talk of the Dorset Pony Club had been Smith's relentless taunts and insinuations regarding Roger and the end of his hasty marriage. Many people thought Elizabeth was heavily involved with Smith's sneering comments, and a fifteen-year-old Katie and her friends had lapped up the allegations, much to their parents' consternation. Katie could even remember her mum marching into her bedroom and snatching the magazine from her hands as she read Smith's column to five of her giggling friends.

'But Mum!' Katie had pleaded. 'Roger's been sleeping with Jessica and Abi, and we need to know which one tried to move in with him.'

'Bloody magazine should be banned – it wrecks lives!' Joanna had shouted back from the kitchen as she hurled *Stable Tattle* into the recycling bin.

'As you've probably read,' Roger stared at his whisky as Katie took another sip to hide the blush creeping up her face, 'my marriage didn't last long after losing Lyric.' He looked up at the painting of the Cottesmore Leap. 'Such an incredible horse.'

'But surely you couldn't blame her for him breaking a leg? It could have happened at any time.'

'She didn't ride like you. She was reckless behind the hounds, and she took him hunting without asking me.'

'There must have been other reasons? You wouldn't split up just because of that?'

He suddenly smiled at her. 'Katie, I have never met anyone like you. You see the positive in every situation.'

'Sorry.' She could feel the heat rising in her face.

'Don't apologise; it's a good trait to have. The truth is, I rushed into it, thinking she would be the perfect back-up that my parents had been, but of course she was nothing like that.'

'What was she like?'

'Sexy, high maintenance, arrogant. I suppose we suited each other very well at the time.'

'Did you love her?'

Roger held her gaze. 'I think so, in the beginning. But I can't say I missed her when she left; I missed Rascal more than her.'

'Who was Rascal?'

'The Jack Russell I gave her as a birthday present.' Roger realised he was quite drunk; the Major's hospitality always included a lot of particularly good Claret.

'Must have been hard losing your parents so suddenly; no wonder you wanted someone to fill the void they left.' Katie watched him open the door to let Otter back in.

'Not exactly a childhood dream, is it? But you must play the hand you are dealt. I should have known no one could replace them.' He put his glass down on the table next to him.

'Do you have a picture of them?'

He got up and handed her a framed photograph from the sideboard, standing over her as she studied it.

'Very pretty lady,' she returned the silver frame to him, 'and your dad was pretty fit too.' She stopped herself from adding that it was no wonder they had produced such a handsome offspring.

'What about your parents?' He replaced the picture and returned to his chair. 'Your father is obviously not keen on you riding horses for a living.'

'He's most definitely not,' she agreed. 'He makes out he's a self-made man, starting as the tea boy and working his way up the ladder to be the company boss,' she took another mouthful of vodka, 'but it was only when he married Mum and Granny and Grandad gave him a huge cash injection that he was able to buy a really small office. Admittedly, he has built it up from there, but it was Mum's family money that set him up. I sometimes wonder...'

'Wonder what?'

'If that's why he wanted to marry her; she was only nineteen when they started going out.' She looked at her glass. 'Dad never really got on with my grandparents; I always thought he was intimidated by their money.'

'What does your mother do?'

'Nothing, she's never had to.' She stroked the top of Otter's silky head. 'I mean, she's on every committee going and rides a lot. Mum's always busy.'

'How did she feel about you moving halfway up the country to work for me?'

'She was okay about it; she was even slavering over your photograph in *Horse & Hound* the day before I left.'

The corners of his mouth twisted into a small smile, making his eyes crinkle.

'Well, it might have been you, or it could have been Paperchase.' She drained her glass.

'Would you like another?'

For a second she paused, wishing she hadn't finished her drink so quickly. 'No thank you, it's getting late.'

He held the back door open for her, and she briefly wavered before standing on her tiptoes to kiss his cheek. 'Thank you for the drink.'

'You're welcome, thank you for bringing me home alive.'

She smiled at him and turned away to the darkness.

Closing the door behind her, he leant against it, closed his eyes and groaned.

Eight

'Oh my God, look at that!' whispered Shelley loudly, her eyes glued on the tall man who was pulling down the ramp of Petra's lorry in the row opposite.

The man was wearing pale-blue jeans and had obviously shunned Petra's yellow team polo shirt, in favour of a dark-blue T-shirt with "this is not what I signed up for" written on the front in pink holographic lettering.

'He is gorgeous – who is that?' Jules was gazing at him.

Caitlyn was busy putting studs in The Mechanic's shoes and, without looking up, she told them it was Tom, Petra's new groom. Working five nights a week in the Cup and Kettle meant that Caitlyn always knew the local gossip.

'Wow,' Katie took in the dark hair that had been gelled into spikes and his beautiful tan, 'he is indeed gorgeous.'

Tom, sensing he was being watched, turned to the Fleming Bowen lorry and flapped both his hands up and down to wave at them.

'Gay,' chorused Katie and Jules.

'No, no, he can't be,' moaned Shelley, 'he's beautiful.'

Katie was putting on her gloves in preparation for Brogue's show jumping. 'If he's not gay, Petra will be shagging him anyway.'

'No, she won't,' snapped Shelley and then, turning back to look at Tom again, muttered that something that gorgeous wouldn't go with a bitter old hag like her.

Roger was shrugging on his jacket inside the lorry, watching his team unashamedly gawking at the new member of Petra's workforce. He was amused by the look of adoration on Shelley's normally passive face, but when he saw Katie also examining Tom critically, he felt a flash of anger, and as he climbed down the lorry steps, he told her coldly that she was cutting it fine for her show jumping.

'Do you have to use those ridiculous stirrups?' He pointed at Katie's rose-gold stirrup irons hanging on Brogue's jumping saddle.

'They were a present from my mum,' she replied calmly, catching eyes with Caitlyn who giggled. 'I'm sorry that you have a pathological hatred of anything pink, but I like them.'

'And for heaven's sake put your tits away, Shelley,' Roger barked as Shelley, wearing a low-cut T-shirt, bent over to screw in Lightoller's studs, giving Tom an eyeful of her cleavage.

~

Deliberately bumping into the gorgeous Tom at the secretary's marquee later in the day, Shelley introduced herself and said he must come for a drink at the Cup and Kettle with her and Katie, so he had some friends in the area.

'He said Petra's going to let him have a crack with Warrior next year,' Shelley told Katie when she got back to the lorry, before adding that she hoped he made an arse of it.

'Gay, then?' queried Katie.

'As a lavender-coloured handbag,' came the swift reply.

Tom in fact was free to join them that very evening in the Cup and Kettle and even offered to drive as he would have to head back to Petra's staff house at the end of the night.

Any faint hope Shelley was harbouring that Tom might indeed be heterosexual was firmly quashed when he arrived at the Dorchester wearing a pink and purple flying suit with a pale-pink Michael Kors crossbody leather satchel over his shoulder.

The three of them got along so well, meeting up in the pub became a regular occurrence, even if it was, as Katie put it, "to see what batshit crazy outfit Tom was going to wear to scare the regulars with". Much to Shelley's delight, Tom was also terribly indiscreet and proceeded to tell them all about Petra's yard, her intense moods and her horses. The new horse, Hoplite Warrior, who Roger was helping Petra with, was a handful and was proving to be much too strong for her. He was also aggressive in the stable, difficult to ride and generally not easy to handle.

'So, I said, "Petra, it's alright for you with your strapping nutcracker thighs that would crush a man to death in seconds, but when you're like me and ride just using your incredible natural sense of balance, that horse is a menace to take up the gallops".' Tom crossed his legs on the bar stool and drained his vodka and grapefruit juice. 'I said, "Petra, perhaps if you actually put them in the field instead of leaving them in the stable all day, they wouldn't have such suicidal tendencies".'

Tonight, to the locals' amusement, Tom was wearing an orange boiler suit, unfastened to the waist with the arms tied around him, and a pale blue T-shirt with the slogan "you're a naughty boy, go to my room" written on the front.

'What did Petra say?' Katie asked as Shelley's mouth dropped open.

'She said, "Tom, if I wanted a six-foot fairy to ride and muck out, would I have to pay them as much as I pay you?" and as she flounced out of the yard in a huff, she told me to get a job as a bus driver if I wanted some form of safety.'

Shelley consciously closed her mouth. 'She's got a point,' she mumbled.

Tom slapped her thigh. 'Now don't you start being nasty with your Rab C. Nesbitt tone, we're here to have a lovely evening after Katie's wonderful third place today.' He waved at Brian the barman. 'Could we have another Salty Dog and two vodka and tonics for the fag hags here.' He flapped his hands at Katie and Shelley either side of him.

'He means a vodka and grapefruit juice for himself,' Shelley told Brian as Tom scowled at her.

'Anyway,' Tom recovered himself and turned to Katie, 'you must be as pleased as punch with Brogue today?'

'Delighted.' Katie poured tonic into her vodka.

'So,' Tom uncrossed his legs and crossed them again, 'who is the Rogerable Roger going to let you ride now?' Tom had a terrible crush on Roger.

Catching Shelley's quick shake of her head, Katie said she didn't know.

She actually knew very well. Roger had already put an entry in for Brogue in the bigger class and had entered Vision and Paperchase at a competition in three weeks' time.

Katie and Shelley loved Tom dearly, but like Mrs Royal, you never told him anything that you wouldn't have put in the *Northumberland Herald*.

'Well, I for one,' Tom placed his hand on his chest dramatically, 'am delighted for you, missy, and I've bought you both a little present for being so kind and allowing me to be your friend.' He rummaged in his new Ted Baker handbag. 'One for you,' he handed Katie a tiny black box, 'and one for you,' he handed an identical one to Shelley, 'you miserable bitch.'

'Tom, they're beautiful.' Katie was looking down at a pair of little silver horseshoe earrings; in each nail hole glittered a blue stone.

For once, Shelley was almost lost for words. 'Tom, they're lovely.' She gave him a hug.

'Well, darlings, if my family can't cope with who I am and want nothing more to do with me, I've got to spend my inheritance somehow.'

'Seriously, Tom?' Katie was putting her earrings in. 'Why have you never told us before? That's awful.'

Tom flapped his hands again. 'I think, sweetie, I've just now come to terms with it. They put money in my bank account every month in the hope that I'll just disappear.'

'You've always got us, Tom.' Shelley was putting the back on her earring. 'You're like an honorary brother.'

The Cup and Kettle was filling up; people who had been in for food were filtering away, and a space had been cleared in the bar for the karaoke to be set up.

'What a lovely handbag.' Mrs Grayson paused to stroke Tom's blue bag before picking up her gin and tonic from the bar. 'My granddaughter would love it, but then again she's only six.'

Tom snatched the bag away from her grimy fingers. 'I'm sure she would indeed love it, but I very much doubt that she could afford it, sweetie,' he said haughtily. 'Oooh I love a good karaoke.' He deliberately turned his back on Mrs Grayson and began thumbing through the lists of songs. 'What should I sing? "I am what I am"? Or should I do something by Sam Smith? Oooh, there's Roger.' He dropped the karaoke list.

'Thought you'd be in here.' Roger signalled to Brian for a beer. 'Jules? Caitlyn?'

'Said they'd be in later.' Shelley took a mouthful of vodka and noticed that Tom's Salty Dog had salt around the rim of the glass, and a there was a yellow cocktail umbrella stuck into a cherry. She raised her blonde eyebrows at Brian who blushed and quickly looked away.

Tom had slid gracefully off his bar stool and was urging Roger to sit down as he must be exhausted after riding five horses at Heathingstone today.

Although no one had expected Jules to turn up, she arrived an hour after Caitlyn, wearing a tiny strappy top and the shortest skirt imaginable above long, brown legs.

'That's why she's late,' fumed Katie. 'Fake tanning everywhere for the lucky Roger.'

In contrast, Caitlyn had rolled up in a pair of jeans and an overstretched T-shirt with the words "I don't work here" printed on the front, in the hope that she didn't get roped into working behind the bar on her night off.

'Pretty earrings.' She pointed at Katie's glittering horseshoes.

'Present from Tom.' Katie pushed her hair back so Caitlyn could admire them. 'Shelley's have got green stones to match her eyes.'

Jules had indeed been planning to avoid the Cup and Kettle, knowing that the entire evening would be the whole lot of them crowing about Katie and Brogue, telling Katie how marvellous she had been. Unfortunately, Jules was so blinkered she couldn't even appreciate the incredible recovery Katie had made after Brogue had got the first part of the combination at the top of the hill entirely wrong. As Roger looked at the photographs, he let out a low whistle and asked Katie how on earth she had managed to get Brogue over the next fence two strides later. She replied that she wasn't very sure, especially as she had had only one foot in a rose-gold stirrup and had dropped her whip.

Jules had swiftly changed her mind about attending the Cup and Kettle karaoke when she had got Caitlyn's message asking her if she was coming, and even Roger was there. So, she had hastily fake tanned her legs, straightened her hair and warned her parents that she might be late.

Brian the Barman had sung "Suspicious Minds" while staring at Tom; Shelley had yelled her way through the only Manically Challenged song that was in the karaoke man's files; Tom had not only sung "I Will Survive" but also several Pet Shop Boys classics when Brian rang the brass bell on the bar for last orders.

Katie, realising that she was absolutely shattered, was sitting talking to Roger, watching the rest of the group dancing to the pub's jukebox.

Roger lifted his bottle of beer to tap her glass. 'Cheers. Are you happy?'

'Very.' She looked up to find Jules, in alcohol-induced bravery, openly glaring at her. 'I just wish everybody was.'

'Ignore her.'

'It's hard to ignore her when she detests me quite so much.' Katie removed the cocktail umbrella from Tom's empty glass and folded it shut. 'Tom says Petra's thinking of letting him compete Warrior next year.'

Roger tightened his lips. 'I like Tom,' he said firmly, 'but I'm not sure he's up to Warrior. The horse is incredibly sharp.'

Katie yawned.

'Come on, I'll give you all a lift home.'

She picked up Tom's Ted Baker handbag from the bar. 'I'd better take this; he always forgets his bag when he's pissed.'

~

As the number of horses Katie was given to ride increased, so did the workload and activity in the yard. Often, they were away competing on both Saturday and Sunday and show jumping at least one night a week at the local equestrian centre. Roger's hours away from Athward Hall giving lessons declined dramatically, as he was so busy with his own horses, and Katie felt she was under his constant scrutiny.

Despite Roger having a part-time secretary, there was still a mountain of paperwork to do for the yard and estate, as well as keeping on top of the entries. In days gone by, the eventing season began in late March and was pretty much over by mid-September. Now the season was longer, and if you weren't doing dressage, show jumping and cross country schooling when you weren't at an event, you were quickly left behind by the competition.

Roger was pleased with the way Katie was riding. It took some of the pressure off him as he was able to give her anything on the yard to ride and know she would make a decent job of it.

'I've had an idea about The Mechanic,' Roger looked across

at Katie in the passenger seat of his Discovery, 'but I'm not sure you're going to like it.'

They had left Shelley and Jules to bring the lorry back from the competition and were hurrying home to ride Bluebell, The Mechanic and Brogue, who were competing back at Easton Mains the following day. From the grass verge, the cow parsley was waving frothy white heads at them in the warm May sunshine, and there were stretches of blackthorn where the blossom was beginning to emerge. Having come to Northumberland at the end of January when the trees were naked and the fields of clay were orangey-brown, Katie thought it was as though the county was finally waking up from hibernation.

She eased herself forward, trying to get comfortable. She'd had a heavy fall with Paperchase when a loose dog had chased them halfway around the cross country course, causing the horse to completely lose his head and bolt. Despite Katie screaming to "get out of the fucking way", a helpful steward trying to slow the pair down by waving his arms had made Paperchase swing around in panic, and the pair had fallen on the flat. The horse had landed on her left leg and then trodden on her ankle as he got to his feet, leaving Katie lying on the grass in her inflated air jacket like an upturned woodlouse.

'How are you feeling?'

'Sore.' She gingerly sat back, wondering how on earth she was going to manage to ride Brogue the next day.

'Did they find the owner of the dog?'

She shook her head. 'They kept appealing for them to come forward, but I suppose they grabbed their bloody Weimaraner and went home as quickly as they could.'

'A Weimaraner?' He was starting to smile.

'Yep. Just my luck, a Jack Russell wouldn't have been able to keep up with us for so long. And then the fence judge gave me a telling-off for my language.'

'Well—'

'You would have said much worse things to him, if you'd been galloping towards him with no control and seen him waving his arms around like a hyperactive mime artist. *And* because my air jacket went off, I'll have to fork out for another canister for it.'

'Do you have a spare?'

'It's in the lorry, but it's the only one I've got.'

'You should always have more than one spare. There are five canisters in a bag in the front locker, just take one of those.'

'Why do you have five spares? Do you expect to fall off that much?'

'Cheeky cow,' he replied with a grin. 'Anyway, I've been thinking about The Mechanic a lot, especially about how he behaves at a competition.' Roger deftly overtook a silver car that was travelling too slowly for his liking.

Katie turned her head to look at him and noticed how brown his forearms were now he had rolled up the sleeves of his shirt.

'I'm going to speak to Charles tomorrow because I want you to ride him.'

She leapt forward, making her seat belt lock, and then winced. 'I can't fucking ride him!' she retorted. 'He nearly bucked Shelley off on Thursday, how on earth will I stay on him? I'm too short in the leg.'

'I've checked and checked, he's never been competed by a woman.' Roger pretended not to hear her. 'Are you up for it?'

He overtook another car and noticed her hitting an imaginary brake.

'I must get this car looked at – the invisible pedals on the passenger side don't appear to be working.'

Katie relaxed her right leg and squirmed in the leather seat. *I can't say no*, she thought desperately.

'You can't say no,' he said, reading what she was thinking.

'Okay, but just once to see what he's like.'

'He's entered at Bellick next weekend; I'll put in a change of rider.'

Katie sighed and changed the radio station, her hand hovering as she listened to what they were playing, her finger ready to press the button again.

Immediately, his hand reached over hers, selecting the CD option, and Lewis Capaldi started singing "Someone You Loved".

'Oh good.' She looked out of the window at the passing countryside, trying as hard as she could to ignore the heat that had shot up her arm when their hands had briefly touched. 'Music to slash my wrists to.'

'I'm starving; if I make a detour we'll go past a McDonald's. A quarter pounder with cheese and a chocolate shake?'

Nine

After the hot weather and hard ground that had engulfed May, the first weekend in June saw Bellick deluged with torrential rain. By mid-morning, the shopping village was a sea of mud, and the spectators' cars and lorries arriving for later classes were being towed onto the field by a tractor.

Watching the windscreen wipers as he waited for the tractor to tow his Mercedes into the owner's car park, Charles Dee wondered idly if he should buy a long, waxed coat and some wellingtons for days like these. He frowned as Miss Mac's tattered Subaru, with the diff lock engaged, swept effortlessly past him and coasted across the roped-off area to the very front of the car park. Charles watched her retrieve a very worn, long, waxed jacket and a hat from the boot of her car and light a cigar inside her cupped hands, before she hobbled off in the rain towards the dressage arenas.

In his first season owning an event horse, Charles was desperately trying to fit in with the other owners but had set the bar painfully high for a horse with a track record like The Mechanic. He was desperate for The Mechanic to qualify for Garwood three-day event at the end of September, and he hadn't told Roger that he had, in fact, already booked accommodation in the small town a few miles from Garwood. Everyone wanted to make the long drive to the top of Scotland for Garwood's end-of-term party, and Charles was enjoying bragging about *his eventer* at every board meeting he held. How terrific it would be if he could tell his board that he was taking time off to watch his horse run at an international event.

To qualify for Garwood, The Mechanic needed to finish in the top three twice before the end of July, and now that Roger had suggested that Katie's womanly touch was going to be the making of the horse, Charles was eagerly awaiting miraculous results.

The Mechanic, cold rain streaming off his liver-coloured coat, detested being wet and cold and was in a foul temper. Thoroughly annoyed and showing his usual pre-performance nerves, he proceeded to buck Katie off in the warm-up to his dressage.

Roger threw his reins to Shelley and sprinted across the mud, warning Katie not to get back on until she had been seen by the course doctor or she would be eliminated.

'What makes you think I want to get back on the fucking thing?' she yelled as he took her arm.

Roger took in her white face and, speaking more gently, said that she had sat the first four bucks brilliantly. 'He's made his point,' Roger watched Tom leading the prancing horse across to them, 'now he'll let you ride him.'

Tom was wearing a blue North Face jacket with the hood up over his spiked hair.

'Oooh, missy, you sat the first ones beautifully; now, have you seen the doctor?' He held his palm up to Roger. 'I've got forty minutes before Petra needs Warrior, so you just leave her with me.' As Roger started to protest, Tom carried on, 'No, you need to be on Bluebell getting ready for your *stressage*. I'll make sure she sees the doctor and gets back on board. Off you pop.'

'Knows more about our times than we do,' Roger muttered as he trudged back across the mud.

Good as his word, Tom stayed with Katie for the doctor's

assessment and gave her a leg-up back into The Mechanic's very wet saddle. As he wiped the mud off the soles of her boots to prevent them slipping in the stirrups, he reminded her not to fall off during her dressage test as they would be eliminated, and Charles Dee would then have to get out of his Mercedes and get his comb over wet.

The rain was so horizontal as Katie trotted down the centre line of the arena, she couldn't even see the judge. Through the mud they trotted, bending and flowing, rain dripping off The Mechanic's neat plaits. The canter was good, and Katie could feel her heart lightening as they changed the rein and cantered in the opposite direction, coming back to walk across the diagonal on a long rein; The Mechanic shook the rain out of his ears and blew through his nostrils. Gathering him up again, Katie was aware of nothing but the horse trotting beautifully around the top of the arena, straight as an arrow down the centre line and coming into a perfect square and balanced halt. Grinning broadly, she saluted the judge who raised a hand back to her in appreciation and turned to leave the arena, slapping The Mechanic's neck in gratitude. The Mechanic, who was delighted with himself and, feeling Katie's mind was no longer on the job, suddenly gave a squeal and hunched himself into two enormous bucks, dislodging Katie from the saddle and firing her onto his long neck. Hearing Tom and Shelley yelling at her to hang on, she managed to cling on somewhere near The Mechanic's ears until he shot through the gap in the white boards, before slithering to the ground.

Cold, wet and covered in mud, Katie opted to change into her spare breeches.

'There's no point in saving them,' she told Shelley. 'He's going to have so many show jumps down, I doubt we'll be allowed to start the cross country.'

Roger had had two fences down with the usually clear Lightoller and advised Katie to take a very wide line at the double of red and white poles, as everyone was having them down. Doing exactly as instructed, Katie rode The Mechanic two metres wider than the muddy hoofprints of the previous competitors and, despite hitting the white planks, which swung and swung in the cup, they went clear.

Roger went clear cross country with Lightoller, and he was happy that Bluebell had settled well and only had one down show jumping. There might be a chance he would qualify for Garwood after all.

Waiting to start her cross country, Katie wasn't feeling nervous, which unnerved her.

Concentrate, she told herself. Reminding herself of the course, and using one of Roger's techniques, she pictured The Mechanic jumping all the fences perfectly.

Roger would order to be left in complete isolation in the lorry so he could mentally visualise his rounds; Katie preferred to do it with her eyes shut while sitting on the horse. Roger had warned her that if someone disturbed her, it could put a break in the imagery which could then put doubt in her mind and, just as she was picturing herself sailing through the combination after the water jump, she was suddenly aware of Charles Dee calling her name.

'Go away,' she shouted and went back to the motion picture in her head.

Do it again, she thought. Riding The Mechanic on the perfect line, he flowed like satin through the combination. When she opened her eyes after completing the course, there was no sign of Charles.

'Thirty seconds.' The starter checked his stopwatch.

She rode The Mechanic in a small circle.

'Fifteen.'

She rode through the gap in the white rails to the start box as he warned her there were ten seconds to go. At the moment when, traditionally, your stirrups feel uneven and you wish you had urinated just one more time, Katie felt nothing but the hammering of The Mechanic's heart through his ribcage.

'Five.'

She turned The Mechanic to face the sodden stretch of grass leading to the first fence, a brush hedge.

'Go!' called the starter shortly. 'Good luck!'

And they were off, galloping to the brush. The Mechanic checked himself and sailed over, landing far out on the other side. Knowing the deep going would test The Mechanic's fitness, Katie steadied him for the second, a set of lashed-together telegraph poles; they flashed underneath The Mechanic's toes, and Katie was already turning him left in the air to gallop up the hill to number three.

They were travelling quite quickly, thought Roger, as he watched them plop down into a very full water jump, the silver pom-pom on Katie's hat the only thing visible from where he sat on Bluebell at the start. The pom-pom cantered through the water, and the pair came back into sight as they leapt up the bank out of the water complex. There was a grey horse refusing at the combination of fences after the water. *Slow him down*, thought Roger desperately, *slow down, give him time to look.*

The grey horse moved off the track, and The Mechanic pricked his ears. He took a huge leap over the first fence and very quickly Katie pulled him to the left, avoiding the second fence; she then cantered a small, controlled circle and presented him to the second fence, which he jumped nicely. They were nearly home but, aware that a slipping concentration could prove disastrous, Katie kept the hammer down, and when she finally dismounted and loosened The Mechanic's girth, Roger thought he had never seen the horse blow so hard.

'My fault entirely, Charles,' she gasped as the owner walked up underneath an enormous green and white golf umbrella, making the other horses in the warm-up shy away. 'I got my line wrong after the water; he might have made it, but I thought it was better to circle and make sure.'

'Quick thinking.' Roger was anxious that Charles saw it for the good round it had been.

Charles was ecstatic. Telling Katie her riding had been "champion" which, as Shelley put it later, was "rich as he couldn't ride in a taxi with the fucking door shut".

~

It was a damp but extremely happy drive home. The Mechanic's red and white rosette for his win lay along the dashboard of the lorry, alongside the purple and orange one that Bluebell had been given for his tenth place.

Mrs Royal was standing in the overhanging doorway of the tack room when they got home.

'The lasses are away home; it's rained all day here.' She watched as the ramp was dropped and Bluebell, on the back of the lorry, gave a soft whicker, knowing he was home. 'Roger, there's a chicken pie that just needs to go in the oven, and I've done you some veggies that just need to go in the dingbox.'

As he thanked her, Mrs Royal thought how tired Roger looked.

'And I thought you'd be tired after such a long day, so I've tidied the flat.' She held up her hand at Shelley's squawk. 'I haven't done *any* washing,' she said carefully, 'I've just done some hoovering and dusting and a bit of tidying for you both.' She winked at Katie as she left.

Although the Dorchester had been cleaned to a standard it had not seen for many years, Shelley discovered the Tampax in the bathroom cupboard had been arranged in order of absorbency, and Katie was silently mortified that the picture of Roger she had torn out of *Horse & Hound* and hidden under her thongs, was now in a little wooden frame on her bedside table.

'Find the keys to our bedrooms now, Roger!' Shelley yelled into her phone. 'Or I'm coming to your house tonight while you're asleep to cut all the buttons off your fucking Hackett shirts!'

Ten

Standing in the tack room doorway with his arms tightly folded, Roger surveyed his four members of staff.

Shelley was lounging in the tatty armchair with Katie perching on the arm; Jules was washing a set of black brushing boots in the sink; and Caitlyn was cleaning Vision's bridle on the hook hanging in the middle of the room.

'What's in it for us?' asked Shelley coolly, picking up Tom's *Gay & Out* magazine from the table.

'Shelley, I detest doing these demonstrations. Watching people who can't ride,' Roger stopped himself from adding "in a taxi with the door shut", 'trying to give them advice as to how their useless horses will suddenly become good enough for the next Olympics. So, I thought if the four of you all rode our horses, I can point out the horse's good and bad points, and we can use Lady Baneford's indoor school for free.'

Caitlyn spat enthusiastically on the saddle soap. 'I'm not riding in front of the Riding Club witches. They're all totally up themselves.'

'I know what they all want up themselves,' murmured Shelley as she flicked through the magazine to the item about stripping away belly fat.

'Jules?' Roger was beginning to sound desperate.

Jules tore the Velcro straps apart on The Mechanic's cross country boots. 'If you really want me to. Who do you want me to ride?'

'Paperchase or Brogue?'

Jules agreed she could ride Paperchase.

'There must be some form of renumeration for this?' Shelley licked her finger and turned the page.

'In my day it was simply called *wages*,' said Roger in despair. 'Katie?'

'Do I actually have a choice?' She was thinking how lovely his face was when he smiled.

'Not really, as I want you to ride The Mechanic and Lightoller.'

'When is this Fleming Bowen masterclass anyway?' Shelley was beginning to read the "should I fake my star sign to make me more employable?" article.

'The twenty-fourth.'

Shelley looked mightily relieved. 'That rules me out because me and Tom are going to the Manically Challenged gig in Newcastle.'

'Right, so just Katie and Jules then?' Roger confirmed.

He took the silence as approval.

∼

Roger was wearing a microphone so that all the sixty-something-year-old ladies from the Athward and District Riding Club could hang onto his every word.

Katie had already ridden Lightoller to his lyrical commentary, explaining to the freshly washed hair and clouds of scent in the gallery that the horse was improving rapidly as the eventing season progressed, and didn't he have such a lovely set on hindleg?

Jules had turned up in brand-new breeches and boots to ride Paperchase, who had behaved beautifully; she now remained in the middle of the indoor school, feet dangling free of her stirrups, as Roger thought Paperchase's calming presence might settle The Mechanic. It didn't, and The Mechanic had produced one of his finest rodeo performances, brutally dumping Katie in the middle of his execution of lengthened canter.

There were gasps in horror as Katie landed on the arena surface, and after she had dusted herself down and Jules had managed to catch the overexcited chestnut, Roger legged her back into the saddle.

'And when it all goes wrong, you have to get straight back up and try again,' he told his raptured audience as Katie picked up her canter again to the sound of tittering laughter. 'You are alright, aren't you?' he added, and there was more laughter as she nodded.

As Katie and Jules were getting the three horses ready for the short journey back to Athward Hall, the whole of the Riding Club descended on Roger.

'Bloody hell,' muttered Jules as she crouched to fasten Paperchase's front travelling boots. 'Why don't they go the whole hog and just shove their phone numbers into his pockets.'

Katie glanced up to see a woman with bleached hair, flesh overflowing from the tightest pair of white jeans, asking Roger if he did private lessons.

Unwilling to risk having both Katie and Jules in the lorry together without Shelley to referee, Roger had tactfully suggested that Jules take her car to the demonstration so she could go straight home afterwards.

In the lorry on the journey home, Katie, feeling stiff and sore from falling off, was not in carnival mood.

'I could shoot it myself,' she told Roger angrily. 'Bloody horse just keeps dumping me.'

'That was quite a performance he gave tonight,' Roger admitted. 'I'm not sure anyone could have sat that. Let's hope that he starts doing it less and less,' he glanced across at her in the passenger seat, 'very soon.'

~

Katie was surprised to see Mrs Royal mooching around the stables with Otter at her heels.

'Well now, I thought you might be late after answering all them questions from the Riding Club ladies, so I popped back to let Otter out.' Otter grinned up at her. 'How was your demonstration?' She followed Katie to The Mechanic's stable.

'Bloody thing bucked me off,' said Katie despondently.

'Now, hinny, he was only showing off. Before long you'll be winning a lovely red, white and blue sash with him. The kind what has golden tassels on and big rosettes with gold ribbons.'

Katie laughed and realised that, like Shelley, Mrs Royal kind of made things alright. 'They don't have posh sashes in eventing,' she replied, 'only rosettes and a salt lick as a prize that would cost you a fiver to buy.'

'Wait and see, lassie, wait and see.'

Finding Roger in Paperchase's stable, she told him there was a beef bourguignon in the bottom of the Aga and some mashed potato ready to go in the dingbox.

'I've done enough for two,' she told him blandly and, leaving Otter with him, she was gone, shouting "ta da, pet" to Katie who was lifting tack out of the lorry.

'Beef bourguignon?' asked Roger as Katie washed out the feed buckets.

With Shelley away with Tom and probably nothing in the Dorchester's fridge but a piece of mouldy cheese and some bottles of tonic, Katie was grateful for the offer.

Going into the Dorchester for a quick shower before supper, Katie found a yellow Post-it note stuck on the inside door. Shelley had written: "pocket of your Barbour jacket – in case you need them. ;) x".

Feeling slightly better after a shower, Katie unearthed a bottle of Shiraz that had been given to Shelley as a present and, as it was starting to spit with rain, put on her wax jacket before heading up to the Hall. As she hung up her coat in Roger's cloakroom, she suddenly remembered Shelley's note and found four condoms in the front pocket.

Roger had showered and was cutting up a loaf of Mrs Royal's homemade bread when she walked into the kitchen.

'How are you feeling?' He poured her a vodka and tonic and put the Shiraz on top of the Aga to warm up.

'Shoulders feel like I landed on concrete.'

'It's the way you landed, right across your neck.' He returned from the freezer with an ice pack. 'Usually reserved for injured tendons, but I think it will help.' He laid it across her shoulders and told her to keep it there until the coolness had worn off.

Too hungry to even put Mrs Royal's mashed potato in the microwave, they devoured the whole bourguignon and mopped up the sauce with pieces of bread. Roger opened the bottle of Shiraz and poured out two large glasses before lifting a huge rice pudding out of the Aga.

'How are you not the size of a house?' she asked incredulously as he handed her a dish.

'When did you last eat?'

Katie had to think for a moment. 'Two pieces of toast and a packet of Hula Hoops at lunchtime,' she said eventually.

'And for breakfast?'

'Full English.'

He looked astounded. 'Really?'

'No not really,' Katie was shovelling in rice pudding, 'two coffees, a KitKat and a handful of Haribo,' she admitted.

He laughed. 'Well, I'm much the same and therefore I always eat everything that Mrs Royal has made for me.'

Roger opened another bottle of wine as the talk came around to horses and then on to the staff.

'Shelley is brilliant,' he stated. 'She just gets on with it and organises everything; I don't know what I would do without her. Caitlyn is an absolute sweetheart and tries so hard, not easy for her being dragged up by her parents and having nothing in the way of money.'

'But she's got her Bogiemobile,' put in Katie, giggling.

'But she's got her Bogiemobile,' agreed Roger. 'But Jules, well, Jules is a strange girl.'

'Strange is not the word. Did you see her laughing when I fell off tonight? She hates me, and she's clearly mental.'

'You've got to rise above it.' He took a mouthful of wine. 'She has been unbearably spoilt by her parents and consequently expects everything to go her way. Why is she so vile towards you anyway?'

'You mean, you've actually noticed how nasty she is to me?'

'I notice lots of things,' he said quietly. He was looking at his glass, twirling the stem around in his fingers; then he looked across the table at her.

There was a pause; the atmosphere had changed, and she could feel her scalp prickling and her heart beating faster. Hastily, she drained the last of her wine and pushed back her chair.

'I'd better go; Shelley is bound to have the hangover from hell tomorrow after drinking with Tom and staying in Newcastle.'

'Have one more,' he emptied the bottle into her glass, 'I'll only end up drinking it if you don't.'

～

Jesus, what a thumping head, thought Shelley. It was all bloody Tom's fault for suggesting they stay in Newcastle after the gig. Beer had led to vodka and tonics; vodka and tonics had led to cocktails and, finally, Jägerbombs and shots. Now, as they raced up the A1 in Tom's BMW, Shelley thought she was going to be sick.

'I need some paracetamol,' she moaned faintly.

Tom, looking as green as the jumper he was wearing, replied there were some in the glovebox, and if there was only one left in the packet, he needed half of it.

'Kill or cure method! Kill or cure method!' he yelled twenty minutes later as he swerved into a layby with a burger van parked in it.

'You can't be serious?' The smell of the bacon frying was making Shelley retch.

'I swear by it, sweetie.' Tom was rooting around on the back seat looking for his wallet. 'What do you want? A bacon roll, or will I ask them to put on a cheeseburger?'

Fortified by the impromptu breakfast, Shelley was rallying by the time Tom dropped her off at the stable gates at half-past seven.

'Morning! Where's Katie?' Shelley shouted across the yard to Caitlyn and her wheelbarrow.

Putting down the barrow, Caitlyn replied that she was schooling The Mechanic.

'No, you bloody don't,' Shelley grabbed Tom by the arm, 'as you've got the day off from Golden Knickers, you can stay and help us muck out.'

Katie sat easily in the dark-coloured dressage saddle as she cantered a figure of eight around the rubber chips of the outdoor school. The horse was going really well, and Katie had almost forgiven him for his unceremonious dumping of her the previous evening. Seeing Shelley and Tom approaching, she eased The Mechanic into a halt and walked across to the school gates on a long rein.

'Oh my God, sweetie,' Tom leant over the fence to stroke The Mechanic's sweating neck, 'you had him going like a bloody Grand Prix dressage horse. Must be the strength in those nutcracker thighs of yours.' He winked.

Smiling, Katie gave the horse a pat and asked how the gig had been.

'Amazing, but I've got a hangover so bad that if I open my eyes, I think I'll bleed to death.' Shelley was looking pale again and regretting the kill or cure cheeseburger with extra onions and barbeque sauce. 'So? How was the Fleming Bowen masterclass?'

'Aside from this fucker bucking me off in the middle of his rather glorious extended canter, it went okay. At least Roger's fan club all seemed to like it.'

Shelley and Tom collapsed laughing.

'The geriatrics at the Riding Club would have loved it if they'd just been sitting in a room in silence with the Rogerable Roger,' sniggered Tom.

Shelley was staring at Katie with a look of dismay but, after closing her mouth, she said that she and Tom would start mucking out with Caitlyn, and once Katie had cooled off The Mechanic, she had better make everyone a coffee.

After turning The Mechanic out in the meadow halfway down the drive towards Mrs Fleming Bowen's lodge, Katie yelled that she was making the coffees and heading to the Dorchester to get some milk. As she closed the fridge door, Shelley suddenly appeared at the top of the stone stairs and shut the door behind her.

'Come on then, out with it.'

'Out with what?' Katie avoided her eyes and put the milk down on the faded blue bench.

'You've shagged him.'

'Shelley! I have done no such thing.'

'Come with me.' Shelley grabbed her by the wrist and dragged her to the bathroom. 'Look in the mirror.'

'Oh no,' Katie moaned.

'Get it now?'

Katie was rubbing an empty earlobe between her finger and thumb. 'I can't believe I've lost one.'

'What?' Shelley glared at her incredulously.

'I've lost one of Tom's lovely earrings.' She took out the remaining earring and placed it on the windowsill.

'I think that's the least of your worries. Look again.'

'What am I looking at?'

'At your *neck*,' said Shelley impatiently.

'Noooo!' wailed Katie as she turned back to her with a hand clamped over the huge hickey to the left of her throat.

'Not quite so innocent now, are we?' gloated Shelley.

Not saying a word, Katie walked past her and sat down on the threadbare sofa in the lounge before getting up and going to her bedroom to search for something with a roll-neck.

'What's he like?' Shelley was laughing, watching her going through drawer after drawer of clothes. 'Is it big? No don't tell me that; I don't think I want to know about the size of Roger's cock. No, I do want to know – is it big? Was he good?'

'I don't want to talk about it.'

'Mmm. Regret sinking in already, is it?'

Katie went into the kitchen and grabbed the half-empty milk bottle. 'You breathe a word, and I mean it, Shelley, you breathe a word and I swear I'll cut off your hair when you're asleep.'

'Fuck's sake I only asked if he had a big cock,' muttered Shelley as she followed her down the stairs.

Katie stopped at the door into the yard. 'Would put most horses to shame,' she said reflectively.

'Thought as much.'

Regret was not the word. Embarrassment, paranoia and guilt were words closer to how Katie was feeling.

She and Roger could have used the vodka, whisky and two bottles of red wine as an excuse; in fact, that was the very excuse Roger suggested when he pulled her towards him and began kissing her neck.

'We shouldn't,' she'd said.

'We certainly shouldn't,' Roger agreed, but as they'd had so much to drink, it could be the perfect reason that they should. He had even, in the most gentlemanly fashion, given her an opportunity to leave, saying that he must take Otter out. But once he had kissed her and she had felt her knees weakening and her body tingling with lust, she had gone with him around the lawn, clutching his warm hand in the dark, and then accompanied him upstairs to his bedroom.

When she unbuttoned his shirt, she saw what an exceptionally strong and superbly fit body he had. Broad shouldered with such a narrow waist, the colour of his skin flattered by the soft, golden glow from the lamp by the bedside.

'You arc fit,' she murmured as she kissed his suddenly exposed shoulder, 'and you're so bloody tall.'

'But only when I'm standing up,' he sat down on the enormous bed and pulled her down beside him, 'and not when I'm lying down.'

Compared to overexcited and infatuated Jamie back in Dorset, Roger had made love to her with incredible energy and a tenderness she had not expected. Too tense and full of alcohol to even contemplate reaching an orgasm, Katie had savoured the sensation of their bodies entwined together and his obvious and utter desire for her.

'I have wanted you since I first met you,' he was leaning on one elbow, smoothing her tangled hair away from her face. 'When you chose to throw yourself at me and almost knock me over, I thought Shelley had sent me a late birthday present.'

She giggled. 'So, it'll come as a shock to you that ten years ago, and much like all my friends at Pony Club, I had posters of you on my bedroom wall.'

He rolled his eyes. 'That's one way to make me feel old.'

'You're not old.'

But too old for you, he thought, tucking her hair behind her ears.

'How do you manage to remain celibate with all those bloody women literally throwing themselves at you?'

'Are you jealous?'

'Yes.' She took her hand from his arm and let her fingers drift lightly down his chest. 'Though not at this very moment in time.'

'There have been one or two women since my marriage ended; I'm not a complete monk.'

'How have you managed to keep that quiet?' She pushed him onto his back and propped herself up to look at him.

'After the shitstorm that blew up after sleeping with most of my grooms, I stuck to married ones, as they will do anything to keep it quiet. And ones like Petra are so pathetically grateful that they won't do anything to rock the boat in the hope that it happens again.'

'Not Petra? Really?'

'No,' he lied, seeing the hurt in her eyes. 'But now I know that my nickname for you is correct, and they are indeed pink.'

'It is my favourite colour, but actually that pair was white until Mrs Royal washed them.'

At four in the morning, she regretfully lifted her head from the pillow and kissed his temple gently. His face was relaxed in sleep, and she stopped to look at him, stroking her fingers down his cheek, wishing she was brave enough to take a photo on her phone so she could relive the moment again and again.

'Where are you going, Pink Knickers?' he whispered, his arms tightening around her as she began to ease herself away.

She kissed him lingeringly on his forehead. 'I'd better get back to the Dorchester before I turn into a pumpkin.'

'Stay a while longer.' His hand caressed the back of her neck softly, and he pulled her mouth down to his. 'Although,' he sat up and rummaged in the drawer of his bedside table, 'I think we used my last one earlier.'

'I'll be back in a minute.'

Giving her a puzzled smile, he watched her pull on his shirt and leave the room before he lay down and waited for her to return.

Fumbling her way through the house, guided by the faint light streaming through the windows, Katie emptied the pocket of her Barbour jacket and raced back to his bedroom. Arms clenched across her breasts to stop them jiggling, she crashed back on the bed next to him and dropped her fistful of condoms.

Screwing up his eyes in the light of the lamp, he started to laugh. 'You certainly came well prepared. Lager and lime, kiwi fruit and banana, bubblegum, curry and poppadum. Where the hell have you been? A vending machine in a nightclub?'

Laughing, she straddled him, and as she leant closer to inhale the orange and bergamot tones of his aftershave, her hair fell forward, brushing his chest. The shirt was hanging open, and he raised his hands to her breasts.

'What an incredible view,' he murmured, knowing it could become addictive but that it must not happen again.

'It is,' she agreed, running her eyes over his face.

'What do you want?' He slid his shirt over her shoulders and ran his hands down her arms.

'What do *you* want?'

He rolled her over and began kissing her neck, his fingers gently caressing her, saying how beautiful she was. Reading the flowing black script tattooed along her ribs next to her left breast, he paused. 'And I again am strong,' He looked up at her quickly. 'Wordsworth?'

She nodded. 'How do you know?'

'One day, I'll tell you.' He lowered his head and let his tongue trail across the wording.

'Tell me now?'

He shook his head and kissed around her navel. 'Not now.'

'Please?'

'No. And if you ask again, I will stop what I'm doing.'

After he had spent ten minutes kissing the inside of her thighs and sliding his fingers in and out of her, he slid a pillow under her hips and caught the look of uncertainty on her face. Promising her it would feel amazing, he sat back on his heels, pulled her carefully towards him and slid inside her. Hearing her sharp intake of breath, he leant down to kiss her before beginning to rub her delicately with his slippery thumb.

'Who taught you this? Someone did.'

'That would be telling, and I never kiss and tell.' He moved his thumb slowly and felt her gripping him more firmly. 'Don't rush, we can take as long as you want. Don't try.'

'But it feels really good,' she replied breathlessly.

'It will feel even better if you take your time.'

'Do I always have to do what you tell me?'

He placed his other hand flat on her stomach to hold her still. 'If you want the best orgasm you've ever experienced, then yes, you do.'

'Okay.' She gasped as he slid fully into her. 'I believe you.'

'Lift your legs higher.'

'Is this another Fleming Bowen demonstration?'

He grinned as his thumb circled. 'You tell me.'

He watched her as her breathing started to quicken and she slowly began to arch her back, hands grabbing his thighs, head tipping back into the pillow, and he began to slide deeper into her. Feeling her muscles tightening on him and her stomach rippling under his palm, he waited until her body had become still and then he stretched his legs straight and lay on top of her, letting his weight pin her down.

'Oh my God,' she said slowly.

Kissing her hard as he drove himself into her, he whispered that her legs around his waist was the sexiest thing ever, but she was going to make him come too quickly.

'Stop being such a gentleman,' she whispered back, wrapping her legs more closely around him and gripping his arms even tighter with her fingers.

Looking down at her beautiful face, he gave in and came, falling on her and biting her neck as the sensation peaked and then faded.

'Again,' she whispered.

Kissing her as he eased himself out of her, he collapsed on the bed, pulling her arm so that she lay with her head on his chest and closed his eyes. 'I think I might need five minutes.'

She looked at the side of his face as she adjusted her head on his shoulder. He was so handsome, and she wondered if this would ever happen again.

'You're looking at me,' he stated.

She traced the outline of his face with her finger. 'How do you know?'

'I can feel it.' He raised his hand to her face, smoothing his fingers over her forehead, before stroking her eyelids closed with his thumb and index finger.

'I don't want to close my eyes; I want to keep looking at you. And you need to tell me how you knew my tattoo was Wordsworth.'

'Another time; it will wreck the moment.'

After half an hour of his hand gently brushing her back and their soft talking, he suggested that if the kiwi fruit and banana hadn't been too bad, why didn't they try the Bubblegum too?

'But I draw the line at lager and lime and curry and poppadum,' he said as she kissed her way down his stomach.

Consequently, it was six-thirty when Katie kicked open the door to the Dorchester, making the horses whinny and whicker for their breakfasts. Feeling slightly tender but not remotely tired or detecting any pain from her fall from The Mechanic after a night of debauchery and two and a half hours sleep, she changed, didn't shower so she could keep the smell of Roger's aftershave on her skin for a few more hours and started feeding and haying the yard. She was already tacking up The Mechanic when Caitlyn rolled in just after seven, full of apologies, saying the Bogiemobile had refused to start and she had had to get her mum and dad out of bed, who had then pushed the car down the main street of Athward village in their pyjamas.

By two o'clock, Katie was seriously flagging with a demanding red wine hangover and, knowing she had two horses to ride at Kinsey Park tomorrow, was furious with herself. Once Roger had schooled Bluebell, they would drive across to Kinsey to walk the cross country course, as Roger felt the times the next day were tight, and it would save them leaving so early in the lorry.

~

Roger was thinking hard as he drove them to the beautiful golden town of Kinsey in the Scottish Borders. What an idiot he had been taking her to bed. He'd been down this route before, and although he didn't think Katie was the type to be bin bagging her belongings, organising his paintings or sliding, sobbing down the window at a dinner party, he was livid with himself. The first time could have been put down to drink but not the second or the third. Captivated by the glory of her fantastic body, he had been ruled by something other than his brain. Now things were going to get awkward. She had made it clear she fancied him; he had bloody well said that he'd always wanted her. He wondered if she could remember that he had said that. He couldn't even blame her for starting it. Christ, he had practically jumped on her last night.

Feeling the friction and seeing a muscle flickering in his cheek, Katie was wise enough to know Roger had realised he had screwed up. After forty minutes of almost silence and Lewis Capaldi, as they crossed the Scottish Border, she quietly told him to forget about last night.

In silent astonishment, he took her hand and squeezed it briefly. 'It should not have happened, and I would rather no one else knew about it.'

'I know.'

'Thank you.'

You utter bastard, thought Katie, as she narrowed her eyes at the road ahead.

Eleven

Five horses were going to Kinsey Park. Katie was riding The Mechanic and Brogue in what would probably be his last event of the season, and Roger was partnering Bluebell, Lightoller and the slight brown mare called Little Vision.

Katie watched as Caitlyn stuck her tongue out the side of her mouth in concentration as she wrote out the list of times.

'There's twenty minutes covering Brogue's, The Mechanic's and Vision's show jumping,' said Shelley, reading over Caitlyn's shoulder. 'We're going to need to be on the ball; one of you two will need to have The Mechanic down at the warm-up for Katie as soon as she's jumped Brogue.' Shelley pointed at Jules and Caitlyn. 'The Mechanic's at the end of section C, and Vision's at the start of section D, so there better not be any balls-ups.'

As Katie warmed up Brogue for his show jumping, she could hear the commentary from the cross country course, relaying Bluebell Folly's round.

'Clear at fences seven and eight,' buzzed the loudspeaker as she cantered Brogue towards the upright fence. 'Roger Fleming Bowen taking a perfect line at nine, jumps it well.'

Jumps incredibly well, thought Katie dejectedly, circling Brogue back to the upright again.

'Bluebell Folly is clear at twelve, looking for a double clear for the Fleming Bowen team.' The commentator switched his attentions to Petra Williams and Warrior who, by the sound of it, was carting her towards fence five at the speed of a formula one car.

Brogue jumped well but had one fence down, putting him well down the order; he was feeling the firm ground, and Katie assumed that Roger would scratch him from the cross country. As she trotted back to the warm-up, Katie was scouring the area for the liver chestnut of The Mechanic. She only had twenty minutes to get him ready to jump, and there was a quarter mile walk back to the lorry. Finally, she saw Jules, denim shorts above long, brown legs, blonde hair flapping in the breeze as she gossiped with Daniel Jobson's groom, India. Jules was holding the reins of Little Vision, who should have been patiently waiting at the lorry for Roger.

Giving a bellow of rage, Katie then screamed at Jules to give the horse to her, and she set Brogue off at a spanking trot, dragging Vision alongside her, back to the lorry. Dodging through horses and bodies in the lorry park, shouting apologies and hearing snatches of conversation as she hurried Brogue on, Katie was riding through a red mist.

Roger was delighted with the white horse's cross country, and as he rode a sweating Bluebell back to the lorry, he wondered if he should suggest to Angela Mac that they put an entry in for the Garwood three-day at the end of the season. He dismounted as he approached his navy lorry and could hear that all merry hell was breaking loose.

'What the hell are you playing at?' Katie was yelling at Caitlyn.

Caitlyn, pale and stammering, was hastily tacking up The Mechanic. 'I'm sorry, Katie – I thought Jules was getting him ready.'

'She got the wrong horse ready! How bloody useless are the pair of you?' howled Katie.

Shelley, holding Vision and Lightoller, was shouting at Katie to calm the fuck down as the whole bloody lorry park could hear her and that it was bloody Jules's fault and not Caitlyn's.

Roger handed Bluebell to Shelley, took off his number bib and threw his body protector onto the ramp of the lorry. Taking his tweed jacket from the locker door, he pulled it on and took Vision from Shelley, as she fastened on his number bib and handed him his velvet hat.

'Calm down,' he told Katie firmly.

For a second their eyes met, and Katie felt a flush descending on her face. 'I've got no time to warm him up,' she said angrily. 'They're holding the course for him.'

'It's okay; let's go.' He vaulted onto Vision.

Shelley legged Katie onto The Mechanic and they were off, trotting through the lorry park.

'For the love of God!' Shelley was fuming. 'I give the pair of you one job.'

Caitlyn wiped away tears. 'Jules said she was on it.'

The steward was calling Katie's number as she and Roger trotted into the warm-up.

'Number four-five-three! You're last to go, go straight in please.'

Katie cantered The Mechanic at the practice fence, cleared it and cantered straight in to jump. The bell rang immediately and Katie, still burning with rage, pointed him at the first fence. The Mechanic, shaken by his bizarre warm-up, dodging people and horses in the lorry park, jumped it cleanly. Over the second, the orange and white poles, around the top of the arena to the white gate again, giving it plenty of daylight, across the middle to the tricky double, pinging through it with ease.

My God, thought Roger, catching the horse's expression. *He's really, really trying.*

Katie was bringing The Mechanic to the set of green planks, placed at a crafty angle from the arena barriers; The Mechanic made nothing of it and cantered sweetly down to the pink and yellow poles of number six, which he popped over beautifully. Roger found he was holding his breath as The Mechanic approached the final double. He jumped the first part, took two level strides and soared over the second part to the sound of applause from the crowd.

As the commentator announced that The Mechanic had jumped clear and was leading the class with a dressage score of twenty, Roger's mouth fell open. Twenty was an incredible score; usually The Mechanic struggled to get a score of thirty something – twenty was phenomenal.

'Twenty what?' Katie was alongside him, flushed with anger and success.

'Just twenty.' He smiled back at her. 'Go on, go and get ready for his cross country. I've asked Miss Mac to withdraw Brogue; there's no point in hammering him around on this ground,' and he cantered off.

Shelley was ecstatic. 'Twenty! Bloody twenty! I thought it was good but bloody hell. You realise that if you win, he's qualified for the Scottish Championship?'

'Don't,' warned Katie. 'Counting chickens and all that.'

'To be honest,' whispered Shelley, 'I'm amazed you can even sit on a horse after the seeing-to you got from the boss on Friday night.'

Katie glared at her. 'You're not supposed to know, so shut up,' she hissed.

Despite Jules's stony silence, Caitlyn was still trying to apologise to Katie.

'You actually did me a favour,' she climbed onto The Mechanic from the lorry's ramp wearing her pink cross country colours, 'he's never show jumped like that in his life.'

Jules looked thunderous.

Shelley watched Caitlyn wrapping plastic tape around Vision's cross country boots and, after a moment, told her quietly to go and watch Katie's cross country.

'Are you sure?' Caitlyn's eyes were rimmed with crimson.

'Yes. I don't for one minute think that Jules will want to watch it, and we can manage here.'

Giving a smile that didn't quite reach her eyes, Caitlyn thanked her and ran towards the exit of the lorry park.

Katie was cantering The Mechanic around the warm-up, occasionally asking him to come back to a halt before demanding he canter on again quickly. She was nervous and wished Roger was there to reassure her, but she knew that he wouldn't be at the start of the cross country with Vision until after she had set off. She jumped the practice fence and saw Daniel Jobson's wife at the side of the arena.

'Good luck!' Sara called out to her. 'Brilliant show jumping!'

Lifting her hand to wave her thanks, Katie saw Caitlyn running past the start and out onto the course. She felt a stab of guilt for bawling her out; it hadn't been her fault, and Katie seethed silently for a second, wondering if Jules had brought her the wrong horse deliberately to mess things up.

Stopping to catch her breath, Caitlyn watched The Mechanic bunny-hopping in the start box, desperate to get on with the job. Katie sat effortlessly as he pirouetted, and when the starter raised his eyes from the stopwatch to give them the order to go, Katie had him facing the right way, and he bounced into a canter. Caitlyn watched them jump the first three fences and made her way up the hill to see them through the combination by the trees.

There was a group of spectators next to the three fences that were decorated with plastic gnomes and pixies, and as Caitlyn approached, there was a blast on a whistle and a man on a grey horse took the long route through the obstacles, twisting and turning to jump the fences, taking up a lot of time.

'It should be Katie Holland next,' a lady wearing a headscarf was studying the programme, 'I do so love her pink colours.'

'I've bought my granddaughter the same hat cover that she wears,' the other lady was holding the lead of a lurcher, 'such a pretty silver pom-pom on it.'

As the whistle sounded again, the group turned to see The Mechanic galloping towards them, Katie looking straight through the combination.

'Looks like she's going the direct route,' stated the headscarf.

The Mechanic pricked his ears as Katie sat down in the saddle to collect him and Caitlyn heard her telling him firmly to "steady". They jumped the first part, took two smart strides, cleared the second part and, with Katie giving him a slap down the shoulder with her whip to keep him straight, cleared the third and were back on their way.

Caitlyn ran back down the course so she could see them over the last few fences while, back at the lorry, Shelley heard the commentator reporting that The Mechanic was clear so far and well within the time.

Roger, riding Vision around the warm-up, watched The Mechanic jumping the huge steeplechase fence as if it was nothing at all and galloping on to the fence adorned with milk churns. The Mechanic stood off the fence a stride, and Roger observed Katie letting the reins slip through her fingers, to give the horse the reach he needed to clear the fence.

'Roger? You're next to go!' called the steward.

'Can you let another one go before me?' he shouted back, watching The Mechanic clear a set of enormous poles and hearing the steward ask if anyone else was ready to start.

Shelley was straining to hear the commentary as the water poured into the bucket from the lorry's water tank.

'The Mechanic is clear at number twelve, one of the few to get through the direct route clear today...'

Shelley turned off the tap and leant against the side of the lorry.

'Cathy Marks is clear at seven, and Katie Holland is home and provisionally clear.'

Grinning and clenching her fists, Shelley then carried the bucket to the back of the lorry and saw Jules sitting on the ramp looking boot-faced.

'What?' asked Jules huffily as Shelley looked at her.

'For God's sake smile, or get a new job,' suggested Shelley.

Caitlyn was puffing madly but made it to the finish to see Katie galloping up the run-in, standing in her rose gold stirrups, leaning forward to pat The Mechanic's sweaty neck in praise. Running across to her, she took The Mechanic's reins as Katie slid pink-faced from the saddle.

'Amazing round.' Caitlyn was grinning, the earlier shouting all forgotten.

'He was amazing,' corrected Katie as she lifted the saddle flap and loosened his girth, hearing the commentator confirming that they had no jumping or time penalties to add.

'I'll take him back if you want to watch Roger?' Caitlyn had unfastened the horse's noseband and was rubbing his forehead.

Katie shook her head. 'You stay and watch him, and I'm sorry I shouted at you – I was panicking about his show jumping.'

'It's okay.'

Katie looked at Caitlyn's kind face. 'How can you be so *nice*?' She unclipped her chinstrap.

Caitlyn shrugged. 'Roger can be a shouty fooker as well when he's stressed.'

As Roger came back on Vision after her cross country, Shelley gave a whoop as she checked the live scores on her phone.

'He's won – The Mechanic's won.' She grinned.

'All the scores can't be in yet, surely?' Roger took off his saddle and dumped it in the locker.

'Doesn't matter, no one left to go can catch him. Scottish Championship here we come!' Shelley's voice was drowned by cheers from Caitlyn and Katie.

'Well done, Pink Knickers.' Roger briefly put an arm around Katie's shoulders, making her blush. 'Maybe all the horse needed was a change of cross country colours.'

Bloody hell, he thought. Charles Dee will insist he goes to the Championship, and how on earth can they replicate today's total fluke?

'Ooh, Katie,' said Caitlyn excitedly, 'you get a lovely set of silver spurs if you win the Championship, and you get training vouchers too, so you can have lessons with someone really good.'

'Really?'

'I wouldn't get too excited about the training vouchers.' Roger was waiting for Shelley to hand him Vision's headcollar.

'Why? Who's the training with?' asked Katie.

'Me,' he replied dryly.

'Well, at least if she wins them,' Shelley was easing off Vision's bridle, 'it'll save you shouting at someone else and them finding out about your foul temper.'

~

Mrs Royal was sitting in the old armchair in the tack room with Otter at her feet. After hearing that The Mechanic had won, she pinned the huge rosettes on the tack room wall above the bridle hooks. As she left the yard, she pointed at Brogue and said that he had a sore foot.

'He's had a long day, and it's hard ground,' said Shelley as she opened the lorry's outside locker to unload the tack.

Calling to Roger that there was a shepherd's pie in the Aga, Mrs Royal was off, calling "ta da" and telling Otter not to follow her.

Shelley announced she was going to the Cup and Kettle for a drink, and who was joining her? Both Jules and Caitlyn offered her a lift.

'Katie?' Shelley hung Bluebell's bridle on its hook in the tack room.

Katie sunk into the armchair. 'Not me, Shell, I'm knackered.'

As Roger put down a plastic box full of dirty cross country boots on the table, he watched Shelley, followed by Jules and Caitlyn, scraping open the door of the Dorchester. Hearing them stomping to the top of the stone steps through the open door, he took a step towards Katie and slowly pulled down her stock. The mark he had left on her neck was almost purple, and he winced when he saw the impression of his teeth where he had bitten her at the point of climax.

'Shit!' he exclaimed. 'I am so sorry.'

'It hurts.' She pulled her stock back up to hide it.

He tugged the silky material down her neck again as if he couldn't believe what he was seeing. 'Christ, I've never done that before in my life!'

'You don't need to look so bloody proud of it.'

'I'm truly not.'

She removed his hand and carefully recovered the bruise. 'Like I just said, it *hurts*.'

'I'm sorry.'

'How did you know?'

'I saw the top of it over your stock this afternoon.'

She dropped her eyes and got up from the chair.

'Please try to keep it hidden.'

'What do you think I've been trying to do for the past two days?' she asked furiously. 'Why do you think I've been wearing a roll-neck since yesterday morning and didn't get changed after competing today? I'm sweating my *tits* off trying to keep it hidden.'

He swallowed; it was the first time he had seen her really angry. 'I'm sorry about everything; it shouldn't have happened.'

'So you've said. But leave me to worry about covering a hickey the size of Hampshire and you can stick to…' She stopped quickly.

'Stick to what?' he asked impatiently.

'Whatever it is you do, alone every night in your enormous house.'

'Katie—'

'I'm going to the pub,' she swung her bag onto her shoulder, 'and don't worry, I'll wear a scarf to keep your reputation intact.'

Seeing the fury in her strides across the yard to the Dorchester, Roger meticulously locked the tack room and slid the key into its hiding place next to the window in the stables on his left. He had been expecting a request for a date or at the very least a replay of Friday night. What he had not been expecting was the anger. She was clearly livid with him for suggesting she try to hide the love bite, because she had been managing quite well without his intervention for thirty-six hours. She was mature for twenty-four, he knew that, but in some ways, she seemed older than him, and that was something he was unfamiliar with. This was different territory, but he felt relieved that she seemed able to put their night in bed behind her.

Her discretion made him want to do it all over again.

As he made his way to the yard gates, Shelley hauled open the Dorchester's lounge window and asked if he wanted to come for a drink with them.

'He's not fucking coming!' yelled Katie in the background. 'I'm not spending all night being lectured on what I've done wrong all weekend!'

Roger gave a shocked-looking Shelley a little shake of his head and continued walking towards the Hall.

Twelve

'Reckon we should have a stab at Garwood as well.' Charles Dee, wearing his new tweed jacket, was sitting at Roger's kitchen table, coffee mug in hand.

Roger held in a sigh of exasperation before telling Charles that after the Scottish Championship at the beginning of September, he felt that The Mechanic should be roughed off and have his shoes taken off for the winter.

'If for some reason Katie can reproduce their form at Kinsey Park, it will be nothing short of a miracle. He's a tricky and an extraordinarily strong-minded horse, and I understand that Daisy wants to compete him next year, but I strongly recommend that you buy her something more suitable.'

'Reckon Daisy will manage him alright.' Charles referred to his seventeen-year-old daughter as he reached for another piece of Mrs Royal's shortbread. 'She's mad keen to have a go at eventing, and the horse is experienced.'

Roger withheld another sigh. 'He's *difficult*, Charles. You would be better making Angela Mac an offer for Brogue or approaching Jennifer Bane about Lightoller. Daisy needs a schoolmaster, not a tearaway.'

'Seems a reformed character now,' Charles wasn't listening, 'you've turned him into a different horse altogether.'

'Katie is a very good rider; she makes it look easy, and the bloody thing has buried her enough times.'

Thinking of the accommodation that he had already paid for, enabling his family to go and watch *their horse* at Garwood, Charles insisted that Roger put in an entry. 'Think of it as an end-of-term party,' he said, as he shook Roger's hand at the door.

Brogue had gone home to the orchard field behind Miss Mac's rose-covered house, and she reported him to be in fine fettle, with her small flock of rare-breed sheep for company.

'I really think I should sell him,' she told Victoria Fleming Bowen as they sat in her garden at West Lodge, drinking Earl Grey one afternoon. 'He's a lovely horse, but I doubt that he's going to achieve much more on the eventing ladder.'

Victoria fed a slice of cake to a drooling Wigeon. 'I hear Charles Dee wants his daughter to event The Mechanic next year.'

Angela agreed that Roger had told her that too.

'Why don't you offer him Brogue on loan for the season?' Victoria lifted her cup and saucer from the glass-topped table.

'Over my dead body!' boomed Angela. 'Bloody little man has no idea!'

'Daisy has though; she's been riding a horse of Petra Williams' at Pony Club. I judged her dressage at the area finals. She's a rather nice little rider.'

Angela handed the last slice of cake to Duke, her Border Terrier, who was lying in the shade underneath her chair.

'You could even stipulate that the horse must remain here.' Victoria reached for the teapot and filled up the two gilt-edged teacups.

Angela looked up, wiping cake crumbs from her trousers. 'Has Roger put you up to this?'

'Not at all, but once one has read *The Telegraph*, *The Guardian* and *The Times*, there's very little else to think about here.'

'Especially as there's only flat racing to watch in the summer.'

They both cackled with laughter.

'I have to say, Katie is making a darn good job of producing Charles's horse.' Angela was reaching for another cucumber sandwich as they had finished all the cake. 'She must have bruises on top of bruises, the number of times the bloody horse has bucked her off.'

Taking an egg and cress sandwich from the cake stand, Victoria replied nonchalantly that her grandson would know exactly where the bruises were.

'Gosh, do you mean?' Angela's second sandwich hovered near her mouth.

'Well, Angela, you know how sleep evades us at our age, and I often tend to be in the garden incredibly early. It's such a good time to deadhead the roses before the flies come out, and if you happen to be at the bottom of my garden, in the rose patch with a set of binoculars, just to watch the birds of course, you can see straight down to the drive between the Hall and the stable yard.'

'How early are you out in the garden?' Angela offered Duke a tiny triangular ham sandwich.

'Oh goodness, usually five, sometimes a fraction earlier. Although I would say it was around half-past six when I saw her.'

'They're making quite a night of it then!'

'I mean it could all be completely innocent.' Victoria raised her hands as she spoke. 'It could be entirely plausible that the young lady just needs to use the telephone or something,' she drank some tea and smiled, 'but I hardly think one needs to borrow an onion or a cup of sugar at six o'clock in the morning, Angela.'

'They are both over the age of consent, Victoria, and I have to confess that I did tell him a few months ago that she would suit him well. He's going to have to think about producing an heir at some point.'

Victoria took a sip of her tea. 'She's very like his mother. The same confident attitude to life and that short-fused temper, much like his own.'

'Do you know, you are absolutely right. I hadn't seen it until now.'

'I think I may need to give him a little nudge in the right direction.'

Angela was reaching for her cigars. 'I wouldn't bother with nudging, just tell him to bloody well get on with it!'

Hearing horses clattering past on the other side of the house, they both stifled their laughter.

'Obviously, Miss Mac and Mrs F.B are having afternoon tea in the garden,' said Shelley, riding around Miss Mac's war-damaged Subaru which was parked half on the grass verge and half across the drive.

Katie, the collar of her polo shirt turned up in an attempt to hide the fading love bite, wished she could have got off Vision and joined them; it was incredibly hot.

'So…' Shelley urged the new brown novice called Murdoch alongside Vision, who viciously flattened her ears at him.

'So?' Katie looked down at Vision's neatly pulled mane, knowing a lecture was about to commence.

Shelley said nothing but kept staring at Katie until she eventually met her eyes.

'You've got to stop it before anyone finds out. It's not worth it, unless you want to look for a new job.'

'I know, I know. And it is stopped,' sighed Katie. 'It's just he's—'

'Let me guess,' Shelley cuffed Murdoch lightly on the neck as he went to take a chunk out of Vision's shoulder, 'he's the most amazing shag ever and you're going to get married and have lots of eventing babies.'

'You got the first bit right.'

'Honestly, Katie, the best shag in the world is not worth your job. It's a fantastic yard; there are no arsehole horses,' she thought about The Mechanic and Bluebell for a second, 'well, there might be one or *two* arsehole horses, but it's a lovely place to work, and I like working with you; I don't want you to have to leave—'

'Hang on a minute,' interrupted Katie, 'who said anything about leaving?'

'You'll have to, if it all goes tits up with you and Roger.'

'There is no me and Roger, what are you talking about?' said Katie indignantly. 'I've slept with him once.'

Shelley opened her eyes very wide.

'Once,' protested Katie, 'and it's not going to happen again.'

'Promise me you'll stop it, for the sake of the yard.' Shelley swatted at the cloud of flies in front of her with her whip. 'I'm serious, it'll just end up as one hell of a mess otherwise.'

'I've just told you, there's nothing to stop, and what do you know that I don't? I know about him sleeping with his staff in the past – how could anyone not know after reading Smith's Gossip Corner?'

'Which you've read religiously since you were fifteen, in the hope that one day you'd get to shag him,' added Shelley.

'In the same way that you read it, hoping to bump into fat old Danny Jenks…' Katie's words trailed away, and she started to laugh. 'Oh my God! How could I not have worked it out? You shagged Danny Jenks, didn't you? And Roger was completely mystified as to why you wanted to leave such a prolific show jumping yard and come to Northumberland.' She laughed even harder. 'You were banging the boss, weren't you?'

Shelley's shoulders had slumped in the saddle, and she muttered that she might have been shagging him a little bit.

'Christ almighty! He's nearly sixty, you slapper.'

'He was fifty-one,' said Shelley hotly.

'Never had you down for being the type to help the aged.' Katie kicked Vision into a trot, leaving Shelley mouthing into thin air.

'He was such a good shag,' said Shelley wistfully as she caught up. 'God, he taught me lots of things I didn't know were possible, and he was so *nice*. He had all those show jumping groupies running after him, and he wanted me. Bloody fit for his age too.'

'That was obviously before Caroline Jenks caught you and

her husband mamboing the mattress in the lorry at the Great Yorkshire Show?'

'Stupid old cow.' Shelley scowled. 'She was meant to be at home that weekend, but she turned up to surprise him with a cottage pie.'

'I bet he got a monumental surprise when she turned up unexpectedly?'

'He did. All I got was covered in cold mince and potato and a split forehead after the bitch threw it at me.' Seeing Katie burst into hysterical laughter, Shelley added earnestly, 'Honestly, it was in a Le Creuset casserole dish – it really hurt.'

'Were you sad?'

'Absolutely gutted. I've always loved cottage pie, and seeing it smeared all over my duvet was sacrilege.'

∾

Roger parked his car at the side of the road and waited for Shelley and Katie. They were trotting towards him, howling with laughter, and he heard Shelley saying something about getting badges made.

'What is so funny?' he asked as they reined in their horses.

Wiping her eyes, Katie said he wouldn't believe it if she told him, and Shelley shot her a filthy look.

'Shelley, when you get back, get the isolation box ready, would you? I might be wrong, but I suspect we might be getting Hoplite Warrior in for a few weeks of schooling.'

'Is that where you're going now?' Shelley slapped her whip down Murdoch's shoulder as he impatiently scraped the road with his foot.

Roger wrinkled his forehead. 'It's very odd, but Tom has just rung me and asked me to come straight over but not to let on that he's called me.'

∾

As Shelley and Katie settled the horses for the night, they heard the lorry starting and watched it roar up the drive towards the West Lodge.

How odd that he's come back to get the lorry but didn't tell us, thought Katie.

Shelley had no such scruples and rang Tom.

Warrior's owner had come to take the horse home, and a huge row had blown up. Petra screaming that she was owed three month's livery fees, Richard Towerlees, the owner, yelling that every time he had seen the horse out in public, it had pissed off with her and reduced the horse's value even further. Then, as he tried to get Warrior into his trailer, the horse had completely lost the plot and had kicked Richard full pelt in the testicles and Petra in the face, breaking her nose and knocking the crowns off her front teeth.

At this point, Roger arrived and offered Richard Towerlees five thousand pounds for the horse, which the owner readily accepted. As Petra began to scream something about poaching her best horse and that he was worth ten times that amount, Roger had uncharacteristically told her to shut the fuck up and be grateful the horse wasn't destined for the meat man, owing to its behaviour in the past.

The whole episode gave fuel to Tom who regaled them with a minute-by-minute version of the entire argument in the Cup and Kettle that evening. Wearing his best non-weekend outfit of a pair of torn jeans, an orange string vest and carrying a Gucci handbag, he was absolutely adoring being the centre of attention.

'So then, Roger walked around the corner looking like something from *Country Life* in his jeans and open-necked checky shirt, and he just took his phone out of his jeans pocket and asked Richard for his bank details. And when Petra started squawking, he just told her to shut the fuck up.' Tom put his hands together. 'It was wonderful; she just closed her mouth and lisped "fank you" as if he'd just saved her from a burning car.'

Katie wasn't so thrilled with Roger's act of gallantry. Warrior had already bitten her, Roger and Shelley, and he had only been on the yard for two hours.

'Do you know what the absolute best thing is?' said Tom dreamily.

'What? Better than Roger telling Golden Knickers to shut the fuck up?' Shelley opened a packet of crisps.

Tom looked from Shelley to Katie with a smug grin on his face. 'I don't have to muck out or ride the evil creature ever again.' He waved at Caitlyn behind the bar for another Salty Dog.

Thirteen

Warrior, like Bluebell Folly had done five months earlier, used violence as a first line of defence against all humans. At Petra's yard, he was used to only being taken out of his stable to be ridden, which meant he also behaved like a toddler having a tantrum when he was turned out in the field. Roger was the person who went into the stable to muzzle him and to tie him up for Caitlyn to brush, and it was Roger who tacked him up and rode him every day.

Thanks to Tom's patient schooling, the horse was supple and responsive and Roger, being a stone and a half heavier than Petra and six inches taller, was able to wrap his long legs around the horse and give him the confidence he so desperately needed.

Katie, thinking The Mechanic was tricky, only rode Warrior once and had careered around the school at a frightening speed, before a well-practised jink to the left had deposited her on the floor.

'You're crazy.' Katie brushed the sand off her breeches. 'He just wants to get you off; you'll never get inside his head.'

'Ah, but I have a secret weapon,' said Roger as Caitlyn came toddling into the school. 'Watch this.'

Asking Caitlyn to cool the horse off for him, she greeted the big brown horse with a Polo from her jeans pocket and proceeded to loosen his tight noseband and begin walking him around the school.

'For God's sake, Roger,' Katie took off her hat, 'he'll savage her; at least warn her.'

'He won't.'

As Katie watched, Warrior visibly relaxed and walked calmly beside Caitlyn as she chattered nonsense to him, pulling his hot ears through her hands and stroking his neck.

'What the hell?'

Roger grinned. 'I have no idea either, but she's the one person he hasn't tried to murder since he got here.'

It was six weeks until the Scottish Championship, and in preparation, The Mechanic was being quietly ticked over at home. Katie was desperate to take him show jumping but Roger, unwilling to watch him decimate a round of coloured poles, knowing it would wreck her confidence, wouldn't hear of it.

'Just one class,' Katie begged as they rode Lightoller and Murdoch in the school one Tuesday morning.

'What part of "no" do you not understand?' Roger cantered Lightoller over a blue and white pole. 'You must have had your teachers pulling their hair out. Taking him show jumping will achieve absolutely nothing.'

'You think it was a fluke, don't you?' Katie halted a sweating Murdoch. 'Why on earth are we bothering to go to the Championship if you think it was a fluke? What a waste of time and money.'

'It's Charles Dee's money.' He popped Lightoller neatly over a cross pole.

Katie's mouth dropped open. 'So you bloody do think it was a fluke, you fucker!' she screamed.

Shelley, pushing a wheelbarrow destined for the muck trailer by the school, saw Katie puce in the face shouting at Roger, who was yelling back at her, and casually turned around and headed back to the yard.

~

'Can I come in?' Roger was standing at the top of the Dorchester's stone steps.

Katie replied that she supposed so, as it was his flat.

Ducking his head to avoid the low doorframe, he went into the lounge and sat down on one of the chairs at the table by the window.

'Shelley?'

'Out with Tom.' She traced the pattern on the throw on the sofa with her index finger.

Wearing only a pair of black shorts and her navy team polo shirt, hair still wet from the shower, Roger was taken aback by how incredibly sexy she looked.

'Where have they gone?'

'Newcastle. There's a Manically Challenged tribute band playing at Bar Ree.' She went to turn off the music playing from the speaker on the arm of the sofa.

'Leave it on.'

She looked him in the eye, her chin raised defiantly.

'I came to apologise about this morning.' He pushed the envelopes across the table so he could rest his elbow. 'I shouldn't have shouted at you, and I'm sorry.'

She looked up mutinously. 'But you're not going to apologise for saying Kinsey Park was a fluke?'

He exhaled loudly.

'Clearly not.' She got up from the sofa and went into the kitchen.

Roger heard her opening the fridge and watched her as she put down a vodka and tonic in front of him.

'So, I guess I'll just have to live with that and prepare to make an utter twat of myself at Auchenruther Castle.'

'I don't drink vodka,' he said evenly.

'I know, but that's actually for me to drink once you've gone. So can you just go?'

'Oh, Katie.' He stood up and pulled her towards him.

'No way, Roger, this can't happen again.'

'Think of it as a farewell,' he said wickedly as his warm hands crept under her T-shirt and he began steering her to the bedroom.

'No, no, no,' she said weakly as he dropped the latch on the door and turned to face her. 'I am not doing this.'

'I promise you that shortly you'll be screaming yes, yes, yes.' His fingers were entwining in her hair, tipping her head backwards.

She closed her eyes as he kissed her neck.

'Just one last time,' he whispered.

Sensing weakness, she asked if she could take The Mechanic show jumping.

'We are not going through that again.' He unfastened the top three buttons of his shirt and pulled it over his head.

'The ground's too hard for him to have a proper run, just one round. Please?'

'I'll think about it. Now, what do I have to do to shut you up?'

She gave a low growl of frustration at the back of her throat and glared at him.

'As I've told you before, you're very pretty when you're angry, but I'm not going to force you.' He took a step backwards and picked up his shirt from the floor.

'Oh no you don't.' She grabbed his hand and pulled him towards the single bed. 'If I'm going to give in to you, it had better be worth it.'

He grinned as he put his mouth on hers, then gently pushed her onto the bed. 'You had better take your clothes off unless you want me to do it for you? In fact,' he tugged off her shorts to reveal a pink thong, 'very predictable, Pink Knickers.'

She giggled. 'They're another white pair that fell victim to Mrs Royal's hot wash.'

Kneeling on the bed, he pulled her polo shirt over her head and kissed along her collarbone. 'Let me guess, the bra was a casualty of my housekeeper too?'

'Yep.'

He rested his chin gently on her shoulder as he unfastened it and, after throwing it to the floor and kissing her neck, he ran his hands over her breasts and down over her concave belly. Seeing the words tattooed on her ribcage, he laid her down on the bed and kissed each word.

'Why did you choose it, the "and I again am strong"?'

'Do you know the poem?' She was running her hands through his hair and inhaling the smell of his aftershave.

'Yes.'

'He's reminiscing, missing his youth, and I loved being a kid. It was the only time that my dad didn't control whatever I did. Did you study it for A level?'

'No.'

'How do you know it then? I didn't have you down as being a lover of poetry.'

'Not now.' He was kissing the words again.

'Why? What's the significance?'

'Not now,' he said firmly. 'What time will Shelley be back?'

'About midnight.'

'Then we don't need to hurry, and if we're going to take our time, it's going to get very hot in here.' He stood up to take off his jeans and opened the window that overlooked the yard, letting the warm summer breeze and the noise of the trees blow in.

'Commando? Not like you.'

His mouth twitched into a smile. 'I saw Tom and Shelley leave, so I knew you were alone.'

'And you think I'm that easy?'

'No. But I knew you would be very easily persuaded.'

Lying on top of the duvet in just her thong, she smiled shyly at him and reached for his hand to pull him down next to her.

Running her eyes over his face as his hand caressed her back, she asked him if she could take The Mechanic show jumping.

'Stop asking,' he laughed, crinkling his eyes at her, 'or I am going to leave you here all hot and bothered.'

'You couldn't do that.'

'No, I don't think I could.' His hand was on the back of her head, pulling her mouth to his. 'I'm not planning on it anyway.'

'What are you planning?' Her hand was stroking its way down his stomach.

'What do you want?'

'A full replay.' She kissed him and, feeling his tongue twirling around hers and his fingers gently pulling her thong to one side and touching her, she gasped.

'You're so wet and I haven't even gone down on you yet.' He watched her bite her lip and his fingers gently increased the pressure.

'I have been thinking about you for a while.'

'Since I bawled you out this morning?' He kept his fingers still and kissed an erect nipple.

'No, since the last time, and don't stop,' she ordered crossly, wriggling out of her thong.

He smiled at her, pulling her on top of him. 'Firstly, you can show me how good your working canter is.'

Ignoring him, she moved down the bed and took him in her mouth, feeling his hands twisting handfuls of her hair.

'It's a good thing I'm not some inexperienced seventeen-year-old,' he told her as she lay fully on top of him to kiss his mouth, and he saw her smirk. 'Did Brett teach you how to do that?'

She jerked her head back with a gasp, eyes wide open in shock. 'How did you know about Brett? What did he tell you?'

'Nothing, I was joking!' He laughed. 'Although I wondered why he was so keen to ask if you were thinking of going back to New Zealand. Have you slept with all your employers?'

'No!' She playfully slapped the side of his head.

'What is it about you girls needing to sleep with the boss?'

She started to smile back at him. 'I think it's more a case of, why do all employers feel the need to bang their grooms?'

'Not *grooms*, just one in particular,' he corrected.

'Well, that's a relief I can tell you,' she said mockingly, her fingers stroking the side of his neck. 'But Jules would be much easier than me.'

'She would,' he agreed.

'But?'

'I'm not into bitches.'

'What are you into?' She pinned him down by his wrists.

'Not you, yet.' He easily pushed her arms back towards her and as he sat up, she wrapped her legs around his waist. 'But I will be, in just a second.' He kissed her forcefully and, feeling her breasts pressed against his chest and her hands loosening on his wrists, he took her face in his hands. 'You don't seem quite so angry now,' he murmured.

'I'm not, I'm quite distracted,' she whispered.

'I hope whatever you've got is better than the lager and lime or the curry and poppadum in my jeans pocket.'

She reached across him to the bedside table, tore open the packet and, putting the rubber into her mouth, wriggled down his body to smoothly slide it on him.

'Did Brett show you that too?' He was still sitting up, watching her.

'You're embarrassing me, stop it.' She straddled him.

Lifting her up slightly, he slid easily inside her. 'Exactly how distracted did you want to be?' His face was close to hers, and she ducked her head to kiss his neck, making him breathe heavily. 'If you keep doing that, I won't be able to distract you for too long.'

Her brown eyes smiled at him through her long, black lashes as he lay down, keeping his hands on her waist to control the pace.

'This bed is too small,' he complained as she moved slowly

over him, her hair brushing his chest. 'I really want to take you from behind, but I want to look at you too much.'

'Is that what you do with the ugly ones?'

'There have been no ugly ones.' An image of Petra writhing under him flashed across his mind, and he quickly tried to put the thought aside. Looking across the room to the small set of drawers, he scooped her up from the bed and, ignoring her squeak of protest, carried her across and sat her on top of them.

'Oh, you feel so hot inside,' he said softly. Feeling her nails scratching the length of his back as she tipped her head back, he kissed her neck and then let his tongue trail down her breastbone. 'How long do you want me to keep you as distracted as this?'

Inhaling deeply, she shook her head. 'I don't think I want to be distracted for much longer.' She kissed him, and he felt her tongue stabbing urgently into his mouth.

'Where do you want to finish this?' he whispered.

'Not on here because I think they might collapse.'

Picking her up again, he laid her back down on the bed and began to thrust harder inside her; watching her face and knowing she was close, he pulled out of her. Rolling onto his side, he pulled her legs over his thigh and entered her again, his fingers expertly rubbing softly until she cried out and her muscles tensed, gripping him even tighter. Staying inside her, he flipped her on to her stomach and pulled her hips towards him until she raised herself on her forearms. Kneeling behind her and slipping a strong arm around her waist, he placed his other hand on the duvet next to hers and pressed his cheek against her face.

'I'm going to come,' he groaned as she pushed harder against him.

As she felt him gripping her hips intensely, she lowered herself on shaking arms and pressed her face to the bed. He kissed her shoulder and gently let his body press hers down to the bed, holding his weight off her with his arms; pushing her hair out of the way with his jaw, he kissed her temple.

'Okay,' her breathing was rapid, 'that was a full replay.'

'It's what you asked for.' He slipped himself out of her, and for a minute, they lay facing each other as their breathing returned to normal.

'Alright?' He brushed her hair off her face.

'Now can I take The Mechanic show jumping?'

'One round.' He lay on his back, and she put her head on his chest.

'Two.'

'You really don't give up, do you?'

'Rarely.' She lifted her head to smile flirtatiously at him.

'Okay, two rounds. But in fairness, if you asked me for anything right now, I would let you have it.'

Except to be with you, she thought ruefully. But said nothing.

Fighting the urge to sleep, Roger ran a hand over her shoulder, telling her they must move, or they were going to fall asleep and be caught by Shelley and Tom. 'Although, there is nothing I would like more than to fall asleep with you.' He kissed her forehead tenderly.

'You do know you're taking advantage of me, don't you?' She looked down at their discarded clothes on her bedroom floor. 'You know I'd quite literally drop everything for you.'

'Well, you do put up *so much* of a fight.' His hand was circling gently on her back. 'If you stop flirting with me, I'll stop making advances.'

'When have I ever flirted with you?' She pushed herself away from him so she could stare him in the face.

'Just this morning, when you asked me who I would rather ride between Lightoller and Murdoch,' ignoring her outraged face he carried on, 'and yesterday when you brought the wheelbarrow to Warrior's box so I could muck him out.'

'Roger, that's me being *nice* and doing my job.'

He laughed. 'Come on, get up. In fact, I might have that vodka after all.'

Admiring her perfect bottom as she retrieved a bottle of tonic from the fridge, he turned to tug open the low kitchen window and heard her give a shriek of warning. Giving her a confused look as she dived towards him, the warm breeze swept through the flat, and her bedroom door slammed shut with a terrific bang.

'Well,' she said calmly. 'I suppose that's the best reminder you'll get, to find the keys to the Yale locks on the bedroom doors.'

Roger looked at her in panic as the realisation dawned on him. 'How the fuck am I going to get my clothes?'

She did the unspeakable and started to laugh. 'There's Tom's boiler suit that he left here the last time he stayed.'

'I'm not bloody wearing that!'

'It's that or Shelley's full-length waxed jacket.'

Sighing, he asked where the boiler suit was and ignored her laughter as he pulled it on. 'It's not bloody funny – you should have warned me.'

'My mind was on other things,' she insisted, 'and Shelley has been at you for ages to find the keys to the bedrooms.' She stood on her tiptoes and tentatively kissed him under his rigid chin. 'On the plus side, you haven't made me look like a vampire victim this time.'

He suddenly smiled at her. 'I'll be back with a lot of keys, wearing clothes that don't make me look as though I have just walked out of a gay club in London.'

It took them over forty minutes to find the right keys to the bedroom locks, and having had another two vodkas while Roger was upturning his study searching for keys, Katie thought the whole thing was hilarious. They had only just sat down with another vodka and tonic when Shelley and Tom came roaring up the stairs.

'Oooh, hello, Roger.' Tom studied Roger sitting at the table as he threw himself on the sofa and crossed his legs. 'What are you doing here? Not like you to visit the Dorchester.'

'You're home early, how was the gig?' Katie poured Shelley a vodka from the bottle on the table.

'They were rubbish,' Shelley added tonic to her glass, 'I would have left after the first five minutes, but Tom said we should give them a chance.'

Roger briefly caught eyes with Katie and realised she was as relieved as he was that Tom had persuaded Shelley to stay on at Bar Ree.

'So? What are you doing here?' Shelley was looking at Roger as she flumped down on the sofa next to Tom.

He held up a key with a smile.

'My God!' Shelley slotted it into the lock on her bedroom door, making the latch go in and out. 'You found them, Roger, that's brilliant. No more Mrs Royal ironing my thongs.' She suddenly frowned at Katie. 'Why are you wearing my jeans and polo shirt?'

Fourteen

As August wore on, the weather got hotter, and the ground got harder.

Caitlyn, with her red hair, was constantly covered in factor fifty but was still moaning that she was covered in freckles. Jules was turning up for work wearing only a bikini top and a pair of shorts, and Shelley and Katie were sharing a huge bottle of gradual tanning moisturiser, in the hope that their legs would eventually match the butterscotch colour of their arms and shoulders. Even Roger had taken to riding in the outdoor school without his shirt and was the most tanned he had ever been in his life, although Shelley wondered idly if this behaviour was for the benefit of a certain member of his staff.

The rock-hard ground was causing havoc with horses' legs across the country, and as a precaution, all Roger's horses were wearing padding that had been soaked in cold water and Epsom Salts, bandaged around their legs every night.

After feeling so at home at Athward and thoroughly enjoying life, Katie was thrown into turmoil when her mother announced that she quite fancied a jaunt up to the Garwood three-day event at the end of September but, as it was so far, thought she would come to the Scottish Championship instead to, in her words, "cheer her on". Despite Katie describing The Mechanic's track record, Joanna was undeterred and booked a hotel five miles away from the venue at Auchenruther Castle.

The routine in the yard changed daily depending on the tide, and even when it was low tide during the heat of the afternoon, Roger took a lorry load of horses to the beach. The sweltering heat was obliterated by the cool breeze constantly blowing off the North Sea and, as Katie admitted, it was worth the sand crunching between your teeth to avoid having to continually swat off the biting horseflies. Praying that the forgiving surface of sand and the astringent seawater would keep his horses sound until the end of the season, Roger used the free facilities as often as he could, ignoring Shelley moaning that absolutely everything was covered in sand, from the tack room floor to the bath in the Dorchester.

Jonny Bell, who trained racehorses at his home right next to the long, stretching bay, was more than happy for Roger to park his lorry at his yard. Jonny's lads were also delighted that there was some eye candy to ogle at, sometimes before eight in the morning.

'Mornin', Shelley.' Peter, Jonny's head lad, slipped lightly out of his minuscule race-exercise saddle and held open the wicket gate for Roger and his team to ride through. 'I've always wanted to ride a dressage horse – do you want to swap?'

'It's not a *dressage* horse, Peter Piper, it's an event horse, and no, I don't want to ride on that slither of leather that you call a saddle.'

Peter chuckled, making his laughter lines deepen. 'I could show you how to crouch over it, any time you like.' He turned his attention to Katie who, leather-booted leg lifted, was checking The Mechanic's girth. 'Katie, I'm sick of hearing Gareth talking about you, why don't you take him for a drink in the Kettle tonight and pop his cherry?'

Seventeen-year-old Gareth turned pink under his blue pom-pommed crash hat and goggles.

'Piper, I'm sure you have better things to do than chat up my staff?' Roger rode Warrior past the girls and through the gate.

'Mornin', guv'.' Peter tapped the peak of his hat with his whip and grinned. 'We'll just watch them as we canter past on our second lot.'

Roger rolled his eyes.

After his horses had schooled or cantered, Roger insisted they walk the length of the bay in the sea, with the waves lapping up to the horses' elbows. If the tide allowed, they would wade to the mouth of the river or, if the tide was extremely low, all the way to the slipway at the nearby village before walking back with the waves breaking over their horses' chests.

Jules, in a tiny, cropped T-shirt above her tanned stomach, was riding Paperchase and thinking about what she was going to wear to go clubbing in Newcastle that evening. She was looking down the horse's shoulder, mesmerised by the swirling patterns of the water, and failed to feel the tension creeping into Paperchase as he watched the chunk of bladder wrack floating towards him.

Giving a snort of fear, Paperchase leapt to avoid it and cannoned sideways into Shelley on Lightoller. Knowing her phone was in her breeches pocket, Shelley yelled at Jules and clung on for all she was worth. Katie, riding alongside Roger behind Shelley, abruptly found that The Mechanic thought the commotion was an excellent excuse to rear up and jump forward into an enormous buck which fired her out of the saddle, up into the air and into the sea with a tremendous splash.

As she completely disappeared beneath the waves, Roger started to roar with laughter. Reaching out for The Mechanic's reins, he waited until she stood up, dripping, shivering and speechless in the waist-deep water.

'Are you alright?' He tried not to look at the wet T-shirt that was clinging to her breasts.

'No,' she pushed the water off her face with her hands, hearing Jules and Shelley howling laughing, 'I'm livid,' she took The

Mechanic's reins, 'and it was your bloody fault,' she shouted at Jules who threw back her head and laughed even harder.

Seeing Jonny's lads coming back onto the sand with their second lot of horses, Roger rode out of the sea, removed his hat and took off his shirt.

'Put it on.' His mouth was twitching into a smile as he handed it to her.

'Thank you, but can you hold him while I empty my boots?' She lay down on the sand and raised her feet skywards.

'You're travelling back with the horses,' Shelley told her as she watched the water cascading onto the sand.

Pulling on Roger's Hugo Boss-scented shirt, she heard Piper shouting to the other lads that they were too late; Gareth had missed his chance, and the wet T-shirt competition was over. Catching Roger's eye as he sat bare-chested on Warrior, Katie saw an expression on his face that she hadn't seen since that night in the Dorchester.

~

Cantering through the sand dunes and along the rough of the orange, scorched grass of the golf course, Katie swung The Mechanic through the gap in the dunes and came back to a trot. The Mechanic was feeling well and, apart from knocking down every single show jump in both his classes at the weekend, he was ready for the Scottish Championship.

In a normal one-day event, having five show jumps down automatically meant you were not allowed to start the cross country, but at the Championship, The Mechanic would have to do his dressage and then go cross country, which meant that if he decimated every fence in the final phase, all that would happen would be that he would end up last. *If they didn't get eliminated on the cross country course*, thought Katie humbly.

Watching Roger schooling Warrior on the firm sand near the

sea, Katie thought the change in the horse was remarkable. *He's really improved*, she thought, as Roger cantered a figure of eight with a flying change of leg in the middle. Warrior already had an entry at Garwood in the three-day event, something which Roger had felt was incredibly ambitious when he first arrived at Athward Hall, but in the four weeks that he had been with them, the horse had settled quickly and clearly felt more at home than he had done in Petra's yard at Low Athward Farm.

There had been an uneasy truce between Roger and Petra. Despite her pig-headedness, Petra knew that Hoplite Warrior was too strong for her, but, unused to seeing her horses sold on and being competed against her – and possibly ending up at a higher level – it rattled her enormously. She was already furious that Roger was doing so well with Bluebell Folly, and she was also outraged that he had told her to shut the fuck up in front of all her staff, leaving her spitting out pieces of crown like a goldfish. Perhaps he had a new woman to influence him, thought Petra; she had never heard Roger use such language in front of her before. Not even in the bedroom.

Roger felt no guilt at all about buying Warrior from literally underneath Petra, knowing he could take the horse further than she ever could, but he was aware that he needed to stay on the right side of her. Not only was she tremendously bitchy, and there was every chance that she could spill the beans on the few liaisons they'd had between the sheets over the years, but as she lived just across the valley from him, she was a handy ally if he ever needed to borrow a lorry or get her staff to look after his horses if his whole team was away at a competition. Bitterly regretting ever having taken the cold old bitch to bed, he felt slightly queasy at the thought of it all coming out.

As she watched him ride through the shallow waves, the horse's feet splashing water high in the air, Katie felt a twinge in her stomach. Good as his word, Roger had not looked near her since the night they had got locked out of her bedroom. She had never told Shelley the truth about that night; she knew she would be furious with her. Although, she had managed to hang on to Roger's shirt and jeans and quietly dropped the snib on her bedroom door on the nights she treated herself to sleeping in his shirt, inhaling the smell of him until she fell asleep.

Roger was like two different people. The Roger who she knew almost inside out from all those long drives alone, the one who joked about her quick temper, comparing her to a Jack Russell who didn't realise it was smaller than the Rottweiler it was about to fight. Asking how her mother was, and had she heard from her dad? Then there was the yard Roger, the boss. Cool and patient, thinking everything through before speaking, very unlike the one she knew who would talk things through with her at length when they were alone. And there hadn't been much in the way of alone together for weeks.

As she only had The Mechanic and the novice Murdoch to compete, and as The Mechanic was waiting for his Scottish Championship in two weeks' time, Katie was usually left at home with Caitlyn while Shelley went off to groom for Roger. The bonus was, with Katie's kind words of encouragement, Caitlyn's riding had come on tremendously. Being too nervous to ask Roger what she thought were stupid questions, she felt she could ask Katie, knowing that she wouldn't make fun of her. As Katie also stuck up for Caitlyn when Shelley began taking the piss out of her, Jules was finding that she was pushed out more and more often. She blamed Katie entirely for this, not realising that if she were less bitchy, the other three would perhaps have more time for her. Jules was also putting herself out of favour with Roger as she now refused to work weekends.

Katie could hear Shelley cantering up behind her on Lightoller.

'He's going well.' She nodded down to the tiny figure of Warrior further down the beach. 'Come on, let's get these two on the lorry; we might be able to nip to Newcastle this afternoon to get you a dress for Roger's owners' party.'

'Do we really have to go?' Katie turned The Mechanic's head towards the dunes.

'It was a laugh last year – Miss Mac ended up driving her Subaru over the ha-ha. It's free champagne, and all you've got to do is carry around a bottle and a tray of nibbles.'

'Can't see Jules being happy about waitressing.' Katie loosened her girth. 'Why doesn't Roger supply us with black dresses and little aprons?'

'Well, you of all people would know if he has an aversion to French maids.'

'Shut up,' snapped Katie.

Roger's drinks party was held on the Saturday night of the August bank holiday weekend. Renowned for its free-flowing champagne and Mrs Royal's excellent canapés, the plain white invitations were proudly displayed on mantlepieces throughout Athward village. The invite stipulated that the drinks would begin at eight and finish at ten, but in reality, the party often roared on until midnight. According to Mrs Royal, on previous occasions, several cars had stood parked on the field in front of Roger's house for two days afterwards while their owners recovered from their hangovers.

Meant as a thank-you to his owners and locals who had worked for the estate, it was always a very lively affair with a cross section of people. Tom had been thrilled to find that Petra's yard was invited and had spent an absolute fortune on a stunning pale-blue silk suit and a silver Miu Miu handbag. On the same shopping trip, Shelley had bought a beautiful sea-green midi dress in Monsoon which set off her flashing green eyes and blonde curls beautifully. It was only Katie who had nothing to wear as Jules had ordered a selection of dresses from ASOS for her to select her favourite and return the rest (they all knew she wouldn't and would keep them all) and Caitlyn, once she had been persuaded that she would stand out like a dog's dick if she insisted on wearing her jeans like she had last year, had found some floral print item in the charity shop on Grainger Street.

Shelley watched as Roger, in his Oakley sunglasses, reversed the lorry out of the parking bay at Jonny's yard.

'Roger,' she began sweetly, 'as we started so early this morning—'

'You need a few hours this afternoon to get Katie a dress for the owners' do,' he finished.

Shelley looked surprised. 'Well, yes. We do.' She frowned at Katie. 'How do you know?'

'Mrs Royal is most concerned that Katie still has nothing to wear.'

'Nothing is secret,' muttered Katie from the window seat.

Shelley rang Tom. 'Tell Golden Knickers you're not feeling well – we're going to Newcastle at one to find Katie a dress.'

'That's almost as bad as poaching staff,' said Roger stiffly.

'But not as bad as poaching horses,' replied Shelley smoothly as she threw her phone onto the dashboard.

～

Katie loathed shopping – all that trying things on did her very impatient head in. Now, as Tom and Shelley lounged in the leather chairs outside the changing room in Fenwick's, she paraded before them in creation after creation.

'Definitely not,' said Shelley as Katie pulled back the curtain wearing a grey smock dress. 'Don't even bother coming out. Next!'

Tom picked up another magazine. 'Who's coming to this bash, anyway? I know all your owners are and us, but who else?'

'Wrong colour,' said Shelley to Katie who was holding up a black tube. 'Well, Major Dawson, old Edwina who has the café in Athward, just some of the locals really. Oh, and the lads who lease Roger's grass parks and arable land.'

'Oooh, *tractor men*,' said Tom excitedly. 'I've always fancied a bit of rough.'

'God no, Katie, you look like Miss Mac.'

Katie sighed and turned back to the changing room in her wide-legged jumpsuit.

'There's only one left to try.' Her voice was muffled from behind the curtain.

'Where can we try next?' Shelley asked Tom. 'She's tried on practically everything in here.'

'Fucking hell!' Tom had jumped up from his seat, his magazine slithering to the floor.

Katie was wearing an orangey-pink dress that was held up with a thin golden band around her neck. Nipped in around the waist, the dress fell to just above her knees, with whispery tendrils floating to her calves.

Fucking hell indeed, thought Shelley. *Roger's going to bust something when he sees her in that.*

'Oh my God, oh my God, oh my God.' Tom was dancing around a blushing Katie. 'It's a-mazing.' He took her shoulders and spun her around so that Shelley could see the incredibly low-cut back. 'Do you know, in that dress you might even bring me back from the *dark side.*'

Katie giggled. 'I feel naked.'

'Wow,' said Shelley at last. 'I think we've found the dress.'

Fifteen

The cars were streaming steadily across the cattle grid and winding along the stony track that led through the rolling parkland in front of Athward Hall. Climbing the hill towards the house, they were parking at the top of the field next to Roger's front lawn, and the noise of chatter as people greeted each other was filling the air.

Tom had swung his BMW into the cobbled yard just before seven and legged it up the stone stairs to the Dorchester carrying a bottle of vodka and a carton of grapefruit juice.

'I thought we'd get a couple under our belt before we go,' he searched for three clean glasses, 'then I can drive you there so we arrive in style through the front door.' He splashed vodka into a glass. 'You don't look very party-ready, missy.' He handed a tumbler to Katie who was still in her dressing gown.

'Loads of time,' she took a sip and was almost choked by how much vodka Tom had poured in, 'I've just got to straighten my hair and slap a face on.' She wandered back to her bedroom and plugged in her straighteners.

She was feeling apprehensive about this bloody party. Sitting in Roger's kitchen discussing horses with Shelley and him was one thing, but she didn't particularly want to go into the rest of the house, anxious that it would take her mind back to the night she had spent with him. She grinned mockingly at herself in the mirror – who was she trying to fool? She thought about being in bed with him on a daily basis, and for a second, she looked at the drawer where his jeans and shirt were hidden under her bras and thongs. His shirt now smelt of her own moisturiser, and she hadn't yet stooped low enough to try hugging his jeans in bed with the door locked. She began straightening her hair and appreciated she was behaving like a stalker; taking a deep breath, she knew she had to move on. Thinking of The Mechanic and the Championship next weekend, and taking a huge mouthful of Tom's Salty Dog, she began to make up her face.

At ten to eight, a giggling Tom put Shelley and Katie in the back of the BMW so he could chauffeur them properly, drove up the drive out of the pillars and, after a hundred metres, turned left over the cattle grid and into the field they called North Hall.

Parking next to the Bogiemobile, Katie saw Caitlyn wearing a green and blue floral dress waving madly on the front lawn.

'Fooking hell, you look amazing.' She hugged Katie, who noticed how much weight Caitlyn had lost with so many more hours in the saddle. 'You look brilliant too, Shelley, and Tom, that's a gorgeous suit.'

'Jules here yet?' Shelley was smoothing down the net overskirt of her dress.

'Yes, she's wearing the tiniest little white smock dress – she looks lovely. She's got the longest legs—'

Shelley cut through Caitlyn's chatter, saying she needed a drink.

Roger was pouring glasses of champagne in the parquet-floored hall, and on hearing them talking, looked up. Shelley noticed, as he welcomed them, he couldn't take his eyes off Katie. *Clearly not over her at all then*, she thought.

As more cars arrived, the house began to fill with people; many spilled into the drawing room and out onto the terrace, enjoying the last of the sun. Katie and Shelley were meandering through the crowd, topping up half-empty glasses and chatting as they went.

'You look wonderful, my dear.' Mrs Fleming Bowen held out her glass as Katie passed where she was sitting in the drawing room.

'Thank you, Mrs F.B.' She took the glass and, holding it at a forty-five-degree angle, poured in the champagne.

'There must be a very lucky gentleman somewhere?' Victoria winked.

'Oh no, not at the minute. You could say I'm married to my horses.'

'How is The Mechanic?' Mrs Fleming Bowen snaffled a blini from Jules's platter as she walked past.

Katie put her hand on the table beside her. 'Touching wood, he's fine. I'm just hoping he's not going to knock down every show jump next weekend.'

As she watched Katie weaving through the group of guests standing in front of the French doors, she saw Roger also observing her departing back. Reminding herself that she needed to have a quiet word with her grandson, she took a sip of her drink.

Petra had tried to arrive fashionably late so everyone could admire her beautiful Emilio Pucci kaftan as she swept in. Unfortunately, as Petra swept in, so did Tiger Lily's owner. Alicia was twenty-eight, six-feet tall and wearing such a glorious black dress slit to the thigh that all the men in the room stared at her and completely ignored Petra.

Seeing Tom chatting with one of her other grooms, Petra promptly ordered them to get her a drink and bring it outside so her face didn't get flushed.

'We're not at work now, Petra – I'm sure you can get one yourself, and I'm quite sure you won't overheat in that gazebo you're wearing,' said Tom haughtily.

'You might not need the money, Tom, but I bloody do,' hissed Josh through gritted teeth.

Miss Mac was having a lovely party. She had enjoyed a nice

chat with Victoria and was now deep in conversation with Jennifer Bane, Lightoller and Murdoch's owner.

Jennifer, sixty, divorced and with a great love of spaniels, had an encyclopaedic knowledge of thoroughbred breeding that was as good as Miss Mac's.

'Of course, the mare has a terrific bearing, and I was lucky enough to have a mare by Henbuthario that I bred all mine from.'

Jennifer nodded, her mouth full of king prawn and cucumber.

'I've always wanted to know how you named your horses?' boomed Miss Mac as she held out her glass for Shelley to replenish.

'They're all connected with the Titanic.' Jennifer skewered a small sausage from the tray Caitlyn was carrying. 'Lightoller and Murdoch were officers on the ship, and so was Lowe, who is the four-year-old I've got at home that I'm hoping Roger will ride next season.'

'How jolly clever!' retorted Miss Mac. 'What a novel idea.'

'Their mother is called Iceberg, and it means I'll never run out of names.' Jennifer held out her glass to Katie.

'Better than "Lettuce" or "Melting", I suppose,' Miss Mac replied.

Charles Dee and his rather pale, thin wife were out on the terrace with Major Dawson.

'Reckon we're going to have a good weekend at Auchenruther Castle; I've even booked a trade stand to see if I can drum up some business. Combine business and pleasure.'

The Major, like most people, disliked Charles intensely and only tolerated him because his garages had a Mercedes franchise.

'Very hard ground at the moment,' he replied. 'Could do with rain, hard going for horses that have been campaigned all season.' He looked around desperately for his wife, willing her to rescue him from Dee's company.

Charles swiped a piece of stilton on walnut toast from Jules, making her jump. 'Ah, but it's the quality of the horse that's important – a stamp of a horse like The Mechanic, well, he's as tough as old boots, him.'

Charles's wife Margaret, knowing he had only learnt the

expression "stamp of a horse" from Miss Mac fifteen minutes earlier, squeezed her husband's arm with pride.

'Roger!' the Major called out desperately as their host appeared on the terrace.

Smiling and knowing that the Major needed rescuing, he strode across to them and shook him warmly by the hand.

'Bally good party.' Major Dawson raised his glass to Roger.

'Pleased you could make it.'

'Wife wouldn't have missed it for the world.' The Major nodded at Mrs Dawson, who was busy taking a cutting of the Wisteria that twisted and climbed over the front of the house.

'How's our horse, Roger?' Margaret was clinging to Charles's arm to ensure everyone knew who she was.

You don't need to impress the Major, thought Roger. *He's got twenty horses in training, one of which was third in the Gold Cup,* but he smiled at Margaret and said that The Mechanic was well and ready for next weekend.

'I've taken a trade stand at Auchenruther Castle, Roger. Hoping to mix business and pleasure!' He roared with laughter as the Major melted away.

'And how are you, favourite jockey?' Charles wrapped his arm around Katie's waist, and she froze for a second as she felt his fat thumb seductively caressing the side of her breast.

'Very well thank you, Charles.' She calmly emptied the bottle into Margaret's glass.

'Are you looking forward to next weekend?' Margaret asked.

'Got your lucky knickers ready?' said Charles in a throaty voice, and as he licked his lips and looked down her cleavage, Roger suddenly saw his straying hand.

'Get another bottle, *now,*' he ordered.

Tom was also having a tremendous party. Roger's owners were lovely people, aside from that conceited Charles Dee and his splinter of a wife, but to his amazement, their daughter Daisy, who had come wearing a yellow dress with daisies on it, was quite funny.

After picking up several champagne flutes and an empty ashtray and hiding them in her handbag, Daisy was now carrying around a bottle of champagne and, in-between topping up glasses, was taking huge swigs out of it as she went from room to room.

'She's going to be shit-faced,' whispered Shelley to Tom as she filled up his glass, 'and try and frisk her handbag before she leaves – she's a kleptomaniac.'

Tom flumped down in a chair next to Miss Mac and Mrs Fleming Bowen; Miss Mac was rummaging madly in her enormous tweed handbag for her cigarette lighter.

'I bloody hate handbags!' she roared. 'I can never find what I'm looking for; I'd be better off carrying a rucksack!'

Tom opened his silver handbag and produced a lighter.

'Thank you, young man, not like your generation to smoke!' Miss Mac handed the lighter back to him. 'What a pretty handbag,' she added.

'Oooh, just you keep it, Miss Mac.' He flapped his hand. 'I don't actually smoke,' he confided, 'but sometimes having a lighter handy is a wonderful way of getting to know someone better.'

'Good Lord, in my day, one just asked someone out on a date,' said Mrs Fleming Bowen.

Katie dropped the empty bottle into the plastic crate and took another from the fridge; it certainly wasn't as painful as she had envisaged, and everyone seemed to be in the party spirit. As she tore off the gold foil from the top of the bottle, Roger came in, closed the door and leant against it.

'Okay?'

'I must have been stuck with Petra for the best part of an hour,' he said despairingly. He didn't add that Petra had tried to continually stroke his thigh with her hand hidden in the folds of her ghastly kaftan.

'I saw.' She didn't look at him as she threw the cork in the bin. 'How did you manage to escape her clutches?'

'She's gone home.' He ran a hand over his hair, picked up a

tumbler from the bench and held it out for her to fill. 'And don't bloody stint,' he ordered.

Watching her as she filled the glass, he told her she looked beautiful.

'Don't,' she said softly.

'Can you not accept a compliment?'

'They're difficult to accept from you,' she said after a pause.

He was about to ask her what she meant when Caitlyn came crashing through the door.

'Oooh, Katie, can I take that bottle and you open another one? Fook, this lot can drink!' She grabbed the bottle and slammed the door behind her.

'You were saying?' Roger was turning the tumbler around in his fingers.

'I wasn't saying anything.' She took another bottle from the fridge and began to open it.

'Don't let him touch you like that,' he said abruptly. 'It doesn't matter who he is, he has no right to do that.'

'What was I supposed to do? Slap him across the face so he can hold up his hands in horror and tell everyone I was overreacting?'

By the way she spoke, Roger knew she was speaking from experience.

'It's not always as easy as a man might think.'

'Wait,' he held the door closed with his hand, 'what did you mean? You said a compliment is difficult to accept from me.'

The corner of her mouth lifted into a rueful smile. 'Because I want more than just compliments from you.'

'I can't do that.' He was held in her gaze and couldn't tear his eyes away from her face, with its beautiful structure and those long, dark eyelashes.

'I know,' she replied honestly. 'Now, are you going to let me out so I can get your guests even more pissed?'

After she had left, Roger stood for a minute staring at the closed door, feeling slightly bewildered. He hadn't expected her to say that, and she probably only said it because she had been drinking. She had always been so cool after they had slept together, as if she could take it or leave it. He knew there was a spark that jumped between them when they were close. He felt it whenever they were alone together, but he hadn't realised that she thought there might be a chance of something more. He was too old; she was too young; and whichever way you put it, the odds were still the same: against them. He finished his drink thinking that it hadn't been an empty compliment – she did look beautiful – and seeing bloody Charles sexually assaulting her right in front of his stick insect of a wife made his blood boil. Wanting to keep an eye on Charles and his grimy, wandering hands, he slammed his glass back down on the bench and rejoined the party.

Miss Mac and Mrs Fleming Bowen were leaving, both leaning on their walking sticks.

'Goodnight.' Roger kissed Miss Mac's cheek. 'Thank you for taking Granny home.'

Victoria had then enveloped him in an embrace and whispered that he must stop gazing at that girl or people were going to notice.

'I don't know what you mean,' he replied smoothly before turning back to Miss Mac and thanking her for coming.

He took one lady on each arm and walked them across the lawn, through the gate and on towards Miss Mac's dented Subaru. As he held the passenger door open for his grandmother, she stared him dead in the eye.

'It doesn't do to get involved with one's staff.'

'I have no intention of doing any such thing,' he replied evenly.

'But sometimes,' Victoria carried on as if he hadn't spoken, 'you need to step beyond the boundaries to ensure your own happiness.'

'What are you trying to tell me?'

Victoria patted his arm. 'In the words of Barnard Thompson, Roger, "it must be horribly challenging to let go of something that is beautiful".' She began to lower herself into the seat.

Roger's face lost some of its colour. 'Who is Barnard Thompson?'

'For goodness' sake, Roger, he was the hotel manager in *Pretty Woman*.'

By eleven o'clock, the canapés had long since been eaten, and the bottles stopped rotating the house in the hope that everyone would soon leave. Outside it was getting cold, but as the heat was so intense in the Hall, Tom, Shelley and Katie were sitting on the patio in the pool of light being cast from the drawing room.

'Charles Dee is such a perv.' Katie shuddered as she took a gulp of champagne. 'How does Margaret put up with him?'

'You have to feel sorry for him though.' Tom sipped his twelfth glass of fizzy. 'He can't have much fun in the bedroom with that scrawny wife; she'd probably snap in half if he jumped on top of her.'

'Yuck, I don't want to think about it.' Shelley picked up the bottle to fill her glass. 'What do you think happens to his comb over when they're at it?'

'It must do this.' Tom put his hand on top of his head and waved it from side to side.

As they laughed, Josh came out of the drawing room, followed by Caitlyn and Jules.

'Joshy, Joshy, come and join us,' called Tom.

Josh had been working for Petra for a matter of weeks, and although Katie and Shelley had seen him riding Petra's horses around the local roads, they had never been introduced. He was a short man in his mid-forties and had a jockey-like stature.

'Having a good time?' Katie asked as he sat down and put his glass on the table.

He nodded. 'You have much more interesting owners than we have.'

'Is interesting a polite word for eccentric?' She handed her glass to Shelley.

Josh laughed. 'Well I suppose it is. That Miss Mac's quite a character, isn't she? She gave me one of her cigars to try.'

People were drifting past them now, heading to their cars, and Katie was sent back to the kitchen to see if there was another bottle of champagne.

'I've had an idea!' Shelley grabbed Tom by the arm and, followed by Josh, Caitlyn and Jules, ran through the house.

'Where the hell are we?' asked Tom as they felt their way along the wall on the first floor of the Hall.

'On our way to Roger's bedroom to apple pie his bed,' hissed back Shelley.

'What's an apple pie bed?' whispered Caitlyn noisily from the back of the line.

'Well,' Tom stopped and turned to her, 'it's when you take the top sheet and—'

'Shut up, Tom!' shushed Shelley in alarm. Turning the door handle, she peered inside the room. 'This is it. Tom, grab the duvet!'

She deftly folded the top sheet and tucked it in under the mattress. Caitlyn and Jules, in silent, drunken hysterics, helped Tom replace the duvet and pull it straight.

'Okay, run!' whispered Shelley loudly and made a bolt for the door, followed by Caitlyn, Tom and a horrified-looking Josh.

Trying not to laugh out loud, Jules began to close the door, checking the bed looked normal so a tipsy Roger wouldn't suspect anything. But the opportunity of being in Roger's bedroom, especially after so much champagne, made Jules pause for just a second, inhaling his aftershave, the light from the landing laying a shaft of light across the bed. She squinted slightly; there was something shiny under the bed. Moving her head from side to side, it twinkled back at her, and she walked back into the room, kneeling next to the bed to reach underneath it, running her hand over the carpet. Her fingers found something sharp and, almost breaking a nail, she teased it out of the fabric; she had it between her fingers when she heard voices coming closer; heart hammering, she swiftly slid under the bed. Oh God. Roger was coming into the room with someone; the light was turned on, and Jules tried to breathe as quietly as she could.

'It was painted at the turn of the century; I believe my great-grandfather bought it shortly after he'd bought the estate.'

'It's a nice piece.' It was a man's voice. 'His paintings of properties are always much sought after, but I think this one has more value on the wall here.'

They both laughed and Jules held her breath until they had turned out the light and closed the door.

She waited for what seemed like an eternity before clambering out and fumbling her way to the door. Bloody hell, she closed Roger's bedroom door and ran down the corridor to the narrow wooden stairs; that was so close she was shaking. As she emerged into the light of the back kitchen, she found she was alone and finally opened her hand. Lying on her palm was a small and somewhat bent silver horseshoe earring with glittering blue stones.

Jules almost laughed out loud. Now she could get even.

Sixteen

Tom, lying on the sofa bed in the Dorchester's lounge, thought he had never felt so ill in his life. Slowly picking up his phone, he messaged Shelley saying he urgently needed a cup of tea.

Shelley, in her bedroom two metres away, read the message, groaned and pulled the pillow over her head.

Katie, woken by Shelley's phone alert, reached out for a drink of water and encountered only an empty glass.

They had sat on Roger's patio until well after midnight, finishing the half-empty bottles of champagne and then, after staggering back to the Dorchester, had finished what was left in Tom's vodka bottle, being forced to mix it with lime cordial when they ran out of grapefruit juice and tonic at four in the morning.

Hearing the radio from the yard below, Katie looked at her phone. It was just after eight. Sitting up slowly so the pounding in her head didn't increase, she began to look for some breeches.

Shelley's phone was ringing; seeing it was Roger calling, she coughed and cleared her throat. 'Morning,' she answered as brightly as she could.

'I just wondered if you were actually planning on coming to work today?'

Shelley coughed. 'Of course, we're just having a coffee.'

'I want to take a load to the beach before it gets too hot. Tell Tom there's a set of chaps in the tack room and my spare hat; I thought he might like to be reunited with his old friend Warrior.'

Katie found Tom groaning like a huge, sick caterpillar in his purple sleeping bag.

'Katie,' he grabbed her hand dramatically, 'I'm dying; I'm dying, darling, please make me a cup of tea. I messaged Shelley ages ago, but the bitch just ignored me.'

'Worse news,' Shelley staggered out of her bedroom still feeling drunk, 'the boss wants you to ride Warrior on the beach this morning.'

Tom snapped upright in his purple cylinder. 'Me? I'm not riding that!' he replied angrily.

'Come on, Tom, it'll give you a chance to get up close and personal with the lovely Roger.' Katie was cleaning her teeth in the lounge doorway.

Tom's face relaxed. 'Oooh, that's a lovely thought, missy.'

~

Cantering along the beach feeling utterly sick, Katie was so off the ball that The Mechanic's customary spooking at the washed-up seaweed turned into a succession of enormous bucks that deposited her on the wet sand. Getting up slowly, pain in her shoulder and knee as well as her head, she watched The Mechanic gallop off along the beach, giving another huge buck and a fart. *Oh Christ, we'll never catch him*, she thought, as Shelley, riding Lightoller and leading Murdoch, roared at them both to stand still.

Tom brought Warrior sweetly into a halt and watched The Mechanic cavorting with the string of racehorses. 'Oooh, missy, that horse can buck. Are you alright? What's he like to catch?'

'Not great,' admitted Katie, resting her hands on her knees, hoping the pain would subside.

After dodging around the outstretched hands of the racing lads, The Mechanic climbed the biggest sand dune and, taking his usual route back through the dunes and along the edge of the golf course without a pilot, he then merrily trotted back towards them, giving Katie a little whicker as he came to a standstill in front of her. Standing hunched, eyes closed in pain, The Mechanic gave her a little nudge as if to say, "I'm back".

Roger, trying not to laugh, asked if she was alright.

'I'll live,' she said weakly as Shelley was sick down Lightoller's shoulder.

'Clearly the drinking continued long after the party was over.' Roger looked at the three green faces.

'Why do you say that?' asked Shelley airily.

'Because The Mechanic has got Bluebell's jumping bridle on and you, Shelley, have put that horse's boots on the wrong legs.'

'Have I?' Shelley stopped quickly and was sick again.

Roger rolled his eyes. 'Is everyone going to manage wading them in the sea? Or should I go back to the lorry for some leading reins?'

There was muttered response.

'Are we just walking now?' The colour was returning to Katie's face. 'Because if we're going any faster than that, I'll have to go back to the lorry for another set of reins – he's broken these ones.'

Roger saw the rein had come away from The Mechanic's bit and was dangling uselessly down the horse's shoulder. 'Swap them with Murdoch's, that's as long as the puking Scottish woman can manage to lead him with one rein?'

Shelley wiped her mouth. 'Of course I can. As long as the smug Northumbrian bastard stops giving us grief about our hangovers, because if he continues, I'm going to have to get off and chin him.'

Roger didn't mind the hangovers; it had been good to see them all having fun the previous evening. Caitlyn had helped to pack up the hired flutes at the end of the night, her chatter even more rapid after a few glasses of champagne, and Josh seemed like a nice man, even giving Caitlyn and Jules a lift back to Athward. He was still livid with Charles being such a bloody letch, and as Miss Mac was going to offer Daisy Brogue on loan for next season with the proviso that he remained at Roger's yard, there seemed little chance of getting rid of him.

Roger was pleased with how his horses were going; he was taking Bluebell and Warrior cross country schooling tomorrow and had suggested that Katie bring Murdoch along as the horse was having an outing at Auchenruther Castle the following weekend. Next weekend was going to be a busy one. Lightoller, Murdoch and Tiger were competing on Saturday, and Warrior and The Mechanic in his Championship class on Sunday. Roger was also wondering what to do about the Garwood three-day at the end of September. He would normally have taken just Shelley and Katie as she would ride The Mechanic, but Warrior was so much more settled when Caitlyn was around him. God, Caitlyn would be a nightmare at a big three-day competition, and he knew that Jules would have a face like a smashed crab at being left home alone. Strangely, Jules had sent him a message that morning thanking him for a great party, which made him speculate if she was up to something, and that something, he thought, was probably another attempt to get him to take her to bed.

Tom couldn't believe the change in Warrior. The strong-willed, argumentative horse he had ridden under Petra's eye was no more, and the new, improved Warrior was sweet and reactive. Tom had ridden circles on the sand alongside Roger who instructed him to lift his hands a little higher and use more leg to ask the horse to really engage his hindquarters. Then Roger had stood Bluebell in the middle of Tom's circle and told him to ask for canter. The first transition to canter was rough and hurried, and Roger ordered him to bring him back to trot and ask again.

'Bring the outside leg back and then touch him with the inside leg for the canter!' he called.

Tom, his hungover dehydrated brain working as hard as it could, was absorbing every word; Petra had never ever helped him when he schooled her horses. Amiably, Warrior began the most delightful canter Tom had ever sat on. Around their circle they cantered before Roger told him to change the rein, which Tom did, trotting for three strides in the middle of the figure of eight before asking him to canter on the other leg.

'Do it again!' shouted Roger. 'This time don't trot – ask him to change in the canter.'

Tom took a breath and, as he crossed the sand again, he sat deeply in the saddle, shifted his right leg behind the girth and tapped his left heel, hoping something would happen. Warrior lifted his back, and Tom felt the immense power as the horse changed his legs in the air and propelled them forward.

'Good,' was all Roger said as they came back to a walk.

'He's so much better,' Tom gushed later as he dismounted at the lorry. 'I can't believe it's the same horse.' He gave a little yelp as Warrior bit him on the arm.

'What's the matter?' Roger was stacking the four saddles into the outside locker of the lorry as Tom and Katie loaded the horses.

Shelley was staring at something and, without a word, she unfastened the broken reins from Murdoch's bridle and handed them to him.

'What?'

'They've come apart, that's why the billet hook came out.'

'Not possible.' He shook his head. 'I don't buy rubbish tack.'

'I know that.' She pushed her nail between the two pieces of leather where the tiny stitches should have been. 'But look at it, only a Stanley knife could have done that.'

He ran his thumb over the hole where the billet should have been on the broken reins. He could see she was right – a blade had been run between the two pieces of leather, cutting the thread, allowing the leather to come apart and the fastening to fall out.

'It's obvious who did this, Roger.'

'We can't prove that.'

'For God's sake,' hissed Shelley. 'This is serious, and it's not the only time it's happened. Brogue's martingale snapping at Tillbridge was no accident.'

'Things break.'

'I showed you the martingale; it had snapped through one of the buckle holes.'

'And? If it was going to break, that's where it would break.'

'It was fairly new, and Brogue doesn't pull; there's no way that horse could have snapped it.'

'He could, if it was on too tight.'

'I saddled the horse myself,' she said angrily.

Roger folded the rein and stuffed it under the boots and bandages at the back of the locker. 'I'll take it to the saddler's this week and get it repaired.'

'But—'

'Don't you say a word, not to anyone.'

She glared at him as she launched the bridle into the locker and slammed the door shut. It was the first time she had wanted to hit him.

～

They arrived at the equestrian centre early the next morning.

Shelley, still suffering from a two-day hangover, was in a foul mood and kept muttering to Roger that she should have been left at home with both Jules and Caitlyn on a day off.

'Shut up, Shelley, or I'll leave you at home when we go to Garwood,' Roger replied.

Katie was pleased with Murdoch; Roger had cantered around with her on Bluebell, offering advice and popping him over some of the smaller fences.

Leaving Katie and Shelley to wash off Murdoch and tack up Warrior, he had then gone on to jump through the water jump again and again until the white horse was jumping in and out without hesitation.

As he handed his reins to Shelley and took Warrior from her, Shelley stated he was in an awful temper and had bitten her shoulder.

'A mood much like your own,' he said as he used the lorry ramp as a mounting block.

'Where on earth are all my breeches?' asked Katie as she jumped down from the living area.

'How on earth would I know?' Bluebell turned his brown eyes on Shelley as she spoke.

Katie frowned. 'Honestly, I can only find my spare competition ones in here and these black ones which are falling apart.'

'Ask Mrs Royal.'

'But she's not been in the Dorchester for weeks. I've looked everywhere.'

Shelley was scraping the excess water from Bluebell's coat. 'You can't just *lose* breeches; they must be somewhere.'

'I know, it's driving me mad. I'm going to have to order a new pair, but I've just spent a fortune on that bloody dress for the owners' party.'

After they had loaded Bluebell, they went to watch Roger on Warrior. The pair were playing through the water complex, in and out they splashed, Roger taking several different routes before cantering up to the big combination of fences that were in the middle of the course.

'Are you over him?' Shelley had her hand by her forehead, shading her eyes from the sun.

Katie paused. 'I think so – it was never meant to be.'

Roger jumped over the first part and circled before riding at the second and third part. He patted the horse's sweating neck and brought him round to jump them again. This time Warrior jumped the first part exuberantly, forcing Roger to circle again before directing him to the second and third elements. The gelding, relishing his newly found power unleashed by his excellent flatwork, fought for his head and ran at the fence.

Katie grabbed Shelley's arm as they watched Warrior hit the top of the fence and, landing almost sideways, make a desperate attempt to stay on his feet before he crashed to the floor, throwing Roger to the side.

Shelley was already running towards them.

Warrior got to his feet and trotted off, reins and stirrups flapping, as Shelley knelt beside Roger, putting her ear down to his face. 'It's alright,' she put her arm up to stop Katie, 'he's breathing; he's just knocked out.'

Katie took her phone out of her pocket with shaking fingers.

'Don't,' Shelley shook her head violently, 'just give him a minute; he'll have a hissy fit if you call an ambulance.'

Biting her lip, Katie held onto her phone defiantly.

Shelley leant over him as he opened his eyes. 'Are you okay? You gave us a bit of a fright.'

Roger took in Katie's white face and Shelley's look of concern and asked what had happened.

'He fell,' replied Shelley gently. 'Any pain or tingling?'

'No.' He started to get up.

'Stay there!' she said forcefully. 'Katie, can you catch Warrior please?'

Roger argued that he felt fine but after finally giving in and agreeing Shelley could drive the lorry home, he vomited violently before he climbed into the cab.

Knowing he would point blank refuse to go to hospital, Shelley took the longer route home, bringing them in to Athward Hall via West Lodge. Jumping out of the driver's seat and leaving the engine running, she hammered on Mrs Fleming Bowen's door. Victoria, taking one look at Roger's grey face and receiving a briefing from Shelley, immediately demanded that her grandson accompany her to the doctor.

'Are you okay?' Shelley checked both her mirrors as she drove off down the drive.

Katie didn't speak.

'Not quite over him then,' Shelley stated. 'I'll ring the physio after lunch; we'll need him to look at the horse.'

~

Tom was standing in the tack room doorway as Katie led Warrior to the washroom.

'Has Golden Knickers given you the afternoon off?' she asked in amazement.

Tom's smiling face fell, and he suddenly burst into tears.

Ignoring Warrior's snapping teeth, she put her arms around him. 'What on earth's the matter?'

Tom wiped his eyes with a blue handkerchief. 'I've been sacked,' he said dramatically.

'What did you say?' Shelley was frozen to the spot on the cobbles holding Murdoch and Bluebell.

'I think you need a drink,' Katie told him.

'Someone told her I'd been riding Warrior on the beach yesterday; she said it was "a conflict of interests", and if I wanted to ride Roger's horses, I should eff off and go and work for him.' Tom was sipping sweet tea in the Dorchester as Katie and Shelley ate crisp sandwiches as they had run out of cheese and ham.

'She can't do that,' protested Shelley with her mouth full. 'Did you tell her you'd stayed here after the party?'

Tom nodded. 'To be honest, I think she was desperate to get off with Roger on Saturday night, and when he wouldn't play, she's decided to spit out her Roger-flavoured dummy well and truly.' Tom put his tea on the table with a shaky hand. 'Petra's given me a week to get my things out of the staff house. I'll have to go home; I've got nowhere else to go.'

Shelley and Katie caught eyes.

'You can stay here,' said Shelley. 'It'll be a bit tight for space, but we can't have you going home.'

'What will Roger say?'

'Shit the bed! Roger!' yelled Shelley and grabbed her phone.

Tom, listening to Shelley's report of the morning's happenings to Mrs Royal, found his mouth falling open.

'Poor Roger, he'll have the most terrible headache, and he'll be stood down for twenty-one days too. But at least that will mean he'll still be fit to ride at Garwood.' Tom looked down at his cooling tea.

'What do you mean "stood down for twenty-one days"?' asked Katie darkly.

'If you get concussion, British Eventing will revoke your rider's licence for twenty-one days. Didn't you know, sweetie?'

Knees shaking, Katie sat down on the sofa. Did that mean she was going to have to ride the whole lot of them at Auchenruther Castle, including Roger's big strong horse that she had just seen cartwheeling over a fence?

Seventeen

Victoria dropped Roger off at the Hall late that afternoon. He had grade three concussion and had been sent home with a clutch of leaflets and told not to undertake any sporting activities for three weeks.

'Bloody stupid,' he complained to Shelley on the phone that evening. 'I've been knocked out lots of times and just carried on as normal.'

'Maybe all those bangs on the head go some way to explaining why you're so cantankerous,' she replied.

Ignoring the jibe, he asked her if Katie was there.

'Yes, and Tom,' she said after a pause.

'Tom?' Roger was opening a packet of paracetamol; the headache was quite spectacular.

'Petra's fired him.'

'*Fired him*?' Roger filled a mug with water. 'What on earth for?'

'Someone's snitched that he was riding Warrior on the beach yesterday. Old Golden Knickers feels it was a "conflict of interests".' Shelley imitated Petra's screechy drawl perfectly.

'She can't do that,' said Roger, feeling dreadfully guilty for Tom's dismissal.

'She has. Roger,' Shelley hesitated, 'he's going to stay with us for a while, just until he finds somewhere to live. Caitlyn thinks there might be a few shifts going at the Kettle.'

'I'll ring Jonny Bell – he might have something temporarily; Tom's really too heavy to be riding racehorses.'

'Thanks, he'll appreciate it. Did you want to speak to Pink Knickers?'

Roger yawned. 'No, ask her to come up, would you? But she better make it quick because I don't think I can stay awake much longer.'

It was another warm and sticky evening and, noticing the drooping leaves on the cherry trees as she walked to the Hall, Katie realised she couldn't remember the last time it had rained. The sound of the combine harvester was coming from the village, and she could smell and taste the wheat dust on the air. There was hardly a breath of wind. The perfect night for sitting outside laughing with friends and a few bottles of wine, but after so much alcohol on Saturday night and Roger's fall and Tom without a job, Katie, Shelley and Tom didn't much feel like it.

She watched the cyclist pedalling down the drive from East Lodge and knew by the yellow Lycra leggings and matching vest top that it was Jules's mum.

'Hello, Katie.' Pippa stopped, took her feet off the cleats on the pedals and placed them on the ground. 'How's Roger? Sounds like he had a lucky escape.'

'I'm just off to find out. How did you know?'

Pippa was spinning the pedals around, ready to restart her ride. 'Jules told me. Give him my best wishes, won't you?'

'Yes, of course I will. How far are you going tonight?'

'Not far.' Pippa smiled. 'Just a quick whizz through here and back home. It's so peaceful cycling around here, no traffic to worry about. Must go, calories to burn!'

Katie watched her cycle away, then turned back towards the Hall. Otter came running out of the open door wagging his tail, and she saw Roger in the doorway.

'Evening.' He was holding out a vodka and tonic.

'You should be taking it easy.'

'I am, I'm not running a marathon. Let's sit on the terrace; I could do with some air.'

'Can you remember what happened?' She sat down in the chair next to him.

He shook his head and winced. 'Not really, just opening my eyes and seeing you both gawping at me. Shelley says he's okay?'

She nodded. 'And the physio's coming tomorrow around eleven; he managed to squeeze him in after he heard what had happened.'

There was a pause and Roger rubbed his temples. 'I want to leave all the entries in for this weekend.' His phone sounded a succession of duck quacks and he rapidly read a message from Jules asking if he was okay. 'The owners are expecting their horses to run, and Warrior needs to go in preparation for Garwood.'

Katie's shoulders dropped. 'But I've only sat on Warrior once, and it didn't end well.'

'I know, but you've got this week to get acquainted with him, and if it's not going to work, I'll withdraw him on Saturday.'

'Then you'll lose your entry fee.'

'That doesn't matter.' For the first time that day he smiled at her. 'You know the other horses well; you just need to learn another dressage test. We'll start tomorrow with Warrior if the physio gives us the all-clear.'

She tried not to hope that Warrior had put his back out.

'Now, Tom. Who on earth would tell Petra he was riding Warrior on the beach, and why the hell has she reacted by sacking him?'

Katie took a sip of vodka and tonic and noticed Roger was drinking water. 'Can I ask you something?' She fished a harvest fly out of her drink.

He shrugged. 'Of course.'

'Did Petra try it on with you on Saturday night, at the party?'

Roger took his time in answering. 'I think that if I had so much as winked at her, she would have, I don't know how you put it…'

'Would have been extremely happy to have been your cougar,' finished Katie.

'That is a horrible expression.'

'It was quite funny how she was trying to hide her roaming hands inside that god-awful tent she was wearing. I thought she was going to unfasten your trousers at any minute.'

'You noticed and didn't think to rescue me?'

'Roger, the whole room noticed what she was trying to do to you.'

He grimaced.

'Tom thinks that because you blew her out on Saturday night, she's determined to get her own back.'

'I wouldn't put anything past Petra.'

'I'd better go.' She drained her glass. 'You look tired.'

His phone rang as they walked through the French doors, and Katie waited in the hall while he talked on his mobile in the drawing room. She glanced at the piano and then walked across to it and lifted the lid, thinking of the night she had played it after giving him a lift back from Major Dawson's. Sitting down on the stool, she quietly played the beginning of "Clair de Lune" and, seeing Roger in the drawing room doorway watching her, she looked at him in astonishment.

'You've had it tuned!'

He gave her a small smile but said nothing.

~

The next day, despite Katie's prayers, Michael the physio reported that Warrior was in great condition and raring to go. Katie had already schooled Murdoch and Lightoller with Roger watching and tomorrow they would take them all, The Mechanic included, to the equestrian centre to show jump.

Knowing Warrior could be incredibly strong, Roger had changed his bit and was watching Katie riding him around the school. He was a bold, long-striding horse, and Katie was struggling to adapt to him. Sweating and exhausted after half an hour in the saddle, she stopped beside Roger on the verge of tears. Slipping to the ground on shaking legs, knee still aching after falling off on the beach, she admitted defeat.

'You can't give up.' He gestured for her to turn around so he could leg her back into the saddle again.

'I can't do it. He's too strong; he's too different, and I'll never hold one side of him on the cross country.'

'You're only saying that because you saw him fall. It was my fault. He's clever, and you don't need to jump him over the same thing twice; once he's been over it, he knows what he's doing. Now, walk on.'

～

That evening, Shelley and Katie went with Tom to Petra's staff house to collect his possessions.

Kind-hearted Josh, who thought Tom was a nice lad, had boxed up his collection of *Stable Tattle* magazines and had put his clothes into bin bags. He had even tipped Petra's golden brushes onto the floor of the tack room and used the big plastic box to carefully pack Tom's handbags. Tom, rooting through it with elation, was devastated to find his blue Ted Baker bag was missing.

Petra, seeing Tom's car outside the house, arrived just in time to see him closing the boot on his boxed handbags and had screamed that it was her storage box and demanded that he return it to her at once.

Tom, snarling that she was a bitter old hag and had better wind her neck in or he was going to bitch slap her, calmly closed the boot and drove off.

'What's eating her?' asked Shelley in awe, watching Petra out of the rear window having a tantrum like a teenager.

'Not your boss, sweetie, and I think that's the problem.' Tom sighed.

~

Show jumping practice the next day was a total disaster. The Mechanic knocked down every single fence; Lightoller took a dislike to a new red-brick wall the centre had recently acquired and point blank refused to jump it; Murdoch, feeling very fresh, raced at everything while staring at the roof; and little Tiger demolished one fence so badly that she ended up hopping lame. Only Warrior put up a good account of himself and cleared everything with inches to spare, despite travelling much faster than Katie would have liked.

On Thursday afternoon, Roger took Katie and Warrior cross country schooling to a different course far inland from Athward. As he drove, it crossed his mind that this was a crazy idea, asking her to ride the horse with so little preparation, but he trusted the horse who, although could be strong, was incredibly talented, and he desperately needed this run at Auchenruther in preparation for his three-day competition at Garwood.

Through frantically chattering teeth, Katie saddled Warrior. Thinking that the horse was about to kill her and overwhelmed by fear, adrenaline, the thought of riding The Mechanic at the Scottish Championship and seeing her mum, she grabbed Roger by the collar of his shirt and quickly kissed him on the mouth.

'If I'm going to die, at least I'll have one happy last thought to take with me.' She turned her back to him and began to pull down her stirrups.

As he watched her ride away, he found he had raised his fingers to his mouth, touching his bottom lip where she had kissed him.

The big, solid horse was interested in his new rider. She was lighter and smaller than the people who had ridden him before, and when he pulled against her hands, she didn't pull back on his mouth the way the others had done. Her light weight was easier to carry too, and he liked her sing-song voice as she asked him to "stea-dy" and the way she raised her tone when she asked him to "go on" when she wanted him to canter more quickly.

'You did well with him,' Roger told her as he started the lorry for the journey home.

'He was easier than I thought he was going to be,' she confessed, picking up her phone from the dashboard.

'What do you want to listen to?' Roger was ejecting the CD from the player.

'Anything, except Lewis Capaldi, Coldplay, Ed Sheeran—'

'So essentially anything, apart from what I like?' He turned to hand her the CD.

'I don't mind your Oasis addiction, but what about my current favourite playlist on Spotify?'

'If you must.'

'You'll like it – I promise.' She opened the app and, as it started to play, she put her phone on the seat beside her. 'There's loads of old stuff on it, so you're bound to like it.'

Roger wrinkled his brow. 'DB Boulevard? How old are you?'

'I love this song.' She looked at him indignantly. 'Give me your phone, and I'll make a playlist for you.'

Roger leant forwards to retrieve it and handed it to her. 'Not too much of your girly pop, Pink Knickers,' he warned.

'You can't have too much girly pop and anyway, I thought you liked a bit of Kylie.' Katie opened Spotify on his phone. 'You've got an email from Daniel – do you want me to read it to you?'

'I liked Kylie in her gold hot pants,' he replied, making her roll her eyes without realising it was a habit she had picked up from him. 'Yes please, read it.'

'Hi Roger, I really fancy your work rider because she's really hot—'

He started to laugh. 'You might have taken me in if it was from Rory, but Dan is besotted with Sara.'

'Alright, alright, he wants to know if you want to go for dinner at his place a week on Friday.'

'Just reply asking if it's at the usual time.'

Katie typed the email and then returned to Roger's Spotify account.

'How can someone who likes ABC and Fleetwood Mac also like the Spice Girls and Rita Ora?' he asked in annoyance forty minutes later.

'"Stop" and "I Will Never Let You Down" are classics,' she reasoned.

'But not quite in the same league as "The Look of Love" and "Go Your Own Way". Are you sure you're only twenty-four? Most of the tracks on here are at least ten years older than me.'

'Unlike you, who listens to music that would drive most people to suicide, I have excellent taste.' She turned up the volume on her phone as Shakira began singing "Whenever Wherever".

'2002,' he stated. 'I was in the upper sixth finishing my A levels.'

'I was five.'

'Stop it,' he warned.

She smiled. 'What did you do for A level?'

'Smoked behind the tennis courts mostly, but I somehow managed to pass English, Geography and History.'

'Very proper.'

'What A levels did you do?'

'Politics, Sociology, Business Studies and Economics.' She grinned as she added Carly Simon's "You're So Vain" to his playlist. 'I wanted to do Spanish, English Literature, English Language and Classics, but Dad wanted me to do the business stuff.'

'Knowing how you don't understand the word no, I'm surprised you compromised.'

She was silent and he glanced across at her.

'Dad always gets his own way,' she said shortly.

There was a silence, and Martin Fry began singing "All of My Heart".

'Is your dad coming up this weekend?'

'I bloody hope not.' She added three Spice Girls' songs to his list.

Roger looked across at her again. 'Don't you think it would help? If he came and saw that you are happy?'

'It wouldn't make any difference; he doesn't think this is a real job.'

It was later in the afternoon when Roger discovered that she had changed his ringtone to "Blue" by Eiffel 65, set his email and WhatsApp alerts to the sound of a woman having a screaming orgasm and had named his new playlist "Boring Boxers".

Eighteen

It was Friday night.

The lorry was packed, and the horses going to Auchenruther Castle the next day had been bathed and put to bed with their bandaged legs. There was an atmosphere of anticipation about the coming weekend – Auchenruther was a big competition and drew big crowds with its shopping village and various demonstrations and parades of previous winners in the main arena.

Katie was feeling anxious, especially about The Mechanic's Scottish Championship on Sunday. She knew that once the weekend was over, she could relax and, as Roger had ridden Bluebell quietly around the fields on Thursday morning, she hoped he would soon be back in the saddle, which would ease the pressure on her considerably. Years ago, in her dreams, she had thought how wonderful it would be to have a yard of horses at her disposal. She had never considered how challenging it was to ride every single horse, how hard it was to get a tune from the ones you didn't click with, and as she closed the door to The Mechanic's stable, she realised how talented Roger was and how simple he made it all look. Her mum had rung that afternoon while she was sitting in roadworks on the M1 in the holiday traffic. They had chatted for five minutes about horses and what Katie thought her prospects were for the weekend of competition. Then Joanna had dropped the clanger that her father had decided to come to the Scottish Borders with her, but as he wanted to look at an estate in North Yorkshire on behalf of a client, they wouldn't make it to Auchenruther Castle until Saturday night.

Annoyed that her mum wouldn't be there tomorrow to watch her ride, Katie consoled herself with the fact that her mother would at least be there on Sunday to watch The Mechanic, even if her dad was in tow, complaining about everything in sight.

Tom had been helping on the yard every day and had also worked a shift behind the bar at the Cup and Kettle. Shelley and Katie weren't sure how long Tom would last as a barman. He wanted to sugar frost a lot of glasses and had mixed a mind-blowing cocktail involving vodka, white wine, sherry, Pernod, Cointreau, orange juice and egg white for Mrs Grayson as payback for her making a joke about his Michael Kors handbag.

Jonny Bell had offered Tom a part-time job riding out and doing morning stables, and he had been and ridden out the second lot with Jonny's lads that morning. Finding him to be high maintenance in comparison to them in their jeans and wellies, they had christened him "Beckham", which Tom found hilarious until Piper had explained they meant Victoria and not David.

Jonny had staff accommodation above his American barn stabling, so Tom's handbag collection, china teapots, matching cups and saucers and myriad of gels, lotions and bath bombs would be moving there with him early next week.

Caitlyn, having rushed away from the horse washing and tack cleaning at quarter to three, now returned to the yard in the Bogiemobile. Making everyone jump as the car horn sounded loudly, she swung around the yard grinning like a Cheshire cat excitedly waving a piece of paper.

'For God's sake, why do you keep beeping your horn?' said Shelley crossly.

'Oh sorry, I didn't mean to, it just goes off on its own whenever I turn left.' She slammed the door shut and a sprinkling of rust fell onto the cobbles.

'What are you so thrilled about, missy?' Tom leant on his broom.

'I've passed my test!' squeaked Caitlyn. 'It's taken three goes, but I've finally passed!' She gave a little boob jiggle.

'What test?' Katie put down her wheelbarrow.

'My *driving* test,' said Caitlyn in an earnest voice.

'Oh, my lord,' said Roger faintly.

After congratulating her, Shelley added that if she wouldn't mind wiping over Lightoller and Murdoch's bridles, they would buy her dinner in the Cup and Kettle to celebrate.

Caitlyn tucked her test certificate under the Bogiemobile's windscreen wiper. 'Tom? Can I borrow this week's *Stable Tattle*? I haven't read it yet.'

Tom looked shifty and mumbled that it was in the tack room.

'Can't believe you read that trash.' Katie carried on with her wheelbarrow.

Caitlyn dismantled the two bridles and dropped the metal bits into a bucket of hot soapy water with a clank. Tom's copy of *Stable Tattle* was lying underneath his riding hat on the table; Caitlyn tugged it out and started to read as she wiped the grease from Murdoch's bridle.

There was a report and photos of the new stallion standing at Grangelands stud farm and an article about different vehicles for towing a trailer. Caitlyn only read *Stable Tattle* for Smith's Gossip Corner, but as she started applying saddle soap to the bridle and turned to find it in its usual place on page fifty-six, she found the page had been ripped out.

Jules, in her strappy top, came in to collect her bag. 'Get a move on, Caitlyn, we're going to the Kettle.' She picked up her empty lunch box and tucked it into her bag.

Caitlyn looked up as Tom, Katie and Shelley came in. 'Tom, there's a page torn out, you need to complain.'

'Hadn't noticed.' He picked up his riding hat. 'Oooh, I'll have goggles on my hat come Monday morning; can you imagine me galloping along the beach looking like a tall, young Lester Piggott?'

Caitlyn was undeterred. 'How could you not notice that Smith's Gossip Corner had been torn out? It's the best part of the magazine.'

Roger, walking into the room behind Shelley and hearing Caitlyn and Tom's exchange, strode quickly into the middle of the room. 'Why is it torn out?' he asked furiously, and Katie gave a little shiver.

'I, I've no idea.' Tom was fibbing and, both six feet tall, they faced each other, their noses inches apart.

'Yes, you do, Tom, what did it say?' Roger was speaking deliberately, and Shelley could tell he was livid.

Tom mouthed wordlessly, and his eyes flicked to the rubbish bin in the corner. Roger was over there in a flash, ripping off the lid and tipping it upside down so the pieces of kitchen roll, Pot Noodle pots, empty coke cans and cotton wool rolled across the floor. Snatching the torn and crumpled page, he smoothed it out and began to read.

'Don't read it!' Shelley made a lunge at him, and in a deft movement, he grabbed her neck to stop her clawing the page from his grasp.

His arm outstretched, almost lifting her off her feet but never taking his glittering blue eyes off hers, he gradually relaxed his grip until she took a step backwards, her hands going to her reddened throat. She glared at him, breathing heavily, then burst into tears and, pushing Katie out of the way, ran across the yard to the Dorchester.

There was a shocked silence before Tom shot after her as Caitlyn looked desperately at Katie, who gave a little shrug and a frantic shake of her head.

Jules was cowering in the corner clutching her bag and now, seeing her escape route was clear, she sprinted for the door, pushing Katie back into the saddle racks on the wall in her haste to get out.

'Well, Caitlyn,' said Roger in a cool voice. 'It was certainly worth waiting for.' He slammed the page on the table in front of her and stormed out.

'What the fook was that all about?' Caitlyn was putting the bridles back together with very wide eyes.

Katie started to read and went cold.

An old friend in Northumberland is being a terribly busy boy at the moment. Not content with having a yard full of event horses to ride, it seems he has also been undertaking some extra-curricular riding. Whilst there has never been a shortage of mares offering themselves for servicing by the handsome thirty-seven-year-old, this coupling is a bit of a shocker as the spritely young filly is thirteen years his junior. She hails from the South of England where the six-bedroomed family seat has twenty-three and a half rolling acres which Mummy gallops around while Daddy pops into the office to play at being the boss between rounds of golf. (£270 a round to non-members.)

My old friend must be ready to settle down after his years of wild oat sowing but with this much younger model, is he really getting his oats, or is it just a midlife crisis?

Caitlyn put her arm around Katie. 'Who would write this? It's horrible,' she whispered.

Katie put her hands to her face, feeling utterly horrified. There was more:

Our friend dallied across the valley once or twice a few years ago but obviously wasn't taken with the more experienced mare, instead preferring to wait for a fresher example which arrived in his yard in January. It's not taken him long to break her in, but what will Mummy and Daddy think of her new sugar daddy? They are all convening at Auchenruther Castle this weekend, so watch out for the fireworks – I hear they are going to be spectacular.

Katie ran to the sink and was sick.

Shaking violently, she shepherded Caitlyn to the door and turned off the light.

'I suppose dinner at the Kettle is off then?' Caitlyn asked hopefully as Katie walked wordlessly away from her to the Dorchester.

She poured an inch of vodka into a dirty coffee mug with a shaking hand and slugged it back in one motion. 'Why didn't you tell me?'

Tom was standing warily by the unlit stove and a tear-stained Shelley was perching on the arm of the sofa.

'You've got so much on your plate at the minute,' Shelley got up and came and sat next to her at the table, 'with taking on all Roger's rides for the next three weeks. We just thought,' she looked across at Tom, 'that it would be better if you didn't know. I knew Roger would go mental when he saw it.'

'I should have eaten it,' said Tom angrily. 'Anyway, as it's obviously not true, I'm sure it will blow over quickly. They'll have found someone else to bitch about by next week.'

Katie fidgeted in her chair then stood up.

'Where are you going?' asked Shelley.

'To talk to him.'

'Are you sure that's wise?' Shelley lifted her hair above her collar to reveal three darkening bruises from Roger's thumb and fingers. 'I thought he was going to strangle me.'

'Well, *I've* considered doing it a few times,' said Tom lightly.

∼

Roger was sitting in the gloom of his unlit drawing room and didn't look up as Otter thumped his tail on the floor in greeting.

'Who did you tell?' he said, at last.

She gasped when she heard the question; she had expected sympathy and some form of reassurance, not an accusation. 'What the hell? You think I took out an ad in the *Northumberland Herald*?'

'Who knew?'

'I can't believe you're even asking me this,' she said furiously. There was a silence.

'Who knew?' he repeated.

'Shelley! She saw the bloody hickey you'd left on my neck before I did. I'm not some hanger-on trying to get my ten minutes of fame.' She slumped into the nearest couch and Otter pushed his wet nose under her trembling hand.

Roger got up and splashed whisky into two glasses; when she didn't respond to him, he nudged her arm gently with the tumbler.

'I don't drink whisky.'

'You do on this occasion. It's medicinal.'

She watched him walk to the door and turn on the lights. 'I didn't tell anyone. Is that really what you think of me?'

'I have been through this before,' he began bleakly, 'and I know that this will not be a one-off. This will continue for weeks until they get either a reaction or someone else to write about.'

She kept her eyes low, remembering the feeling of excitement and anticipation in the days when she had been reading about Roger and Elizabeth in *Stable Tattle*. It had all seemed so innocent at the time, like watching a soap opera, and she and her friends had given no thought to the people whose lives were being scrutinised and dissected.

'I don't think I have the energy to fight them this time; I really don't want to go through it all again.' He waited until she lifted her eyes and looked at him. 'And I don't want you to go through it either.'

'They've only accused you of sleeping with me; they haven't written horrible things about your family.'

'Because I don't have one,' he said quietly.

'Sorry. Didn't think.' She mentally kicked herself, what a bloody stupid comment to make.

'I will never give them the satisfaction of threatening them with court action; it's best to ignore it, but it's difficult to ignore the knowing looks in the lorry park.'

'But how do they *know*?'

'A lucky guess.'

She swallowed the last of the whisky and felt it burning in her stomach.

'Do you need a hug?'

She smiled weakly as she stood up and he wrapped his arms around her.

'Let's just get this straight. This is me as a concerned employer, trying to offer support to an employee.' He felt her give a sob and squeezed her tighter. 'We just have to deny everything – it will blow over eventually.'

'Dad will go ballistic if he sees it; he'll probably threaten to cut me out of the will unless I go home.'

'He's hardly likely to read it, especially if it's true and he spends most of his working week on the golf course.'

'Don't try and be funny.'

'I'm not.'

There was another silence, and Roger held her more tightly against him; his hand on the back of her head was beginning to tingle as he stroked her hair.

'I assume the dally across the valley was Petra?'

Knowing her face was buried in his chest, he admitted it was.

Looking up at him with tears drying on her cheeks, she asked if Petra had been a "double bagger".

'What's a "double bagger"?'

Katie pulled away and wiped her eyes with her sleeve. 'You know, you put a bag over your head and one over theirs, in case yours falls off.'

He nearly laughed.

Nineteen

On Saturday morning, as the lorry ate up the miles towards Auchenruther Castle in the Scottish Borders, Mrs Royal was busily hoovering the red-patterned carpet of the upstairs landing of the Hall. She had been away since Monday morning, staying with her sister in Newcastle, and although she always enjoyed visiting Betty and her husband, she was always more than happy to return to East Lodge and her own space.

Humming her favourite Cliff Richard tune, she flung open Roger's bedroom door and plugged the hoover into the socket by the bed. Taking a yellow duster from the front pocket of her apron, she lifted the lamp from the bedside table and gave the top a quick dust. There was a strange feeling in this room, she thought, someone's been in here and they shouldn't have. Frowning and feeling drawn to the other side of the bed, she walked around and, after slowly getting to her knees, gazed underneath it.

The earring was gone.

She had managed to carefully hoover around it for the past eight weeks, and now it was gone. Running her gnarled hand across the carpet, her fingers grew cold, which told her that the silver earring had not been taken by its rightful owner, and whoever had taken it was going to use it to cause harm. Clambering to her feet, she stood still for a moment and sucked her teeth. She decided she would speak to Roger when he was home tonight.

~

Katie had an abysmal day. Both horses did mediocre dressage tests, had four show jumps down and, although she got Lightoller around the cross country with only time faults, Murdoch was eliminated.

'I'm so sorry.' She slumped against the side of the lorry to speak to Jennifer Bane as her five spaniels turned her into a maypole.

'They are both going home safely, and that's the main thing.' She hauled on her handful of dog leads. 'To be honest, after I read Smith's column, I'm impressed you've even come out of your house.'

Petra was there with a lorry load of horses, and although Josh gave her a grin and wished her luck at the start of the cross country, Petra shot her a look of pure hatred.

'Bitter old hag,' she told Roger as he tightened her girth.

'If you think that's bad, you want to see her face when she's having an orgasm.'

'Did both your bags fall off?' she enquired.

~

Once back at Athward that evening, Katie schooled Warrior and, while Shelley was settling him in for the night, she took The Mechanic into the school.

Roger, sitting on the fence of the arena to watch her, was getting crosser and crosser.

He was discovering he was very easily tired since his fall, and after a long day at Auchenruther, refusing to let Shelley drive home because he was "fine", he was now struggling to keep his eyes open. Used to his usual level of fitness and mental strength, he was frustrated by this creeping fatigue and prayed to God that it didn't last much longer.

'No, no, no!' he yelled, jumping down off the fence, all thought of "no physical exercise for three weeks" forgotten and stalking across to where Katie had hauled The Mechanic to a halt. 'If you ride like that tomorrow, Smith's column is going to be the least of your problems! Do it again!'

After her third attempt at the walk to canter transition, Katie, also absolutely exhausted after a punishing week and two rides that day, lost her temper.

'You fucker!' she howled. 'I'm absolutely shattered trying to cover your arse – you could at the very fucking least be constructive!'

'You ungrateful bitch!' he roared back. 'I'm giving you a massive opportunity to prove yourself, and if you ride tomorrow the way you rode today, you'll be getting your fucking P45!'

Eyes full of tears, she blushed as she grasped that the level of his temper had way surpassed hers.

'Oh, for fuck's sake, please don't turn on the waterworks,' he said wearily.

Telling him she was going for a ride, she rode past him and unlatched the gate. Ignoring his shouted order for her to come back, she trotted The Mechanic around the outside of the stable yard and headed towards East Lodge.

∼

Mrs Royal was hovering at the back door, and Roger greeted her by asking if she had enjoyed her week away and wondering if she had heard the foul language coming from the school five minutes earlier.

'Sorry to bother you so late, could I have a word?' She was wringing her hands as she spoke.

Roger led her into the kitchen, and Mrs Royal refused a cup of tea and launched into a speech that lasted almost four minutes. As the sermon came to an end, he looked at her in bewilderment, and Mrs Royal wrung her hands even tighter.

'Why?'

'Now, it's not my place to ask why a lady's earring is under your bed, Roger,' she straightened the stack of paperwork on the table, 'and that's why I left it where it was, and I didn't want to embarrass you by picking it up and leaving it on your bedside table.'

'But it's gone now?'

Mrs Royal nodded. 'I had a cold feeling.' She sucked her teeth.

When she left with her usual "ta da, pet", he went into the drawing room and poured a whisky. Although it was getting dark, it was still warm, and he pushed open the patio doors, letting in the night air. Walking around the edge of the lawn with Otter and squinting down North Hall to the babbling river, he could make out Katie and The Mechanic running through their dressage test. Katie was adding an additional movement here and there so The Mechanic would not think to anticipate when they performed it for real in the morning; he watched as she walked the horse up the hill to the front of the house and led him through the wicket gate.

Going back to his drinks table, he poured himself another whisky and a vodka and tonic and went down to the yard. He found her in the tack room cleaning The Mechanic's dressage saddle, and he blinked as his eyes adjusted to the harsh electric light after the darkness of the night.

'Why don't you do that in the lorry on the way there tomorrow?' he asked.

'I'd rather do it now.' There were tears on her cheeks, but she accepted the tumbler and held it steady as he chinked his against it.

He hitched his hip onto the sink and watched her as she soaped the girth straps of the saddle.

'I'm sorry,' her voice was choked, and she didn't look at him, 'about before. I'm shattered, and I'm trying so hard.'

He put his glass on the edge of the sink and rubbed his eyes. 'I've put you under a lot of pressure this week, and I don't want to broadcast it, but I haven't really felt like myself since the fall. I've even noticed that I've been on a shorter fuse than usual.'

She gave him a watery smile.

'I need to ask you something.' He sipped his drink.

'Roger, I've told you before, when a man and a woman love each other very much—'

He laughed. 'I'm serious, and it could be important.'

'Okay.' She used a clean cloth to wipe the brass nameplate on the back of the saddle.

'I think someone found your lost earring at the owners' party,' he said slowly.

She looked at him sharply.

'The silver horseshoes that Tom gave you, have you lost one?'

She nodded.

'It was under my bed.'

She frowned at him. 'Why didn't you give it back to me?'

'I didn't know it was there.' He ran a hand over his hair. 'Mrs Royal didn't want to pick it up for fear of embarrassing me.'

'Does she know it's mine?' she asked in a subdued voice.

'I would imagine so, but she's very discreet.'

There was a silence as she sat down in the armchair and finished her drink.

'I think, if we find out who took your earring,' Roger reached for her empty glass, 'we will also find out who has been talking to Smith's Corner.'

She said nothing, thinking of Shelley howling with laughter as she relayed the story of the gaggle of them apple pie-ing Roger's bed.

Twenty

Sandwiched between Caitlyn and Tom on the sofa in the living area of the lorry, Shelley was watching the leafy hedgerows flash past as they made their way back to Auchenruther Castle.

Yesterday had not been a good day – Katie hadn't ridden Lightoller or Murdoch with her usual gusto, and she looked absolutely knackered. Thinking Roger was partially insane to give Katie the ride on Warrior, her thoughts then turned to Jules.

Jules had messaged Roger at five that morning to say she was ill and devastated, as she had been looking forward to the day out for ages. Although Shelley had done nothing but raise her eyebrows at Roger as she digested this information, she instinctively knew Jules was up to something. There was no way in hell Jules would have missed a day out with Roger, especially when there would have been the opportunity to stay with him all day as he had no rides.

Shelley had quietly tried to find out if Jules had another job somewhere, but whoever she tactfully asked always knew nothing. Even Edwina in the café in the village, who knew everything, had told her that as far as she was aware, Jules only worked for Roger and lay in the sun in her parents' garden the rest of the time.

The lorry slowed as they approached the junction at Upper Newtown, and as they had to wait for a gap in the traffic for Roger to pull out, Shelley noticed the ruby-red berries of the hawthorn mingling with the bright crimson holly berries, signalling the end of summer. In four weeks, when the sloes would be busily ripening on the blackthorn bushes, they would be heading to Inverness and Garwood's international competition. After that, there were just a handful of local events before the horses were let down for the winter and sent home. After a busy season, Shelley was looking forward to some time off and wondered if she and Katie should think about booking a holiday abroad.

Glancing forwards to the cab of the lorry, Shelley saw Katie's head was lolling to the side as she slept. Katie had been in an odd mood since last night, and Shelley wondered if it was nerves about competing, seeing her parents or the ferocity of the row with Roger in the outdoor school that had put her friend into silent mode. Shelley knew she was not overjoyed that Eddie was coming to Auchenruther. Bloody Eddie didn't usually need an excuse to put the boot in with Katie, and Shelley hoped he wouldn't be hanging around the lorry today, although she knew he would be desperate to suck up to Roger and all the trappings that went with him.

As Shelley got The Mechanic ready for his dressage, Joanna and Eddie appeared bearing an enormous picnic hamper which Caitlyn, in her new denim shorts above her fake-tanned legs and Tom in his distressed designer jeans, were now devouring for their breakfast.

Joanna thought how fit and well Katie looked and hugged her tightly. 'What's the cross country like?'

'Absolutely huge,' she replied. 'I'm terrified.'

'It can't be that hard; it's not Badminton, is it?' Eddie laughed as he briefly hugged her, making Katie grit her teeth to keep in her response. 'And where is this famous man that you're working for? I'm looking forward to meeting him.'

On the well-watered, lush green grass of arena number four, The Mechanic produced a brilliant dressage test, which put him into fifteenth place on the Scottish Championship leader board. Delirious with happiness, Katie then proceeded to attempt to produce a similar result with Warrior, who carted her around the white boards and flowers and was so rigid with tension that she ended up with a mark of forty-four, putting her in thirty-eighth place and bringing her brutally back down to earth.

'He is very handsome.' Joanna was watching Roger talking to Cathy Marks at the lorry opposite as she fastened Katie's number bib.

'Isn't he just?' said Tom dreamily. 'You want to see him when he's schooling without his shirt on – if you took a photo in black and white, you could sell them as posters.'

'For heaven's sake, Tom!' Katie snapped. 'Mum, he's nearly forty.'

'Oooh but is lovely,' Tom was pulling down her stirrups, 'and he doesn't look thirty-seven. I bet he could go all night.'

Glaring at Tom, Katie led The Mechanic away from him.

After Roger had legged her into the saddle, he led her away from the noise and chatter of the lorry. 'Now look,' he checked her girth and rested his hand on her boot as he talked, 'it's a big course, but there's nothing that you're not capable of jumping.'

She nodded.

'Make sure you stick to your line at every fence; don't change what we've walked and what we've talked about. The water and the combination before the ditch are going to catch a lot of them out, and you need to go clear if you're going to be in with a shout.'

'Before he decimates the show jumps,' put in Katie.

'Focus on the cross country,' he said harshly. 'Make sure you give him time to look at the drop fence; don't rush him; and take your line at the snake's head and stick to it. Ride forward all the way. Alright?'

She nodded again, teeth chattering with nerves.

'Come back safe.' He patted The Mechanic, who swung his head towards him for a head rub.

Joanna watched as Katie dropped a grateful hand onto Roger's shoulder. *The lady doth protest too much*, she thought.

Down at the start, Daniel Jobson was warming up his brown and white horse and, seeing Roger walking alongside The Mechanic, he lifted his hand in greeting, calling across to him.

'Shitty piece in Smith's last week.' Daniel ran his hand down Rock On's neck.

'Bastards,' replied Roger shortly.

'We've all been there – last year Smith's said I was shagging someone who worked in a bank. Turns out it was my own bloody wife!'

Roger laughed; hearing that Smith's had also written about Daniel and Sara made him feel slightly better.

'Anyway, if it was true, no one would blame you, mate – she's a stunner.'

Charles had left his trade stand in the hands of his head salesman and walked with Margaret up the hill in the middle of the course. Daisy had disappeared into the Pimm's bar next to the water jump and was now sitting on the grass with her friends, clutching a pint glass half full of fruit.

'I'm going to ride next season,' she told them boastfully. 'I'm starting with Miss Mackenzie's Brogue, and after I've done a few events with him, I'm going to compete The Mechanic.'

Roger's phone was ringing. Annoyed with himself that he hadn't turned it onto silent mode, he pulled it from his pocket and saw it was his own landline number on the screen.

'Yes?' he said sharply as he watched Katie give The Mechanic a longer canter down the far side of the warm-up area.

'Roger,' Mrs Royal didn't wait for him to answer her, 'that lassie needs to check her tack.'

An icy feeling was rushing over him, and he began to run across to The Mechanic.

Pulling the horse up, Katie looked at him in annoyance. 'What?'

He put his hand on the rein. 'Get off,' he said quickly.

'Roger, we're about to start – what the hell are you playing at?'

'Get off him, now.'

Seeing the set of his face, she slipped to the ground. 'I don't need this, not now.'

'Be quiet, will you?' He was looking at the inside of the reins, the buckles on the bridle as The Mechanic sidled around him, feeling the change to the normal pre-cross country warm-up.

'What are you doing?' Katie had her hands on her hips and was clearly furious with him. 'You know how bloody nervous I get; I don't need this now.'

'Just check your girth and stirrups.'

Her face dropped and she pulled her leathers through the T-bar on the saddle so she could check the stitching and examined her girth. 'It's fine, Roger; everything's fine.'

He pushed her out of the way and lifted the flap of the saddle. She was right – the girth was safe and secure, buckled onto the first and third straps of the saddle. But there was something that made him lift the flap higher and, being taller than Katie, he could examine the webbing that the girth straps were stitched to, where it emerged from the innards of the saddle.

It was fine, absolutely fine.

But the nagging doubt was still there, and Mrs Royal was never wrong. He saw Shelley running across to them as he ducked under The Mechanic's neck to look at the offside of the horse. Again, he lifted the flap of the saddle, Katie's rose-gold jumping stirrup flying to the side of him and hitting The Mechanic on the shoulder.

And he found it. The synthetic fabric that held the first leather strap into the guts of the saddle had been slashed and was desperately frayed – there was only a two-millimetre sliver of material holding the girth in place. He rapidly unbuckled the girth from the damaged strap and fastened it onto the second one.

'What is it?'

'I just had to check.'

'What was wrong with my girth?' she asked quickly.

'Nothing.' He smiled at her as he walked around the horse to give her a leg-up. 'Close your eyes and take a breath – you need to focus.'

He stood beside her as she shut her eyes and breathed deeply, her hands on The Mechanic's ribcage, and he watched as her face relaxed.

'I'm ready,' she said finally as she turned, gathered up the reins and placed her hand on the saddle for the leg-up.

'God, I bloody hate those stirrups,' he told her as he watched her nose her toes into them.

She gave him a grin. 'But as I've told you before, *I* really like them.'

He watched her ride away and beckoned to Shelley. 'Check everything twice.' He was still watching The Mechanic. 'The webbing has been cut on one of the girth straps.'

'What the *hell*?' Shelley asked incredulously. 'Did you tell her?'

'No. But she'll soon realise when she goes to let her girth down after this.'

'What made you check?'

'Mrs Royal rang me.'

'You've got to report this. This is crazy.'

'Who do you suggest I report it to?' he enquired. 'Just make sure everything is checked twice.'

She nodded.

'And I think we need a keypad on the tack room door. We shouldn't leave it unlocked as often as we do.'

'You can keypad it as much as you like; it won't make a shred of difference if the Stanley knife slasher is part of your own team,' said Shelley sarcastically.

'She might be a huffy cow, but she wouldn't stoop this low.'

'She's changed, Roger. There's something different about Jules now.'

'Care to elaborate?'

She shook her head. 'I can't. It's just a feeling.'

As the starter began to count them down from fifteen seconds, Katie circled beside the start box.

Please God, let us get around, she prayed.

Please God, let them go clear, prayed Shelley.

Please God, let Roger stand a little bit closer to me, prayed Tom.

The Mechanic exploded from the start box with the ferocity of a caged lion. Steadying him for the first set of rails, he jumped them exuberantly.

No way, thought Katie, *if you jump them all like that, I'm going to fall off.*

They cleared the brush fence and galloped up the hill to the Irish bank, popped neatly on and off and galloped on to the huge table decorated with wooden teddy bears and tea plates. Katie could hear the wonderful sound of The Mechanic's high blowing as he exhaled every breath and the clack of his overreach boots in an otherwise peaceful world. There was no talking, just the occasional whistle from the fence judges to keep the course clear and this wonderful horse pulling like crazy, so keen he was to get to the next fence. They jumped the wooden bank of potato boxes, followed by a skinny single potato box three strides later, and thundered down the hill to the miniature thatched cottage.

'He's jumping well,' Roger murmured.

Caitlyn was transfixed; they were going awfully fast.

After the thatched cottage, it was the water complex – Katie slowed him as they approached it so The Mechanic could get a chance to look at the task in hand and work it out. He jumped over the upturned boat into the water with Katie leaning well back in the saddle, took four splashing strides before clearing the wooden Loch Ness Monster and jumping up the step and over the log.

There was applause from the gathered crowds expecting drama as the commentator reported that The Mechanic was safely through the water on the direct route; Shelley reported that her knees were knocking. Answering that she was not the only one,

Roger watched as The Mechanic cleared the rails at eight and the chess set at nine before they disappeared behind the hill.

'Ouch.'

Tom realised he was gripping Roger's arm. 'Sorry.' He blushed.

As Roger and the team were left with the commentator to chart The Mechanic's progress, Charles and Margaret saw their horse galloping towards number ten, the sequence of jumps that, as Roger had indicated, was causing elimination after elimination. The fence judge blew her whistle and Katie, standing in her stirrups, gave a fierce tug on her reins. Reluctant to slow down, The Mechanic shook his head from side to side in disagreement; still she pulled until he finally relented and slackened his speed to a canter. Sitting down in the saddle, both legs pressed to his sides to keep his body as straight as an arrow, she released him to jump the first element – The Mechanic landed, took three strides on a slight arc and popped over the second part.

'The Mechanic and Katie Holland are clear at ten.'

There was an audible outburst of relief from the Fleming Bowen team.

Maybe, thought Roger, *just maybe.*

Urging him on, she swung The Mechanic right after twenty metres and jumped a brush fence with a ditch in front of it. Running away slightly down the hill, she struggled to anchor him, and he jumped the corner at number twelve, her knee knocking down the red flag on their right. There was another fence decorated with smiling pumpkins and then they were galloping over the top of the hill back into Roger's view towards the colossal drop fence. Trotting him onto the wooden box that was built into the side of the hill, giving him time to assess it, he popped off the drop neatly, making Katie feel as though she was in freefall before the jolt as they landed.

The tricky snake combination had already caused huge problems, and there was a big crowd around the fences that were built on swirling lines, giving the riders many different options as to how to jump them. As they galloped on towards it, Katie was looking for the tree on her right that would put her on the right line for the fastest and most direct route. Lining him up perfectly, The Mechanic cleared the first part, jumped the second and, with a shout of encouragement from her, cleared the third with a bang, catching his near hind foot on it. Thumping his neck in praise, she rode away from the applause; they were nearly home. They cleared the next hedge, an enormous tree trunk and a set of tractor tyres.

'They're going to do it!' Shelley's face was flushed as she grabbed Tom's hand.

The Mechanic sailed over the strawbales, took the final set of white rails and galloped up the run-in to stop the clock within the allocated time.

Led by Roger, Shelley, Tom and Caitlyn were running towards her as she swung The Mechanic in circles to pull him up. Jumping off to walk alongside him, she found she hadn't the strength to loosen her girth and bent over to catch her breath.

'Brilliant!' Shelley yelled, taking The Mechanic's reins from her and placing her arm around her friend's shoulders. 'Great round!'

'What a round, missy!' Tom was doing a little dance.

Placing a gloved hand on Caitlyn's arm, hearing her excited congratulations as she caught her breath, Katie was looking at Roger for approval. His eyes crinkled in joy; he banged lightly on the top of her hat.

'What a brilliant ride.' He looked delighted. 'Your line through the water was perfect, and you rode through fifteen really well.'

'He was perfect.' Katie tucked her whip under her arm and unfastened her chinstrap. 'He was absolutely perfect, and I don't even care now if he knocks down every single show jump.'

The Mechanic was blowing hard, nostrils extending like trumpet bells, sweating white foam where his breastplate had rubbed against his rich-coloured coat. Katie had never been so proud of anything in her life.

Riding with the confidence from The Mechanic's round,

Warrior had only one fence down show jumping and managed to get around the cross country with only a run-out at the unforgiving twisted snake fence.

Joanna was having a marvellous day and was pleased to see Katie looking incredibly happy, so much happier than she had been in London, and she wished Eddie could appreciate it. Seeing a copy of *Stable Tattle* discarded on the grass as she made her way back to the lorry from the cross country course, she picked it up, rammed it in the nearest bin and threw her half-full coffee cup on top of it.

She had read Smith's column in the hotel last night as the proprietor, knowing they were attending the horse trials the following day, had thoughtfully purchased a copy of the magazine and left it in their room alongside the complimentary coffee and shortbread. Unsure which element Eddie would be most offended by, she had hastily hidden it under the mattress and reassured herself that there was little chance of her husband seeing a copy of the magazine.

Unfortunately, as Eddie drifted around the trade stands looking at Charles Dee's Mercedes cars and the numerous agricultural stands, he came across a red-fronted stand where some very pretty girls wearing red baseball caps and very tight catsuits were handing out paper cups of Pimm's and giving out free copies of a magazine called *Stable Tattle*.

'Everybody reads it just for Smith's Gossip Corner on page fifty-six,' the blonde girl confided, flashing a lot of cleavage before asking him if he would like to take out an annual subscription.

Flicking through it as he strolled, taking swigs from his complimentary Pimm's, he spat out a mouthful of fruit when he read Smith's. Working out immediately who it was referring to, and recognising his wife, who spent most of her day on horseback, and his own golfing habits, Eddie threw his paper cup in a wasp-infested bin and stomped back to Roger's lorry.

Caitlyn was leading The Mechanic around to cool him off as

Katie, sitting in the doorway to the living area, cleaned her jumping saddle.

'You are such a clever boy.' Caitlyn sponged the horse's face and dried it with a towel. 'Now you must be a good boy and not knock any show jumps down, or we might just leave you here.' She tied him up and stood on a plastic step to redo one of his plaits that had come undone. 'Are you excited?' she asked Katie.

Katie looked at her glumly. 'I wouldn't exactly use that word,' she replied as Roger handed her a bottle of water.

'Dad!' Katie put her water bottle on the step. 'You must meet Roger,' she jumped down and went to greet him.

Eddie, fortified by a glass of wine at the John Deere stand and his weak Pimm's from the blonde in the half-unzipped catsuit, gripped his daughter by her arm.

'Oh, I definitely need to meet Roger,' he said carefully, 'if *this*,' he shook the magazine in her face, 'is right, we need to have a little chat.'

Recoiling, Katie stammered that of course it wasn't right; Smith's column was renowned for printing untruths and was regularly having to print apologies.

'How did this *Smith* person know about our house?' He tightened his grip and shook her. 'Who on earth knows it's exactly twenty-three and a half acres? And *Smith* is bang on the money with the cost of a round of golf for non-members at Caperlees, and if that's all factually correct, I think it's safe to assume that the rest is as well.'

'This is the biggest day of my career so far, and you're determined to ruin it,' spat Katie. 'Why did you even bother coming?'

'It's not a career, Katherine,' Eddie replied sharply. 'It's buggering about with horses, which is all you have done since you left school.'

Roger, being forced to offer an ecstatic Charles and Margaret a glass of wine after they had turned up at the lorry, glanced out of the window and saw his work rider being gripped by her obviously furious father who was also waving a copy of *Stable Tattle*. Murmuring that he would be back in a minute, he got to his feet.

Charles, looking out of the window, surveyed the scene. 'No one blames you, Roger; if I was a few years younger and didn't have this one,' he patted Margaret's hand who gave a titter of laughter, 'I would've had a crack at her myself.'

Roger shot him a look of pure loathing as he closed the door on them.

'Mr Holland,' Roger strode towards them with his hand extended, 'I'm Roger Fleming Bowen, Katie's boss.'

Caught on the hop by Roger drawing himself to full height and towering above him, Eddie found himself letting go of Katie and shaking his hand. Crickey, he was tall, and Eddie noted the strong, broad shoulders and flat stomach beneath the checked shirt.

'I understand from Mrs Holland that you broke the journey from Dorset by staying overnight in Malton? Nice area, I have a friend who trains racehorses near there.' Roger turned to Katie. 'If you wouldn't mind speaking to Shelley? She needs to know which bridle you want on The Mechanic for your show jumping.'

Knowing full well that The Mechanic had only one competition bridle, Katie gave him a small smile and took her escape.

'I understand you aren't keen for Katie to follow this line of career,' Roger said the words as a statement and not a question, 'but she's exceptionally talented and rides extremely well.'

'And when she's too old to do all this?' Eddie waved his hand at the enormous lorries and glossy horses swishing their tails at the flies.

'That's when you start teaching morning, noon and night.'

Eddie laughed sarcastically. 'And what do you, Roger, charge for this teaching?'

'£120 an hour,' said Roger easily. 'I've just opened a rather good bottle of Chablis; would you care for a glass? We've got some time before The Mechanic's show jumping.'

Katie was cantering circles in the far corner of the emptying lorry park, breathing deeply into her stomach thinking calm thoughts. Refusing to take The Mechanic to the frantic scuffle of the show jumping practice area, she intended to warm him up away from the electrical tension in the lorry park and go to the main arena at the very last minute. Now, after twenty minutes in the saddle, Tom came running over, panting that there were three more to go before her and she had better hurry.

Trotting sedately between the lorries, people were shouting good luck to her as she passed.

Daniel was walking Rock On back to the lorry on a long rein. 'Good luck, Pink Knickers!' he called as she trotted by. 'Take it steady down the last line; it's causing problems.'

She shouted her thanks and asked how he had got on.

'Two down!'

Oh no, she thought. Rock On was usually a good show jumper, and hearing he had chalked up faults did nothing to help her nerves.

She brought The Mechanic to a walk as a grey horse trotted in to start his round, the electronic scoreboard showing the number before hers. Roger was lowering an upright in the middle of the roped-off warm-up, calling for her to jump it. She sent The Mechanic forward, and he sailed over. Now Roger was altering the big parallel on the other side; she rode a circle and, as soon as he was clear of the fence, touched her legs to the horse's sides and pointed him at the green poles. Cantering on, she jumped the upright again, which Roger had raised, and came to a halt at the entrance to the arena.

As Caitlyn wiped a cloth over The Mechanic's gleaming coat, Katie noticed her cheeks and nose were red from the afternoon sun. Shelley was quickly repainting The Mechanic's feet as Katie looked frantically around for Roger. He was walking across from the practice fences and, seeing he was squinting slightly, she knew he was tired.

'There have been very few clears; everyone seems to be

demolishing the last double, and the gates are falling easily. Just relax and keep to your line.' He tried to ignore the sense of foreboding as he thought about the partially severed girth strap. 'Try and enjoy it.'

The arena steward unlooped the rope across the entrance and told her to go to the top of the arena and wait for the bell. Smiling consolingly at the rider coming past her, she knew she would have to wait for the course to be rebuilt and took her time getting to the far end. Watching as the arena party painstakingly reconstructed both parts of the double, Katie waited until they were putting on the final pole before taking The Mechanic out of a trot and popping into canter.

The bell rang almost instantly, and she was through the start, triggering the electronic clock. The Mechanic jumped the first one easily, and Katie had to sit deeply to curb his enthusiasm to get to the blue planks that made up the second fence. Coming back to the bottom of the arena, they jumped the black and white sponsor's fence; crossing the middle of the grass, they cleared the double of white gates with The Mechanic giving an extravagant flick of his tail as he made nothing of the second one.

'How's she doing?' Tom was puffing after running back from the lorry park.

Roger announced he couldn't watch and walked away.

'Roger!' said Caitlyn in a shocked voice.

'Leave him alone,' growled Shelley.

Katie had ridden a beautiful dog-leg from the gates to number five, the red-brick wall with the white poles above, and The Mechanic backed himself off and jumped it carefully. They cleared the next, coming tight to the ring's border of advertising boards to get a clear line at it, and cantered a swinging loop to bring them to the pink and yellow poles of number seven.

Glancing around, Shelley saw Roger watching intently on the other side of the warm-up, his hands clasped on top of his head.

As The Mechanic landed over the pink and yellow fence, there was just the double between him and a clear round. Katie slowed the canter as they rounded the top of the arena, steadying him with her hands and voice and then, seeing the stride she wanted, she let him go forward.

'I can't watch!' Shelley buried her head in her hands.

'He's clear over the first,' said Tom in a trembling voice, and then he let out a yell of delight as The Mechanic landed safely over the second part and Shelley, looking between her fingers, saw Katie was looking up at the scoreboard as though she couldn't quite believe it herself.

Seeing a zero next to The Mechanic's name, she dropped the reins and, with a shriek of elation, raised both her fists and shook them in triumph to the gods of show jumping above her.

The crowd gave them a thunderous applause. They hadn't seen many clears, and this slight girl and her horse with the coat the colour of raw liver had floated around the course like thistledown.

Hardly able to speak, she slid out of the warm saddle and ignored all the words of congratulation as she put her arms around the hot, damp neck of The Mechanic, whispering her praise and adoration for him.

'How on earth did you do that?' asked Shelley in awe. 'That was fantastic.' She squeezed her tightly.

'Oooh, missy, what a round!' Tom thumped the top of her hat.

Roger, knowing that Eddie Holland was sitting in the stands watching his every move, told her she could now do no more.

'How many more to go?' Katie was taking a bottle of Lucozade from Caitlyn.

'Twelve.'

Caitlyn had slackened The Mechanic's girth and was leading him calmly around to keep his muscles moving. Whatever happened, it was looking like they were going to be in the top six and would need to go back into the arena for the prize-giving.

'What are you doing?' Katie noticed Tom and Shelley had their eyes shut and were moaning softly to themselves.

'Shush, shush,' chided Tom, still with his eyes shut.

'We're voodooing,' added Shelley.

'You're what?' Katie dropped the empty Lucozade bottle into the bin.

Shelley used her must-be-patient-with-the-idiot voice. 'Voodooing. This one,' she pointed at the man in the ring on a chestnut horse, 'is five penalties ahead of you so needs two fences down.'

They watched as he knocked down a gate and had both parts of the double.

'We did better with that one than we meant to, Tom. This one,' Shelley looked up the scoreboard as a young girl on a small black horse cantered past, 'is level with you and needs a cricket score.'

The young girl had the planks, a gate down and both parts of the double.

'Getting my eye in now,' crowed Tom.

'That's not very sporting,' said Katie grumpily.

'Oh, give the cat another goldfish; The Mechanic could do with a bit of luck.' Shelley closed her eyes again.

It came down to the final round. Rory Davison was one penalty better off than Katie after a textbook dressage and a clear cross country. His horse, Peethofsky, was a brilliant show jumper, and as he cantered easily around waiting for the bell, Caitlyn thought how nice it would be if The Mechanic won.

Katie was oiling The Mechanic's feet – they were going to be second, what a result for the faithful old Mechanic, he had produced more than she had ever dreamed he would. She tightened his girth as Caitlyn wiped him over again, and Roger came forward to leg her up.

As Rory came down to the final double, he pulled Peethofsky into a springy canter, knowing he had to get it right. They cleared the first, took two strides and cleared the second and cantered through the light beam, stopping the clock.

After the rumble of applause, Roger heard a groan of sympathy from the crowd and, looking up at the yellow digital figures on the scoreboard, saw Rory had collected penalties for taking his round too slowly, and The Mechanic was the winner by half a point.

He grinned at Katie. 'You've won it, darling, you've only gone and won it.'

She too was looking at the scoreboard in silence, and then she looked at him, her eyes wide with shock. Her mouth opened briefly as if to say something, before she burst into tears and flung her arms around him.

Laughing, he ducked down to avoid knocking her hat and kissed her on the cheek. 'Come on, get on, you've got to lead them in.'

As he threw her up into the saddle, The Mechanic disappeared beneath a sea of patting hands as the grooms and riders in the collecting ring, knowing the horse's history, came to touch the new Scottish Champion. Rory Davison rode Peethofsky alongside and kissed her cheek, laughing that never had time penalties been so important.

Liver chestnut, bay, brown and grey, their coats gleaming and polished in the sunshine, the prize winners lined up to face the packed stands. Katie rubbed The Mechanic's neck gratefully with her knuckles; her heart felt as though it was about to burst. She had managed to stop crying but knew the tears of pride could start again at any second. He hadn't let her down; The Mechanic had been incredible today, and maybe that's what he needed to show jump clear, just a calm warm-up away from the arena to get his muscles flexible and then a couple of practice fences and straight in to jump. For now, it didn't matter, he would be finished for the season after winning today; she knew Roger would insist on it.

Gavin Brooks had left his commentary box and was in the arena with the winners and his roving microphone. As the competition's main sponsor, in his very smart suit, shook her hand and began to clip the huge red and gold rosette onto The Mechanic's bridle, she saw Gavin was walking towards her.

'How does it feel to win the Scottish Championship with a horse who has, to put it mildly, a bit of a chequered record with British Eventing?' His eyes were encouraging, and he waited for her to answer.

'I adore this horse,' she said after a pause. 'He's tried his heart out today, and I'm grateful to Charles and Roger for allowing me to ride him.'

'Did you expect him to show jump clear?'

She watched the sponsor fastening the black and white tartan rosette to the other side of The Mechanic's bridle. The horse nudged him with his nose, as if he was hoping for a treat, and she smiled, running her hand under the neat plaits on his muscular neck. 'We tried a different tactic with him today and brought him over here at the last minute. And it seemed to work – he was very settled and a joy to ride. It was all him; I just had to sit here.'

Across at the entrance to the arena, Roger felt a lump rise to his throat.

'So,' Gavin's eyes were twinkling, 'can we expect to see you both at Garwood International?'

Katie had known the question was coming and she grinned at him. 'I will leave that decision to the horse's owner and my boss.'

'Speaking of your boss,' Gavin turned to face the stands, 'for those of you who perhaps aren't familiar with eventing, Katie works for Roger Fleming Bowen, who is this year's accredited trainer connected with the Scottish Championship and therefore, Katie has just won herself twelve hours of lessons with her employer.' There was a ripple of laughter from the stands before he resumed, 'Are you looking forward to your lessons with this year's accredited trainer?'

Katie chuckled. 'I might put the training vouchers on Ebay; I'm not sure I could stand being shouted at for another twelve hours.'

The crowd laughed and she looked across to the arena exit where Roger was standing, smiling and shaking his head.

The sponsor was struggling to fasten the Velcro on a red, white and blue sash around The Mechanic's neck, and Katie leant out of her saddle to help him. Then he presented her with a box. He showed her the velvet top with the white saltire on a navy-blue field, and when he opened it, she saw the coveted silver spurs for winning the Scottish Championship lying on the satin lining. She had read that they would have the date and the occasion engraved on the inside, and she could see the tiny Scottish flags etched on the outside of them.

She looked at them for a moment and then touched them with her gloved hand. 'They are beautiful.'

'Well done, you must be very proud.'

'I am. He's a fantastic horse.'

'You should be proud of yourself as well.'

'I just steered him.'

He smiled and posed for another photograph. 'That's not true; it's always a partnership.' He handed her a bunch of white lilies and said he would give the spurs to the arena steward so she didn't have to risk carrying them on her lap of honour.

Charles, Margaret and Daisy were being escorted into the arena, and the sponsor presented them with a huge silver cup, as Gavin congratulated them as the winning owners.

As the suit moved on to give Rory his blue and gold rosette, Katie saw her mum in the stand and gave her a grin and a wave. Her dad was smiling broadly and telling the lady next to him that that was his daughter, the winner.

'You gave us a thrilling end to the competition, Rory.' Gavin was standing in-between The Mechanic and Peethofsky. 'It came down to time penalties on your show jumping round, but you must be pleased with how your horse went today?'

'Delighted,' drawled Rory. 'The aim was always Garwood, so this is a huge bonus. Although I'm hoping the winner will give me some kind of *consolation prize*, for losing to her by only half a point.' His eyes were firmly on Katie, and he gave a suggestive smile and raised his eyebrows.

Across in the warm-up, Roger felt the heat of his temper rising through his chest and waited as Gavin held up the microphone for Katie's reply.

'You can have my training vouchers, Rory,' she quipped.

Setting out in a slow canter, she led them on their lap of honour as the spectators loyally clapped and cheered. Tom, Caitlyn and Shelley had battled their way to the front of the crowd that lined the arena, and when Katie saw them, she rode The Mechanic closer to the barriers and carefully tossed her bouquet of lilies to Shelley. As she cantered to the arena entrance, the ring steward, in her tweed suit, held her arms outstretched, asking her to wait and, once the other horses had trotted out, told her to "take him around again".

Loosening him up, Katie sent The Mechanic off in front of the stands at a gallop, with Gavin inviting the spectators to show their appreciation for the new Scottish Champions. Steadying him around the far end as the crowd roared their approval, people were hanging over the barriers urging them on. Galloping down the long side, with ribbons flying, she raised her hand to thank the crowd who clapped and cheered; The Mechanic put his head down and gave a buck – he was absolutely thrilled with himself. She laughed out loud, tears of joy and emotion pouring down her face as she clung on to her neck strap under the sash as he bucked again. Bringing him back to a walk to leave the arena, she saw Roger standing alone in the middle of the empty warm-up ring; he was smiling at her, and she briefly bit her lip as she felt a tightening in her stomach. She knew now for absolute certain, that after winning the Scottish Championship, there was only one other thing that she really, really wanted.

The steward was calling her name, and as she turned in the saddle, the tweed suit came running across to her.

'Your spurs,' she panted.

Clutching the velvet box, she turned The Mechanic and rode up to Roger. 'For you.' She held out the box to him.

He frowned and shook his head. 'They're yours; you won them.'

'You gave me the ride on him. They belong to you.'

'I wouldn't have won it with him; he didn't go for me the way he goes for you.'

'I want you to have them.' She dismounted but kept her hand outstretched towards him.

He took the box from her and looked at it. 'It's not right, Katie, I've never won the Scottish Championship.'

'We couldn't have won it without you. Please, take them.'

He gave her a grin. 'They are the wrong colour for you.'

'What do you mean?'

'They should be rose gold, not silver.'

'True, but I've looked everywhere for a pair of rose-gold spurs with pink Swarovski crystals, and I can't find a set anywhere.'

'Thank God for that!' Opening the box, he admired the spurs glittering in the late afternoon sun.

'I hope they bring you luck.'

'Thank you.' He rested his hand on The Mechanic's hot neck, feeling proud but also slightly envious about how perfect their partnership was. 'I know they will.'

And they walked, side by side with the liver chestnut, rosettes fluttering, along the roped-off track towards the lorry park.

Twenty-One

The Cup and Kettle had not seen such champagne consumption since Roger's British Team selection.

Charles, Margaret and Daisy arrived first, brandishing the enormous silver cup, followed by Eddie and Joanna, Miss Mac and Mrs Fleming Bowen, Roger, Caitlyn, Shelley, Tom, Katie and, finally, Jules, who said she was feeling much better.

Miraculous recovery, thought Shelley, as she took in Jules's suntanned face and the smudges of mascara under her eyes.

'What a day,' sighed Katie as Tom handed her a drink.

'Brilliant day,' agreed Tom, who was wearing a pair of skinny leopard-print jeans and a pink T-shirt with "no photos please" on the front.

'You'll sleep well tonight,' said Mrs Fleming Bowen, who fleetingly wondered if Katie would be sleeping alone after such a big win.

When they went through to their table, Charles deliberately sat at the head, and Margaret and Daisy took the two seats to his left. This flummoxed Jules, who, fully expecting Roger to sit at the top of the table, suddenly found herself sitting on Charles's right. Roger held out a chair for his grandmother at the other end of the table, settled Miss Mac to her right and took the seat next to her.

Katie, keen to put herself as far away from Roger as she could, and not just for her father's benefit, sat down next to Caitlyn, who was manically chattering at Mrs Fleming Bowen. To her dismay, Katie then found she was opposite Roger, and her mother was sitting next to him.

Shelley, on a mission to find out why Jules had cried off coming to Auchenruther Castle, casually sat down next to her, with Tom on her other side next to Katie.

'What are you going to have, missy?' Tom opened the menu and called to Brian for another Salty Dog.

'I haven't had a Salty Dog in years,' sighed Mrs Fleming Bowen to Caitlyn and asked Brian if she could have one too.

'Have whatever you like,' Charles was pouring champagne into flutes and handing them down the table, 'tonight is on me as way of a thank-you to you all.' He listened to the chorus of praise before he carried on, 'Reckon Athward Hall has been the making of The Mechanic, and me, Margaret and Daisy are looking forward to seeing him run at Garwood now.'

Katie caught eyes with Roger and quickly looked away.

Miss Mac had no such tact and asked Charles why in the name of God he wanted the horse to go to Garwood after he had gone so well today.

Charles shrugged. 'Reckon the form he's in he might be in with a chance of another win at Garwood; after all, he's now the Scottish Champion.'

Roger raised his glass of champagne to Katie across the table before taking a sip.

'Exactly,' boomed Miss Mac, 'now he doesn't owe you a thing!'

Frantically, Roger shook his head at her.

Mrs Fleming Bowen was looking at the drink Brian had put down in front of her. 'This isn't a Salty Dog,' she complained stiffly.

'Yes, it is Mrs F.B, vodka and grapefruit juice.'

'No, that's a Greyhound. A Salty Dog must have a salt-frosted rim.'

'I would have his shoes off and turn him out for the winter,' Miss Mac was continuing despite Roger's attempts to discourage her. 'A three-day takes great strength from a horse.' She pushed her champagne away and returned to her brandy.

'What do you do, Daisy?' Eddie was scanning the menu.

'I'm doing my A levels next year.' She slipped her dessert spoon and several packets of tomato ketchup into her handbag.

'Then what are you going to do?'

Daisy was bored and wished she was sitting on the other side of the table.

'I want to be an event rider like Katie,' she replied, making Eddie choke on his champagne.

'Feeling better?' Shelley was trying to decide between the chicken and the lamb.

Jules nodded. 'I really wanted to go today too.' She buried her face in the menu.

'You missed a good day out.' Shelley decided on the chicken and placed her menu on her placemat. 'What was wrong with you anyway?'

'I had a migraine, probably too much wine last night.'

'Steak for me,' said Tom finally. 'What are you having, missy?'

Katie yawned. 'The chicken and more alcohol to keep me awake.'

'Would you like my Greyhound?' Mrs Fleming Bowen handed her cocktail to Caitlyn to pass to Katie. 'It isn't as good as I remember them being.'

'Probably because you had already drunk several Dirty Martinis before ordering a Salty Dog,' said Roger before turning to Joanna and asking her when she and Eddie were heading back south.

'Tomorrow morning, after breakfast. We've managed to get a room here tonight, so we'll call in and see Katie before we head off.'

'Come and have coffee on the lawn.'

Saying that would be wonderful, Joanna buttered a bread roll and looked over the ice bucket at Katie, stating she looked tired.

Lowering his voice and leaning closer to her, Roger encountered the same slanted brown eyes and high cheekbones he had become accustomed to fantasising about. 'She's had a tough week with me being confined to barracks and did incredibly well with Warrior today, considering before last week she had ridden him only once before.'

'Who owns Warrior?' Joanna looked around the table.

'I do.'

'I didn't realise.'

Roger said it was a long and complicated story.

'He's a nice horse, will you keep him or sell him on?' Joanna thought about taking a bite out of her bread roll, then decided against it.

'I think he could be a very good horse in a few years, but it's hard to keep hold of them, especially when the price is right and there's a yard to run.'

'Eventing is not a cheap sport,' agreed Joanna, 'and my husband would tell you it's not a sport at all.'

'Is he really so against his daughter doing something she loves?' Roger took the bottle from the ice bucket and refilled her glass.

'Absolutely. He wants Katie to work for him and cannot understand that office work is not for her. I haven't seen her look this happy for an awfully long time.'

Roger flashed a look across the table to where Katie was laughing helplessly as Tom performed his famous impression of Petra throwing a strop, and Joanna noticed his eyes changed as he looked at her.

'I don't suppose you would be interested in someone buying a share in Warrior?' she asked quietly.

He picked up his champagne and watched the bubbles rising. 'I might be. It would depend on who was interested and what sort of percentage they wanted.'

'It would obviously be entirely on your terms.'

'And I would want to keep the ride on him.'

Joanna looked at him inquisitively. 'She's not at that level yet, Roger.'

'But she will be, in a few years.'

As the food arrived, Charles, who had spent the first part of the evening paying attention to his wife and plying her with over half a bottle of champagne, turned his attention to Jules.

'Do you compete?' He filled her half-drunk glass to the brim.

Jules shook her head, making her blonde hair sway. 'I applied to be Roger's new work rider, but he gave the job to Katie instead.'

'You're young; I'm sure your time will come.'

Jules sliced the mushroom on top of her steak. 'I'm two years older than Katie, so I'm not sure that's true.'

'Did you see Smith's column this week?' Charles was leaning in to look down Jules's low-cut top, and he spoke so quietly that she had to lean closer to him to hear.

'Me and the rest of the world.' She moved on to her grilled tomato. 'They're both denying it, but I know that it's true.'

Shelley, listening with one ear as Tom on her other side asked if anyone had a chainsaw handy to enable him to cut up his steak, gave nothing away and continued to eat her Hunter's chicken as if she was in a world of her own.

'You *know* it's true?' Charles was speaking softly. 'How?'

Jules looked into his eyes and smiled arrogantly but said nothing.

Twenty-Two

A little after ten the next morning, Eddie drove his purring Jaguar through the pillars at Athward Hall.

Joanna, nursing a headache after so much champagne, thought how much she had enjoyed Roger's company the previous evening. He had the most wonderful ability to make whoever he was talking to feel as though they were the only person in the room, and although she got the impression there was a flashing temper hidden beneath those impeccable manners, as he kissed her goodnight, she thought how easy it would be to forgive him for anything.

Eddie, in the same way his daughter had done seven months earlier, drew in his breath as Athward Hall, in its glittering sandstone, peeped through the trees.

What a place, he thought. No wonder the six-foot-tall bastard was so smooth, living somewhere like this.

The stable yard was quiet. The horses that had been at Auchenruther Castle were in the field looking like medieval jousters in their fly sheets and mesh masks, and when Joanna peered inside the stables, there were doors standing open with wood shaving trails escaping them, indicating everyone was out on a ride.

They returned clattering into the yard through the tunnel to the outdoor school, the sound of their conversation and laughter bouncing off the sandstone walls as Joanna inhaled the smell of hot horse and deodorant.

Roger, riding a small black horse with four white feet, slid to the ground and greeted Joanna by kissing her cheek and Eddie with a firm handshake. Asking Caitlyn if she wouldn't mind sorting out Cooper for him, he swept Eddie and Joanna up to the Hall.

Sitting on Roger's terrace, the three of them were halfway down the first pot of coffee when Katie, Shelley and Caitlyn appeared.

'Where's Jules?' Roger handed Caitlyn a cup as she drooled longingly at Mrs Royal's thistle-shaped shortbread biscuits.

'On the phone, said she would follow us up.'

'Is Tom off today?' Joanna asked.

'Tom doesn't actually work for me, despite the number of hours he spends here. He works for a racehorse trainer on the coast.'

'He's moving his stuff to Jonny's this afternoon.' Katie sat down on the balustrade that separated the terrace from the front lawn.

'Does he have much to move?' Roger was handing the plate of shortbread to Caitlyn.

'Seventeen designer handbags, lots of face cream and some teapots,' replied Shelley. 'And he's most upset that he can't find his orange boiler suit that he swears he left at the Dorchester after staying over. We've had the bloody place upside down and can't find it anywhere.'

Joanna caught Roger giving Katie a quick glance.

'Anyway,' Shelley carried on as Jules sauntered into the garden, 'a couple of carloads should get his stuff to Jonny's, and Katie and I will regain control of our bathroom.'

'He's taken over every surface,' agreed Katie. 'He should have shares in Clinique.'

'Especially their Surge Intense seventy-two-hour lipid replenishing hydrator cream,' added Caitlyn.

'I'm afraid, Jules, if you want a coffee, you and Caitlyn will need to make another pot.' Roger handed her the coffee pot and watched Caitlyn grab another piece of shortbread from the plate before they headed inside.

Offering to give Eddie and Joanna a tour of the garden, Shelley watched as Roger led them across the lawn before looking over her shoulder into the house. As Eddie and Joanna began their inspection of the long border, Shelley grabbed Jules's phone. Swiping it open, she tapped the screen a few times and took out her own phone to photograph it.

'What the hell are you doing?' hissed Katie.

'Just shut up and keep a look out – I've got a theory.' She took more pictures, quickly closed Jules's phone and slid it back on the table where she had left it.

'And all this land is yours?' Eddie took in the rolling terrain at his feet as it fell away down to the river and trees.

'Across to Low Farm on the left and the village on the right. It's all leased out as grass parks and arable; I don't need much for grazing, and we use the fields off the drive as they're nearer the yard.'

'I hope you've got a good agent getting you top dollar.'

'Very good.' Roger smiled.

After another coffee, Joanna announced that they must go.

Hugging her mum, Katie asked her to come again soon.

'I might come to Garwood after all,' Joanna whispered back.

∼

With Tom's car full of bin bags and his favourite teapot seat belted onto the passenger seat, he took the last of his possessions to his new home above Jonny's stables. Katie and Shelley had accompanied him on his previous trip to see his room, and although Tom had described it as a "bedsit", "flat" would have been a better word.

Standing on Tom's bed and looking through the window in

the roof, Shelley could see the sea, and he had a shower, sink and toilet behind a partition on one side of the room.

'It's really nice, Tom,' said Katie, bouncing on the bed, making Shelley hit her forehead with a *thunk* on the Velux. 'Promise you'll still come and visit us in our scruffy Dorchester?'

'You try keeping me away, sweetie.' Tom squeezed her arm. 'I'll have to get my Roger fix somehow now I'm not living there, and I can't use my bath bombs in a flippin' shower.'

Watching Tom driving away with the last of his teapot collection, Shelley announced she was going for a shower and, grabbing her phone, the notepad that usually lived on the table in the lounge and a pen, she proceeded to lock herself in the bathroom.

Trying to stay awake to watch *Emmerdale*, Katie picked up her phone, hearing the message alert. *I have an idea of where the orange boiler suit is.*

Laughing to herself, Katie replied that it might be best if Roger kept quiet about that.

Shelley's hands were shaking. She swiped to the gallery on her phone and wrote down some numbers from Jules's call lists from the past nine days that she had photographed that morning. Then she sat on the closed toilet lid with the shower running, tapped one-four-one and made her first call.

There were several calls to different names that must be Jules's friends; alarmingly, there were two to a Petra, and when Shelley called it, she heard Petra Williams' unmistakable rasp and hung up. Other unidentified numbers included a clothes shop in Newcastle and a local garage and restaurant. But there was another number that kept coming up again and again on the list; Jules must have made and received at least ten calls from this number. Feeling sick, she tapped it into her phone and almost dropped it when the call was answered.

She put her phone on the windowsill, took off her clothes and got in the shower. She needed to think.

Half an hour later, Shelley emerged from the damp, steamy bathroom wearing Katie's fluffy dressing gown and went to the kitchen to pour two vodka and tonics.

'What's this?' Katie threw down *Horse & Hound* in mock distress. 'What happened to limiting vodka to weekends?' She imitated Shelley's Scottish accent.

Shelley didn't smile.

'What's wrong?' Katie sat up.

'I need to double check something.' Shelley swallowed. 'If I read out a number, will you ring it? I just need to know I'm right about something.' As Shelley read the number from the piece of paper in her hand, Katie punched it into her phone.

The phone rang a few times before the answering machine cut in.

'*Welcome to* Stable Tattle *magazine. For features, press one. For advertising, press two. For—*'

Katie hit the red button and sat staring at Shelley. '*Jules?*'

'Yes.'

'Did you look at her emails?'

Shelley shook her head. 'Didn't think.'

Roger ducked his head under the doorframe at the top of the Dorchester's stairs; he assumed something was wrong as Shelley had insisted that he come to the flat and had refused point blank to come to the Hall.

'Jules's call list from her mobile,' said Shelley shortly, handing him her scribbled numbers.

'How did you get that?' he asked in astonishment.

'Photographed it this morning while she was making coffee and you were trying to impress the hell out of her parents.' Shelley tipped her head towards Katie.

'Do you pick locks as well?'

She considered for a moment. 'I do,' she said eventually, 'but I'm not very good at it, takes me ages.'

'Your point is?' Roger was looking at the scrawls of numbers.

Shelley walked over to the table. 'This one,' she picked up a pen and circled a number, 'I think you'll find very interesting.'

'I don't drink vodka,' he said automatically as Katie handed him a glass, but as she stood there waiting for him to look up, he saw she was holding a glass of whisky.

'Tom left you a bottle as a thank-you for letting him stay here. I took the liberty of opening it for you.'

Roger took out his phone and dialled the number. There was a silence as he listened to the answering machine. 'The fucking little bitch,' he said softly as he ended the call. 'It was her. Her who found the earring. What a snake.'

Shelley was puzzled. 'What earring?'

'The earring I lost when...' Katie stopped and blushed. It was suddenly very embarrassing having this three-way conversation. Shelley might indeed know the exact dimensions of Roger's cock, but she didn't particularly want Roger to know exactly how much Shelley knew.

'Tom's earring that you lost?' Shelley narrowed her eyes. 'Where was it?'

'Under my bed.'

'Wait, wait!' Shelley was marching around the room. 'She,' she pointed at Katie, 'loses an earring under your bed and Jules finds it? What in the love of God was Jules doing in your bed?'

'She wasn't in my bed,' said Roger irritably. 'It was apparently under my bed until the night of the owners' party when it disappeared.'

The realisation sunk in, and Shelley dropped whimpering into the sofa. 'Oh God, it's my fault.' She looked at Roger, feeling quite ill. 'We apple pie-ed your bed.'

'That was you? You and who else?'

'It was me,' groaned Shelley. 'It was me, Tom, Caitlyn, Jules, and I think Josh was there too.'

After spending the last forty-eight hours not knowing who to trust, Katie was starting to feel relieved, although it was now clear that Jules was going to stop at nothing until she was fully humiliated.

'You complain about my housekeeper ironing your knickers, yet you thought it was alright to take a hoard of people into my bedroom?'

'I'm sorry; I was drunk, and I thought it was funny at the time. When we got back downstairs, Jules wasn't with us, said she'd got lost.'

Roger closed his eyes; he was tired.

'What are you going to do?' Shelley was sitting next to Katie on the sofa.

'I will have to go and see her.'

'If you'd kept it in your pants, we wouldn't be in this situation,' said Shelley coldly.

'Mind your own business, Shelley.' Roger swirled the last of his whisky around the glass.

'It could be worse,' said Katie resignedly. 'You could be shagging Danny Jenks.'

Shelley shot her a look of disgust. 'Thanks, Katie, thanks a lot.' She downed her vodka and tonic.

Roger started to laugh. 'Oh my Lord, Shelley, you weren't?'

'She was, until Mrs Jenks clobbered her with a Le Creuset casserole dish at the Great Yorkshire.' Katie got up and gestured for Shelley to offer up her glass so she could pour her another.

'I bet that hurt.'

'In every sense of the word,' Shelley watched Katie go into the kitchen, 'but at least I didn't shag Petra,' she finished.

He shot her a venomous look as he left.

~

Parking his car in front of the double garage at Jules's parents' home the next morning, Roger was trying to hide how wretched and betrayed he felt.

She had taken him in entirely. He knew she was a spiteful bitch, but he had in no way anticipated the treachery lurking beneath such a pretty exterior. He thought she was just a spoilt, huffy woman, and the Smith's story had shocked him – he had meant what he said to Katie; he wasn't sure he had the mental strength to deal with Smith's all over again.

He should have listened to her. She had told him again and again there was something devious about Jules, something bitter and twisted that extended way beyond the black hatred of her. Shelley had also warned him there was something distinctly wrong with Jules, something which had escalated since Katie came to Athward at the end of the winter. But he had felt nervous about getting rid of her. She would have heard on the underground drums that she had been replaced, and Roger had been worried that Jules would turn up on his doorstep screaming unfair dismissal. It was also bloody hard to get good staff, and he had unwittingly put his other staff at risk by not being brave enough to let her go. He thought about the broken tack. There was no way to prove that it was Jules, but he felt resentful that she was going to get away with her attempts to cause what could easily have been a horrific accident.

As he knocked on the white front door, there was the sound of a dog barking and a woman's voice as she cajoled the dog away.

'Roger!' Pippa Patterson-Holmes opened the door and stepped aside to welcome him inside. 'Jules is at the gym, but she's due back at any minute.'

'I'll wait, if that's alright?'

'Of course, of course.' She led him past a closed door where the dog was growling on the other side and into the lounge at the back of the house.

'I just need to speak to Jules,' he said as he refused Pippa's offer of a seat.

'Would you like a cup of tea, while you're waiting?'

Roger shook his head. 'Perhaps you should leave us alone to talk.'

Pippa folded her arms and stared at him. 'This doesn't sound good – is there a problem?'

'I just need to talk to her.'

'Tell me, Roger. Maybe I can help.'

'I'll just wait for her, thank you.'

Almost on cue, there was the sound of the front door being opened and then slammed, and Pippa called out that she was in the lounge.

There was a silence as Jules came into the room and saw Roger standing stiffly by the ornamental fireplace.

'Hi,' she said easily, 'do you need me for something?'

Roger was seeing her through new eyes, and he wondered how any man could ever find her attractive with her haughty expression and downturned mouth. She had obviously showered after her gym session – her blonde hair was freshly blow-dried, and her make-up was as perfect as ever. The tight black T-shirt was low enough to give him a glimpse of cleavage, and Roger found himself wondering if the shape of her body was the same when she took off her too-tight clothes.

'Why don't you sit down,' he suggested.

'No thanks. Do you want me to work this afternoon? I can, but I'll need to make a phone call—'

'I don't want you to work this afternoon.'

Jules raised her shaped eyebrows and looked at Pippa.

'Roger, what is this all about?' Pippa was frenetically scratching the inside of her wrists.

'Pippa, I really think you should leave us.'

He saw the change in Jules's face; just for a second, a shadow passed across her eyes before she recovered herself, and the blue eyes took on a look of insolence.

'I think I should stay,' said Pippa uncertainly.

Roger shrugged. 'Alright then. Jules, I believe you have been speaking to *Stable Tattle* magazine, and I think it was you who persuaded them to write about me in Smith's Gossip Corner.'

She started to laugh. 'Why on earth would you think that? I've got better things to do.'

'You made over ten calls to the offices of *Stable Tattle* last week. Were you fine-tuning the copy you had sent them? Would it not have been quicker to send your amendments by email?'

'Is this true?' said Pippa, scratching her wrists even harder.

'No! It's none of my business who he's shagging or not shagging.'

'I can WhatsApp you the photograph of your call list, if you like?' Roger began taking his phone out of his pocket.

'How the hell did you get that?' Jules's face was turning red. 'That's an invasion of my privacy; I could go to the police.'

'And I could sue you for breaching the terms of your employment contract.'

'Piss off,' spat Jules.

'The terms clearly state that you are to have no contact with the media regarding your job or any aspects of it.'

'I haven't said anything to the *media*,' she snarled.

'It was you who found her earring. That's how you knew. It wasn't just a lucky guess, was it?'

'Just admit it, you're all over her, and she's like a lovesick puppy trailing along behind you.'

Pippa saw Roger's jaw tighten dramatically.

'All the time you spend with her, and you think no one knows that you're fucking her?'

'That is none of your business.' He was clenching his teeth, knowing he couldn't afford to lose his temper.

'What?' asked Jules in disgust. 'You're practically old enough to be her dad!'

'You told Charles Dee you knew what Smith's had written was true. Do I need any more proof that it was you?'

'Fucking Shelley!'

'Do you want to sabotage her tack as well?'

'W-what do you mean?' Pippa was looking shocked; it seemed to be the most dramatic thing that had ever happened in her life.

Roger turned to her. 'Suspiciously snapping martingale, stitching cut on a set of reins, a severed girth strap on Sunday, which I found seconds before the start of the cross country. I'm sure there's more; we just haven't found it yet.'

Pippa's nails were scraping her wrists more quickly.

Jules turned her head slowly and looked blankly at Roger; then she shook her head. 'I didn't do that.'

'Sure,' he replied mockingly.

'I didn't,' she said fiercely. 'I might hate that stupid, stuck-up cow from London, but I would *never* put a horse in danger.'

'I don't believe you.'

'I would *never* do that to a horse,' she was looking straight at him, 'and I wouldn't do it to you either.'

He ignored her last comment. 'I'm sure you have more in your poison pen for *Stable Tattle*, so I doubt you need the money, but your wages up to today, and any holiday pay you are owed, will be in your bank account by close of business tomorrow. I will never see you on my land ever again – is that clear? If I see you anywhere near my house or my yard, I'll call the police.'

'Whatever,' said Jules in a bored voice.

'I'll see you out.' Pippa was out of her seat and holding open the lounge door with a shaking hand.

Giving Jules one last threatening look, he marched out and strode down the hall to the door. The dog was barking again, and he hesitated. It was a deep bark from what was obviously a big dog. He reached out and began to open the door.

'Oh, leave him, Roger.' Pippa was tearing at the insides of her wrists again. 'He'll jump all over you.'

He ignored her and pushed the door open. A large, silver-grey Weimaraner burst into the hall and leapt around him, jumping up and clawing at his legs through his jeans. He patted the dog's silken head and gently pushed him down.

'Did you enjoy your day out at Easton Mains, Pippa?' he asked softly. 'You could have come with us in the lorry and got in for free.

Then you could have had a day out with your daughter, instead of being out on the cross country course, alone with your dog.'

Pippa's face had gone white, giving Roger all the confirmation he needed.

'It was you.' He glared at her. 'It was *you*, you stupid, dangerous cow. Do you have any idea of what you could have done?'

'I think you need to leave.' Pippa's face had hardened, and she was holding open the front door.

Roger clutched his head. 'It was you. Cycling around my yard at all hours of the night, no wonder you had time to find your way around the tack room. Did Jules tell you where the key is hidden? Did you mean to just damage Katie's tack? Did you get mixed up and cut the reins on Bluebell's bridle by mistake?'

'Leave.' Pippa pulled the door even wider.

'Does Jules know it was you? You do realise that *she* could have been riding in your handywork?'

'Leave!'

'Is there more?'

He caught the flicker across her face, the manic look of pleasure before her usual features settled back into place.

'There is, isn't there? You've done something else we don't know about.'

'Get out, now!' Pippa rattled the door, making the keys in the lock jangle.

'I'm going. If I stand here for another second, I'm going to be done for assault. No wonder your child is deranged.'

Getting into his car, he rang Shelley – Christ, his hands were shaking he was so angry. What a stupid bitch; he shuddered as he thought about the partially severed girth strap on The Mechanic's jumping saddle. How the hell it had even held for Katie's warm-up was a miracle.

'Where are you?'

'Malaga,' replied Shelley sarcastically.

He was reversing rapidly off the drive at Sweet Meadows.

Christ, the irony of the house name. 'Shelley, where are you?'

'We're riding out, the three of us. I'm assuming it didn't go well?'

'Did you check the tack before you got on?'

'Yes, like you told me to,' she said patiently.

'There's something else; she's done something else that we haven't found. I could tell by the look on her face.'

'I've checked everything; I can't find anything else.'

'Don't say anything to the others – I'll be there in five,' he said and hung up.

∿

Roger looked at the three faces staring at him across the tack room table. 'Any questions?'

'But we're not to say anything?' asked Caitlyn cautiously.

'Not a thing.'

'So, we say nothing about an ex-member of staff who's gobbed off to the press and her psychopathic mother who's tried to kill you both?' confirmed Shelley.

'I don't want to be done for slander.'

'What if she's done more?' Katie had been silent throughout the whole debrief.

'We've checked saddles and bridles until we're blue in the face – there's nothing else.' Roger gave Shelley a warning look.

'Why did she do it?'

'I don't know if it was some crazy attempt to stick up for Jules; we'll never know.'

'Or it could just be that she's completely off her tits.' Shelley had picked up Tom's *Gay & Out* magazine.

'It could be that too,' acknowledged Roger. 'So, are we good?'

He waited until all three heads nodded.

∿

On Thursday morning, as Katie and Shelley were riding The Mechanic and Bluebell along one of the tracks through Roger's woods, Shelley's phone rang.

'Stand by your beds, sweetie.' Tom was sitting in Jonny's kitchen, watching Mrs Bell piling bacon onto a yellow plate. 'The Rogerable Roger is going to go absolutely mental when he sees what Smith's has come up with today.'

Shelley groaned. 'What does it say?'

'I'll send you a photo of it.'

Tom need not have bothered. Because when they returned to the yard, Caitlyn handed Katie an envelope that had just arrived by courier, inside which was a copy of *Stable Tattle* and a very bent silver horseshoe-shaped earring with blue stones.

'Come on,' Katie opened the magazine on the tack room table and braced herself, 'we may as well read it together.' She turned to page fifty-six.

Last week I revealed that an old Northumbrian friend was cavorting with a spectacular new filly thirteen years his junior, and I warned of fireworks at Auchenruther Castle as Mummy and Daddy were going to be in attendance.

One and all had done a simply sterling job keeping my column hidden from Daddy, so imagine my glee when he collected a complimentary copy from our very own trade stand. Despite a brief altercation with the filly, Daddy was quickly placated by my old chum, and it seems the way is clear for the stallion and the filly to resume.

I hear the Dally across the Valley is not pleased, perhaps as she knows she won't be getting the super stud servicing any time soon.

'Christ, Petra's going to go crazy,' said Shelley.

After the filly's roaring success in the Merlish-Waller sponsored Scottish Championship, the celebratory party was a champagne-

fuelled affair. Not only did my old mate enjoy the close company of the filly's dam, but an incredibly happy owner got up close and exceedingly personal with the young filly and even enjoyed a quick frolic. Either the young filly will do anything to keep a ride or has a penchant for stallions nearer Daddy's age.

I'm sure the lucky owner does not regret his pleasurable experience getting under the filly's wrappings, but things could get tricky next season when his own produce starts riding from the stallion's yard. The haylage will be flattened from all the rolling.

Roger, seeing Katie retching in the sink and Caitlyn with her hand over her mouth, knew Jules had not failed him. He had been expecting something horrendous and now, as he read it, the poison almost oozing out of the page, he felt white hot with anger.

'Bloody little cow!' he roared, making Caitlyn tremble. Turning to Shelley, he asked her and Caitlyn to give them a minute.

Katie turned to face him, and he saw her take a shuddering breath. 'It's not true, before you even ask.'

Roger was shocked that he felt so thankful.

'There was nothing between me and your mother; we were just talking. Talking about you, mostly.'

'She even returned my poor earring.' Katie picked it up and turned it idly between her finger and thumb. 'This is all because of you,' she told it.

'Jules's way of admitting responsibility.'

She shook her head. 'Jules's way of sticking another knife in.'

'Are you alright?' He was leaning against the doorframe, looking very tall.

'I guess so – nobody's died. I suppose I should be pleased to be described as a "spectacular filly".'

Roger smiled at her.

'And not the "Dally across the Valley",' she finished with a smirk.

Twenty-Three

There was a vicious and bitterly cold north wind blowing off the sea and howling across the Athward Valley. Having dug out her winter jacket, Katie felt it was having little effect, and as she and Shelley turned Cooper and The Mechanic through the pillars at West Lodge, she suggested they trot to warm up.

'Going to be colder in Scotland,' Shelley warned as they jogged on towards the Hall. 'Have you got plenty of layers packed?'

'I haven't packed anything yet; I've got that to do tonight.'

Shelley watched the yellow leaves on the sycamore trees being whirled and spun around by the wind. 'It'll be bloody cold at night too. Are you taking your winter pyjamas? Or are you expecting something else to keep you warm in bed until me, Tom and Caitlyn get there on Thursday night?'

'Don't be stupid,' replied Katie hotly.

Shelley held up her hand towards her, stopping the barrage of insults. 'I'm just saying that you and Roger are going to be alone for a few days—'

'He in his hotel room and me in the lorry,' said Katie firmly.

'Well, you know, I just think you should be prepared. It's different being away from home.'

'I'm fully prepared thanks, and I don't need a pep talk from you.'

Shelley sighed. 'I just mean that you've managed to resist him for ages – don't give in to him now.'

'I don't intend to; I've got too much to think about, riding in my first three-day without any added complications.' Katie crossed the fingers of her left hand as she pictured Roger running out of the Dorchester in Tom's orange boiler suit.

'We could go to the pub tonight.' Shelley slowed Cooper to a walk. 'As you're not leaving early and you don't have to drive tomorrow, we could get very drunk.'

Katie shook her head. 'I can't; I've got to pack.'

A lot had happened since the Scottish Championship.

Katie had given an interview to *Horse & Hound* and had been given a whole page to herself with a very glamorous photograph of her holding The Mechanic's reins outside Roger's photogenic tack room. *Stable Tattle* had also asked to come and interview her, an offer which she had flatly refused, and The Mechanic's red, white and blue sash, complete with its golden tassels, had pride of place above the bar at the Cup and Kettle next to Roger's faded green and white European Championship rosettes.

Smith's column had continued to sneer at Roger and Katie, with the occasional dig at the bitter "Dally across the Valley", as Golden Knickers was now more commonly known. Despite appearing to shrug off Smith's comments, Katie was feeling more and more wounded as the weekly insinuations continued, especially when they alluded to her affair with Charles Dee, something which he was absolutely thrilled about.

While Roger wanted to take Caitlyn to Garwood to keep the fiery Warrior calm, without Jules to pick up the slack, he had been forced to tell her that he needed her to stay at home and look after the yard. Roger thought she had taken it very well until Shelley told him she had found Caitlyn weeping and wailing in the big horse's stable, with her arms around his neck.

'Then as I tried to give her a hug, the sodding animal bit me.'

'I haven't got an alternative,' he told Shelley crossly. 'I can't leave you at home and expect Caitlyn to groom at a three-day; she would probably load the wrong horses onto the lorry if I left it up to her.'

'There is an alternative.'

'I'm not poaching Tom from Jonny.'

'Tom's booked the week off; he's coming with us,' said Shelley airily.

'Christ almighty, Shelley, it's not a booze cruise for you and your friends. Would you like to traffic some illegal immigrants across Scotland in my lorry as well?'

'Tom's driving up in his car,' she objected, 'and he's a good groom – he'll help us.'

'Alright, what's your alternative suggestion?' Roger clamped his phone between his ear and his shoulder before quickly taking it in his hand and straightening his neck.

'You hire agency staff.'

'What the hell? Do you know how much that would cost for six days of cover? I'm not some bloody millionaire! Are you going to have a whip round in the Kettle to pay for them?'

Shelley reasoned that he and Katie could take the lorry to Garwood on Tuesday; there was nothing to do on Wednesday except exercise the five horses and walk the courses. Thursday was The Mechanic's dressage and Cooper's novice one-day when Katie could groom for him, and Friday was Bluebell and Warrior's dressage and Katie riding Lightoller in a one-day.

'Meaning, me, Tom and Caitlyn could drive up after work on Thursday and you would only need three days of cover.'

Realising that this was a remarkably good idea, Roger booked a lad from the agency.

That evening, with clothes littered all over her bedroom, Katie opened her biggest bag and began working through her list.

Roger, arriving at the Kettle and hearing from Shelley that

Katie was in the Dorchester packing for Garwood, left his bottle of lager and picked up his keys.

Following him out of the pub and ignoring Tom's knowing look, Shelley hung onto the car door as he went to close it. 'What are you doing?' she asked sharply.

'Going to get her so she can join us all for a drink,' he replied in a startled voice and wrenched the door out of her hands.

Hearing Roger calling her name from the top of the Dorchester's stone steps, Katie threw another pair of jeans into her bag and shouted for him to come in.

'I'm not coming for a drink,' she told him. 'I've got to pack, although I have no bloody idea what to take.'

'Then I'll help.' He moved a heap of polo shirts, sat down on the bed and picked up her list.

'You're not helping me pack my clothes,' she said in horror.

'Be quiet; empty your bag; and start again.' He scrutinised the list. 'Why do you need eight sets of underwear for five days?' he asked in bewilderment.

She giggled. 'Because I'm a girl.'

'Okay, jeans, five pairs. *Five pairs*? What are you going to do? Change your clothes three times a day?'

'Roger, you aren't helping.' She grabbed the list from him.

He snatched it back. 'As you were. Five pairs of jeans, these?' He held up the heap that was on the bed and she nodded. 'Four hoodies, seven polo shirts.' He counted them out and threw them into the bag.

'Don't you have somewhere else to be?' Katie rescued her favourite pink polo shirt from the pile he had discarded and added it to the bag.

'No.' He looked again at her list. 'Not until you've packed and will come for a drink with us all. Four pairs of breeches, four shirts and your stock.' He looked up at her as she added them to the bag.

'I suppose Mrs Royal has already packed all your navy clothes?'

She lifted an armful of socks from the floor and dropped them into the bag.

'She does many things for me, but packing is definitely not one of them.' He picked up the heap of pink and black thongs from the bed. 'All of these?'

'Do you have to? I'd rather handle my own knickers if you don't mind.'

'I have handled them before.' He saw her blush. 'What are you wearing for the cocktail party?'

'The dress I wore to your owners' do.' She pointed to the carrier hanging on the wardrobe door.

'Then I'll need to chaperone you; I don't want to see Charles mentally undressing you again.' He returned to the list. 'Pyjamas?'

She picked up two T-shirts and threw them in.

'*They* are your pyjamas?'

She lifted her hands in despair. 'Okay, okay, you win, let's go to the pub. I can't stand the embarrassment any longer.'

Laughing and throwing her list on top of the bulging bag, he said they should get three rounds in before last orders.

Twenty-Four

The journey to Garwood took them over the Forth Road bridge and along the wandering A9, skirting the edge of the Cairngorms National Park. Having never been as far north before, Katie was watching the scenery slip past in-between climbing into the living area to make yet another coffee for Roger and typing his dictated emails on his phone as he drove.

'Do you want me to ping one off to Petra too, inviting her for a drink tonight?'

'Some things are never funny enough to be joked about.' He momentarily looked away from the road to narrow his eyes at her. 'Why don't you have a sleep?'

Katie laughed. 'You might see the funny side in about ten years' time.' She yawned and put her feet up on the dashboard.

Although she wanted to stay awake, so she didn't miss a single minute of having him all to herself, five minutes later, she was sound asleep.

Roger had made the 250-mile trip to Garwood many times before, and although the A9 was a painful road, he still loved the drive and the scenery. Seeing Katie fast asleep across the two crew seats and wishing he could watch her instead of the road, his thoughts turned to his horses.

He had schooled The Mechanic a handful of times at Katie's request. The horse was vastly different to the hot-headed chestnut he had competed in the spring, and Roger acknowledged that Katie had made a good job of him. Warrior continued to be a strong and bold horse, very quick to learn and very impatient when asked to repeat things. Bluebell Folly had mellowed over the past few months and, although not as naturally talented as Warrior, was still an exceptionally good horse. Roger had high hopes for the pair of them for next season, presuming that they both came out of the winter sound.

Miss Mac was driving up in her beaten Subaru on Thursday and had booked into the same hotel as Roger in the town a mile and a half from the Garwood Estate. To both Miss Mac and Roger's horror, Charles, Margaret and Daisy were also booked into the same hotel. Roger hoped the Dee family wouldn't expect to have dinner with him every evening. He stood up behind the steering wheel to stretch his back.

They arrived at Garwood a little after four, and after Roger had taken the clutch of passports to the stable office, they were allowed to unload their horses into one of the dome-shaped marquees that housed the lines of the sliding metal doors of the stables.

After removing the travelling gear from the five horses, Katie shook out bales of wood shavings, filled water buckets and completed the stable cards which slotted into holders on each door. Roger was unloading the lorry and carting boxes of equipment, bridle and rug hooks and plastic bags of haylage, laying them outside his stable doors.

Wheelbarrows were upended between stables; there were rugs and bridles hanging from every spare ledge; and, as many competitors wouldn't arrive until tomorrow, the empty stables were marked with two yellow bags of wood shavings outside.

Further down the row of boxes, India was walking Rock On into a stable, calling out a greeting to Martin who groomed for Cathy Marks.

Cathy stopped to speak to Roger as she led her best horse, Travallio, to his stable. 'Have you seen the forecast?'

'I have. It's not great.' Roger lifted a bale of haylage off the stack in the wheelbarrow and threw it next to Cooper's door.

'Not great is putting it mildly,' snorted Cathy. 'We'll all have webbed feet by Saturday.'

The sound of the rain battering down on the roof of the lorry woke Katie at five the next morning. Cathy wasn't joking – it was absolutely pouring. Snuggling deeper under her duvet, she shivered. Garwood was renowned for its undulating cross country course, and as it was forecast to rain for the next three days, the cross country was going to be bottomless.

After riding in the torrential rain that day, Katie was on to her second set of waterproofs before lunch. In-between brushing The Mechanic and Cooper, she rang Shelley.

'Have you got everything?' Shelley was bringing Murdoch in from the field in glorious sunshine. 'Is there anything I need to bring?'

'A snorkel,' she replied.

❧

Charles Dee swung his Mercedes into the gravel car park behind the Croft Hotel. It had rained all the way since the Scottish Borders, and he was pleased he had packed his new full-length waxed jacket and wellingtons with their little silver buckles on the side.

Margaret, in the passenger seat, looking pale and drawn in her primrose-yellow dress, was not in a good mood. She had found a heap of *Stable Tattle* magazines hidden in Charles's wardrobe, in the space usually reserved for his porn magazines that he thought she didn't know about. Margaret had read all four of Smith's Gossip Corner's with shaking hands. Switching between intense fury that her husband was having an affair with Roger's work rider and panic that she would be destitute if he left her, she had been icily silent for the entire journey. It irked her even more that Charles hadn't even noticed and had chatted away to her for the whole duration of the drive.

Sitting behind her mother, Daisy could tell she was in one of her sulks; perhaps she had finally seen Smith's Corner. She put on her headphones and tapped her favourite playlist.

∾

Back in Northumberland, Miss Mac had called in to see Mrs Fleming Bowen.

'Are you sure you won't come?' she bellowed as Victoria poured Earl Grey into teacups. 'I've booked a twin room.'

Victoria thought for a moment. It would be quite nice to have a trip up to Garwood, and she hadn't been to the event for years.

'Do you know, Angela, I rather think I might – what time tomorrow are you leaving?' She sawed at a jaded lemon with a very blunt knife.

The satnav in Joanna's hire car told her she would arrive at the hotel around four, meaning she would have time for a long bath before meeting Katie and Roger for supper.

Eddie had decided that he could not miss his Friday morning meeting with a new and extraordinarily rich client, so Joanna, deciding that the six-hundred-mile drive without an overnight break was a ridiculous idea, had booked a return flight from Southampton to Aberdeen.

∾

After Charles had checked in and asked the receptionist the name of the best restaurant in town, he immediately rang and booked a table for dinner that night. Roger and Katie were just finishing up in the stables when he rang.

Roger rolled his eyes as he answered his phone. 'That's incredibly kind, Charles, but Katie is meeting her mother for supper this evening and has invited me to tag along.'

Katie swept the absconded wood shavings off the grass into Lightoller's doorway.

'Yes, alright, that sounds perfect, we'll all come.'

She stopped sweeping and looked at him in disgust, mouthing, 'What the hell?'

'No don't wait at the hotel; we'll see you there.'

Katie slid Lightoller's door shut with a bang. 'How could you? I don't want to have dinner with that bloody creep.'

'Sometimes you need to stroke your owners' egos.' He put his mobile in his pocket. 'Get your things from the lorry – Daniel's going to give us a lift back to the hotel.'

The little restaurant of El Camino, knowing there was an international horse trial a few miles down the road, had removed its usual Italian flags and had strung world flag bunting around the empty wine bottles and paintings that adorned the dining room. Seeing Charles, Margaret and Daisy already sitting at the table, Katie baulked.

'Please, Mum, will you sit next to him? He's the most awful letch and stares at my tits all the time.'

Roger grinned as Joanna declared that he certainly was not going to stare at hers in her new cashmere jumper.

'So, Katie,' Charles called across the table as she finished her calamari starter, 'anything good going to be in Smith's Corner tomorrow?' He sniggered and took a glug of wine.

Katie paused, spinning her fork around in her fingers.

'It's been belting, the past few weeks.' He took another swig from his glass. 'I'm not sure how we had time to fit each other in.' He laughed loudly.

Roger saw Margaret's face turning to her husband in horror as Daisy quietly slipped her knife, fork and the table's pepper grinder into her handbag.

'I hadn't noticed; I don't read it.' Katie put down her fork and tore up her bread roll.

'You must! All you youngsters read it – Daisy here is addicted to it.'

'Whaaat?' asked Daisy, pulling out her headphones.

'Do you know, I'm not very hungry after all.' Katie scraped back her chair, kissed her mother and walked out of the restaurant.

Joanna threw down her napkin, rising to follow her, but found Roger, placing a warm hand on her arm, and after whispering to her to keep the peace, went after her.

Outside, Katie was on her phone googling taxis.

'Bloody wanker,' she fumed. 'I feel sick at the thought of him… of him… of him even thinking about me. When he looks at me, I could throw up.'

'I know.' Roger took her phone out of her hand. 'Come back inside, finish your dinner and I'll book a taxi to take you back to Garwood.'

She slowly hugged herself, shuddered as though someone had just walked over her grave and then glared at him. 'If he makes one more comment about bloody Smith's, I'm going to smack him.'

Charles's leering comments didn't stop when the pasta arrived, and when they eventually left El Camino and he used his pudgy hand to stroke Katie's bottom, Roger finally flipped.

Grabbing Charles by the cape of his new waxed stockman, he rammed him up against the wall. 'Keep your filthy hands off my fucking staff!' he howled.

As a shocked-looking Charles, an ecstatic Margaret and Daisy staring at her phone with her headphones in, plodded off to the Croft in the rain, Joanna handed Roger her car keys.

'You've only had one beer – why don't you drive her back to Garwood? It would save the taxi fare.' She gave Katie a hug. 'I'll see you in the morning.' And, giving Roger a smile, she unfolded her umbrella and set off for the hotel.

'Thank you,' said Katie quietly as she fastened her seat belt. 'I liked seeing the shock on his face when you slammed him against the wall; he thought you were going to punch him.'

'It's a pleasure. I've wanted to hit him since I saw him pawing you at my owners' party, but unfortunately, I knew I couldn't go that far.'

They checked the horses using the light from Katie's headtorch and walked back through the rain to the hire car parked next to the lorry.

'I have a question,' said Roger, and as Katie began her "when a man and a woman love each other very much" speech, he told her to be quiet and open him a beer.

Turning on the lights in the lorry, Roger took in the double bed made up from the usual seating and table. 'Expecting someone?' he asked mockingly.

'I'm not sleeping on the Luton.' She made a face as she forced the cap off the bottle. 'It's claustrophobic.' She sat down next to him on her duvet and handed him his beer. 'What was your question anyway?'

He leant over and kissed her, for a moment enjoying the feeling of the softness of her lips and the way she responded to him so willingly. It turned him on just knowing that she wanted him so badly.

'That's not a question,' she said evenly, and her eyes followed him as he moved his face away and then began kissing her neck.

'The question was lager and lime or curry and poppadum?'

His fingers were stroking the back of her neck, and she could feel his hot breath close to her cheek. She kept her eyes closed, knowing what she should do but finding that the warm fizzing sensation in her stomach was making her feel dizzy.

'I assume by your reaction the answer is "neither".' He sighed, stood up and put his beer on the bench.

'You know I can't say no to you, but we shouldn't.'

He turned slowly and then knelt on the floor between her knees and kissed her again, his hands holding her head still as he kissed her cheeks and her mouth, before inclining his head and sucking gently on her neck, making her take a low, shuddering gasp.

'Get into bed,' he whispered, 'because I really want to take your clothes off and it's freezing.'

~

He woke at quarter to five and, as he swiftly dressed, was amused to find her sitting up watching him. He looked at his watch, realising with some regret that there wasn't time for a second round.

'I'll go, get a shower and my gear and then I'll be back. What time is your dressage?'

'Ten-fifty.'

'Plenty of time, Cooper doesn't start until one.' He pulled his jumper over his head and noticed her face had dropped. 'What's the matter?' He sat down on the bed and faced her.

'I just wish you could stay longer.'

He kissed her forehead fondly and then dropped his chin so his cheek gently rubbed against hers. 'So do I,' he said softly, 'but if I don't leave now, I'm going to get caught driving out of here and sneaking into my hotel room wearing last night's clothes.'

'And you don't want anyone to know you've been fucking your groom.'

'Don't,' he said sharply. 'It isn't like that!'

'What is it like?' She looked down and pulled her knees towards her, hugging them through the duvet. 'What exactly is it like?'

He paused and then said it was complicated.

'Why is it complicated?' Her voice was low.

'Katie, I am thirteen years older than you – if you were older or I was younger, it might be different.' He raised his eyes from her hands clasped around her knees. 'It *would* be different.'

'I don't care how old you are—'

'But it matters.'

'Not to me it doesn't.'

'It matters, and I shouldn't be here.' He kissed the corner of her mouth, and she pulled away.

'The thirteen years between us didn't seem to bother you last night. I'm not a toy you can pick up and play with whenever you feel like it.'

'I never meant to make you feel like that.'

'It's exactly how I feel. How can you be such a hypocrite?'

'I'm a hypocrite?' he asked fiercely. 'You behave as though I am practically invisible but are happy enough to roll over when it suits you.'

'How can you say that? I have never instigated anything – it's all been you.'

'And no wonder it's been so infrequent when you behave like the fucking ice queen after we've slept together.'

'For God's sake! You're the one who doesn't want anyone to know, as if it's some kind of dirty secret. You're like two different people, and I'm never sure which version I'm going to get.'

'You asked me to stay away from you, and I have. I should have just dropped you off here last night and gone back to the hotel.'

'Yes, you should. I'm sick of being your plaything.'

'Are you trying to tell me that you don't enjoy it?' He saw the blush spreading across her cheeks as he spoke. 'Because you seem to come awfully quickly, for someone who is hating every second of it and is simply going through the motions.'

She could feel her face burning. 'Doesn't that make you realise? Doesn't that make you stop and think for a minute? You can't keep doing this to me – I would do anything for you, and you clearly don't feel the same way about me.'

There was a silence, and as he looked at her sitting with her head lowered, eyes beginning to spill tears, he felt a darkness come over him. He wanted to protect her from every bad thing in life, to look after her so no one would make her cry. It dawned on him that he had completely overstepped the mark and had led her on, making her think there was more to come from their relationship.

He hadn't meant to; he liked her, and he liked being with her – now he felt his stomach churn with guilt.

'I'm sorry.' He lifted his hand and gently touched her chin with his fingers, encouraging her to meet his eyes. 'You are beautiful and bright and funny, but you need to find the right man, and I am too old to be him.'

'Do I have any say in this at all?' She bit her bottom lip as it started to tremble. 'Do you actually want to hear how I feel?'

'No. I don't.' He clenched his jaw and she saw the muscle flickering in his cheek.

'No one has ever made me feel the way that you do. Even just being alone with you makes me feel different.'

'I am too old for you. You said it yourself, the day I took you and Warrior cross country schooling. I was finishing my A levels when you were five years old—'

'I wasn't begging to be your girlfriend when I was five.'

'Begging won't make any difference,' he was speaking quietly, knowing she didn't want to hear what he was saying, 'it's not going to happen.'

'You should go,' she said finally, easing her hand away from his.

'I'm sorry. I should never have got involved with you.'

'*Involved*, that's a great way to put it. I feel so much better hearing you say that. It means a lot,' she said bitterly.

'I didn't mean—'

'Just go, leave me alone.'

After a moment, he put his arms around her and, after holding her tightly, expecting her to push him away, he felt her rigid body relax against his. Stroking her hair, he told her that he would always be there for her, whatever she needed – wherever she was in the world, he would be there. For a minute they sat locked together, Roger gently rocking her back and forth as she quietly cried.

'And when you find him, I'll be happy for you.' He brushed the tears from her cheeks and wondered if he was trying to convince himself that he was speaking the truth. 'I'll even threaten to ram him against a wall if he steps out of line.'

She closed her eyes tightly and two more tears ran down her cheeks. 'He will never match up to you.'

'He will; he will be everything you want him to be. He will give you more, much more than I ever could.' He looked into her eyes, knowing he was saying the right thing but aware that he must leave before he said anything more.

'Roger—'

'Stop,' he placed his index finger on her lips, 'leave it there. We both need to leave it there.' He stood up and looked at the wet tracks the tears had left on her face. 'You are so different to anyone that I have ever met.'

'But not enough.'

'More than enough, but in a different time.'

'If I could change it, I would. I would do anything.'

'I need to go.'

'Wait,' she got up and, after reaching into her bag, handed him his neatly folded jeans and shirt, 'the ones you left in the Dorchester, I couldn't think of a way of getting them back to you.'

He smiled. 'I had only worn them for an hour, you didn't need to wash them.'

'I-I did.' She looked up at him awkwardly. 'I wore your shirt in bed until it didn't smell of you anymore.'

'Oh, Katie,' he rested his forehead against hers and felt her shivering, 'I wish you had given it back to me smelling of you.'

'Don't say that; I know you don't mean it.'

He helped her back under the duvet and stroked her hair off her face.

'Is there nothing I can do? To change your mind?' Her face was crumpling, and she was beginning to cry again.

He shook his head.

She turned her back to him and felt him briefly entwine his

fingers in her hair. He hesitated at the door as if he was going to say something and then, switching off the light, he was gone.

She heard him close the outside door and listened to him jumping down the steps and the sound of the car starting. She pulled the duvet tightly around her and wept in earnest.

Roger drove quickly back to the Croft with shaking hands and a strange feeling in his stomach. He hoped he wasn't coming down with something; he really couldn't afford to be ill this week.

At ten-fifty, The Mechanic produced a particularly solid test and put himself in sixteenth place. In the afternoon, after a respectable dressage, Cooper had one down show jumping and, after a clear cross country, was ninth.

It was still raining.

Twenty-Five

Miss Mac and Mrs Fleming Bowen arrived at the Croft Hotel at quarter to five after a journey that involved four toilet stops and many phone calls to Miss Mac's bookmaker.

Buoyed by two good wins at Chester and Ripon, she reserved a table in the à la carte restaurant in the hotel and rang Roger.

Roger was holding Cooper while Katie washed him off and, as he answered his phone, he examined a small cut on the horse's knee. 'Yes, I would be delighted to join you.' Roger was now pulling the elastic bands from Cooper's plaited mane. 'Is Charles joining us?'

'I didn't invite him,' replied Miss Mac in a shocked voice.

'Thank God for that,' muttered Roger as he hung up.

News of Roger flattening Charles to the wall of El Camino had spread around the showground like raging wildfire.

'Did he really punch Charles because he groped you?' India asked Katie in awe.

'It wasn't really like that.' Katie flushed.

'Ahhh I'd love your boss to pin me up against a wall.' India's face had taken on a dreamy expression. 'He could keep his muddy wellies on, and I still wouldn't kick him out of bed.'

~

'For the love of God, Tom.' Shelley covered her eyes as Tom undertook yet another car and hurtled the BMW on towards Aviemore.

He patted her arm. 'Just close your eyes, sweetie; I'll have us there in no time at all.'

Caitlyn, with her mouth full of crisps, added that they must arrive there alive or they would miss Warrior's dressage tomorrow morning.

'Now,' Tom took his hands off the steering wheel for a moment to flap his hands wildly in Shelley's direction, 'do you want to message Roger's favourite work rider to say we'll bring a Chinese? Or do you want to heat up Mrs Royal's quiche in the oven in the lorry?'

'For fuck's sake, Tom.' Shelley shielded her eyes again as he hurtled across to the fast lane to overtake a postal wagon and a cement mixer. 'Can we just get there alive and then decide?'

'It's going to be after eleven when we get there – let's get Chinese. Ring ahead and order it.'

Katie, watching YouTube videos of previous Garwood cross-countries on her phone, was delighted when they arrived brandishing a bag from the local takeaway.

As Shelley unloaded more of Mrs Royal's supplies into the fridge, full to bursting point with chow mein, Tom unrolled his purple sleeping bag and threw it above the cab onto the Luton.

'I hope you don't snore, sweetie.' He flattened his pillow next to Caitlyn's feet.

The pair of them were asleep in minutes.

On the double bed below, Shelley angrily ordered Katie to swap pillows with her.

'You might want to reek of Hugo Boss in the morning,' she savagely punched her pillow, 'but I don't.'

~

'Oh my God, oh my God, oh my God.' Tom was standing outside the stables in the rain, gazing at Roger dressed in his peaked hat and black tailcoat.

'He is handsome, isn't he?' said Caitlyn distractedly as Shelley led Bluebell towards him.

'Sweetie, he's *divine*,' slobbered Tom, 'such incredible legs.'

'And Shelley's plaits are so neat.' Caitlyn screwed up the paper from her bacon roll.

Tom swung around to glare at her. 'Not the horse, you fool – I meant Roger.'

'Oh, I suppose. He's quite fit but a bit old though.' Caitlyn watched Katie leg him into the saddle and wipe his boots with a towel.

As Roger rode away through the drizzle, turning heads in every direction, Shelley handed Tom her bank card and told him to go and buy the ice creams.

'An ice cream in this weather, sweetie? Are you mad?'

'Welcome to Scotland,' she replied coldly.

Following Katie back into Bluebell's empty stable, Shelley closed the door, trapping them both inside.

'So, you've either drenched your pillow with a secret bottle of Hugo Boss or you've slept with him again,' she stated. 'Have you completely lost your mind?'

'Just leave it, Shelley.' Katie was forking through the wood shavings.

Shelley folded her arms. 'I thought this was all over – you *promised* me it was all over.'

'It was, and it definitely is now.' She slumped against the wall, sliding into a sitting position on the bank of shavings, her eyes closed tightly as she fought the tears that were threatening to spill out.

Shelley had been planning to completely bawl her out over this but, seeing Katie so obviously upset, she faltered. 'What's happened?'

There was a silence, and they could hear Shawn Mendes singing "If I Can't Have You" on India's radio hanging on its hook across the walkway.

Katie swallowed and took a deep breath. 'He's made it quite clear that it would be different if I was older or he was younger.'

'He's not going to ask you out because of the age gap?'

'Yes.' She put her face in her hands. 'Can you just stop now?'

'What a bastard! I presume he told you that afterwards?'

'I really don't want to talk about it.' She groped in the pocket of her jacket for a tissue.

Shelley crouched down beside her. 'I'm sorry. I know how much you like him, but he's a stubborn git who always has to do the right thing.' She used her fingers to put quote marks around the word "right".

'I really like him, Shelley.'

'I know you do,' she hugged her and felt the silent sobbing lurching through her, 'but if that's what he thinks, you've got to stop giving in to him. You'll end up cracking up if you keep sleeping with him.'

'I know.' Katie rummaged for another tissue as the original one had disintegrated on her jeans. 'I just thought… I don't know what I thought. I don't know what to think anymore.'

Shelley watched her as she resumed tidying the bedding. 'Are you thinking of leaving?' she asked suddenly.

'I can't stand seeing him every day. It hurts too much.'

'Don't make any sudden decisions, will you?' She slid open the door as Katie shook her head.

Bluebell did a good test in the light rain, and Roger found he was lying twenty-fourth as he warmed up Warrior. The big horse had been soothed by the arrival of Caitlyn, who had got him ready all on her own.

'One day he's actually going to open his mouth and answer you,' remarked Katie, listening to Caitlyn's endless stream of chatter as she plaited his mane.

'Probably just to tell her to shut up,' added Shelley.

Warrior did an astounding test and, as Katie watched while Shelley videoed it on her phone, she thought that he must be well up the leader board.

'He's ninth,' Tom told her later as she plaited Lightoller's mane, 'and that bitter old hag Petra is bloody seventh with that new bay horse of hers.'

'The one with the stupid name?' Katie teased an elastic band from her mouth to secure the plait in her fingers.

'It's called "Absolutely Naked", which I think is hilarious, and I don't think the stupid woman has worked it out yet.'

'I don't get it?' Katie began to plait the next section of mane.

'Think about the cross country commentary, sweetie.'

Lightoller was feeling the effects of a long season but was his typical reliable self.

'He was a star,' Katie told Jennifer on the phone later. 'He had a show jump down and was still seventh and the going on the cross country was really deep.'

Sand had been put down on every take-off and landing on the cross country course, but still Katie was worried about how the going between the fences would affect The Mechanic, especially as the much faster Lightoller had struggled to get around.

The Mechanic, Bluebell and Warrior were due to cross country the following day and, as she walked the bigger course with Roger again that night, she could feel the all-too-familiar nerves creeping in. The course was huge, and when she looked at the fences Roger was going to have to jump with his two, she felt quite sick. She was struggling to concentrate. In fact, she wished she could just curl up in bed and never get up again. After talking to Shelley, she had tried to pull herself together. Okay, so Roger didn't want her, but there were plenty of other fish in the bloody sea. She could go home and look for another job and, after almost nine months of working on the hallowed ground that was Athward Hall, she knew there would be other eventing yards who would want to snap her up. But the feeling in her chest, the feeling that was similar to homesickness, was atrocious and now, walking the course with him, the smell of him close to her, was making her hate him. How could he? He knew how she felt about him and had been happy to sleep with her and then announce that she meant nothing to him. Dully, she dragged her mind back to the rain-ravaged ground and The Mechanic's cross country. Bastard, she could win with The Mechanic – that would make her feel better, to achieve something with The Mechanic that Roger hadn't been able to.

The rain had finally stopped as they walked the final stretch of the course and Roger, the collar of his coat turned up, pointed down the hill to the last fence. 'Keep a hold of him here – if he's got any petrol left in the tank, he'll be running on down the hill, and you need to be in control and balanced to jump it.'

'Okay.'

'Are you alright?' Roger's eyes ran over her face.

'Fuck off,' she said grimly and marched off the course, leaving him gritting his teeth.

～

Shelley, Tom and Caitlyn were going to the Friday night party in the huge marquee which housed the canteen and doubled as a bar in the evenings. Katie had been invited to the owners' and riders' cocktail party in Garwood House and, after spending most of the day keeping as far away from Roger as possible, was more eager to go to the marquee with the others.

'You can't,' argued Shelley. 'Your owners are expecting you to be there – you have to go.'

Tom paused dramatically in his pink "what the actual f*ck?" T-shirt. 'Get a shower, sweetie, and I'll do your hair.'

'Her hair?' Shelley's head swivelled in his direction.

'I used to do all the girls' hair at school.' He turned to Katie. 'Go on, missy, quick shower and then we'll get you ready.'

Grumbling that she would rather go with them to the marquee, she grabbed her towel.

Tom, rummaging through the drawer beside the oven that housed the cans of deodorant, hairbrushes and Katie's dark-coloured hairnets, was overjoyed when he found the packet of hair grips that she used to secure her neat competition bun. After blow drying her hair, he set to work and, after twenty minutes, Caitlyn gasped.

'Why have you never done my hair before?'

'What have you done?' Katie put her hands to her head, her fingers feeling the perfectly messy bun and the tendrils teased out of it.

'It would be neater if I had some mousse and hairspray.' He held her head still as he stabbed in another grip.

'Bloody hell, Tom,' said Shelley in amazement. 'You're wasted riding out for Jonny; you should be a hairdresser.'

'I have many talents.' Tom combed down Katie's long fringe. 'Do we have any scissors?' After Caitlyn had handed him the pair from the cutlery drawer, he used his fingers to cut it diagonally across her face. 'There, missy. You look fabulous.'

Standing up, Katie viewed herself in the mirror that Shelley was holding up.

'Tom!' She turned and hugged him. 'You're amazing.'

He flapped his hands at her. 'Come on, Cinderella, do you want me to escort you to the ball? Or are you happy to yomp through the mud on your own?'

At the door to Garwood House, Katie pulled off her wellies and added them to the long line of boots in the hallway. Leaning against the wall next to a Munnings print in a gold frame, she slipped on her pink satin stilettos and checked her reflection in a huge spotted mirror.

'At last. I was just coming to look for…' Roger's words faded away, and she saw him catch his breath.

'I wasn't going to come, but they persuaded me that I had to.'

She took the champagne flute from his hand, drained it and, after handing him back the empty glass, walked past him into the party.

'My dear!' Miss Mac, wearing a trouser suit that was much too big for her, took Katie's hands and asked if she had a drink.

'Not yet, but I'm fine at the moment, thank you.'

Glancing across the packed hallway, Miss Mac saw Roger's furious look and suspected there had been a row.

'Evening, Pink Knickers.' Daniel handed her a glass. 'You are gorgeous in that dress; if I didn't love my wife, I would seriously want to get you out of it.'

She laughed. 'I think that's a compliment, so thank you. Where is Sara?'

Daniel tipped his head to the left. 'Talking to Charles Dee.'

'Oh, for God's sake, you can't leave her alone with him – he's a total letch!' said Katie impatiently. 'Go and rescue her. It's not funny, Daniel – he's a creep. Go.' She pushed a laughing Daniel towards Charles and Sara.

'You're late,' Rory Davison kissed her cheek, 'but now you're here, would you like to dance?'

'I've just got here,' she insisted, 'at least let me have a drink and schmooze my owners first?'

'Later then.' He kissed her shoulder before wheeling around to face Roger glowering at him. 'I'll dance with her later, Roger, when you've gone to bed. Then you won't have to watch us.'

'Where the hell have you been?' Roger steered her away from the crowd. 'Charles has been asking for the past hour where you were.'

'I told you – I didn't want to come, but Shelley and Tom told me I had to.'

'Do you think I want to be here? It's what you have to do to keep your owners happy.'

'I know that,' she snatched her arm away from his grasp, 'but I didn't particularly want to be in the same room as you, either.'

'Katie, I am sorry, but we need to work together—'

'No, we don't,' she interrupted, 'you don't own me.'

Grabbing her hand, he dragged her past the dancing couples and the chatter of the people drinking, past the line of wellington boots and out of the door. Ignoring how she was struggling against him, he pressed her against the cold stone wall of the outside of the house and leant down to look into her eyes.

'What do you *want*?' Her voice was shaking.

His hands softened on her arms, and he kissed her strongly. For a second, she kissed him back, before she placed her hands on his shoulders and pushed him away.

'That's enough.' She shivered. 'I'm sure there's someone nearer your age that you want to sleep with.'

He stood for a moment looking at her, his eyes blazing in temper. 'Why don't you go and dance with Charles,' he whispered evilly, 'and don't look for me to stop those roaming hands of his.' He turned on his heel and walked back into the house.

She took a minute, breathing calmly and telling herself to be the grown-up, and then followed him.

'Looking forward to tomorrow?' Charles's comb over was flapping over his red face, sweat beading on his brow and trickling down his temples.

'Of course.' Katie had deliberately waited for an upbeat song before asking him to dance, knowing it was the only way to keep away from his sweaty hands, but he kept trying to talk to her, so she had to lean towards him.

'Great stuff!' he shouted over the music. 'I can't wait to see my horse go clear!'

To her relief, the song finally ended, and while everyone was still politely applauding, the band struck up "Moon River".

'One more dance, eh?' Charles stared at her breasts.

'No thanks, Charles – I must go.'

'Shame.' His hand went around her waist and, just as she expected, his hand landed slightly too high and his fingers rubbed her breast firmly.

Trying to wriggle out of his grasp, she jumped when she heard Roger's enraged voice directly behind her.

'Touch her like that again, Charles, and I swear, I'll break your fucking nose.'

Charles raised his hands in mock surrender. 'No harm done, Roger.' He laughed and wandered off to find Margaret and his car keys.

'Are you alright?'

'Yes, thank you.'

'Why the hell were you dancing with him?'

'You told me to,' she said sulkily.

'I didn't mean smooch with the slimy bastard; you know what he's like.'

'I wasn't!'

'Keep away from him. We don't need this, not this weekend.'

'Except there's no *we*, is there?' she said nastily, before turning away from him and striding her way out of the room.

Roger watched her. Her head was held high in defiance, and she strode through the middle of two groups of chatting people before he lost sight of her.

Letting out his breath, he turned and walked back to Daniel and Sara.

'Are you okay, Roger?' Sara looked at him closely.

'It's all such a bloody mess,' he muttered.

'What is?'

'My supposed *private life*.'

Sara thought about Roger's flight path across the dance floor when he had seen Katie dancing with Charles; it had been like Moses parting the Red Sea. 'She's really nice, Roger.'

'Who is?'

'Katie,' she said impatiently.

'If you want another drink, we'll have to go to the marquee. The shutters are well and truly down here.' Daniel sat down on the winged chair opposite them.

'Thank God,' said Roger with feeling.

'Marquee, then?' asked Daniel hopefully.

Roger shook his head. 'Katie is on with The Mechanic in the morning, so we've got to walk the course again early. You guys stay; I'll get a taxi back to the hotel.'

Twenty-Six

The weather gods looked down on Garwood more favourably on cross country day. The sky was a glorious azure blue, marred only by fluffy aeroplane streaks, and there was a gentle breeze to keep the flags fluttering and the day cool.

Katie, quaking with nerves, was listening to Roger's last-minute instructions. His two rounds were both after lunch, and their final course walk at seven o'clock that morning had done nothing to ease her concerns.

Shelley was leading The Mechanic around them as they talked. She had a strange sense of apprehension; it was certainly the biggest course The Mechanic had ever faced, and she hoped they would both be alright. The ground was terrible. There had already been a number of casualties taken away in the horse ambulance, and the air ambulance had taken one rider with suspected spinal injuries to the Trauma Unit in Aberdeen.

Katie, Shelley thought, was obviously a tangle of nerves as she always was before cross country, but today was different. There was a blackness to her that she was trying her best to hide from the others, but Shelley knew she was hurting badly. She had arrived at the party in the marquee last night very sober, and when Shelley had asked her about the cocktail party, Katie had suggested that the edited highlights would be more interesting.

'Argument with the boss, tits fondled by Charles, followed by another row with the boss.' She drained her first vodka in one gulp. 'Perfectly sums up my entire life at the moment.'

After another vodka, Shelley had found her snogging Martin and had tried to prise her away, knowing damn fine she would regret it today. Initially, Katie was adamant in telling Shelley to mind her own business, but when Shelley made it back to the lorry half an hour later, Katie was already tucked up in bed, hiccupping tears.

Charles Dee, red faced with excitement, wearing his long, waxed coat despite the glorious sunshine, was standing where he could see the start and finish. He noticed Daisy taking selfies for Instagram and Margaret, sweating in her new tweed suit, studying Roger and Katie through her binoculars. He briefly wondered what the hell they were doing, standing in the middle of a muddy field in Scotland, and looked down the hill to where his horse was circling around the tall figure of Roger and Katie in her bright-pink colours. The horse was costing a fortune, and he still hadn't broached the subject of sponsorship with Roger. The idea of the Dee Garages' logo on the side of Roger's lorry had once excited him enormously, but that was before Katie had appeared on the scene, and now it was her that excited him. Three times she had ignored his subtle advances, and he wondered how he could speak to her alone and make it clear that if she fancied a bit of rest and recuperation time with him, he was most certainly up for it.

He glanced at Margaret gazing through her binoculars at the gaggle of people around their horse. Her hair had been coloured in preparation for their weekend away and, despite also being waxed to within an inch of her life, she still slept in a full-length nightie, an eye mask and a set of ear plugs to block out his snoring. It didn't really matter anyway, he thought. Even if she came to bed wearing stockings and suspenders, it still wouldn't disguise the fact that she looked like a famine victim. Picturing Katie in red suspenders and black fishnets, he smiled at his wife as she lowered her binoculars. Margaret, seeing the look of unrestrained lust in his eyes, wondered if he'd been watching porn on his phone again.

'Ride forward, but keep a hold of him.' Roger put his hand under Katie's knee and threw her into the saddle. 'If he's struggling, don't think twice about pulling him up. Not many are getting around, but if he is getting tired, stay off his back and see if you can nurse him home.' He watched her collect her reins and gave The Mechanic a little pat, unexpectedly feeling a sense of trouble. 'Good luck.'

'Thank you.' She said it automatically and kept her eyes on The Mechanic's ears.

Having had no appetite for the past few days, Roger refused Caitlyn's offered bacon roll and went off to watch Katie's cross country alone.

He was trying to keep his thoughts together and had fought with his concentration during their final walk around the cross country course that morning. He had his own course to remember and was desperately trying to make sure Katie was confident about her own course, as if in a stupid way to try and make up for breaking her heart. Katie's mood was shifting from being desperately needy and spitting fire at him in the blink of an eye. He knew she was hurt, and he felt dreadful and annoyed with himself for becoming so close to her.

The thought of her leaving was too awful to contemplate. Not only would he lose a brilliant rider, but Shelley would lose her best friend and he would be back to being on his own with only Shelley or Daniel to bounce his ideas off. Reserved ideas. There was always a part of him that he held back, the part of him that he had let Katie see. Talking to her was like talking to Daniel, only he never felt the need to guard his feelings because he knew she was as deep as the ocean. He could talk to her about anything, and she always gave both her honest opinion and a sensible solution. She was a source of reassurance to him that was both constant and positive, and they had been able to idle away the many hours travelling together very easily. He sighed heavily, clenching his jaw and his fists, and wished he had stuck to his resolution of never getting involved with his staff. This was a mess, and it was all his doing. He had lost grooms before after crossing boundaries but had never lost a rider as good as her. This wasn't just a mess, he thought, this was a total disaster.

He saw the tension in her shoulders as she rode The Mechanic around behind the start box, and he closed his eyes briefly, wishing he could go across and talk to her. As if she felt what he was thinking, she halted The Mechanic, rolled her shoulders back and tipped her chin upwards towards the clear sky. In his mind, he could hear the deep click that would have been emitted from the bottom of her sternum and, suddenly, she glanced across at him as if she could feel him watching her. She held his stare for a moment before she turned The Mechanic away.

'Two minutes,' advised the starter.

Miss Mac and Mrs Fleming Bowen were waiting at the beginning of the course on their hired off-road mobility scooters. They had planned their route across the course meticulously, with the aim to see The Mechanic jump every fence. Miss Mac checked her map one last time.

Joanna had kept out of the way, accepting that Roger seemed much better at keeping Katie calm, and cross country day was always fraught with nerves and drama. Seeing Roger standing alone, she walked across and stood beside him.

'Would you rather be on your own?' she asked politely.

He shook his head, giving her a tight-lipped smile. 'Are you nervous?'

'It's more nerve-wracking watching, than doing it yourself.'

'Did you event?'

She nodded.

'To what level?' He was watching The Mechanic circle closer

to the start box as the starter called out there were thirty seconds to go.

'Advanced.'

He gave a low whistle and glanced at her with a new-found respect. 'Katie never told me.'

'She's always wanted to reach the top under her own steam, not by being her mother's daughter.' Joanna adjusted her engagement ring instinctively before adding that she hadn't been that good and had only been placed at Burghley twice.

'Five, four, three.' The starter was gazing intently at his watch.

Katie turned The Mechanic's head, and he leapt from the start box. *Come on, mate*, she thought, *let's show them what we can do.*

Charles Dee snatched his wife's binoculars from around her neck and almost strangled her. Miss Mac and Mrs Fleming Bowen set off on their scooters, and Caitlyn clutched Tom's arm.

The Mechanic soared over the brush fence at number three, and Katie sent him on up the hill to jump the whisky barrels of number four.

'Sweetie, you're going to have to cut your nails before your darling Warrior goes around.'

Caitlyn looked down and saw nail marks in Tom's arm.

The Mechanic had jumped up through the sunken road at six and Shelley, holding her breath, saw him bounce cleanly over the hedge at seven and the black rails of eight before he disappeared out of sight behind the hill.

'Katie Holland is clear at nine,' the speaker crackled above Tom and Caitlyn's head as Shelley, wishing she smoked, walked aimlessly around staring at the grass. 'And we have a new starter, Rory Davison and Peethofsky, who are safely over the first, as The Mechanic is clear at ten and eleven.'

Joanna gripped Roger's hand.

'Peethofsky clear at two, and on a dressage score of twenty-four while out in the country, The Mechanic is clear at twelve and taking the direct route at thirteen.'

Miss Mac and Mrs Fleming Bowen were being thwarted by the throng that had gathered around the water jump.

'I'm very old and disabled!' boomed Miss Mac, and the crowds parted to let them through to the front.

Shelley saw The Mechanic coming back into view splattered with mud, Katie's face turning pink with exertion.

Sitting well back as he jumped down into the water, she sat up to drive him over the tree trunk and then hung left to jump up the step, bringing him neatly to the narrow rails.

'Bloody hell, that was good.' Roger realised Joanna was hanging onto his hand and gently let it go.

'Rory Davison is clear at fence number six, and The Mechanic is through the water, again taking the direct route, Katie Holland riding for Charles and Margaret Dee, on a dressage score of twenty-eight.'

Katie patted The Mechanic's neck as they galloped on. He was jumping superbly, that wonderful sound as he exhaled, and he was hardly pulling at all. She sat down as they approached the enormous wooden mushrooms that were number fifteen; he was starting to labour slightly, and she jumped the fence to the right where the ground was less churned.

Miss Mac watched closely as The Mechanic passed her; the horse was starting to look tired in the heavy going.

'We're nearly home,' Katie told him. 'We're nearly there and you are brilliant.' They jumped down the drop fence; Katie, clinging tightly to her reins, knew she was going to have to ride him carefully to get him home. He hit the next fence hard with a loud bang and twisted to the left as he landed. *Two more*, she thought, sitting down and closing her legs around him to hold him together. *Two more*. She again took him to the very right of the roll top for the better ground and let him ease down a gear so she could balance him down the hill to the final fence. She positioned him to the right of the hedge and realised that, unless she had stuffed up somewhere or had missed a flag, they were going to go clear.

'He's very tired,' observed Joanna as they landed over the hedge.

'But they're clear, and Charles will be a happy man.' Roger was beginning to relax.

'As long as he doesn't stroke her bottom again,' mused Joanna.

Katie let The Mechanic gradually slow on the run-in, completing the course in a sluggish, exhausted canter to the applause of the crowd along the ropes. Laughing with joy and relief, she patted his sweating neck again and again. Shelley was running alongside the horse as his trot became a walk, patting his neck as Katie hung out of the saddle to put an arm around her friend's shoulders.

'There's something wrong with him.' Roger was watching the horse as Shelley and Katie celebrated and Joanna looked at him in alarm. 'He's…'

The Mechanic's walk suddenly became disjointed and, as he began to stagger, his hindquarters sank to the ground. In slow motion, his shoulder fell sideways and, as Katie found her left foot on the ground, she jumped away from him in panic. Not knowing what was happening, she flipped the reins over his head and started to encourage him to get up.

Swearing, Roger started to run towards them as The Mechanic, now almost fully on his back, hindlegs sticking straight up in the air, rolled deliberately back onto his side, his uppermost hindleg sticking out poker straight.

The sandy-haired vet waiting at the finish to check The Mechanic's heart rate was quicker than Roger and, as he sprinted across to where The Mechanic lay, radioed for a doctor and the horse ambulance.

'There's no time, get back!' he shouted as Katie gathered up the reins at the horse's head.

'What's happening?' Caitlyn asked Tom in horror.

'It's a heart attack sweetie.' He put his arms around her and turned her away. 'Don't look.'

Daisy was covering her mouth with her hands.

'What is he doing?' Margaret was looking through her binoculars.

Charles didn't answer.

The Mechanic's limbs went rigid, and then he began to jerk violently. Roger grabbed Katie's shoulder and pulled her back as the horse's front legs thrashed aggressively towards her. Within ten seconds, The Mechanic was completely still.

The horse ambulance was racing across the turf, and the commentator announced that there was a hold on the course. Shelley was covering her face with her hands, and Katie could hear crying from the crowd. Someone was trying to pull her away, and she looked down at Roger's hand on her arm.

'I'm not leaving him.' She prised off his fingers and knelt beside The Mechanic's head, stroking his face, covering his glassy, unseeing eye with her hand.

The crew from the horse ambulance were rushing around them, holding the green screens up as high as they could, trying to hide The Mechanic's lifeless body from the anguished eyes of the crowds. Roger heard someone shouting that no one was allowed past the screening as Tom and a sobbing Caitlyn fought their way past the vet's assistants. Shelley was standing looking at The Mechanic in shock, watching tears pouring down Katie's face as she crouched over his pretty head. Roger dropped his arm from Katie's shoulders and sat back on the mud, pressing his forehead to his bent knees.

'How long do we have?' he asked the vet.

'As long as you need. Would you like me to take the bridle off?' The vet looked around the ashen faces.

Roger shook his head. 'No, I'll do it.' He got to his feet and, after calmly lifting Katie's hand from the flat cheekbone, he carefully pulled the headpiece over the floppy ears, tucked The Mechanic's tongue back into the half-open mouth and smoothed down the soft lips with a gentle hand. Looking at Shelley, he quietly asked her to take the horse's boots off and went to remove the saddle.

He unfastened the girth and with the help of the vet, they pulled the muddy saddle out from underneath the horse. Shelley was snapping the plastic tape off The Mechanic's boots, automatically putting the pieces into the pouch of her hoody. Katie still knelt at his head, and she leant down and kissed his hot face, still unable to comprehend what had just happened and just how rapidly it had happened.

'We should go.' Roger hitched her saddle onto his hip.

Shelley put down her armful of boots, crouched down to give The Mechanic a final kiss on the side of his soft nose and, after asking for a pair of scissors, cut off a strand of his muddy tail.

Roger watched Katie as she pulled a few hairs from the unplaited mane and silently handed them to a sniffling Caitlyn. She then pulled out some more, tied them neatly in a knot and zipped them securely into her breeches pocket.

'Come on.' He put his arm around her shoulder. 'You don't want to see him loaded; let's go.'

She looked at him, as if seeing him for the first time, and shrugged off his arm.

There was a collective moan from the bystanders as Roger emerged from a gap made in the screening, carrying the saddle and bridle. The uninitiated now knew for certain, seeing the saddlery and boots being brought outside the hastily erected tent, that the horse was not going to get up again. The horse ambulance was being reversed up to the screens, and Shelley saw the shocked faces of the spectators.

'Go to the lorry, all of you. Wait for me there.' Handing the saddle to Tom, Roger turned to speak to Charles.

Charles and Margaret were in complete shock. Margaret was shaking and Charles, who up until that moment genuinely thought horses just galloped and jumped all their life without encountering any complications, could not grasp what he had just seen.

'It's not common, but it does happen, and I am sorry that everyone had to witness it. Nothing could have been done.'

'What was it?' Margaret was hanging onto Charles's arm.

'Most usually it's a ruptured aorta; it's very quick.'

Strangers were offering their sympathies as Roger walked off the course, and he was glad to reach the inner sanctum and familiar faces of the lorry park.

Shelley had boiled the kettle and put four spoons of sugar in Katie's coffee. India, having heard the news, flung open the door and, with tears pouring down her face, told them she was so sorry. Receiving a nod of acknowledgement from Shelley, she quietly closed the door again. No one spoke, and Katie was trembling so badly she was holding her mug in both hands.

'Why did it happen now?' cried Caitlyn.

Shelley turned away from them on the sofa and pulled down the blind above the sink. They needed a moment to grieve.

There was a silence as Roger came in, his phone ringing madly. Rejecting the call, it immediately rang again.

'It's an awful thing to happen,' he said at last, 'but I've got two horses to ride this afternoon, and I need you all to focus.' His phone rang again and he switched it off. 'There was nothing anyone could have done.'

'It's alright – we know the drill.' Shelley's voice was thick, and she kept her back to him. 'What time do you want to be on Bluebell?'

'Quarter past.' He glanced at Katie. Her hair was plastered back with sweat, face drained of any colour, and her eyes were black with grief. 'It could have happened at any time.' He felt a wrench in his chest as she looked at him, and he saw the pain in her eyes.

Shelley turned to face him. 'We'll have Bluebell ready at quarter past, what about…' Her voice trailed away as she saw the look of fury on Roger's face.

'What is it?' Katie put her mug down on the table with an unsteady hand. 'What are you staring at?'

'Roger?' Shelley looked from him to Katie. 'What's wrong?'

'It didn't go off.'

'Help us out here, Roger?' Shelley was frowning.

'Her air jacket didn't inflate. The lanyard disconnected from her saddle, and it didn't bloody go off!' He took two strides across the living area and hauled Katie to her feet. Instinctively, she grabbed his arm to stop him and, seeing the blistering fury in his eyes, she tried to push him away.

'What are you doing to her?' Tom was struggling to get his long legs out from under the table. 'Roger, she's had a terrible fright, we all have!'

Roger stopped. His hand was gripping the shoulder of her body protector and, as Katie's grip on his arm slackened, he touched her cheek gently with his other hand. It was a tiny gesture, but it was so tender and intimate, it made Shelley want to look away. He unzipped the pocket on the front of the pink jacket and, with a push and a twist, he removed the air canister. Examining the bottom of it, he saw there was a hole where the trigger had previously hit it. It was empty.

'You changed this, after you fell with Paperchase. I watched you do it. I watched you reset the trigger.'

She swallowed and nodded.

'I said Pippa had done something else! I told you to check everything!'

'We thought we had, Roger.' Shelley could tell he was about to lose it altogether.

Giving a yell of rage, he threw the canister as hard as he could to the floor and stormed out.

Shelley looked at the vacant cylinder that was slowly rolling to a stop. 'We thought we'd checked everything. We checked every stitch in every bridle; we checked stirrups, girth straps, boots and hats.' She looked at Katie. 'We didn't check air canisters.'

'It's okay,' Tom's voice was calm, 'she didn't need it to inflate today.'

'But it might have been like that for ages.' Caitlyn's face was still pale after Roger's outburst.

'Can you get Roger's air jacket out of the wardrobe, please?' said Katie quietly. 'I need to check it.'

Shelley went into the back of the lorry to call him.

'What?' he asked sharply.

'Yours was a used one too. We've changed it. Well, Katie has.' She bit her lip; she could hear the commentary in the background of the silence.

'Thank you.'

'Stay here or go out onto the course to watch Bluebell,' Shelley told Katie. 'We can get them ready for him; you need some time.'

'I think I'll stay here for a while.' Tears ran down her face. 'Poor Mechanic, he's almost been overshadowed by some crazy woman disabling air jackets. I can't believe what's happened and he's gone too.'

Tom took her hand. 'And what better way to go, after a glorious clear around such a tough course? He was brilliant today, and so were you.'

'There'll be your video and photos.' Caitlyn dabbed her eyes.

As Tom bore Caitlyn off to the photographer's stand, Shelley took a deep breath and headed off to what she knew would be the shocked silence and wary glances of the stables.

Tom bought every photo of The Mechanic on the cross country course and then, heading down the line of stands to the little antique stall, he bought a silver frame. The picture of Katie, eyes wide open as they jumped down into the sunken road, The Mechanic, ears fiercely pricked forward as he assessed the jump out, fitted perfectly. He would wait, he thought, he would give it to her at Christmas once the pain had lessened.

Back at the lorry, Katie stood in the shower crying uncontrollably.

Looking down at the foam circling the plughole, she took a deep breath. Roger, the total bastard, was right. She couldn't ignore the fact that he had two rides this afternoon and, turning off the water, she wrapped herself in last night's damp towel, padded across the muddy floor in her bare feet and pulled down the blinds. Hearing the outside door being opened, she pulled her towel higher around her and almost cried with relief when Joanna opened the inner door.

'I'm sorry – it was horrible to watch, and I can't begin to imagine how you're feeling.' Joanna hugged her.

After struggling to hold it all together in front of everyone else, in front of her mum she let her emotions surge out like a flash flood. The emotion was too much for her to contain: the loss of The Mechanic, the empty cylinder in her jacket, the feeling of unrequited love. It was all a complete mess.

'It's been the most terrible week,' she sobbed. 'I really like him, and he said it would be different if I was older or he was younger.'

'Roger?' she asked, knowing that it was and feeling awfully guilty for suggesting he drive her back to Garwood after dinner on Wednesday evening.

Katie nodded against her shoulder. 'I don't know what to do. I can't stay.'

Joanna sat for a moment, holding her tightly. 'I wouldn't make any rash decisions; it's different when you're away from home and in the competition bubble.' She moved away and they met eyes. 'It's very different to being at home.'

Katie got up, tore off a piece of kitchen roll and blew her nose. 'I don't think I can stand seeing him every day.' She opened the cupboard door under the sink and threw the tissue in the bin. 'He's everything I ever dreamed he would be.'

'You can still be his friend,' Joanna's words were unhurried, 'and he is an awful lot older than you.'

'Don't.' She sat back down, shivering slightly in her wet towel. 'I shouldn't have told you.'

Joanna hugged her again. 'I was young once – I do understand. And you were obviously going to be attracted to him – he is very handsome – and as Madonna once said, "power is the greatest aphrodisiac".'

'It wasn't like that, Mum; I'm not some stupid groupie. He's just… he's *wonderful*, and I have never felt like this before about anyone, and now, to top it all off, I've lost The Mechanic too.' She started to cry again and used her towel to wipe her eyes.

'Do you love him?'

Katie looked at her and then gave a tiny nod.

They sat for a moment, and when they heard the outer door being opened, Katie hurriedly wiped her eyes again.

Roger opened the door slowly and took in a tearful Katie wrapped in a blue towel and Joanna giving him a very cool look. He knew immediately they had been talking about him.

'Sorry, but I need to change.' He put down his breeches and navy top.

'We'll talk later.' Joanna gave her daughter a final squeeze and left.

'You can stay; I don't mind,' he said, as Katie got up to go into the shower to get dressed.

'I mind.' She picked up some clothes from her open bag. It seemed an awfully long time since Monday night when he had helped her pack.

'Katie?' He sounded tired.

She gave him the same cool stare that her mother had administered a minute earlier.

'I'm sorry about The Mechanic, and I really meant what I said, about things being different if I was younger.' He put his hand on her bare shoulder and gently stroked her collarbone with his thumb.

'I didn't think you could make it any worse,' she turned back to look at him from the doorway, 'but you just have.'

Bluebell Folly looked magnificent in the start box. Gleaming white in the sunlight, he stood rock solid, white tail fanning out in the breeze, heart hammering, his kind, dark eyes on the roped-off track he was about to gallop along. The starter counted out loud from ten to one and, with a leap, Bluebell burst out and was on his way. In the lorry park, Katie slid open the window above the sofa so she could listen to the commentary.

The water jump was Bluebell's undoing. As he jumped the log in the middle of the pond, he didn't lock onto the narrow fence on the exit and ducked around the side. Knowing that, with an extra twenty penalties to add for the refusal, there was little point in rushing the horse, Roger proceeded to give Bluebell a lovely confidence-giving round. He finished well over the optimum time but was delighted with the horse, giving him enormous slaps of praise down his shoulder as he trotted around to cool him down.

Shelley and Caitlyn had washed him off by the time Katie returned to the stables. She noticed someone had hung The Mechanic's rug over his empty door and, pushing it out of the way, she removed the card with The Mechanic's name on and put it in the back pocket of her jeans.

Roger was sitting on a plastic box outside Cooper's stable drinking a bottle of water, his blond hair damp with sweat.

'Is Bluebell okay?'

'He's lost a shoe, but he's alright.' He wondered if this was the start of a truce. 'How are you feeling?'

'Terrible,' she replied and gave him a cold glare as he offered her the bottle of water.

Josh led Petra's bay horse past, kitted up in its yellow cross country boots.

'Good luck,' called Roger.

'Sorry about The Mechanic, horrible thing to happen. Martin says if you need cheering up, Katie, he's up for a rematch.' He winked.

'Martin?' Roger saw Katie's face turn scarlet.

'Come on.' Tom ushered Roger up from where he was sitting. 'We all need cheering up, and Petra's about to go cross country.'

As Warrior was ready and waiting just to be tacked up, Tom ordered Caitlyn outside as well to listen to Petra's round.

'I don't understand.' Caitlyn was itching to get back to her charge.

'Shush, shush, just listen, sweetie.' Tom was clutching the metal security fencing that surrounded the stables, and even Roger was looking amused.

Gavin Brooks, sitting high up in the glass-fronted commentary box, was doing the afternoon shift.

'And away from the start is number three-four-two, this is Petra Williams and Absolutely Naked, on a dressage score of thirty-one; Cathy Marks and Travallio are clear at twelve and heading strongly on to fence number thirteen.'

'Come on, come on, bloody say it,' muttered Tom.

'Rory Davison and Seascape Artist are home with provisionally no jumping penalties to add, while Petra Williams, riding Absolutely Naked...'

The rest of Gavin's sentence was drowned by hysterical laughter.

'Did you give her that horse to ride, Roger?' Tom was wiping his eyes.

Once Gavin had also found the joke in Petra's horse's name, he proceeded to use the same words at practically every fence.

'Petra, riding Absolutely Naked, is clear at five; Cathy Marks has had a problem at fifteen but she's bringing Travallio quickly around for a second attempt, and he jumps it well. Petra Williams, riding *Absolutely Naked*, is clear at six and seven.'

Shelley was hanging onto Tom, saying she had never laughed so hard in years. Laughing his head off, Roger suggested they had better get Warrior saddled.

Despite nearly bucking Roger off as he entered the start box, the powerful gelding ploughed through the mud to produce a fantastic clear and made himself the overnight leader going into the show jumping the next day.

Twenty-Seven

'I know you're heartbroken, sweetie, but it will do you good. You shouldn't be on your own.' Tom was wearing his Saturday night party outfit of black and lilac camouflage-print trousers and a yellow T-shirt with "S*** my D**k" written on the front.

'I know, Tom, but I just need a bit of time; I'll come down in an hour.' Katie opened the fridge for a bottle of tonic.

'An hour and I'm coming to get you, missy.'

In honour of the cross country day party, the main marquee was decked out with greenery around its metal framing, and the tables and chairs had been cleared to one end, making half of the marquee available as a dance floor. Roger, flying high from Warrior's fabulous clear cross country, was dancing with Joanna and ignoring Petra's hostile stare.

'You must be pleased with Warrior.' Joanna leant close to his ear to make herself heard over the disco.

He grinned at her. 'I am. And I will be even more pleased with him if he passes the trot up and jumps clear tomorrow.'

Charles and Margaret had put in their apologies, Charles telling Roger that they would just have dinner at the hotel. Daisy was furious as she wanted to get off with Martin and had pestered and badgered her father until he gave her the money for a taxi to and from Garwood. Miss Mac and Mrs Fleming Bowen, knowing the Garwood Saturday party could end messily and that they would not be able to hear themselves think, had booked a table at El Camino.

Shelley placed a clutch of glasses on the table and took a bottle of vodka out of Tom's yellow Mulberry satchel. Ignoring Roger's warning that she would get kicked out of the party if she got caught, she carefully added vodka to each glass before handing them out.

'Aren't you going to ask me to dance, Roger?' Tom tucked the Smirnoff bottle back into his satchel.

Roger laughed. 'Perhaps after another beer, Tom, I need to dance with my staff first. Caitlyn?'

'Oooh yes please!' she squeaked.

Petra wasn't quite so annoyed when she saw him dancing with Caitlyn in her torn jeans and green T-shirt, but that bloody Katie had just walked in, looking pale and beautiful in a dark-blue polo shirt and black jeans. Petra, in her smart trousers and floating top, wouldn't have been seen dead in jeans. After she had dragged a blushing Martin to dance and clasped him to her ample bosom, she manoeuvred him across to where Roger was dancing with Shelley.

'For the love of God, poor Martin's been snared by the Dally across, er, I mean, Golden Knickers,' finished Shelley quickly. She swung Roger around so he could see Martin disappearing into Petra's cleavage.

'Is that Martin, who works for Cathy?' When Shelley agreed it was, Roger continued, 'He was very keen to comfort Katie this afternoon.'

'I bet he was; he's been desperate to get off with her for months and was sticking his tongue down her throat last night.'

I shouldn't have told him, thought Shelley, seeing his body stiffen and his face harden. What a mess; she'd bloody warned Katie this would happen.

Feeling Shelley's mood had changed, Roger led her back to the table and then tangoed Tom around the dance floor to the sound of shrieking laughter as Shelley poured more vodka.

'Go on, Katie,' urged Caitlyn mischievously, 'you're the only one who hasn't danced with Roger.'

'I don't want to dance with you,' she said crossly as Roger took her arm and pulled her to her feet. 'No, I really don't want to dance with you.'

'Just for once, you are going to do as you are told,' said Roger firmly and bore her off, still protesting, to the dance floor.

'I suppose "Bad Romance" is the most appropriate song,' she mumbled as she finally stopped fighting him.

'Brutal,' observed Joanna and, seeing that Shelley had quickly turned to face her, she added that he didn't come across as being a player.

'He's not like that; he just worries about what people think, and he can't see what's bloody well right in front of him.'

'He likes her?'

Shelley poured more vodka into Joanna's plastic cup. 'More than he realises; I hope he works it out before it's too late. Men are so *dense*.'

Pulling Katie onto the dance floor by her wrist, Roger finally let go of her and turned to face her as Lady Gaga faded into Tom Walker singing "Just You and I". Slowly, he pulled her towards him, holding her hand against his chest and putting his other arm around her. As they started to dance, she gave a little sigh and leant her head against his chest.

'Are you alright?'

'No,' she answered.

'You're going to have to stay here for a little while longer.'

'Why should I?'

'Firstly, you smell absolutely amazing and secondly, you have given me the biggest hard-on that I have ever had.'

She moved deliberately away from him. 'And yet still I am not good enough for you.'

'If you recall the conversation correctly, I said you were more than enough but in a different time.'

Resting her head back on his chest, she closed her eyes.

'I'm sorry,' he said quietly.

'For what?'

'The Mechanic, me, that bloody awful cocktail party, Charles, some crazy woman sabotaging our kit. Everything.' He could feel the heat of her body through his shirt.

'It doesn't help.'

Tom and Caitlyn had their eyes pinned on them as they came in and out of sight between the other couples.

'Oh my God, you can tell they've had sex.' Tom folded his arms.

'They're just friends,' said Shelley, glancing across at Joanna who was watching them intently.

'Sweetie, I have friends, and they don't dance with me like that.'

'Any closer and he could slip it in,' agreed Caitlyn. 'Tom, why have you got "Sack my Duck" blurred out on your T-shirt?'

'For the love of God,' Shelley rolled her eyes, 'it's like working with Dougal from *Father Ted*.'

As Lewis Capaldi began singing "Someone You Loved", Roger felt Katie take a sharp intake of breath.

'What?'

'Do you know how many hours I've had to suffer Lewis bloody Capaldi with you in your car? It's as though there's no escape from him.'

'I like him and, as you've told me, he is better than my Ed Sheeran addiction.'

'You need better playlists.'

'With less Spice Girls and more Coldplay.' He squeezed her hand gently.

Petra had also noticed Roger and Katie dancing so closely that you couldn't have fitted a flattened cigarette paper between them. Grumpily, she grabbed her handbag and went to the bar.

'Gin and tonic.' She ignored Tom waiting to be served next to her and rummaged in her handbag for her purse.

Tom eyed Petra's bag for a second before giving a screech. 'That's my Ted Baker handbag, you thieving old bitch!' He snatched it from her. 'It is mine, it's got the scratch on it where I fell over pissed outside the Kettle!'

'It's not yours,' Petra snarled, snatching it back.

'Fucking is!' Tom grabbed the bag and held it high above his head so Petra was unable to reach it, making her jump to try and seize it.

'Dear God, what is going on over there?' Roger turned around on the dance floor so Katie could see.

'I should make a citizen's arrest!' yelled Tom and, in one motion, tipped the entire contents of the bag onto the floor.

As Petra scrabbled to collect her spilt possessions, Tom picked up a tampon. 'Do you just carry these to make yourself look younger?' He threw it back on the floor and marched back to the table.

'There's clearly no love lost between Tom and Petra,' observed Roger, watching Petra marching away from the bar with the contents of her handbag clutched to her chest.

Katie was watching Daisy snogging Martin in the middle of the dance floor. 'She's wearing my breeches,' she said faintly.

'Who is?' he turned to look.

'Daisy's wearing my breeches!' she said incredulously. 'I knew they were disappearing, but what the hell?' She looked back at Roger. 'Am I going to wake up in a minute and find this is all some crazy dream?'

'I would rather you stayed in this moment,' he whispered in her ear.

He felt her chest rise and then she pushed him away.

'I can't do this, Roger. It's too much. You can't dance with me like this and think it's okay.'

'Can't we even be friends?'

She looked at him for a moment, her eyes filling with tears, finding that the dancing couples around them had morphed into a swirling kaleidoscope along with the lights of the disco. 'I can't do that, and this isn't how *friends* dance with each other.'

'Pink Knickers!' Daniel took her arm and spun her around. 'I thought you were going to dance with the boss forever.'

She burst into tears and buried her face in Daniel's shoulder as he put his arms around her.

'Hey, are you okay? Shit luck today, the old horse was quite a character.'

'Thanks, Dan,' she sniffed and wiped her eyes, 'but there's a lot going on at the minute, and it feels like I've lost a friend.'

'You idiot,' he said softly, 'that's because you have.' He looked across at a shell-shocked Roger dancing with Sara and suspected that there was more than just the emotion of losing The Mechanic at play. 'Do you want a drink?'

'No, I think I'll just go to bed, Dan. Thanks anyway.'

Daniel watched as she walked out of the marquee, wondering if he should have offered to walk her back to Roger's lorry.

'Is she okay?' asked Sara. 'She doesn't seem her usual self. I mean, I know it's tough losing a horse, but she looks terrible.'

Daniel nodded at Roger racing out of the marquee after her. 'I think that's more the problem.'

Katie was halfway across the lorry park when Roger caught up with her.

'Are you alright?' He grabbed her arm to stop her.

'What do you think? Just leave me alone.' She began to pull away from him, and he roughly pulled her back to face him.

'I've said I am sorry – what else do you want me to do?'

'Nothing. There's nothing you can do,' she said simply. 'But I'm sure you have never dumped anyone and then complained that they have given you a hard-on.'

'For Christ's sake, I know this is difficult, but if we can just sort it out—'

'How do we do that?' she asked flatly.

Roger inhaled, and when he spoke, his tone was calm. 'We've lost a horse today – emotions are high – can we please just get tomorrow out of the way and then we can try?'

'I don't want to try. I want to leave. Now.'

'Katie, we're in the middle of a field; you can't leave now.'

'I can. I can get the taxi with Mum back to the hotel and fly home with her on Monday.'

'Now you're being fucking ridiculous.'

'I mean it!' Her voice was rising and, conscious that people were starting to leave the marquee and head back to their lorries, Roger navigated their way across to his wagon.

'You need to go to bed – there's been too little food, too much emotion and too much vodka. You need to sleep.'

'I'm not drunk,' she spat.

'I didn't say you were.'

As she opened the door to the lorry, she saw The Mechanic's boots neatly packed away in their plastic box and began to cry. Guiding her by her elbow towards the double bed, Roger handed her the kitchen roll from the bench and sat down beside her.

'I'm sorry; I am so sorry.'

'What for?' He was wiping away her tears with his fingers.

'I should have pulled him up.'

'It would not have made any difference.' He shook her irritably. 'Look, now is not the time. Go to bed.'

He tried not to watch as she stripped to her underwear and pulled on the T-shirt that was stuffed under her pillow. Pulling back the duvet, she crawled across to the far side of the bed and lay down, her slanted brown eyes looking warily at him.

'Did you mean it, you want to leave?'

'How can I stay?' she whispered sadly.

There was a moment of understanding in his eyes, and he nodded.

'I'm sorry for being such a bitch.' She scrubbed her face with the piece of kitchen roll in her hand, leaving a black streak of mascara down her face. 'I don't mean to be.'

'I'm the one who has screwed everything up; it's me who should be apologising.'

'Will you stay with me?' she asked hopefully as he smoothed the bedding around her.

'I can't,' he said shortly.

'Please? Just until I'm asleep, then I can pretend you're still here.'

He turned off the lights, leaving just the one on above the cooker, and sat down again on the bed. 'You rode a brilliant round on him; no one could have ridden him better.'

'He was so easy, just like you think I am.'

'Stop it,' he said impatiently. 'I don't and you're not.'

'I only snogged Martin to make you angry, but you don't care anyway.' She turned her head away from him and he listened as her breathing slowed into sleep.

He pulled the duvet more firmly around her and stood up, thinking of how they had been entwined under that quilt a few nights ago and how wrong everything had been since. It was a night he knew he was never going to forget, and for the first time in his life, it wasn't about mind-blowing sex. Wednesday night had been a completely new experience for him – the way they had fallen asleep spooned together had felt more precious than the act that had happened previously. He thought about the smooth curve of her waist as he had slid his hand over it to pull her warm body closer to him and how she had threaded her fingers through his as she nestled his hand against her breasts. He looked down at her sleeping form and, after a moment's hesitation, he kissed his index finger and lightly pressed it against her cheek.

Closing the outside door quietly, he walked down the steps and collided with Shelley in the darkness.

'How is she?'

'Asleep.'

'Roger…' She faltered, running her fingers through her curls.

'What is it?' She had sounded as though she was about to break the news that she had another job.

'Look, Roger, I don't want to interfere.'

'Then don't.'

Still, she stood in front of him, blocking his escape. 'I'm not the only one who's noticed.'

'Noticed what?'

'For the love of God, why are men *so thick?*' she asked in exasperation.

Roger, having an idea where this was going, hurriedly pushed her out of the way, but Shelley grabbed the arm of his shirt and swung him back around to face her. Bravely, she took a step up the lorry steps, so her eyes were level with his.

'I've seen the way you look at her. You don't look at me or Caitlyn, or even your grandmother, like that, and I saw the look on your face when you realised Pippa had tampered with her air jacket.' She took a deep breath. 'Roger, she's crazy about you, and you need to do something before someone else snaps her up. Stop worrying about a bloody stupid age gap and about what other people think.'

They glared at each other in the darkness, and Shelley had the awful feeling he was going to slap her.

'What the fuck do you know about it?' He spoke through gritted teeth as he took a step upwards towards her.

Shelley climbed a step higher, opened the door and stepped inside. 'For God's sake, Roger! You've been feeling odd and haven't been able to face food for the past three days because you're in love. You bloody *moron!*'

He stood very still as she slammed the door in his face.

Twenty-Eight

The remaining competitors in the final class at Garwood would show jump in reverse order, meaning Bluebell Folly was to jump early afternoon and Warrior last of all. Roger had no penalties to spare with Warrior, and a single fence down would drop him to sixth place. He walked the course early on Sunday morning with Daniel and Cathy and found it to be a twisting course, cleverly thought out, and he knew immediately that Warrior, with his flowing long stride, was going to struggle.

Cathy, lying in fifteenth and one place higher than Bluebell Folly, was pleased with the course, knowing it would suit her neat little Travallio. Daniel crossed his fingers and hoped Rock On would be passed fit by the ground jury at the final veterinary inspection in an hour's time. The horse had ripped off both front shoes during yesterday's cross country, and India had been out three times in her headtorch to add fresh ice to the poultices through the night.

Looking at his two beautiful horses, their manes and tails neatly plaited, Bluebell Folly a dazzling white and Warrior's gleaming coat the dark brown colour of Katie's eyes, Roger felt a surge of pride. Whatever happened, his horses looked fit and happy, and his team had performed amazingly well, considering they would be travelling home with an empty stall in the lorry.

Bluebell trotted along the gravel strip in front of Garwood House under the scrutinising eyes of the judging panel and was passed fit to complete the final stage. Daniel's Rock On was sent to the holding box, and it was quickly announced that he had been withdrawn from the competition.

'I thought he would pass.' Daniel and Roger watched Shelley with Bluebell, and India leading Rock On, going back to the stables. 'At least we can get loaded and ready for home.'

After Warrior had squealed and tried to bite the arm of Roger's expensive suit, he proceeded to buck and cavort on his trot up, making the judges ask Roger to do it again to check he was sound. He was duly passed fit and, as Caitlyn took him back to the stables, telling him what a naughty little rascal he was, Roger went to the lorry to change.

Since Tuesday night, the area where the horses travelled had been used as a feed room and now Roger retrieved the partitions from underneath the lorry and slotted them back into place. Katie was stacking boxes of kit in the empty stall at the front of the lorry, and Caitlyn and Shelley were arriving with wheelbarrows full of rugs and saddlery that weren't now required at the stables for Roger's two rounds of show jumping that afternoon.

The pop-up village of Garwood International was beginning to fold. The traders at the stands around the main arena were discreetly packing away some of their wares, and across in the campsite, tents were subsiding, and caravans were being hitched onto cars. Within twenty-four hours, the stables would be down; the grandstands would be gone; and the sheep would return to the grass that had seen both tragedy and triumph over the past four days.

Miss Mac and Mrs Fleming Bowen had arrived and, after a drive around the trade stands on their mobility scooters, were parked up at the side of the show jumping ring watching the dog agility.

'Are you pleased with Bluebell?' Victoria held her melting ice cream to the side, so it didn't drip on her lap.

'Golly yes!' replied Miss Mac. 'So much to look forward to for next season – I'm wondering if he might go to Bramham. Pleased you came for the jaunt?'

'Absolutely, I've had a marvellous time. I must do it more often. There's Roger.' She gave a little wave.

Roger kissed his grandmother in greeting as she asked him what the course was like.

'More suited to the quicker, smaller horse. I'm not sure how I'm going to get Warrior around.'

'Rather like turning the Queen Mary in a bathtub,' agreed Miss Mac, who had driven her scooter around the course while Victoria was powdering her nose.

'How is everyone this morning? Was it a good party?' Victoria crunched up the last of her cone.

Roger shrugged. 'We weren't really in party mood.'

'How is Katie this morning?' asked Miss Mac.

Victoria saw his face change for a fraction of a second and, although his phone began to ring, for once he ignored it and quietly said Katie was thinking of leaving.

'Don't let her,' said Miss Mac in a startled voice.

'I'm not sure it's as easy as that,' he conceded. 'I had better go and get changed; I'll see you both later.' He stooped to kiss Victoria's offered cheek.

'She is a very nice girl,' she whispered.

'She is,' he whispered back.

'And as James Hammerton said, "you won't know unless you try".'

'What part did he play in *Pretty Woman*?'

Victoria shook her head crossly. 'He was the Scottish one in *Sliding Doors*! Now for God's sake, man, pull your finger out!'

Roger walked away wondering if his grandmother had been alluding to his show jumping.

Bluebell jumped well on the twisting course and had only one fence down; Cathy, jumping immediately after him, went clear. They now had a wait of an hour and a half before Warrior would jump, as there was a parade by the local Pony Club before the top ten show jumped.

The sun was high in the sky, making Caitlyn's nose turn red and Tom buy a panama hat from one of the trade stands.

'Do I look like an English gentleman?' he asked hopefully.

'I'm not sure they wear leopard-print skinny jeans,' Shelley replied.

'Perhaps if you carried a croquet mallet it might help,' said Katie soothingly.

Bluebell's tack had been taken back to the lorry, and the stables were almost empty. The horses' travelling gear was placed neatly outside the stable doors as the bare minimum of grooming and plaiting gear was kept out for the final hour and a half of the competition. As the Pony Club cantered in and out of the enormous fences dressed as *Harry Potter* characters, the trade stands started packing up in earnest as the crowds surged forward to watch the final ten battle it out.

Despite Tom and Shelley's voodooing, Petra annoyingly went clear, even though Gavin introduced her to the crowd as "Petra Williams, delighted to be riding Absolutely Naked", leaving everyone in fits of laughter. Joanna, standing with Miss Mac and Mrs Fleming Bowen, found she had torn her catalogue to shreds.

Cantering around the collecting ring, Roger wished Warrior felt more awake. Despite his rodeo at the veterinary inspection that morning, he was feeling the effects of a big three-day and had lost a lot of weight during his six days away from home. Climbing over an upright and knocking it down like an arthritic donkey, Roger saw Katie run forward and replace the pole, shouting to him to "come again". Warrior jumped it cleanly the second time and, as Roger walked him alongside her around the others crashing over the practice jumps, she kept a soothing hand on the horse's shoulder.

'I don't think you had him balanced enough as you came off the corner,' said Katie delicately, knowing she might get a bollocking for even suggesting it. 'You came at it a bit quick.'

Roger said nothing, and when she timidly raised her eyes to look at him, she saw he was smiling at her.

'You're absolutely right.'

'Just not absolutely naked,' she murmured despondently.

Rory Davison was in third place, and he too needed a clear round to hold his position. Jumping his big bay around the course immaculately, as he walked Seascape Artist out of the ring, he blew Katie a kiss and shouted that there were no time faults this time.

'Stay with me until I have to go in.' Roger kept his eyes on the grey horse in the arena.

'If you want.' Katie eyed him curiously, knowing it wasn't like him to need reassurance. 'Is everything alright?'

'Just stay beside him.'

'Don't you want Caitlyn?'

'No,' he said quickly. 'I want you.'

Wishing it was true, she dropped her eyes to try and contain the emotion and centred her vision on his boot resting lightly in the stirrup. The spur was glittering in the sunlight and, looking more closely, she saw the tiny saltires engraved on the silver, flashing and sparkling in the light. It was the first time she had seen him wear them. She started to speak and then realised he had closed his eyes, and she knew he was visualising his round one last time. Placing both her hands on Warrior's shoulder, she breathed deeply, feeling the heat from the horse's skin prickling her hands as Warrior exhaled deep, relaxed breaths from his nose. She remained there, absorbing the electrical power of the horse and rider through her palms, focusing on returning the energy back to them until Roger opened his eyes and she felt her hands beginning to cool.

This is the last time, she thought, *the last time I'll stand beside him as part of his team.* She hastily swallowed, but the lump in her throat didn't move. *You could stay*, she told herself. *You could stay, if you could only see him in a different way.* But she knew that would never happen; it was impossible. Her idol was gone; the man she had thought she loved as a teenager no longer existed. Now, the man sitting on the horse beside her was a real person, a short-tempered man with true and good qualities and a gentleness under the tough exterior that she had never expected.

And she loved him.

Roger finally glanced down from Warrior's majestic height but, seeing her teeth raking over her bottom lip and her eyes full of tears, he quickly looked away.

'Should I go over?' Caitlyn was looking across at Roger and Warrior.

Tom saw the tight expression on Roger's face and shook his head. 'Just leave him with Katie, sweetie.'

'But—'

'She's the best one to deal with him at the minute.' He was thinking that Roger was looking strangely nervous, and Katie looked as though she was about to burst into tears.

'But I could just go and stand with them?' Caitlyn looked at Shelley pleadingly.

'Caitlyn,' Shelley was hiding her impatience, knowing how much the younger girl loved Warrior, 'you know how cutting he can be when he's under pressure.'

'Oooh yes. Like at Kinsey Park when he said that if my brains were dynamite, there wouldn't be enough to blow my hat off?'

'Yes, just like—'

'Or like at Heathingstone, when he said that I was the reason there were instructions on bottles of shampoo?'

'Yes—'

'And when he told me to go to sleep and pray for brains?'

'Caitlyn—'

'And that time when I forgot to put Paperchase's dressage saddle in the lorry, and he said I was about as useful as a crocheted condom?'

'Caitlyn!' Shelley's tone was sharp. 'Just shut up and enjoy watching your bloody horse!'

Sophie France-Chambers was in second place and, as Tom and Shelley's moaning voodoo increased in decibels, her grey horse, with its white-bandaged legs, knocked down the second part of the yellow double, giving Roger one fence in hand.

Katie was still standing beside Warrior, her hand on his silky shoulder, when the steward opened the barrier for Roger to ride in.

'Good luck.' She gave Warrior one last pat and stepped back.

'Katie,' the word came out as a croak, 'I've made a mistake.'

'Roger, they're *waiting*.'

'Don't move; wait here.' He touched his heels to Warrior's sides.

Cantering into the arena, he brought the horse to a solid halt to salute the judges. The chatter from the crowd was settling, and they were becoming quiet; he took a breath and patted Warrior's neck before he asked him to move off into canter.

The Fleming Bowen team had congregated, and just as Roger had done four weeks earlier, Katie announced she couldn't watch and turned her back to the arena. There was a collective groan, and she swiftly turned back to see the poles from the first fence clattering to the ground.

'Don't you turn away again, missy – you need to bring him luck.' Tom stood behind her and placed his hands on her shaking shoulders.

After hitting the first fence hard, Warrior shook his head angrily and cleared the second by a mile. Roger was using every inch of space available around the curving course but, knowing that he would get time penalties if he rode too far off the normal jumping line, he was letting the horse bowl along as best he could but not allowing him to stretch his naturally long stride too far.

They cleared the third and the blue and white poles that made up the fourth. Katie closed her eyes and heard Warrior's hind feet rattle number five, but she knew the fence must have stayed up as there was no sound from the crowd. Crossing the arena, Warrior suddenly lit up and started to lean on his bit, pulling against his pilot's hands, wanting to get on with it. Roger blocked the tension with a slight check before releasing his hands again, and they jumped the next, which Warrior rattled so hard, the plank was still swinging in its cup as he cleared the next and turned to jump the final line.

Caitlyn, having chewed her fingernails almost down to the quick, walked away and shut her eyes.

He's going to have another one down, thought Shelley, *he's touching everything.*

He's going to have another one down, thought Tom, *he's been lucky not to have four down until now.*

He's not going to have another one down, thought Katie, *he's riding beautifully.*

Warrior put in an enormous leap over the first part of the double and, with a sharp twist in the saddle, Roger put him slightly left as they landed, giving the horse the room he needed to take two strides and jump the second part. They cleared it with an effort, and Roger rode a slight arc to approach the final fence.

The crowd held their breath as they watched the brown horse canter down to the white poles and, aware that he needed to accelerate to stay inside the time allowed, Roger let Warrior go on more quickly, softening his hands on the reins to encourage the horse to stretch out. Warrior pricked up his ears as he neared the fence, and Katie saw the look of concentration on Roger's face as he steadied him for the last two strides before they took off.

There was a second of hushed silence after Warrior landed before the crowd erupted with a roar that almost lifted the roof off the stands. The noise told Roger he had done it. By some miracle, and despite rattling almost every show jump, the unforgiving cross country through the bottomless mud and the dressage in torrential rain, they had won. He looked over his shoulder to check the scoreboard, and when he saw the number one beside his name, the feeling of euphoria rushed to his head, and he urged Warrior on to gallop an unofficial lap of honour.

Pandemonium was breaking out in the warm-up area as Roger's team jumped up and down, screaming and hugging each other, yelling that he had won.

Seeing Caitlyn openly crying, Katie hugged her. 'Are you okay?'

'He did it – he fooking did it!' Her voice increased to a scream.

Katie grinned at her. 'He did.'

'How does it feel? To win like that?'

'Almost better than sex.'

'You must have really good sex.' Caitlyn wiped her eyes.

Petra felt the rush of air as Warrior thundered past her and huffily turned away from the ringside to order Josh to get Naked ready for the presentation.

'I think I have to wear something,' he spluttered back.

Roger brought Warrior back to a walk and saluted the crowd before turning to leave the arena, slapping the horse's neck with joy, a huge grin plastered on his face. There were people surrounding them, shaking his hand and patting Warrior's neck, but his eyes were searching through the hordes trying to find her. Caitlyn was pushing her way through the people, tears pouring down her face and, as Roger dismounted, she flung her arms around Warrior's neck.

'Thank you.' He briefly hugged her, and she looked at him in surprise.

'Have I done something wrong?'

'You keep him calm, and you've turned him out beautifully. We couldn't have won it without you.'

'Fook.' Caitlyn opened her eyes very wide. 'I thought you were going to say your grandad could do better than me, and he's dead.'

'Brilliant!' Shelley launched herself at Roger and gave a burst of laughter as he caught her.

'It's you at home that make things like this happen.'

'That's true,' she laughed, 'but nobody could have ridden him better than that.'

'Oh my God, Roger!' Tom was clasping his chest. 'That was so tense, I think I might have accidentally leaked some wee.'

'You did some hard work with this horse, even if it was for Petra.' He put his hand on Tom's shoulder. 'I'm pleased you're here today.'

'Oh, for heaven's sake,' said Tom impatiently, grabbing Roger and kissing him. 'I'll just take advantage of the opportunity because it's *never* going to happen again.'

As they crowded around him, he was aware there was someone missing, and he turned to look at her. She was standing further away, her face looking drawn as she watched them congratulating him. He took off his hat and found Shelley was holding out her hand to take it from him.

'Don't mess it up,' she said desperately.

He half smiled at her, and she saw his hand was shaking as he handed his hat to her.

The six steps he took to reach her would be imprinted forever on his memory. She looked so pale and tired, as if the events of the week had finally taken all the force from her. When he finally stood in front of her, he found he couldn't speak. The adrenaline was still coursing through his veins after the crackling tension of his round, but all he could think about was how fragile she looked.

'You were brilliant,' she said quietly. 'How you got him out of trouble at the combination was just brilliant.'

'I asked you to wait for me, over there. Why do you never do as you're told?'

'I didn't want to be in the way of your fan club.'

'I thought you were one of the founder members?'

'I was.'

'Was?'

'Still am.' She gave him a weak smile. 'I always will be.'

'Always?' He suddenly took her face in his warm hands, his thumbs gently stroking her cheeks and, as she took a sobbing breath, his brow creased in anguish. 'Always, Katie? Are you sure?'

It was as though the world had stopped around them; the chatter behind them was fading, and all she could think about was how much she wanted him to kiss her. His face was centimetres away from hers, and she felt his breath on her lips as he looked at her.

'Always,' she whispered.

'I should have done this a very long time ago.' He wiped away a tear from her cheek with his thumb and kissed her forehead tenderly. 'I'm sorry – I've put you through hell this week.'

'Are… are you trying to tell me—'

'I am desperately trying to tell you how I feel about you.'

'How do you feel about me?' She was trembling, and her heart was hammering so hard inside her ribcage she thought he might be able to feel it.

'Like this,' he said softly and kissed her quivering mouth.

'Oh my God! Form a queue, form a queue!' squealed Tom, frantically trying to push Shelley and Caitlyn behind him.

When Roger finally pulled away, he rested his forehead against hers. 'Will you stay?'

'Are you sure?' she asked shakily.

'I'm sorry.' He shook his head. 'I didn't realise how I felt about you. I am such an idiot.'

'Are you *sure*?'

'About being an idiot, or how I feel about you?'

'Both.' She slowly smiled.

'I'm sure about both.'

'You're not an idiot.'

'That's good to know.'

'You're an absolute bastard.'

'I am that too,' he agreed.

'You're wearing my spurs. You've never worn them before.'

'You noticed?'

'I notice lots of things.'

He smiled back at her, remembering the night he had used those very words to her, just before he had kissed her for the first time. 'I thought I might need some luck today.'

'You didn't need luck.'

'I need you.'

Seeing them standing together, Roger's hands cupping Katie's face as she listened intently to what he was saying to her, Mrs Fleming Bowen turned to Joanna.

'Your daughter.'

'Your grandson.'

'You can tolerate a compromise if you manage to get something accomplished.'

Joanna frowned. 'Is that—'

'Yes, my dear,' Victoria placed her liver-spotted hand on Joanna's arm, 'President Whitmore in *Independence Day*.'

'I hate to break up what should have happened about three months ago,' Shelley nudged Roger's back pointedly with his hat, 'but *The Scotsman* is waiting to speak to you, and they've nearly finished clearing the jumps for the presentation.'

'You need to go,' said Katie gently. 'Enjoy the applause.'

'Wait here and don't move. I want you to be exactly here when I get back.' He kissed her forehead and turned to climb into Warrior's saddle, adding that perhaps this time she could try a little harder to do as she was told.

Rory rode alongside Roger at the arena entrance and gave him a grin. 'Next time, if I win, do I get to kiss her?'

Roger threw back his head and laughed. 'No, you bloody don't, Rory, so don't even try it.'

'Are you alright, missy?' Tom put his arm around Katie's shoulders. 'You look very pale.'

'I feel absolutely exhausted.' For a moment she bit back tears.

Tom touched her arm comfortingly. 'We'll get you some

Lucozade and a big can of Monster, sweetie, because after seeing the way the Rogerable Roger is looking at you, I doubt that you're going to get much sleep tonight.'

Shelley grinned. 'Happy?'

Katie nodded and smiled, her eyes glistening with tears.

'Don't cry.' Shelley gave her a hug. 'I should be the one who's crying. My God, he took some bloody prompting, I can tell you.'

'What do you mean?'

'I've told you before, my wee Southern friend. If you want a man to notice something, you need to use a flipchart and a PowerPoint presentation.'

'You don't,' pouted Tom.

'Tom, you're gay. Gays don't need a flipchart or a PowerPoint presentation.' Shelley was watching Roger cantering into the arena with a kite tail of horses and riders following him.

'What exactly did you put on the flipchart?' asked Katie.

'Edited highlights?' Shelley gave her a small grin.

'They'll do.'

'That it was bloody obvious to everyone apart from him.'

Katie looked across the empty warm-up. There was a line of grooms standing along the arena fence, their buckets of brushes and hoof oil standing beside them. Caitlyn was standing at the head of the line, as close as she could be to the entrance, waiting to greet her winner as soon as the presentation was over.

'Go on,' Katie turned to Shelley and Tom, 'go and watch. I'll wait here.'

'You'll give him a heart attack if you start doing as you're told now,' retorted Shelley.

Twenty-Nine

Warrior's enormous rosettes were lying on the dashboard of the lorry. The precious cargo, legs wrapped in travelling boots, were loaded, and Shelley was making a final sweep of the stables. Miss Mac, Mrs Fleming Bowen and Joanna were staying another night at the Croft Hotel and would make their way home tomorrow, one journey involving an aircraft, the other several toilet stops and a detour to the food hall at the House of Bruar.

Charles and Margaret had come to Garwood to wish the team a safe journey, and Charles handed Shelley fifty pounds, telling her to make sure they all had a drink on him. He then turned to Roger and handed him a heavy cool box.

'We couldn't bring all of him home, but the Kennelman suggested we take his heart. He was happy at Athward, and we thought you might be able to bury it somewhere he liked.'

Taking the box from him, Roger felt the immense weight of The Mechanic's heart. 'Did they say?'

'Ruptured aorta,' said Charles flatly.

'I assumed.'

Charles stretched out his arm and, after Roger had switched the plastic box to his other side, they briefly shook hands, before

Roger realised it was the same hand he had seen caressing Katie's backside and stroking her breast and immediately let it go.

Deciding that there was every possibility that he wouldn't be able to stay awake for the eight-hour drive home, Roger asked Shelley to travel back in the lorry in case he needed her to drive, leaving Tom and Caitlyn to go home in the BMW.

'At least the other fag hag is there to chaperone you.' Tom kissed Katie's cheek. 'We don't want Roger tearing off your clothes with his lovely white teeth.'

It was long after midnight when they crossed the border into England and Shelley, with her favourite squashy pillow sandwiched between her head and the window, stockinged feet on the dashboard, had been asleep for almost an hour.

'What do you think?'

The question came out of the silence, and Katie turned to look at him. His face was illuminated by the lights on the dash, and he briefly took his eyes off the road to glance across at her.

'What do I think about what?'

'Can you cope? Being with me?'

'Did I just hear you actually ask me out?'

'Are you deaf?' Shelley rearranged her cushion. 'I heard him from here.'

Roger smiled in the darkness. 'Shelley, put your headphones in please?'

He waited until she had picked up her phone, selected a playlist and settled back down again.

'Well?'

'What do you mean *cope*?'

'You know what my life is like, Katie, it's not always easy to be part of it.'

'Especially with that foul temper of yours.'

'That's rich, coming from the woman who hasn't the patience to wait for a kettle to boil.'

'At least I don't threaten fat, red-headed men with violence.'

'That, was completely justified.' He realised she was laughing, and he took her hand and gently kissed her fingers. 'I'm sorry if I embarrassed you, but I couldn't wait any longer, once I'd realised. I thought you might not come back with us and fly to Southampton with Joanna.'

Feeling a rush of elation that was better than winning the Scottish Championship, she drew his hand back to her face and brushed it against her cheek. 'I'm sorry I made your weekend so horrible.'

'But Wednesday night was a highlight,' he admitted.

'It was.' She giggled.

He reached out his hand in the darkness, and she entwined her fingers with his. 'Curry and poppadum?' he asked softly.

'I just hope it's a vast improvement on the lager and lime.'

After guiding the lorry through the pillars and past East Lodge, Roger took his hands off the steering wheel and stretched as they slowly rolled on down the drive to Athward Hall. Shelley had laced up her boots and was rubbing the crick in her neck. She checked her phone and read a message from Tom asking if they had made it home safely and if she had had to drive so Roger could have his wicked way with Katie. Replying "FFS", she then climbed over into the living and began emptying the fridge.

There was soft whickering from Tiger's stable as the ramp landed gently on the cobbles. Warrior came out first, looking weary and, as Roger led him to his stable, he saw that the bedding in The Mechanic's stable had been pushed off the rubber matting and the door was tactfully closed. They had been through the mill at this year's Garwood, and Roger wondered what Charles Dee's plan was now.

Katie was settling Cooper in his stable on the far side of the yard. As soon as she had removed his travelling boots, he sank to his knees and rolled and rolled in the fresh wood shavings. Snorting through his nostrils as he got to his feet, he shook himself like a wet dog and turned to his haynet.

Shelley watched Lightoller tugging hungrily at his hay. They had lost The Mechanic in such awful circumstances, but at least it meant that the conceited Daisy wouldn't be badgering Charles to ride the horse next season. It would have been a total disaster; Daisy would never have managed him. She turned off the light and went to get her bag from the lorry. The smell of woodsmoke was drifting down from the Dorchester's chimney; Mrs Royal had obviously lit the fire, and Shelley hoped to God she hadn't done any tidying; although, with their bedroom doors locked, the damage shouldn't be too tragic. Seeing the lights still on at the top of the yard, Shelley dropped her bag and walked across the cobbles; her feet were killing her, and she was absolutely shattered.

Roger was closing Warrior's door and Shelley thought he looked more drained than she had ever seen him look before.

'We'll have a late start tomorrow; I'll message Caitlyn and tell her to come in at half eight.'

'What do you want to do tomorrow?' Shelley picked up a broom and swept a handful of shavings towards Murdoch's stable; he stopped eating his hay for a second in the hope of a Polo.

'Apart from sleep all day?' Roger bolted the stable door. 'First thing, get these boys turned out, muck out and we'll take it from there. Murdoch and Tiger are show jumping on Wednesday night so will need to jump on Tuesday.'

Katie was hauling her bag out of the lorry as it ticked itself cool. 'I honestly think I could sleep standing up.'

'You're not alone; I'm off to bed.' Shelley turned and went to pick up her bag. 'And if your housekeeper, Roger, has colour-coded my Tampax again, I'm going to write to my union.'

Watching Shelley closing the Dorchester's blue door behind her, he turned to Katie and took her hand. 'Come on, I cannot wait to fall asleep and wake up with you.'

After the heat in the lorry, the night air was cold, and she felt the welcome rush of warmth as Roger pushed open the back door to the Hall.

'My housekeeper must think I have shares in a bloody kerosene producer,' he complained as he sorted through the pile of post on the kitchen table. 'I can't believe she has turned the heating on when all I want to do is go to bed.'

Katie dropped her bag on the floor and yawned.

'Do you want a shower? I need to go through this heap and check my emails.'

'Can't you do that tomorrow?'

'There'll be more by tomorrow, and the press will be chasing me for a quote in three hours if I don't respond to them now. Go on, I'll use the shower in the cloakroom so you can take as long as you want. Towels are in the cupboard by the sink.'

After the shower in the lorry, where you had to use the water cautiously, she stood under the hot torrent and felt the mud and negativity of Garwood rinsing away. A delirious feeling of happiness washed over her, and she smiled – what a week it had been, talk about highs and lows. Then her face fell as she thought about The Mechanic. She felt guilty that she had been so preoccupied with Roger, she hadn't begun to grieve for the loss of her favourite partner. She had wanted to take the horse to a higher level next season, and now she had nothing to aim for. She knew he would continue to let her ride the novice horses, but Roger was short of intermediate horses, and she wondered briefly if Charles would buy another horse. She shuddered when she thought about Charles. She couldn't see Roger letting her ride anything he owned in the future, and that was something she wouldn't lose sleep over. She dried herself, put on the fluffy white robe that was hanging behind the door, wrapped her hair in a small blue towel and made her way to Roger's bedroom.

'Did you not want to get out?' He was sitting on the bed rubbing his hair dry.

'Much better than the shower in the lorry,' she agreed, pulling the turban from her hair. 'Incidentally, how was your amazing power shower in your warm hotel room?'

'Good,' his eyes were twinkling, 'but I much preferred Wednesday night in the lorry.'

She dropped her eyes and reached for his hand.

'What's wrong?'

'Nothing.'

'Yes there is, I can tell.' He frowned as he stood up. 'Have you changed your mind? Because it's alright if you have—'

'I haven't changed my mind, I'm just…' She twisted her fingers carefully around his and watched their hands interlock.

'First night nerves?' he asked gently.

She hesitated and then nodded. 'Sorry, I know it's stupid; it's not the first time—'

'It's not stupid. It is, however, very flattering.' He gave her a small smile as he put his hand on her cheek, his thumb gently touching her chin, lifting her face towards him. He kissed her forehead and let his fingers stroke down the back of her neck, encouraging her to put her head on his chest. 'And anyway, I am so tired, I don't think I could shag you tonight if my life depended upon it, so I'm not sure you need to be nervous.'

She started to laugh and then put her forehead against his chest.

'Katie, standing here now, especially knowing you are naked under my dressing gown, I can honestly say I feel the same as I did when—'

'When you plied me with wine and seduced me?'

'Is that what I did?' he asked in surprise.

'No. But it does sound better than "got drunk and ended up in bed together".'

'Alright, I'll admit to that. But I was actually referring to that day in January, in the snow, when you flung yourself at me outside my tack room.' He kissed her hair. 'And falling asleep with you last Wednesday night was the most incredible thing. Even though you kept pushing yourself closer to me to steal my heat.'

'It was cold,' she exclaimed.

'It was, but I had to concentrate very hard to stop something rising to attention.'

She smiled at him and kissed his shoulder as she carefully unbelted the robe and let it slip to the floor.

'Oh Christ,' he looked down at her and swallowed, 'now you're making me feel nervous, looking at me like that.'

'Like what?' She was sliding her fingers into the tuck of his towel, and it fell from his hips.

'How are those first night nerves?' His hands were shaking as he tucked her wet hair behind her ears.

'I don't know what you mean,' she whispered, 'but I am pleased Mrs Royal turned the heating on.'

Thirty

Hearing Roger opening the bedroom curtains, Katie forced her eyes open and lifted her head from the deliciously soft pillow to look at him. 'What time is it?'

'Six.' He sat down next to her on the bed. 'Sleep well?'

'Six? You kept me awake until after three, and I thought we were having a late start this morning?'

'I kept *you* awake?'

'Okay, maybe that's not entirely true, but you told me we weren't starting until half-past eight.' She yawned and stretched her arms towards the ceiling.

He flicked back the covers and planted a kiss on her stomach. 'Get up – we've got a job to do – and wrap up warm; it's cold outside.'

'It's too early,' she objected.

'I'll give you five minutes to get dressed, Pink Knickers. Otherwise, I will carry you out of here naked.'

In the kitchen, there was a wicker basket standing next to the cool box, and suddenly she understood.

'Where are we going?' She shivered as she fastened her seat belt.

'Somewhere I think The Mechanic was at his happiest. You can correct me if you think otherwise.'

There was a frosty feel to the early morning air, and the condensation on the Discovery was running in little streams down the windows. Roger drove down the drive to East Lodge and took the main road to Athward, before turning left over the cattle grid into North Hall.

It seemed a lifetime since Tom had driven them along the rough track to Roger's owners' party. The night that Jules had discovered her secret, the night they had met Josh, the night they had sat carefree, swigging champagne on the patio before Smith's Gossip Corner had poked a stick into the hornet's nest. She half smiled as she remembered The Mechanic bucking her off on the beach the day after the party and cantering back to her, believing he was so clever. Two tears rolled down her cheeks and, not wanting to cry in front of Roger, she hastily wiped them away.

He put his hand over hers. 'You're allowed to cry; The Mechanic would have expected it.'

Following the stony road down the hill to the trees, he then drove across the grass towards the river.

'I was schooling here, the night before Auchenruther Castle.'

He put on the handbrake and met her eyes. 'I was watching you.'

Katie looked up the hill to the front of Athward Hall; the wisteria had long since finished flowering, and the leaves of the horse chestnut trees were crimped and brown.

Telling her she could set up camp, Roger produced a spade from the boot of the car and handed her the basket, inside which was a blanket, a flask of coffee, a bottle of Taittinger and two champagne flutes. She spread out the blanket over the silken spiderwebs and unscrewed the lid of the flask. Filling it with coffee, she watched Roger digging a neat hole in the old turf and wrapped her hands around the cup to keep them warm.

'Why here?' she asked.

'Don't you think it's right? Where you practised your dressage the evening before you made him Scottish Champion?' He threw the spade into the ground.

'I didn't make him Scottish Champion – he did that all by himself.' She took a sip of coffee and pulled a face. 'Why didn't you put sugar in this?'

He laughed as he walked across to her and threw down his coat on the blanket.

'You are never happy.' He knelt and kissed her. 'Don't you understand? The Mechanic had been in a million different yards, and no one else worked out how to get him to concentrate for long enough to do a good dressage test, and no one else managed to jump a clear show jumping round on him.'

'That was bloody Jules who taught me how to get him to show jump. The only good thing she ever did was bring me Little Vision instead of The Mechanic at Kinsey Park.' She looked down at the coffee. 'He just needed to be loved.'

Roger took a mouthful of coffee, thinking that he had never felt like this before about anyone. What the hell was happening to him? He felt like a teenager at the launch of their first crush.

'I need to tell you something.' Katie drew her team jacket more closely around her.

Roger noticed there was horse dribble on the sleeve, and there were dark hollows under her eyes. He waited.

'I love you. And I'm sorry, I'm really sorry because I never meant to fall in love with you, but I've loved you for years, and now that I *know* you,' she raised her head and looked into his eyes, 'I love the person far more than I ever loved the pictures of you.'

He sat down beside her and put his arm around her shoulders, brushing his lips against her temple. 'I think I love you too,' he said lightly.

She was smiling. 'You *think*? Only you could say something like that and get away with it.'

He wrinkled his brow. 'I've never ever felt like this before.

When I married Elizabeth, I really thought I loved her, but it didn't feel anything like this.'

'How does it feel?'

'As though I can't live for a minute without you.' He raised her chin with his index finger and kissed her longingly.

'My mum's going to be seriously jealous.'

'I'm not sure your dad will be very happy; I don't think he's a member of my fan club.'

'He'll get over it.'

'I think that may take him some time. Now for heaven's sake, stop distracting me. Let's finish the job.' He got up and took the cool box from the grass beside the car. 'Do you want to see?'

She shook her head.

Lifting the plastic bag from the cool box, Roger felt the bulk of The Mechanic's enormous heart in his hands. It must have weighed twelve pounds, and he thought that maybe it was true what people said about good horses having big hearts. He placed the package on the grass and took a penknife out of his pocket to make a long slit in the bag. Carefully lifting the heart out of its wrappings, he placed it in the hole and, for a moment, his mind was full of images of the liver chestnut. The Mechanic had come good in the end; the delinquent that many people had tried to tame had turned into a good horse with Katie. They had been a wonderful partnership, and Roger felt immensely proud of being a part of it.

After he had refilled the grave, he laid the square of turf neatly on the top of the earth and walked over to the river to wash his hands in the icy water. Looking at the overhanging trees on the opposite bank, he tried to gather his jagged thoughts. He had never undergone anything like the emotions he had experienced over the past few days. He had tried to hold the team together after the untimely death of The Mechanic; he had tried to ignore the feeling of unadulterated defeat when he thought Katie was going to leave and return to Dorset; and he had tried his best to ride Warrior to win the class. He had ridden the horse like a man with a mission because he knew Katie was watching, thinking that if he won, then maybe he could persuade her to stay in Northumberland. Now that the adrenaline and tension had gone, he felt depleted to a level that he had never been to before. He wanted to close his eyes and sleep.

'Hey,' she had her hand on his back and could feel the rigid muscles through his shirt, 'okay?'

'Garwood has been quite something this year.' His eyes were glossy when he turned to look at her.

'I know.'

Closing his eyes, he felt the gentle movement of her palm. 'I love you,' he said quietly.

'You think?' Her tone was mocking, and he smiled at her.

'You're different; you don't try to be something that you aren't. You see me for who I am.'

'A bad-tempered bastard.'

He laughed. 'And I can always rely on you to bring me down to earth.'

She wrapped her arms around him and rested her head under his chin, telling him his hands were freezing. She then gave a shriek as he slid his still-wet hands under her coat. Grinning, he led her back to the blanket and sat down, pulling her towards him. She offered him the flask cup of coffee, but he shook his head and said that something stronger was required. Reaching into the basket for the Taittinger, he tore off the gold foil and, after easing out the cork with a loud pop, he filled both glasses.

His voice wasn't altogether steady when he proposed a toast to The Mechanic and, after taking a mouthful of champagne, he got to his feet, walked back to the square of grass that stood proud and poured the rest of his glass over it.

Still sitting on the rug with tears dripping off her chin, she refilled his glass as he sat down.

'There'll be other horses, much easier than him.' He slipped a reassuring arm around her shoulders.

'But they won't be him.' Her bottom lip was trembling.

'They won't,' he agreed, 'but no one else got a tune out of him the way you did. You should be proud of what you achieved.'

'It's just such a shock, him going like that. I wanted to stay with him, until they… until they got him off the track.'

'They were very respectful; they always are. They knew he was someone's pride and joy.'

She leant her head against his soft cheek. 'Did you sleep at all last night?'

'A little.' He kissed the top of her head. 'Why do you ask?'

'Because you've shaved; you must have been awake for hours.'

'I just wanted to look at you; you look more beautiful than ever when you're sleeping.'

'Roger?'

'What?' He felt her shivering and reached for his coat to wrap it around her.

'What happens now?'

'Well, it's much too cold to make love to you on a blanket by the river,' he lifted the bottle out of the basket to top up her glass, 'we'll save that for a warmer day.'

She dug him in the ribs. 'I meant you and me.'

'What about you and me?'

'What's everyone going to say?'

'At least we don't have to worry about Smith's; they've already written it.' Roger was more concerned about how Eddie was going to react when he heard the news.

'Do you know, eleven months ago I moved to London, and I had never been so miserable in my life, and yet now, I'm so happy.' She ran her eyes over his handsome face. 'I feel like I'm going to wake up in my horrible cold bed in Stamford Hill any minute.'

'I'd much rather you woke up in mine.' He took out his phone and took a photograph of her.

'Couldn't you have waited until I had my make-up on?' she grumbled.

He flicked through his gallery until he found the picture of her, standing in his drawing room at the owners' party, wearing the beautiful orangey-pink dress that seemed to cling to her frame in all the right places.

She frowned. 'When did you take that? I don't remember it being taken.'

'I had to pretend I was taking one of Tom in his suit and then I cropped him out.'

'Tom would be most disappointed. How often have you looked at that photograph?' She nestled closer to him.

'Oh, you know, just every morning, every lunchtime and for most of every evening.'

'Mrs Royal rumbled me fairly early on.' She took a sip of champagne. 'I'd hidden a picture of you that I'd torn out of *Horse & Hound*, and I came home to find it *framed*.'

'Good old Mrs Royal – where had you hidden it?'

'In my underwear drawer. It's the only place Shelley doesn't go looking for things to wear.'

'Where is it now? Still hidden under your pink thongs?'

She hesitated for a second and then unzipped the phone pocket on the front of her jacket; taking out a tightly folded piece of glossy paper, she handed it to him. 'You can have it; I don't think I need it anymore.'

He took it from her fingers and slid it back into her pocket. 'But I quite like the idea of being so close to your heart all of the time.'

'What changed your mind?' she asked slowly. 'Something must have?'

'A lecture from Shelley on Saturday night, my grandmother quoting lines from every romantic film she has ever watched, Miss Mac telling me back in April that you were a nice girl, making love to you in the lorry last Wednesday night, which is something I vowed I would *never* do. Should I continue?'

She laughed and shook her head. 'Shelley was livid with me.'

'How did she know?'

'I got the pillows the wrong way around and gave her the one that smelt of Hugo Boss.'

'Ah.' He took a drink and then smiled. 'At least now I don't need to make up an excuse to be alone with you.'

'What do you mean?'

'There were plenty of times I took my car, when we could have travelled in the lorry.'

'Sneaky, but impressive. And I enjoyed every minute of it.'

There was a silence, and she took his hand and entwined her slender fingers with his.

'What are you thinking?' he asked.

She looked at him for a moment before she spoke. 'You've never told me how you knew my tattoo was Wordsworth.'

His fingers stopped moving, and she felt him become still. He was staring straight ahead towards the river, and she watched him swallow and blink, as if he was deciding whether to answer her or not.

'I'm sorry; I shouldn't have asked.'

Still his fingers were motionless, and he composed himself before he spoke. 'The wording on my parents' headstone is from the same poem,' he said quietly.

'Oh God!' She placed the heels of her palms to her eyes. 'I'll get it removed.'

'Which? The inscription on the headstone or your tattoo?'

'I'll get it lasered.'

'No, don't,' he said quickly. 'It's *you*, and in a sort of strange and weird and non-incestuous way, it's quite comforting to see it.'

'No wonder you didn't want to tell me.'

'I wish they were here. To see you, to hear you laugh…' His voice faded as a robin flew down and perched on the handle of the spade that he had left speared in the soil.

They watched as the bird puffed out his chest and gave a brief burst of song before it flew in a darting fashion towards them, landing on the handle of the wicker basket. Staring at the bird in astonishment, Roger caught a quick movement out of the corner of his eye and saw another robin land on the grass beside The Mechanic's heart. It ruffled its feathers meticulously for a few seconds, sang a line from its autumn melody and then Roger watched it flying off towards the huge oak tree on the riverbank.

The first robin was still on the basket and, after another snatch of music, it shook its plumage confidently and flew down to the rug. It hopped across the blanket towards Roger's feet, where it momentarily paused to look at them both, its head flitting from side to side, and then it was gone.

'Wow,' she looked at him, 'I've never seen two of them so close before. Normally they're really territorial.'

'But they carry the souls of our loved ones,' he replied softly, and then he started to laugh. 'I think, perhaps, you've just been given the seal of approval.'

She couldn't think of a reply and found tears were stinging her tired eyes.

He smiled at her for a minute, before saying he had something for her, and he went to his car.

'They were meant to be a celebratory present for winning the Scottish Championship, to replace the silver ones you gave me.' He sat down beside her and handed her a palm-sized leather box. 'I just never found the courage to give them to you, but you must promise me faithfully that you will never wear them at a competition. These are only for riding at home because, as you know, I detest all things pink and glittery.'

She grinned at him and then looked down and opened the box. There was a set of rose-gold spurs lying on the blue satin lining. They glinted in the light, and the pink Swarovski crystals sparkled as she stared at them.

'Do you like them?'

'I love them; I *love* them!' She grabbed his shirt and kissed him.

'I've looked everywhere for a set like this – where did you find them?'

'I had them made for you.'

'You had them made for me?' she asked in disbelief.

He nodded.

'Thank you. They're beautiful.'

'So are you.'

'But I don't promise to only wear them at home.' She slowly reached into her coat pocket and handed him a small box.

'What's this?'

'I bought it on Saturday afternoon when I was feeling fairly miserable. It was meant to be a peace offering, but then I realised that I wanted to make more than just peace with you, so I didn't give it to you in the end.'

The bracelet was three braided strips of soft brown leather with a silver clasp, and Roger was genuinely touched.

'No one has ever bought me anything like this before.'

'Not even Elizabeth?'

When he shook his head, she told him to read the inscription on the inside of the clasp.

'Fate whispered to the Warrior, "You cannot withstand the storm," and the Warrior whispered back, "I am the storm.".' He looked up into her incredible brown eyes.

'I read it and thought it summed up everything. Warrior included.'

Holding her closely, he thanked her and then took the bracelet out of the box for her to attach around his wrist. Watching her fasten it, he knew that looking at it would always take him back to this moment.

She leant her head against him, listening to the chattering river and the song of the robin, feeling the chill of the morning on her face. As she saw him look at his watch, she begged him not to move, asking if they could be alone for a while longer.

His arm tightened around her. 'We've got a yard of horses to see to in an hour, but I think we've all earned an afternoon off. Come on, let's go; we can collect Otter from Mrs Royal on the way back.'

Shelley was going around the stables with two buckets of feed and, as she fed the last scoop of mix to Cooper, Roger and Katie, both looking distinctly starry-eyed, walked into the yard.

Katie heard the Bogiemobile screeching to a halt outside as she started mucking out Warrior, next to The Mechanic's empty stable.

Shelley, pushing a wheelbarrow towards the stables underneath the Dorchester, saw Roger standing thoughtfully in the middle of the yard. 'Finally,' she told him quietly.

He turned towards her and smiled.

'You will take care of her, won't you?'

'I'm too scared of her best friend to do anything else.' He began to walk away. 'You were right,' he said abruptly as he turned back to her, 'what you said to me.'

She gave him a grin. 'I know I was.'

Running his hands down Warrior's legs, checking for any injuries, he heard Caitlyn approaching with a trolley piled high with haynets. Katie's phone was pinging constant alerts of new WhatsApp messages, and Caitlyn said she was either extremely popular or the news of her new boyfriend had broken.

'I've known for ages,' Caitlyn confided as she tied up Tiger's hay.

Roger straightened up and looked at Caitlyn through the bars of the stable wall.

'Oooh, sorry, Roger, didn't know you were there.'

'How have you known for ages?' he asked dryly.

Shelley took one of the haynets off the trolley and looked enquiringly at Caitlyn.

'Well, Katie told me to get fitter because she said it would help my riding, so I've been riding my bike at nights when I'm not working in the Kettle.'

'I think he just wants a straight answer and not an essay,' suggested Shelley.

'I'm getting to the point,' said Caitlyn crossly. 'And on my bike, it's such a nice loop to come along the main road from the village to here, around the outside of the yard and then up to Mrs F.B's and back along the main road home.'

'Caitlyn, please get to the point.' Roger sounded irritated.

'Well, I was riding through one night and I saw you,' she pointed at Roger, 'looking pretty flustered, I must say, running up to the Hall wearing Tom's orange boiler suit.'

'Do you know how many hours I have wasted turning the Dorchester inside out looking for that bloody boiler suit?' ranted Shelley.

Katie started laughing and found that she couldn't stop.

'And?' Roger looked blandly at Caitlyn.

'Well, I wanted to cycle a bit further that night, so that was my second loop around here.' She suddenly smirked at him. 'And on my first loop, I saw you opening the Dorchester's kitchen window, and you were absolutely starkers.'

Roger's face was turning red.

'I nearly fell off my bike, I was so shocked,' said Caitlyn slowly.

'I bet you were.' Shelley tried to stifle a snigger.

Caitlyn turned back to Roger. 'No, I mean I was so shocked because, for forty, you're actually quite fit.'

'Thank you, Caitlyn,' said Roger weakly and added that he was thirty-seven.

'Oh God,' the realisation was dawning on Shelley, 'that was the night Tom and I were at the Manically Challenged tribute act, wasn't it?'

'Might have been,' blushed Katie.

'The night you gave us the keys to the bedrooms?' Shelley was looking incredulously from Katie to Roger. 'The night you, Pink Knickers, were wearing my jeans and polo shirt?' Shelley was starting to laugh, 'Oh Lordy, I would have paid a lot of money to have seen you in that boiler suit, Roger. Have you worn it since?'

'My clothes were locked in her bedroom, what else was I supposed to do?' asked Roger in annoyance.

'I'll donate fifty quid to a charity of your choice if you wear it to the Kettle,' laughed Shelley.

'Can we just get these horses out, get mucked out and the lorry emptied, so we can have the afternoon off?' Roger's cheeks were still burning as he reached for Warrior's headcollar. 'In fact, if it shuts you all up, I'll buy you lunch at the pub.'

'Oooh lovely.' Caitlyn pushed the trolley back out onto the yard. 'The special today is shepherd's pie, and I love shepherd's pie.'

Thirty-One

Being a Monday, the Cup and Kettle was quiet, and now that most of the tourists had gone home, there was just a scattering of locals sitting at the bar and a couple with two small children sitting inside.

Roger's team had the beer garden to themselves and, after Brian had arrived with a tray of drinks and the lunchtime menus, Tom appeared from the back door of the pub. After asking Shelley if any more of her friends required a free lunch, Roger put his foot on the chair opposite him and pushed it out for Tom.

'Sorry I'm late,' Tom put his Salty Dog on the table, 'I was sweating my balls off after the third lot, and I had to have a shower.' He folded his arms over his grey "the only gay in the village" T-shirt and tightened his eyes at Katie. 'You look knackered, missy; you should try going to bed and actually doing some sleeping. Now, what's everyone having?'

'Shepherd's pie,' said Caitlyn without opening the menu.

'Burger,' chorused Shelley and Katie.

Having eaten practically nothing during the days at Garwood, Roger looked at the menu and found he was absolutely starving. Shelley noticed his arm was lying along the back of Katie's seat, and she smiled to herself at such an obvious gesture of possession.

'What are you doing this afternoon?' Tom closed his menu.

'Going to bed until I have to get the horses in at four.' Shelley yawned.

'I think we should do that too,' whispered Katie to Roger, who glanced at her quickly and then slowly smiled.

'You've got no stamina,' said Tom angrily. 'What are you doing, Caitlyn? Are you behind the bar here tonight?'

'No, I'm not here until Friday night.'

'Well why don't we all go back to the Dorchester and have a few cheeky vodkas in the sun? Celebrate the end of summer.' Tom removed the cocktail umbrella from his Salty Dog.

'I suppose I could be persuaded if you stay and help get the horses in and do their cold water bandages at nine o'clock.' Shelley looked at Tom sweetly. 'Except I think we're low on vodka, so you'll have to go to the shop.'

Tom patted Shelley's arm. 'I've got a whole case and four cartons of grapefruit juice in the car, sweetie.'

'Have you planned this?' asked Roger in amazement.

'No, Prince Charming.' Tom raised his right hand in a three-fingered salute. 'I was a Scout, and it always pays to *be prepared*.'

An hour later, and leaving only clean plates, empty glasses and a tip, the yawning group made their way out of the Cup and Kettle.

'Right, who's coming with me?' Tom was standing by his BMW, which was parked half on the pavement outside the door, as if he had half-heartedly attempted to ram-raid the pub.

'Do you even need to ask?' Caitlyn pushed the case of vodka across the back seat.

'Well, darlings,' Tom watched Roger holding the Discovery's passenger door open for Katie, 'I don't think we'll see much of them this afternoon.'

'I think you could be right.' Shelley fastened her seat belt as Tom started the car. 'It's about time he took himself off the shelf.'

'At least it's *finally* out in the open.' Tom reversed off the pavement with a bump.

'What do you mean?' Shelley frowned at him.

Tom slapped her leg. 'Come off it, sweetie, that night we went back to the Dorchester and Roger was there with the keys to your bedroom doors, the night Katie was wearing your T-shirt and jeans?'

'What about it?'

'Roger's shirt was buttoned up all wrong, so he'd obviously got dressed in a hurry. And way before that, in fact, it was the morning after the Manically Challenged gig, by the state of her neck, she looked like he'd practically eaten her alive.'

'You *noticed*?'

'Lucky girl,' replied Tom wistfully. 'What I wouldn't give for an hour in Roger's bed. I wonder if I could spike his coffee with Rohypnol?'

'You definitely wouldn't get much action if you slipped him some of that.' Shelley gripped the handle above her head as Tom tore past a tractor.

'But you could wrap him in a blanket and feed him chicken soup if he was a bit sleepy.' Caitlyn put a steadying hand on the case of vodka as Tom shot around the right-hand bend out of Athward village.

'I could,' agreed Tom dreamily. 'Do you want to help, Caitlyn? Now you've admitted he's fit?'

'No thanks, Tom – he is definitely fit, but he's only four years younger than my dad.'

'For the love of God,' muttered Shelley.

∾

Pulling up at the back door to Athward Hall, Roger jumped out of the Discovery, raced around to open the door for Katie and pulled her into his arms.

'You have had all your clothes on for at least eight hours, and we really need to do something about that.'

'What's happened to you?' She laughed.

'You have.'

'So, do you want me to rearrange your paintings and furniture and open your post?'

'Do you know, I wouldn't mind if you did.'

'That's a bigger compliment than telling me you love me.'

As she pulled off her shoes, she received a WhatsApp from Shelley telling her to check her pockets. Shaking her head and knowing what she was about to find, she unzipped her jacket pocket, took out a handful of condoms and started to laugh.

'What is so funny?' Roger twisted her hair in his hand and dropped a slow kiss on the nape of her neck.

'Every single one is lager and lime flavoured.'

Acknowledgements

Currently, there are a number of different competitive levels within the British Eventing structure. As *Silver Spurs and a Twelve Pound Heart* is a work of fiction, I have deliberately avoided using the correct terms, to make it easier for a reader who is unfamiliar with the sport to comprehend. To those eventing buffs among you – I hope you managed to suspend your knowledge of qualifications and minimum eligibility requirements, to ride at Intermediate level and above.

There are so many people who have helped with the facts needed for this book and I cannot thank them all enough for their help and guidance. Any errors are mine and should in no way reflect upon the advice that I was given.

Rebecca Maitland deserves an enormous thank you for her help regarding Katie's music choices, slang terms and giving me an insight into the thoughts of a twenty-something-year-old in today's culture.

Ian Murray and Andrew Tate gave me guidance concerning Roger's taste in music – and although I was somewhat surprised by their answers – I thank them both for their input.

The wonderfully kind and patient Fiona Fell, offered excellent veterinary information on the subject of an Aortic rupture, and how an equine heart attack would be dealt with should it occur during a competition. I have to admit that Fiona's horse, Rocky, was also the inspiration for Daniel Jobson's Rock On.

I must express my thanks to Jenni 'Jennimoose' Heard, Caroline Stewart and Henny Cooper, for keeping me up to date with the British Eventing rulebook. These ladies are at the coalface of BE and their views and opinions were invaluable.

My very tall and beautiful friend, Imani Hazelhurst, read a very rough first draft and also ploughed through a much more final version of the manuscript. Imani, you have been the best Beta reader that the world could ever have provided – thank you.

Louise Fairbairn was the most incredible help, offering professional advice and giving me real inspiration for my writing. Lou, you are a superstar and one day, when you have eased off your blog tours and your endless panellist and judging work, you will have your Bookshop.

I have to mention the lovely Claudie, the creator of *Peonies & Bees*, for inspiring the slogans on Tom and Caitlyn's tee shirts. Yes, some of these are a product of my own imagination and terrible sense of humour, the rest are all available in the real world. I will leave you to work out which are which.

Roy Todd – ex-Head Teacher and long-suffering English teacher – you once told me (frustratedly), that I should be writing, and not working for a firm of Chartered Accountants. I think you may have had a point.

A huge thank you to my very dear friend, Karen Redfearn, for giving me the opportunity to groom for her all those years ago, where the idea for the book originated. The days were long, but we had numerous laughs as we traversed Northumberland, Yorkshire, Cumbria and Scotland with various horses in *Colin* – her eighteen-ton lorry. With Karen, I learnt a great deal about British Eventing and also discovered that *Colin* had to be perfectly level for the gas fridge to work, ensuring we had ice cubes for that end of day Gin and Tonic.

Massive love and thanks to my husband Marcus because quite simply, the book wouldn't be what it is without him. Likewise, my daughter Tabitha, who is wise beyond her years, was also the most brilliant help when it came to creating the Spotify playlist which accompanies the book.

Finally, to all the amazing event horses and their hardworking grooms – who all take the highs and lows and the long hours, with the most incredible energy and enthusiasm. To the owners, who continue to pour money into the sport and to the riders who persevere with broken ribs, metal plates holding shattered joints in place and a love for the sport which borders on an addiction: you are insane but brilliant. May you all come home from each day and every competition safe and sound, and continue to work hard, and play hard.